THE
ACTOR

DOUGLAS GARDHAM

To Arlene,
Enjoy the journey!
Happy Birthday!
Doug Gardham

iUniverse LLC
Bloomington

THE ACTOR

iUniverse Star
an iUniverse LLC imprint

iUniverse books may be ordered through booksellers or by contacting:

iUniverse
1663 Liberty Drive
Bloomington, IN 47403
www.iuniverse.com
1-800-Authors (1-800-288-4677)

Because of the dynamic nature of the Internet, any Web addresses or
links contained in this book may have changed since publication and
may no longer be valid. The views expressed in this work are solely those
of the author and do not necessarily reflect the views of the publisher,
and the publisher hereby disclaims any responsibility for them.

ISBN: 978-1-9389-0866-8 (s)
ISBN: 978-1-9389-0867-5 (e)

Library of Congress Control Number: 2014906695

Printed in the United States of America

To Laura, Zach and Sammi
without whose love and support
The Actor would not have been possible.

PROLOGUE

All the world's a stage,
And all the men and women merely players:
They have their exits and their entrances;
And one man in his time plays many parts.
                    —William Shakespeare, *As You Like It*

Ethan's Timeline
October 1991—Redondo Beach, California

The elevator door was open as he entered the lobby of the apartment building that had been his home for the past several months. He'd been wary of an open elevator after finding a mutilated cat in the compartment a few weeks back. Nothing had ever happened again, outside of a sleeping drunk, but he still hesitated. As he slowly approached from the side, he found the compartment empty. He pressed the button to the eighth floor, just as an attractive blonde woman wearing horn-rimmed glasses joined him.

"Hi," he said as the elevator door closed. "What a great day!"

She turned and looked at him for an instant, as if he was a drifter begging for money, and then her stare returned to the closed elevator door.

He didn't allow her reaction to bother his mood. He wanted to share his news with the world, but she was the only person in his presence. She was going to hear about the contents of his envelope whether she liked it or not.

He was perspiring from the heat outside and his hasty walk up

Bronson Street. He never lacked for energy, and today was no different. He moved with the frenetic energy of a child on a sugar high. In his hands, he held a manila envelope containing the fulfillment of a dream he'd had for as long as he could remember. It was all he could do to stand still. "Ethan Jones," he said as he thrust his free hand toward the woman. Her faded Levi's were frayed to threads around the back pockets and seams. Her white cotton T-shirt was only partially tucked into her denims, yet she stood erect with perfect posture. "Glad to make your acquaintance."

There was a moment's hesitation before she turned to face him. Startling blue eyes glared at him from behind the pink-framed glasses. There was something strangely familiar about her. "Katharine Davenport," she replied, her voice calm and professional, with a why-are-you-bothering-me edge to it. She squinted at him as the hint of a smile curved her lips. Her hand was petite, soft in his but surprisingly firm. "So you won the lottery?"

Ethan combed his fingers through his light brown hair, something he did unconsciously in moments of anxiousness. "No, better than that," he spoke excitedly. "I'm gonna be a movie star." It could have sounded like he had his head in the clouds, but to Ethan it was as real as the clothes he was wearing. He held up the manila envelope, now stained by his damp fingertips. "And in here is the script that's gonna take me there."

It took willpower for him to suppress screaming right there in front of this unknown woman. On many levels, this surpassed winning a lottery. This was a ticket to the dreams he'd fought to achieve for so long. His insides were ready to explode.

"I'm happy for you," she replied, maintaining her professional air, but her face brightened, reflecting his enthusiasm. "Maybe I'll get to see your movie sometime. What's its title?"

"*Browning Station*. Oops—I'm not supposed to tell you that. I'm the bad guy."

"*Browning Station*," she repeated. "I won't tell a soul, even if I see it. How's that?"

The elevator stopped as the number eight lit up the panel above the sliding door and the bell rang.

"Suspend your disbelief until I see you again," he said, smiling and ignoring the slight, "but remember Ethan Jones, whom you met in an elevator before he was famous." He laughed at his words and stepped out of the elevator. He normally wouldn't have started a conversation with a stranger, but today was different—he was on a high after finally winning a big character role. "Nice meeting you, Katharine Davenport," he said, exaggerating a bow as the heavy elevator door tried to close. It knocked him sideways and then retracted.

"You too, Ethan Jones," she replied, smiling at his awkwardness. "I'll watch for you."

Eighteen months ago, he'd left a secure job in Canada, even when all of his friends told him he was crazy. ("California, Ethan? Have you lost your mind?") Well, if he had, he'd found it at last.

Ethan walked quickly toward his apartment, his feet barely touching the threadbare carpet. He shared the apartment with his girlfriend, Christa White. His roommate from university, Robbie, who had helped bring him to California, was staying with them, as he was between jobs. As Ethan approached their apartment door, he noticed it was ajar. His hesitation was brief as a smile formed on his thin lips—Christa must be home early. He didn't notice the slash of red above the doorknob or a similar spot on the carpet just inside the door.

"I got the part!" he shouted, pushing the door open and slipping off his worn deck shoes. No answer. Not a sound. The apartment was dim. "Hey, anybody home?" he called, his voice at once losing its excited edge. Something wasn't right.

A trace of Christa's Givenchy fragrance hung in the air. He grew anxious as he connected the open door and her absence—but maybe she'd only stepped out and inadvertently left the door open.

Later, his memory would fail as to what happened next. In the dark, his hand swept the wall and hit the light switch but not before touching a wet tackiness on the switch plate. As the apartment lit up, he saw the crimson substance on his hand. *Blood?* He felt light-headed as he grabbed at the wall to stay upright. His heart pounded in his throat. *It can't be real,* he told himself. *Such foolishness. It can't be blood. Not here. You're in a nightmare, Ethan. Wake up!*

As he looked around, however, his heart nearly stopped. Their apartment was a sea of destruction. Shards of glass from their full-length mirror were scattered everywhere. A lamp lay broken on the floor, its shade crushed like an extinguished cigarette. The doorframe to Robbie's room was cracked and splintered, the pieces of wood askew. The bookcase was upended, its contents strewn across the parquet floor. The television screen was smashed. And the blood … it was everywhere—on the walls, the doorframes. His feet moved of their own volition. He stepped around the shattered remnants of an antique vase that Christa had bought with money they didn't have—she'd been so pleased at the deal she'd struck for the piece.

He walked slowly past the partially open door to Robbie's room. Blood splatter was on the walls, the bedspread, the bureau, and the mirror.

Ethan stepped backward, afraid of what he would find on entering, and nearly tripped over the white plastic deck chair near the doorway. In horror, he looked into the bedroom he shared with Christa. He heard himself repeating her name again and again, like a sacred chant. His own voice was unfamiliar to him, as if coming from a distance. Through the doorway his glazed eyes fell on Christa's feet, naked but for the small gold toe ring he'd given her.

His feet stopped moving as his eyes caught a full red handprint on the wall beside the bed, directly above the word he'd written to inspire himself: *Act.*

Another step forward and he saw the rest of her—or what remained of her. A vibrant crimson filled the bed where Christa lay motionless in the center, her broken hands held behind her head in what looked like an attempt at protection. Her long, beautiful brunette hair was a mixture of coagulating blood and bits of bone and skin. Ethan prayed for the strength to turn away, yet his body remained rigid. His eyes were transfixed on the disfigured head he no longer recognized—the partially torn scalp, the white skull bone. *God, please.*

He dropped to his knees at her bedside. His whole body screamed, unloading in shocked grief. He reached out to touch her, hoping, praying for a sign that by some miracle, life might still be inside her broken body. She just couldn't be gone.

"God!" he screamed in agony as his life crumbled before him. "You can't take her away! Not now!"

Sobs wracked his body as the room swirled about him. Books and clothes were scattered everywhere. His prized book of *Homes and Cars of the Stars* lay in shreds at the foot of the bed. He was numb to the broken glass on the floor that cut his knees.

He had no memory of how long he remained with Christa's lifeless form. Somehow, he managed to struggle back through the living room to dial 911. Later, he would recall little of what happened before the LAPD's arrival on the scene. The police found him at Christa's bedside, her lifeless fingers entwined in his own.

There were many questions with few answers. The constant motion of emergency personnel taking charge overwhelmed him—mass chaos to his grief-stricken mind. One officer, noticing Ethan's disorientation, pulled him out to the hallway, away from the scene and further trauma. Ethan's only response was to say, "It should have been me."

Paramedics arrived moments after the police had secured the apartment. Ethan sat on the floor in the hallway with a blanket wrapped around his shoulders. Shock and a strong sedative kept him calm and listless. Ethan slowly raised his head as someone came off the elevator. He stared in disbelief as Robbie approached.

"*Ethan?*" Robbie shouted from halfway down the hall. His face strained with concern. "What the hell's going on?"

Ethan looked up, recognizing Robbie. He reached forward and touched his friend's shoulder. Robbie was real. "But I thought ..." Ethan shook his head, confused. "Christa's dead, Robbie," he sobbed, embracing his friend and sorrowfully adding, "How could he hate her that much?"

ACT I

It was the best of times,
It was the worst of times.
　　　　—Charles Dickens, *A Tale of Two Cities*

CHAPTER 1

Ethan realized he'd made a grave mistake. It wasn't the sort of mistake you go back and erase, like spelling a word wrong. There was much more at stake than that, like the rest of his life.

Attending university had been as much of an assumption in his life as marriage or buying a car might be to others. It wasn't a question of whether he wanted to go or could afford it. Postsecondary education was simply expected, a part of his destiny. His parents didn't see education as just important; it was a requirement for life. They knew the privileges of education and had fought too hard without them. They weren't about to let their only child suffer through those same hardships.

His parents were distraught when school became secondary to a rock band he'd formed with a few of his buddies. He'd been groomed for adulthood and a successful career since preschool and was expected to know better. University required good grades that weren't achieved by staying out all night strumming an electric guitar to a drunken audience. So when his band broke up in the final days of his high school senior year, no one was as happy—maybe ecstatic was a better word—as his mother and father. "Things always work out for the best," he later recalled his mother repeating more than once at their dinner conversation. His father, in a strange reinforcement of his mother's words, added something like, "I never thought you were any good anyway."

The breakup was devastating for Ethan. He'd loved the band. Nearly all his hopes and dreams had gone into its creation. He loved

1

writing songs, creating something from nothing. There was magic in playing songs they'd created themselves. What could be more exciting than making a living doing what he loved? He would remember forever the fateful Monday night of their breakup. They were sitting around the pool table that supported their eight-track mixing board in Greg's parents' basement. Greg was their drummer. After a couple of beers and shootin' the shit, Greg announced he'd been accepted at MIT. Ethan's jaw dropped.

"So what the fuck does that mean?" Ethan demanded, his disappointment displayed in anger.

"It means that I'm fuckin' outta here, come September," Greg answered, shaking his long black hair and raising his bottle in celebration.

"I thought we were a fuckin' band, man," Ethan shot back, upset by the obvious betrayal. "What's the deal? Fuck."

Greg proceeded to unload a barrage of faults that insulted everyone— they'd never made money, they'd never recorded, they didn't sound any good, and Ethan couldn't sing. They had to get on with their lives. On and on he went. If it wasn't wrong before, Greg found a way to make it wrong by the time he finished. Ethan could still remember standing in stunned disbelief beside someone he'd called his friend.

"Fuck, Greg, if you felt this way," he cried, not far from taking a swing at him, "why the fuck did you hang around so long?"

Greg shook his head. His decision was made. There was nothing to talk about.

They never played again as a band. From then on, Ethan floundered. Some quick decisions got him into university and four months later, he was on a bus to Ottawa.

The most difficult part of the university experience for Ethan was never feeling connected. Like an outsider, his mind was always on something other than the point at hand. The engineering curriculum was rigid and demanding—it had to be; the world didn't need bridges and buildings falling down, or planes falling out of the sky, or ships sinking.

Engineering was his program of choice because of his flair for mathematics and love of the automobile—two reasons that were as good as any.

Mid-November in Ottawa found bare-branched trees and grass covered with leaves. Ethan's roommate, Robbie, had come back to their dorm room after breakfast and invited him to play touch football in the commons. Ethan had refused to get out of bed. He wasn't feeling well and was trying to sleep off the bug. In truth, he was depressed over the decision he'd made to be there. His pain was due to his foolhardy reasoning that university was a lesser evil than facing the wrath of his parents if he dropped out. He spent the entire day in bed, attempting to escape the inevitable dreariness that lay ahead. It was dark when he finally got up and dressed. Being a Sunday night, there was little action in the quad. He decided a walk was in order and left the dorm for the briskness of the mid-November evening.

It was just past seven when he stepped off the cement steps of the entrance. With little in the way of destination, he headed toward the bridge over the Ottawa River. A sense of calm settled over him in the darkness of the night. Utterly alone, no one knew who or where he was. He gained a sense of power, knowing he could do as he pleased without interference. The night belonged to him.

Ten minutes later, he crossed the bridge toward Billings. Few cars were on the road. The whole world seemed to move in slow motion. He'd stopped on the sidewalk in the center of the bridge and peered over the rusting metal railing, down into the water below. He shivered in the cold breeze. Winter was on its way.

The flowing water seemed so free, a part of nature. Why wasn't he? Why couldn't he fit in? The water seemed to speak to him in a way he'd never heard: *Come join me.*

Without consciously making a decision, Ethan found himself climbing the railing and leaning over the edge in a very precarious position. *Come join me,* the water repeated. He sensed the words more than hearing them; his grip on the railing loosened.

Then a calm female voice spoke to him. *Ethan, you're not finished yet.*

The words, which would return in moments of indecision, turned him around, panic-stricken, as he wrapped his arms around the rusty railing. Fear weakened him. He barely held himself upright. Gravity teamed with the water to pull him down. To maintain his grip seemed impossible, yet he fought back. Nearly incapacitated, he pushed hard with his legs and dragged himself back over the railing. Shaking but safe, he listened as the water rushed past below. Shock overtook his muscles as he realized, shamefully, how close he'd come to certain death. He collapsed to the cement sidewalk and wept. Deep sobs shook his body; sweat cloaked his skin.

After a few minutes of catching his breath, he got up and continued along the bridge. He walked toward Bank Street. He wanted a drink, and there'd be something open on Bank. It didn't take long to find his way into a small club. The entrance led him to a downstairs bar, where half a dozen people were sitting around, drinking and talking. Quite thirsty, he approached the bar and stood beside a young couple who looked to be students, although he didn't recognize them. Ethan ordered a draft and stood quietly watching. A draft appeared in front of him. At the same time, the girl beside him tapped him on the shoulder, held out her cigarette, and asked him for a light. On reflex, he checked his pockets, knowing he didn't have a match, but liked the girl's pretty face. It was hard not to look at her deep brown eyes. She was dressed in torn denims, a faded jean jacket, and a pair of red high-tops, and he didn't want to stop talking to her just because he couldn't light her cigarette. He asked if she was a student as he kept digging in his pockets.

She said she was a sophomore in dramatic arts. She was supposed to be rehearsing but wasn't in the mood. "What are you in?" she asked, her eyes darting around his face. She was a natural beauty without makeup. Her brown hair was tied back in a loose ponytail. The red sweatshirt under her jacket was ripped just below the neckline.

Ethan couldn't take his eyes off her. "Engineering," he answered, passing his hand through his hair. Her brown eyes seemed to hold the light in the dimness of the bar.

"Engineering?" she said, amazed. "You must be in environmental or systems engineering."

He smiled. "Why do you say that?"

"Because you don't look like a jerk."

Ethan paused and took a sip of his beer. "Is that a compliment or a shot?" He was suddenly more comfortable than he'd been in weeks.

"Probably a compliment," she said and smiled, nodding her head, "although I'll reserve the right to change my mind."

Mila then introduced herself and her friend Sean, who was seated next to her. They were both from Ottawa and in the same program.

"Sean's like a brother," Mila said, as if needing to explain their relationship. "I keep telling him if he hangs with me, he'll never have a girlfriend."

Ethan wasn't entirely sure that Sean saw things the same way that Mila described them, but he didn't care. Her brown eyes and smile were kindling something inside him.

"So what kind of engineering?" asked Sean, speaking for the first time. "I've got two friends in mechanical."

"And they're assholes," Mila was quick to add. "Don't tell me you're a gear-head too." A smile trickled across his lips. "I knew it!" she cried, while Sean smirked beside her. "Another gear-head! Is there no justice? You seem so normal. You're the first human I've met in mechanical engineering. It's not too late to change, you know."

It was Ethan's turn to laugh.

Their conversation continued. They talked about movies and actors. What was hot and what was not. Mila told him of her dream to go to Hollywood and become an actress. That was the real reason she was in the drama program.

Ethan asked why she didn't just go to Hollywood, if that was her dream.

"I'm not ready yet," she replied matter-of-factly, as if it were obvious. "Why are you in engineering?"

"I didn't know what else to do. I'm good at math and science."

Ethan hated his response after hearing that she was chasing a dream. It didn't matter, though. He just liked talking to her; she was like a friend he'd known his whole life. "I like to know how things work," he added. He surprised himself with his next question. "Mila, do you think you're a good actress?"

"Yes," she replied without hesitation. Something flashed in her eyes when she said it—a raw excitement, an inner strength. "You should come and see me. *Another Color Blue* starts in three weeks."

Another Color Blue was the university theater group's stage production just before the Christmas break. He'd seen the posters but knew almost nothing about it.

Sean stood up. "Mila, I gotta get going. I've still got stuff to catch up on for tomorrow." He leaned forward to give her a hug, but Mila didn't reciprocate. There was a brief awkwardness as his arm went around her back. Ethan again sensed that Sean had different ideas about Mila's company than she understood.

"You know, I'm in the same boat," Mila added.

"No, Mila, it's okay. You stay. It's just I've—"

"I'm already late," Mila interrupted. "Great to meet you, Ethan. See you around." Then she paused. Her forehead wrinkled, as if she was confused about something. "Sean, give me a sec. I really need to pee."

She headed to the toilet.

"You really ought to come out and see her in *Another Color Blue*," Sean said abruptly. "They've had poor ticket sales, but that's just the university. Mila's incredible. She's the show. I've only watched rehearsals, but she's incredible. An alumnus wrote the play."

"Hey, who knows?" Ethan said noncommittally. "Maybe I'll check it out."

An uncomfortable silence fell between them.

First impressions were difficult to break. Ethan could already see the word *weirdo* forming on Sean's forehead. Each of Sean's gestures seemed to be an effort to be cool. Tall and wiry with a constant smirk on his face, Sean sported gold rings in each earlobe. The thought that crossed Ethan's mind was how often beautiful girls hung around goofy guys.

Sean picked up his book off the bar.

Mila rejoined them. "Okay, let's go," she said.

"See you around, Ethan," Sean said without expression, staring at Mila.

"You too," Ethan added, reaching out to shake hands. Sean had already turned toward the stairs. Ethan stepped back and bumped Mila. "Sorry," he said.

"It's okay," Mila replied. "My fault. It was nice to meet you, Ethan."

She followed Sean to the stairs. At the bottom, she paused and turned. Ethan expected a wave. Instead, she glanced his way, winked, and then hustled up the stairway.

Ethan leaned against the bar. There still were a few people around, but he decided he'd go too. Raising his glass to finish, he found a piece of paper—a note—stuck to the bottom. He realized he'd bumped into Mila because she was slipping the note under his glass.

Ethan

I'd love to talk more. Come see my rehearsal tomorrow.
You won't be sorry. We're in the Aud at seven.

Mila

CHAPTER 2

Real Time
November 1983

Ethan hardly slept that night. Mila never left his mind. Having dozed for most of the day, he didn't need the rest. After his physics lab on Monday afternoon, he headed to the Aud.

The Aud was the main auditorium on the university grounds, located at the far end of the campus, away from the dorms. Walking in the cold autumn air, Ethan hardly noticed its icy bite; he had one thing on his mind—Mila.

It was strange to see the main doors into the reception area of the auditorium open when he reached the building. Clusters of people were loitering at the front. He proceeded through the entrance doors and was greeted by a gust of warm air. The maintenance staff was struggling with the inside temperature. The heat in the foyer was stifling, which explained why the main doors were open on such a cold evening. Ethan slowed on entering and then headed to an open door of the auditorium.

The front floor lights of the stage were lit. A number of people were in conversation on the stage. As he walked down the aisle, a handful of people were seated, but he didn't recognize anyone. Ten rows back, he cut in and moved to the middle. The lap of the wooden seat banged loudly as he sat down, and several people turned around, but he reacted as if nothing had happened. He leaned forward, forearms on his knees, and hunted through the faces on stage for a glimpse of Mila.

As he searched, activity started to take place. A spotlight lit up two guys on the front right side of the stage. The main lights dimmed and the auditorium went quiet. The two were talking about a beautiful

8

girl. The spotlight faded and then lit up another actor, farther back to the left. A female, wearing a kerchief around her head, was sweeping the floor. Ethan was quick to recognize Mila, although her face was obscured by the kerchief. Her character spoke with a French accent about how happy she would be if a certain boy would ask her out. Her accented voice mesmerized him, like music to his soul. With each move, she became more beautiful, amplifying his memory of the night before at the bar. To Ethan, she was the only one on stage. In what seemed like minutes, the house lights came on again. But it was eight thirty. It didn't seem possible he'd been sitting for so long.

Mila had enthralled him. The stage was hers, and the cast supported her. He'd never experienced anything quite like it, and he couldn't pull away from her spell. It was rare to be in the presence of greatness, but the impact would change his life.

"Ethan, what a treat to see you!" exclaimed Mila, coming up the aisle where he was sitting. He stood up. "Are you okay?" she asked. Her hand touched his arm.

He blinked a couple of times. "Just great," he answered, staring at her. Unexpectedly, he pulled her close and kissed her. She felt light in his arms and didn't resist. Her lips were soft and salty from perspiring under the stage lights. He held her close for a moment. When he released her, her fellow cast members applauded. Ethan's face flushed, having momentarily forgotten where he was and the many eyes following the star performer. Despite the attention, he was not about to trade places with anyone.

From the corner of his eye, Ethan also noticed Sean, leaving the auditorium alone.

It was Wednesday before he saw her again, and by then he'd been driven to total distraction. His ability to concentrate on his course material had disintegrated to the point of futility. His interest in anything to do with engineering had evaporated. Mila filled his head, as did—with what little space was left—the idea of acting. His fascination grew beyond simple curiosity. The bug of performing had bitten him in high school with his band. Now, after watching Mila's performance, he could think of nothing else. Now he wanted to give it a try or—more to the point— *had* to give it a try. Not only that, he would get to spend more time with the one who made his heart beat faster and his knees feel weak.

On Wednesday, he met her outside McKinnon Library on campus, and before they'd said two words, they were embracing. He'd not only found a new friend but a destiny, seemingly impossible to refuse.

"Ethan, wait a minute," Mila said, breaking their embrace. "This is crazy!"

"I know," he agreed, a big, stupid grin lighting his face. His arm was around her back. "I'm out of control. What can I say?"

"I don't know," she replied, kissing his lips again.

"Come on; let's go," he said, lifting her knapsack onto his shoulder. He put his arm around her shoulders. "Burgers or pizza?"

"Let's go back down to Charly's," she suggested, naming the place where they'd first met. "I'm in the mood for a beer. It's been a busy day."

"Sure," he replied. "It's on me."

"I've no problem with that."

Her head pressed against his chest as they walked on the sidewalk that edged the canal toward Bank Street. She fit comfortably right by his side. He held her close. His hand slid down from her shoulder to her slim back, her woolen winter jacket soft beneath his fingers. There was a good breeze blowing the cold November air across campus, but they didn't notice, nuzzled as they were in each other's warmth. The wind blew her brown hair into his face, tickling his nose and cheeks. It was heaven.

Approaching the bridge, a chill ran through him as he saw himself leaned out over the icy water. How close had he come? It seemed crazy how unpredictable life could be.

"What is it, Ethan?" Mila asked as they walked across the bridge. She must have sensed something as he thought about it.

"Thought I forgot my wallet for a second," he lied, touching his pocket, embarrassed by the images in his head. "No worries."

A lot had changed since that evening. An angel had touched him and spared him certain tragedy, like George Bailey in *It's a Wonderful Life*. He didn't dare look over the railing. Mila's closeness comforted him.

"When did you start acting?" he asked when they reached the other side. Her arm moved across his back. He felt her fingers on his ribcage. Life was grand.

"My parents got me started when I was eight," she replied, looking up into his eyes. "Local theater stuff. I loved it. They couldn't keep me away. They didn't push, though; I just wanted to do it. I love getting lost in someone else."

They stopped to cross the street. Traffic was heavy at this time in the afternoon, with commuters returning home to their families. For an instant, Ethan saw a scene of Mila and him having a family. He smiled. *Slow down, big boy. Don't scare her off.*

Mila continued as they reached the other side. "What I didn't like were all the kids who were there on account of their parents. Most were like that. I didn't understand but felt sorry for them." She paused for a moment, reflecting on the memory and then went on. "It quickly became my dream. I've pursued it ever since."

"You've been given an incredible gift, you know," Ethan added.

"Thanks. I'm grateful for it every day."

When they reached Charly's, Ethan opened the door and followed her in. Downstairs, they squeezed into a spot at the bar and ordered.

"Have you ever tried acting?" she shouted to him above the din of the crowd.

"Almost every day," Ethan laughed. "I need to, just to get through the day. My skin's too thin." In trying to be funny, he wondered where his answer came from. Upon seeing Mila's wrinkled forehead, he realized that she wondered too. "I just mean … you're chasing a dream and I'm not."

The bartender slid two glasses of beer in front of them. Ethan placed a five on the bar.

"You know what?" Mila shouted again. "Let's drink these and go. It's too loud in here."

Ethan leaned his head back and swallowed half his glass in one gulp. He smiled and razzed her with his eyes.

They left and headed to The Kitchen, a greasy spoon Ethan had been to a few times. It wasn't far and was on the way back to campus. They each ordered the student special—a burger, fries, and a bottomless glass of soda for three bucks. They sat across from one another in a booth with a chipped wood-veneer tabletop and cracked green-vinyl upholstery. What it lacked in décor, it made up for in character, even down to the bride and groom salt and pepper shakers. It wasn't luxury, but the price was right and the food was good. Neither of them was interested in the surroundings anyway. They wanted to talk.

"So no acting and no dream," Mila said, bringing them back to what they'd started at Charly's.

"I took drama in high school," Ethan began. "It was my best mark. The teacher really liked me. But nothing came of it. I was very serious about my band and being a musician." He explained his love of music and performing live.

"Wow. Why the hell did you pick engineering?" she asked, amazed by his story. "Sounds pretty messed up."

"Life is a paradox, isn't it?"

"I'm serious, Ethan." She leaned over the table. "You only get to go through this once, you know. You got to make it count."

Ethan didn't know how to respond. Mila was serious. He'd blocked out most of his previous self to focus on engineering. It was like she knew what she was chipping away at. "Mila," Ethan said, taking her hand and remembering her transformation at the rehearsal, "can we talk more about you? I've never experienced anything like what I saw the other night. Everyone in the auditorium was watching you, including those on stage. You make it all seem real."

It was Mila's turn to become uncomfortable. Her hands went to her lap, and the color rose in her cheeks. "Thanks, Ethan," she said, avoiding his eyes. "That's nice of you to say, but I can't explain what I do. It just feels right."

The waitress brought their Cokes in scuffed, old-fashioned Coke glasses. The phrase *Coca-Cola* was almost faded away. Mila took a quick sip from the end of her straw.

"Good try, but you're not getting off that easily," Mila added. "What about your drama class in high school? You didn't continue 'cause someone said you were good in science, right? Fuck—that pisses me off! The sciences always win. It's like the arts don't matter in the real world, and it's the only thing that's real."

"Mila," Ethan said, preparing to defend the decisions about which he himself often second-guessed, "you're kinda putting words in my mouth."

"Tell me—did you like drama?"

"Yeah," he admitted, "but it was nerve-wracking."

"Oh, come on. I can see it in your eyes. You loved it. You're just too afraid to admit it because people would think you're a pussy."

Ethan didn't know what to say. Truthfully, he didn't really like where he was, and he was tired of trying to save face. "Okay, acting was cool. I love the movies. The thought of being on the big screen thrills me. But it's a pipe dream. It's not real." He paused but only for an instant. "Did you ever see a movie called *The Warriors*? That was the first movie I wanted to be in."

"Ethan," Mila interrupted before he could go on, "why don't you join us. We need a replacement for Luke. He quit after the rehearsal on Monday. Says he's too busy with school but partying's more like it. You'd be perfect. And there aren't a lot of lines." She waited while he thought about it. "You have natural instinct," she added. "I saw it the first night we met. It's a rare quality my father told me about years ago. What do you say?"

Ethan was trying to keep up. Engineering was why he'd come to Ottawa, yet the arts seem destined to find a way back into his life. What if he did take the role? Would he get too distracted? Was it really a choice? "Sure," he said, surprising himself. Whether he could pull it off with school remained to be seen, but he'd get to spend more time with Mila. "When?"

"Wow!" Mila cried grabbing his hand. "I mean—that's great! I was afraid you'd say no. We can go back and start reading now."

Their food arrived. They munched away on the burgers and fries, but Ethan didn't really taste them. He was trying to figure out how he was actually going to do it.

"Mila," Ethan said, taking the heavy brown paper on which his burger was served and crumpling it into a ball, "what makes you think I can do this?"

Mila looked back at him, holding a fry between her thumb and forefinger. "You do, Ethan." She grabbed his hand again and squeezed it. Smiling, she said, "It's just a feeling but a really good feeling."

He just shrugged his shoulders, at a loss for words.

As they walked back to the university, Ethan wondered what he'd gotten himself into.

CHAPTER 3

Real Time
December 1983

"You've got to be more forceful!" Mila cried. "You're pissed at her. She's destroying herself, and it's breaking your heart. Pretend you're pissed at me. What would you say?"

"I love you," he replied smugly.

"No!" Mila exclaimed. "Be serious. That's not what you'd say. Come on. You're really pissed at me. You'd curse, something like, 'Damn, Mila, what the fuck are you doin'?'" Mila then paused and looked at Ethan like he had somehow detached his head from his body.

"*I love you* is exactly what I'd say," he repeated, realizing Mila was suddenly hearing him.

"You would too," she replied. "That's the line." She grabbed the script and crossed out what was there, replacing it with Ethan's response. "Perfect. I like it. I knew you'd be great. It's uncanny. You're a natural."

"Oh, I'm a natural all right," he repeated, chuckling. "A natural choke artist. Just you wait." Ethan was joking, but he slowly was getting comfortable with the idea of performing in front of a live audience without holding a guitar.

It was midnight. They'd been going over the script for the better part of the evening—a good four hours. A break was more than overdue.

"Mila, what do you say we call it a night?" he suggested, tossing the script on her unmade bed. "This is good, but I don't want to wear myself out."

Mila looked back at him. Her eyes were magnificent, so alive with

15

excitement. Her whole being was absorbed. Ethan could almost touch her love for the craft; it was so real.

"It's okay; you won't," she replied, sitting on the corner of her bed, flipping through several pages of the script. "There's another part I want you to take a look at."

Ethan stood up from the director's chair in the corner of her small dorm room and sat down beside her on the bed. "I could really use a break," he whispered near her ear.

Mila dropped the script on the floor, turned her head, and kissed him. She kissed him deeply as his hands tightened around her shoulders, pulling her close. He couldn't get close enough. His hands slipped under her sweatshirt, his fingertips spreading across her smooth skin. Her stomach was hard. His hands slipped beneath the lace of her bra and caressed her breasts. Her warm breath against his neck felt exquisite. She helped him pull her shirt over her head as he adeptly unhooked her bra. His dreams were coming true. She was so beautiful. He kissed her neck from behind as her head slowly swayed from side to side in rhythm to a secret melody. His hands cupped her breasts again and again. Their hungry mouths came together. Her fingers found his chest and pushed, squeezed, and clawed off his Reebok T-shirt. She kissed and tongued his chest. His quivering hands slid down her sides and over her hips. Her skin was so silky; he couldn't get enough of it. Their fingers, lips, and tongues devoured each other with an insatiable appetite.

Destiny had brought them together—they were meant to be.

Ethan awoke in the early hours and slipped from her bed. Mila looked heavenly; wisps of her brunette hair were splayed across her forehead. The script lay on the floor where she'd dropped it. He retrieved it and left.

A week later, Ethan was on the stage for the third time. Most of the cast gave Mila a "what's this crazy broad up to?" look when she brought him to the first rehearsal, but that changed quickly after Ethan spoke his first few lines. The looks turned to stares of amazement as Ethan took on his role and became increasingly comfortable with the script and interacting with the other actors. His initial nervousness faded as he transitioned into his performance and his lines became more natural. Each night, they would rehearse—he and Mila—until the early morning hours, when they then would make love until, exhausted, they fell asleep in each other's arms. It was an incredible time. Ethan finally had found where he fit, like that perfect pair of shoes that slide on right out of the box. The stage was his, and he shared it with the one he was falling in love with.

"Let's take five," announced Alexander, the director of their production. "Ethan, can I see you for a second?" Ethan walked over and sat down on the side of the stage. "Ethan," Alexander said, turning to face him, "you seem to be enjoying yourself up there."

"Can you tell?"

"No question," Alexander replied. "You've really taken to the role."

"Thanks. I've had a lot of help. Mila's a remarkable teacher." Ethan shifted on the stage, just in time to glimpse his roommate, Robbie, walking toward the auditorium exit. He threw up his hand to signal Robbie to come down front. It'd been a couple days since they'd last talked.

"Listen, Ethan," Alexander said, his voice becoming noticeably quieter and serious. "Would you be interested in auditioning for a show a friend of mine is producing downtown?"

Ethan hesitated, flattered by the request but uncertain of how to answer. "I'd be interested, but I've got no time. I've hardly cracked my books since I started on this thing."

"Ethan," Alexander continued in a low voice, "I don't need to tell you. You're a natural."

"Thanks," Ethan replied, catching Robbie approaching behind Alexander, "but all the credit goes to Mila. I'll have to think it over."

"Yeah, for sure," Alexander added, "but I have to know soon—like in a couple of days. If not, we have to find someone else."

"Okay. And thanks again."

Alexander got up and pulled a pack of du Mauriers out of his pocket as Robbie joined them. "Time to support my habit," Alexander said, placing a cigarette between his lips. "See you in five."

Ethan was trying to think of something smart to say but couldn't, so he just waved. He turned to Robbie. "How you doin'?" he greeted him.

"Just fine, guy. You look like you've finally found something you're good at."

Ethan laughed. They were always trying to get at one another.

Robbie was an outgoing, affable kid who couldn't quite understand Ethan's reserve but respected it. While Ethan was quiet and bookish, Robbie was a clever extrovert who needed little sleep and constant interaction with others. "Hemingway," Robbie had announced one day, picking up one of the books on Ethan's desk. "*The Old Man and the Sea*. I wonder if ol' Ernest ever imagined this little book would make him a star."

"It did restore his literary prowess," Ethan had replied.

Their talk of books then had turned to movies. "*The Philadelphia Story* with Cary Grant was the first movie I ever watched," Robbie had said. "There's nothing like the old black-and-white pictures." Robbie had seen a lot of movies, from *Casablanca* to *Star Wars*.

Now, Robbie's eyes followed Alexander as he left.

"You know it feels like I'm good at it," Ethan replied seriously. "It's kind of magical. I've looked a long time to find this. I get to become someone else for a brief moment in time."

"Well, I'll tell you something," Robbie admitted, looking Ethan straight in the eye. "You appear to be someone else too. It's like your mannerisms and everything change. It's pretty good for a jerk-off. But don't let it go to your head. You're still fucked up."

"You up for a beer later?" Ethan asked, ignoring the shot.

"You know," Robbie answered, "that's the first intelligent thing you've said."

"We'll be another hour or so," Ethan continued, "if you can stay up that late. Say, why are you here anyway?"

"Ah, you know," Robbie replied. "Kinda thought I should support the school and see how my roommate gets so fucked up."

"Well, thanks," Ethan said, flattered by Robbie's left-handed compliment.

"I was talking about Little Miss Muffin up there," Robbie said, nodding toward the stage. "She's unbelievable."

Ethan turned to see Mila standing a few feet away, beside the stage. "You mean Mila," he said. Mila must have heard him say her name, as she came over and put her hand on his shoulder. "Robbie Johnson, meet the genuine Miss Mila Monahan."

Robbie's eyes widened as he shook hands with Mila.

"Robbie's going to join us for a beer after rehearsal."

"Hey, that's great," Mila said in welcome. "Ethan's told me about you. It would be good to hear the truth."

They all laughed. Robbie said he'd stick around to the end, and they could head out together. Robbie then found a seat a few rows from the front.

Mila had the script in her hand.

"Tired?" Ethan asked, sitting down on the side of the stage.

"A little," she replied as he rubbed his hand down the middle of her back. "We've a lot to do and no time to do it. Another week, and it's showtime."

A chill went up Ethan's back, raising gooseflesh on his arms. He was just getting comfortable with rehearsals. The thought of performing in front of an audience terrified him. He forced himself to think of something else. "Hey," he said with a serious expression on his face, "you got me into this, so don't even think about abandoning ship now."

A look of horror crossed her face. "Ethan!" she exclaimed. "Don't even suggest such a thing. That's not what I meant." Mila seemed hurt.

"I'm sorry. I didn't mean anything by it. My feeble attempt at humor."

"Ethan," she whispered, moving closer to avoid being overheard, "I don't like anything that could jinx the show."

"All right, everybody!" shouted Alexander from the front of the stage. "Let's get back to our places. Scene two—let's move it!"

The next hour went by with only a handful of miscues. Performing in front of an audience kept creeping back into Ethan's head. Mila said it was the most exhilarating part of the whole experience for her. He didn't doubt it for a minute, but it still scared him shitless.

CHAPTER 4

The final week of dress rehearsal came and went without a hitch. Ethan became increasingly comfortable. His lines began to appear almost magically before his eyes as the words became his own. Mila and Alexander both remarked on his transformation. Alexander told Ethan it often took actors years to accomplish characterization; some never did. Flattered, Ethan wasn't sure he understood exactly what they were talking about. "*Whatever works*" became his motto.

There was a lot to do in the remaining hours before opening night. Alexander was up for the better part of two days from the last rehearsal, arranging and rearranging, meticulous in his attention to detail. The show was part of his master's degree in dramatic arts. He wanted everything perfect. They ran on a sparse—really, nonexistent—budget. Everything from costumes to the set design was minimalist in nature. Ethan was astonished by the tremendous effort required to bring it all together on opening night. Nervous anxiety ran at a fever pitch.

Ethan paced around the backstage room the actors used as a dressing room. They all had their own way of dealing with pre-show jitters. Some talked incessantly about nothing. Others were quiet, refusing to speak to anyone as they played and replayed scenes, lines, actions, and whatever else was in their heads. Excitement and tension filled the room. Like expectant fathers, they waited and watched the clock tick down the minutes before the big event.

Ethan became very nauseated an hour before curtain time. He had visions of puking at center stage in front of the audience.

Furthering everyone's tenseness was Mila's absence. She was never late; in fact, usually she was there before anyone else. The stage action she lived for was closing in, yet she was nowhere to be found—several of them had looked on campus for her—and no one had heard from her.

Alexander was freaking out, pacing backstage and cursing her lateness. For him, it was becoming unbelievable. "Where the fuck could she be?" he hissed, staring at his watch. "You have no idea what she's up to? Like picking up a cake or champagne for opening-night celebrations?"

Ethan shook his head and shrugged. "She didn't say anything to me. I'm as shocked as you are."

It was starting to scare Ethan. He couldn't believe she hadn't called anyone, especially him. It wasn't like her not to show, especially for something so important to her.

Alexander finally made the decision that no stage director wants to make, particularly five minutes before curtain time. Mila's understudy would have to step in. Ethan knew they would have to make it happen—the show must go on—but outside of meeting the girl and exchanging a few lines, he had practiced very little with her.

Now it was Ethan's turn to freak out. He was concerned for Mila's safety. He scanned the theater every few minutes for some sign of his love. His pre-show jitters were replaced by a fear that harm had come to her in some way. He felt wretched. This was not what he'd signed up for. He could only pray. With no Mila and an understudy who was nervous beyond words, the curtain rose.

From the first spoken words, opening night turned from one disaster into another. Alexander was beside himself with frustration. Ethan was so distracted that at one point, with his lines forgotten, he looked to the sky in character and asked for strength. After the final scene, rather than return to the stage for his curtain call, he ran out of the auditorium to Mila's dorm.

Numerous times during the performance, different members of the cast had called her room. After several tries with no answer, Ethan had called the dorm superintendent to check her room, who only returned to say there was no answer at her door.

"Well, fucking go in and check!" Ethan had yelled into the phone. "This is an emergency!" A sickening feeling seeped into his already cramped stomach; he was certain something was very wrong and was helpless to do a thing about it until the performance was over.

When he reached her dorm, he found two police cruisers parked outside the entrance. His heart dropped to the bottom of his gut. His feet stopped moving in his worst nightmare. Inside the foyer of Mila's dorm, several students were standing around. A police officer was writing on a black pocket-sized notepad. Ethan's mouth opened to ask the officer what had happened, but he didn't hear his own words come out. Stricken expressions of fear were written in the faces of the students he recognized from the dorm, reflecting his own fear as they turned to look at him. Verbal communication was unnecessary.

Ethan was terrified that it was Mila—and it was bad. He heard someone say her name.

"Mila who?" asked one of the students from the throng of voices. "Mila on third?"

"Oh, my God!" Ethan screamed, hearing the name he most feared, his emotions releasing his tightly strung feelings. His legs grew weak as he slumped against a wall.

Many of the students turned, confusion on their blood-drained faces.

"Someone broke a window on the third floor tonight, son," stated the police officer in an officious tone. "You know anything about that?"

Ethan realized he knew something about the room but couldn't speak about it—because he couldn't remember exactly. His mind already was changing what he knew. Maybe he'd find Mila up in her room with a major case of the flu. God, he prayed that would be the case. He tried with all his might to picture her thin, beautiful body curled up on her side in her small dorm bed, resting after another bout of vomiting.

"You called earlier," stated the dorm superintendent, appearing from behind a column beside the desk. His voice trembled like someone who had seen something so horrific that shock made it difficult to speak. "You wanted me to check her room."

Ethan shook his head. "Jesus Christ!" he exclaimed. "Where could she be?" At odds with himself, he didn't know what to do. His mind was in a quandary. Why couldn't he remember what had happened? He saw the stage with Mila on it.

On seeing Ethan's distress, the dorm super directed Ethan to a chair in his office. The officer followed, carrying his open notepad.

"Son," the officer said in a low, controlled voice, "why the makeup?"

Ethan looked back at the cop and realized he was still in character. He ran his sleeve across his lips. "It's not what it looks like, sir," he replied to the officer.

"Why do you say that?" spoke the officer, staring at him. "What's not what it looks like?"

Ethan thought for a moment before continuing. Had the dorm super said something about seeing him around earlier? "My girlfriend is not in her room," Ethan said, keeping the tone of his voice level and controlled.

"Is that unusual?"

"Normally, no," he answered. He had to be careful with what he said. He was being observed. Something *had* happened to Mila, but he couldn't remember what. "But tonight, yes."

"I'm listening," said the officer in a no-nonsense tone. Ethan imagined the officer's patience had more than run its course over the years when dealing with the shenanigans of spoiled university shits, wasting his time and Mommy and Daddy's money.

"I'm part of the university's theater group," Ethan began, passing his hand through his spray-stiffened hair. "We opened our show tonight. My girlfriend, Mila, is the lead. She didn't show."

There was little else to add.

"And no one has seen or heard from her tonight?" the officer asked, seemingly more interested in what Ethan had to say.

"Not as far as I know."

The officer jotted something in the notepad. He looked backed at Ethan without expression. "Your girlfriend's name is Mila?"

"Yes, Mila Monahan," Ethan replied. An image of Mila lying at the side of some road, crying his name as the lifeblood drained from her slashed throat, floated to the surface. He knew it wasn't real, but he couldn't help himself. The thought carried his emotions over the edge. Tears rolled down his cheeks. "Sir, I don't know what's happened to her. I fear the worst." He paused and then added. "She's a free spirit, for sure, but her dream was acting. She wouldn't have missed tonight for the world."

"It's gonna be okay, kid," the officer said with a tight-lipped smile. "We'll find her. These things have a way of working themselves out. It'll be okay."

The officer's words did nothing to calm Ethan's nerves or the churning that gnawed at his stomach.

"God, I hope so," Ethan stated, lost and all but powerless to control where he was headed. "She means the world to me, sir."

"I'm sure she does, son."

The officer removed his cap—that lessened his dominant appearance—and asked Ethan when he'd last seen Mila.

"Just after lunch," Ethan replied; it was all he could remember. "She was on her way to class." He provided a brief description of what she was wearing.

"Do you have a picture?" the officer asked, closing his notepad.

"No, I don't," Ethan answered, cursing himself that he hadn't pushed harder to get the photo he'd asked her for.

The officer left, saying he'd keep Ethan posted on their search. He left Ethan with a contact card and said, "If anything comes to mind, give me a call."

With little else to say, Ethan left and headed back to his room. He couldn't sleep. Robbie wasn't in the room; somehow, Ethan knew he wouldn't be. Things were mixed up, like he'd woken from a deep sleep and his brain was fuzzy. Despite the cold, he decided to walk around campus. Around 3 a.m., he returned to his room. Robbie was there and asleep.

Ethan woke him up. "Hey, man."

Robbie grumbled, "Go to sleep."

"I can't," Ethan said, moving to Robbie's bed. "Mila's gone."

"What? What do you mean? She's probably at a party. Go to bed, man."

Ethan shook his head as he pulled off his coat. He turned on his bedside lamp. "No, Robbie, she never showed up tonight. It was opening night."

"*What?*" Robbie cried, knocking off his blankets and sitting up.

"She never showed for the performance. She's gone. MIA. Something's happened to her. I just can't believe she'd miss opening night."

"You haven't heard anything?" Robbie asked.

"Nothing. No one has."

Stripping down to his underwear, Ethan lay down on his unmade bed and stared up at the ceiling. Each time he shut his eyes, he heard Mila crying out his name.

Shortly after 6 a.m., their room phone rang. Ethan jumped across the room, believing it would be Mila's voice at the other end. Instead, it was Alexander.

"She's vanished, Alex," he said. "I've not heard anything. The police are looking for her."

Alexander said little, expressing the same concerns running through Ethan's head: something tragic had happened.

Robbie was standing behind Ethan when he hung up the phone.

"I'm supposed to give this to you," Robbie said, frowning, passing a folded piece of paper to Ethan.

Ethan took the proffered page and opened it.

The writing seemed unmistakable, although something didn't look quite right to Ethan's eye. Mila's name was written at the bottom, with a small star dotting the *i*. Mila usually dotted the *i* with a heart. The note read:

Ethan,

I couldn't wait anymore. You're right. I need to go where the action is to make it. I'm just playing here. I have to make it real.
I'm going to New York.
Good-bye, my love.
Mila

After reading the note, Ethan nodded his head. It was hard to fight his disappointment, but his hope was renewed that she was alive. A good feeling crept in, but still he knew something wasn't right ... *didn't he?*

It didn't make sense. The note made it sound like going to New York was the only way to get what she wanted, but he couldn't believe she would do it. She'd not spoken of it or even hinted. He wasn't about to believe she really felt that way. Not a chance. But whether he liked it or not, it didn't change the fact that he had a note in his hand.

"Thanks, Robbie," he said. "I see it, but I don't believe it." He didn't know what else to say.

It was eight o'clock in the morning.

CHAPTER 5

The officer Ethan had spoken with the night before called him back to the superintendent's office in Mila's dorm.

Ethan left their room in a hurry. His head was spinning. Robbie dressed and came with him. There were four police cruisers in the dorm's visitor parking lot when they arrived; double the attention from his last visit. It couldn't be good.

"Dude, it'll be okay," Robbie said as he pulled open the dorm's entrance door.

"I don't know," Ethan replied. None of it seemed real.

The dorm super was waiting, standing beside the table outside his office.

"I need to ask you a few more questions," the officer said, coming out from behind the column by the front desk. "Alone."

Ethan nudged Robbie with his elbow and walked in the dorm super's office.

The officer closed the door and pointed to a chair for Ethan to sit down. "This is a real tragedy son," the officer began. "I'm so sorry. I understand the girl was your friend."

Ethan nodded, confused by the officer's words of "tragedy" and "so sorry," especially after the note Robbie had shown him earlier.

"I don't understand," Ethan said haltingly, looking into the officer's face.

"It defies understanding," the officer replied, "but we'll find who's responsible."

Ethan shifted in the wood chair. *Who's responsible?* he thought, *It isn't Mila? New York is her dream.*

The officer's gaze had dropped to the floor and then shot back at Ethan. "New York?" the officer stammered in surprise. "What do you mean?"

Ethan hadn't realized he'd spoken out loud. "She's in New York," Ethan replied matter-of-factly.

"No," the officer replied, again seeming to adjust his words as he spoke. It discomfited Ethan. He added, "Why do you say that?"

"Because of the note." Ethan's voice faded as his thoughts began to collide.

"What note?" the officer asked, shifting his feet.

Silence followed as Ethan tried to put together how Mila could possibly be in New York without his knowing or why she would have left on opening night of *Another Color Blue*. But there was something else that didn't make it seem real. "My friend showed me ..." Ethan heard himself say and then stopped.

"Your friend who's outside?"

"How would I know?" Ethan shot back, his voice sounding guilty.

"Because you said it," the officer replied.

Ethan could feel the intensity of the officer's eyes trying to read his mind. Ethan couldn't concentrate. "I don't know anymore. It was something I said to her once."

The officer bit his lower lip. "Are you sure, kid?"

Ethan wanted to say yes but couldn't. Things weren't fitting together in his head. God, he missed her. After a prolonged silence Ethan spoke. "Can I go?"

"Yes, Ethan," the officer replied, his tone again friendly. "Of course."

In the days that followed, Ethan could not bring himself to believe that Mila had left for New York. It didn't make any sense to him. For every question he posed to himself, he had an answer. Her clothes still hung in her closet. Would she leave without packing? And why a note? If she really left to chase her dream, she would have told him. And why would she leave before her big debut on the stage?

Ethan wasn't satisfied. He wasted little time in checking out the ticket sellers at the bus station. He even went so far as to take a trip out to the airport to ask around, all to no avail. No one recognized a female of Mila's description who'd bought a ticket to New York. Ethan knew it didn't end there. Someone could have driven her, but that would be nearly impossible to uncover.

"This isn't right!" Ethan uttered aloud, alone in the room he shared with Robbie. "I know it's not right."

The image of a bare bulb in a light socket, just like the light in Mila's bathroom, kept returning to his thoughts.

And blood. Blood. Blood always seemed close now, but whenever he tried to see more, the images dissolved.

CHAPTER 6

To Ethan, the feelings expressed on campus for Mila's disappearance were those of shock and disbelief—certainly beyond anything expected of a student's dropping out of school and chasing a dream to New York City. It was a very difficult time for him. He was convinced, despite the lack of evidence—other than the letter, which he was certain had not come from her hand—that she was gone. He prayed for her but was incapable of explaining what had happened. Somehow, he believed, she would find a way to communicate with him. Her going to New York to chase her dream made sense to him. *If you can make it there, you can make it anywhere.* Maybe she just couldn't wait any longer. But it didn't answer why she'd left without telling him or anyone else—that was a huge missing piece. Ethan only knew that she was gone and that he couldn't bear her absence.

Still, he knew—as Mila would demand—that the show must go on. The theater group played to six sold-out performances in four days, exactly as scheduled. After the upset and disaster of opening night, Alexander led the cast in regrouping, first asking whether they should continue without Mila. It was unanimous to go on with the remaining five shows, each dedicated to Mila. Ethan was grateful but at the same time surprised, as dedications were usually reserved for those absent due to circumstances beyond their control. Mila had quit the show. The cast's reaction fluctuated between a melancholy sadness and silent remembrance of their fellow actor, but perform they did.

It was most difficult for Ethan. Every word of every line seemed to bring Mila close but never touchable. He questioned whether it was right to put himself through such an ordeal. Time dripped by, as thoughts and vision melded together and produced a world only he could see and control, going in and coming out. Tears would roll down his cheeks during a performance, smearing his stage makeup. After one performance, he caught a glimpse of himself in a mirror, looking like an Alice Cooper rip-off with mascara running down his face. With each sold-out performance, the local community's support was astounding. Mila's absence, sadly, seemed to generate more publicity than if she'd actually been there to perform.

At the beginning of their final performance, Ethan delivered a special dedication to his mentor, Mila, in which he vowed to carry her dream to the world and, God willing, allow her to attain hers. He stood straight and erect as he delivered the speech, holding his voice strong amid the tears rolling down his cheeks. His heart was in pieces. Mila's absence was beyond his comprehension, yet he remained strong for her. She would never accept any thumb-sucking, sympathy-laden drivel. *"Shake life's foundations until it gives you what you want,"* she'd told him on several occasions, even the night before leaving. The theater troupe's final performance was magnificent; Ethan was truly inspirational to those who attended. He had found his place beside Mila and would do his all to bring her back. Her spirit was with them on the stage. Their performance tingled the senses and left the audience breathless.

Despite his attempts to deal with it, Ethan could not bring himself to believe Mila was gone. There was something unreachable, put away and inaccessible, that drove him to his wit's end and kept the police listening. Did he have the energy and wherewithal to keep going? He vowed he would never stop chasing the dream Mila had inspired in him.

In the days and weeks that followed the end of the show, life on campus began to reshape itself, and Ethan found no new information on Mila. Many of those closest to her stopped talking to him. "She's gone, Ethan. You have to let her go." Ethan maintained that he couldn't make sense of it. How could she make her dream come true by being invisible? It didn't make sense.

During this time, her class friend Sean came forward about a phone call he'd received from her the night prior to her disappearance. Sean had been questioned by the police, but Ethan really didn't understand why. Sean told Ethan they'd met at Charly's, as Mila needed to relax; she was so uptight and nervous about the big performance. Under the scrutiny of police interrogation, it turned out that Sean had made up the story—there'd been no meeting—to keep the police on Mila's case. Sean had an alibi—he was with a friend in the audience to watch Mila in *Another Color Blue*. Ethan didn't see much of Sean after that and continued to believe Sean knew more than he admitted.

Ethan fought to finish his engineering studies. Machine-like, he worked an incredible schedule, determined to complete his year so he could go on to graduate. His anguish seemed to translate into intense focus on his studies. Mila was with him; each night he could hear her whispering his name, telling him to go on and never stop. Life would give him everything; he had to persevere.

Still unable to answer what had happened, he sought counsel at the university's health services.

Ethan described the extent to which he missed Mila. It was beyond anything he'd ever dealt with. She was with him. He often felt her presence beside him. There were times when he could almost reach out and touch her, only to have her vanish like vapor. The same sense of emptiness would overcome him as he'd experienced when he'd first learned of her disappearance.

"It's a difficult time for you," the doctor who saw him empathized at their first meeting. "It doesn't make sense. Grieving for those we're closest to is difficult."

"I pray she's alive and okay," Ethan said, "but fear she's not." Pausing a moment, he then added, "And I'm helpless to do anything about it."

"Ethan," the health services doctor replied, "I would like to set up an appointment for you to meet with Dr. Katharine at the Royal Ottawa Hospital."

"Okay," Ethan replied. "But why, exactly?"

"It's standard protocol," the doctor answered matter-of-factly, "but after any traumatic event in a person's life, it's good to speak with a professional who can sometimes lessen the burden. Dr. Katharine is exceptional at what she does."

CHAPTER 7

Initially, the police would contact Ethan by phone, ask him a few questions about Mila, and probe for anything, endlessly looking for clues. As time passed, the calls became less frequent; more often than not, Ethan was the one initiating them. Had they made any progress? Were there any new facts or clues? But the end result was always the same—if they uncovered anything, they'd let him know, and he should do likewise. The weeks became months, but Mila's memory remained alive inside him.

Ethan and Robbie became much closer. They would do anything for one another. Their friendship helped Ethan become aware that certain people were meant to do certain things; that they were wired in certain ways—Robbie, for example, was gifted in math and science. Ethan would spend hours studying and completing assignments, but Robbie would hardly crack a book, yet he'd walk away with the top mark in the class.

"I don't know how the fuck you do it," Ethan stated late one night in their sophomore year. Robbie had just come in to the room they shared with a Bud Light in one hand and Oscar Wilde's *The Picture of Dorian Gray* in the other. "I'm studying my fucking head off, and you're out drinking and reading literature. Fuck—what gives?"

"It all makes pretty much sense to me," Robbie replied. "You've got a gift. You just don't see it. Have a beer, man."

"I can see it. I just can't remember it," Ethan chuckled. "And beer doesn't improve that."

"How do you know? You've never tried it."

"Yeah, right, just what I need—Lampwick in the flesh."

Exams were tough, but Ethan persevered and made it through. At the start of the spring term, the police still were not forthcoming with any new information on Mila's disappearance. Ethan was coming to grips with admitting that Mila wasn't coming back. Even though at times he felt she was there, he had to move on. To help let go, he decided to audition for another school theater production. He hadn't lost his knack.

"I know you," said the director, one of two people evaluating his performing skill. "You were part of *Another Color Blue*, and that girl—such a tragedy. Ever find out what happened?"

The question caught Ethan off guard, but he didn't miss a beat.

"Nothing. She just went away."

The play they were tackling was *Twelve Angry Men*. Ethan was reading for the role of Juror No. 8, a role played by Henry Fonda in the 1957 movie. The jurors are faced with the task of deciding whether a son is guilty of murdering his father.

Nothing more was mentioned of Ethan's previous experience. He began to read for the audition, and it was quickly evident he would win the part. He became the juror right in front of them. He really embraced the role and hoped it would help distance his thoughts of Mila; it didn't. In many ways, it brought him closer to her. He could hear her direction to be more forceful with his words or to lighten up as his character tried to understand what really happened. Often, during rehearsals, she seemed right by his side on the stage. All he had to do was follow her direction. It worked beautifully. The cast and director again were often mesmerized by his ability to transform himself so completely into character.

Nights remained the worst. Despite the accolades for his performances, the play only served to make Mila more prominent in his mind. He longed to hold her, to touch her smooth skin, or to kiss her soft lips. On nights when he felt her memory coming on strong, Robbie was by his side. As often was the case, they did not leave the room. They'd purchased a small refrigerator that they kept stocked with beer. On the nights when beer didn't dull the edges enough, out would come Robbie's Black Russians and Ethan's rye and Coke. Some nights, they went down to Roosters or the Bin, but their return to their room always was followed by a couple of nightcaps.

Ethan knew he was on a dangerous slope but couldn't help himself. *Mila wouldn't leave*, he thought on more than one occasion. She had introduced him to the world of acting; she had brought him to the stage. Wherever she was, he was sure she was watching him.

Sometimes Ethan would talk to Robbie about her vanishing act.

"How does someone just fucking disappear like that?" he commented late one evening at the end of their sophomore year.

"What do you mean, Eth?" Robbie replied. "She just signed out."

"But why did she leave?" Ethan asked. "Was our whole relationship just made up?"

"I don't know, but things do happen for a reason."

"How so?"

"Well, for instance, our friendship," Robbie answered. His eyes locked on Ethan's. "Before you only needed me for the answers to physics and math. Now you need a drinkin' buddy."

Ethan laughed and raised his bottle.

"Don't worry," Robbie added. "I'll still give you the answers, 'cause I love the drinkin' part. Besides, I never saw you when she was around."

They'd drink into the early hours, just the two of them in their room, with a small wooden night table between them, where they set their drinking glasses and liquor.

In the final performance of *Twelve Angry Men*, Ethan saw Mila for the first time in over a year. Backstage beside the curtain, she stood watching the cast perform. Ethan's character was facing the other jurors, explaining his point of view. When his character was asked a question, Ethan looked off in the distance away from the audience. For a moment, he was dumbfounded, and then his heart lightened upon seeing his love. If it wasn't for her hand rising and hearing her whisper, "The show must go on," he would have left the stage. She distracted him enough that one of the stagehands had to hiss, "Ethan!"

He continued with the scene, but as he came off the stage, he cried out to Robbie, who was working as a stagehand, "Did you see her?"

"See who?"

"Mila!" Ethan shouted, exasperated. "She was standing right here, smiling, and watching the show."

"I don't think so," Robbie said, astounded to hear his friend say such a thing.

"She was right *here*," Ethan insisted. "How could you have missed her?"

ACT II

Do not go where the path may lead,
Go instead where there is no path
And leave a trail.

—Ralph Waldo Emerson

CHAPTER 8

Ralph was one of a handful of engineers with whom Ethan worked at NewTec, a small engineering firm in the west end of Ottawa—Ethan had joined NewTec following graduation.

Ralph had just finished presenting his latest idea on a new cooling system for NewTec's newest Tech2 engine when David, their boss and engineering manager, left the meeting to answer a call from the company's president. Without the presence of the "dictator," as the engineering group referred to him, the discussion digressed to comments on David's wife's pert breasts, which recently had been revealed at the office Christmas party.

The incident had become the talk of the office following the party when David's wife, Martha, some fifteen years his junior, removed her blue fox-fur coat in the main reception area of the Ramada Renaissance Hotel, where NewTec held its annual Christmas party. While taking off her coat, it snagged the front of her dress, pulling the gown off her shoulders for a most revealing view of her chest—while she was not particularly attractive, Martha was well endowed. Martha's cheeks had flushed, but she carried on for the rest of the evening, unperturbed, and no one within earshot of the dictator would admit to having seen her. In the weeks that followed, however, the male population of the office could not leave the subject alone.

As in many meetings that went off the rails in David's absence, Ralph desperately tried to get the meeting back on track before David returned to assume control. "We've reduced the number of restrictions

41

within the manifold," Ralph stated, pointing to the drawing posted on the wall of the conference room, "by 30 percent."

"Well, her manifolds looked just fine to me," said Sam, one of the younger members of the team, like Ethan. Sam was a year out of college and single. Since the party, Martha's breasts made up a significant part of his conversations. "Forget 30 percent. I'll take them as they are."

"Get a life," retorted Ethan, tired of the discussion and the meeting. "What you need is a set of your own."

"You're just—" Sam started to say but stopped abruptly when David re-entered the room and assumed his seat at the head of the cherry wood table.

David shot Ethan a look of grave disdain. "So it's settled? You've decided?" David said in his condescending manner. "I'd like to think this team can work independently, at least once in a while."

Ethan was of the same mind but knew better; it was David's team. No one said a word as Ralph moved back to his drawing. "This, in turn, exceeds our 15 percent cost-reduction target."

"Great," replied David, always pleased with cost savings, "but what about the control system? How is it going to work? Tell me again why we should reposition the temperature sensors."

"There's no question we want them as close to the heat exchanger as possible," explained Ralph, "for optimizing the fuel–air ratio."

"Well, I think there is a question. The temperature farthest from the cooler is the most stable," David remarked, pausing to clear his throat. "Surely we want to control the engine around this temperature."

This was the third time they'd discussed this point in as many days. Ethan couldn't believe they were at it again. His patience had run its course. "The temperature is *definitely* stable at that point, David," Ethan interjected, surprised at the loudness of his voice. "We have to look at the system as a whole. We don't want a meltdown. Measuring the temperature that far away, though stable, will not indicate soon enough when cooling is required. We'll be into an overheat situation before it can be corrected." The room was silent as he continued, trying to control his temper. "This is the third time we've been through this. Can't we just decide and move on?" He turned toward the dictator among looks of surprise and continued. "David, let's go with mounting near the cooler, and change it if it becomes too erratic."

It's not your company, Ethan. Let it go. Again, the voice.

The meeting was a waste of time, as the outcome of the previous two meetings had proved. They all had more than enough work to do and little time to finish it—and still there was no decision. Ethan knew to whom he was speaking but went on anyway.

Sam's eyes were wide, reflecting his own shock, but he was beyond caring today. No one else said a word. The tension grew in the room. Ethan wanted to leave and get on with his day, and he wondered now why he'd started. His face was flushed with earnestness. Was this really a battle he wanted to fight? If he'd stayed quiet, the meeting would already be over, with plans for another one. No one else was going to say anything. Everyone knew better than to wade in now. Staring at David, whose eyes were fixed on the engineering drawing posted on the wall, Ethan looked across at Ralph, whose balding head was shaking back and forth in vexation.

"Well," David began, when there was no further input from anyone else, "it appears we have some disagreement on how to settle this matter."

That's one way to put it, Dave, Ethan thought cynically.

Could David even make the decision?

"This is important," David stated, turning to address Ethan. "We need to consider the position carefully because it *does* have serious implications. I would like some additional temperature readings around the reservoir."

Ethan remained quiet, barely able to contain himself. They were in production on the first engines, but here they were, still finalizing the design. It was unbelievable! The first were to ship in two days. They needed decisions, not more testing and another meeting.

It's not your company, Ethan. Let it go, the voice repeated.

This wasn't about engineering.

"So what are you waiting for?" David announced after a moment when no one moved.

"A decision," Ethan replied. The words were out of his mouth before he had a chance to check them.

Ethan was in turmoil that evening. His anger at his situation had grown steadily. His bouts of frustration with work were increasing. His thoughts kept returning to Mila. Her case remained open, and despite his attempts to bring closure to it, she continued to resurface again and again in his mind. Tonight, outside his apartment building, he saw her walking into the lobby. She was standing outside, looking off in the distance. He knew it was her, because she smiled at him. Her brown hair was shorter than before. Screeching tires jarred his attention. When he turned back, a woman stood by the entrance door, but it wasn't Mila. Mila was gone.

As of late, he'd lost heart in his work. He loved the creativeness of design, but the dream of car design had been replaced by the drudgery of engineering practice, reconfiguring the same designs over and over again. The excitement of innovation seemed missing from his world. He'd simply failed to understand why he was doing what he was doing. Meetings and posturing had replaced meaningful discussions on new products. Disillusionment with what the profession represented—and his role in it—sat heavily upon him.

"You seem distracted tonight," Beth commented. She set the box of lukewarm chow mein she'd picked up on her way home in the center of their small pinewood kitchen table. "Work okay today?"

Ethan had moved in with Beth a year after graduation. He looked up at Beth and wondered what life would have been like with Mila; a life with love. "Yeah, you know, David in indecision. He wouldn't know if good design came up and bit him in the ass." Using chopsticks, Ethan shoveled some chow mein onto the white Corelle dinner plate.

In a few scattered sentences, Beth spewed out her messy day at the office. They were losing a major account after months of planning. Beth was responsible but blamed her team for not capturing the "magic." Failure to secure the account would impact management's view of her ability to deliver. Her facility to perform would be questioned in the future. Discouraged, she was contemplating quitting. "I'm going to circulate my CV," she stated.

"Whatever you got to do," Ethan agreed, putting some of the limp bean sprouts into his mouth.

Beth was two years his senior and very career-minded. Ethan wanted to be with someone, and the two of them got on well. Both were looking for a relationship. Neither was ready to settle down, but living together fit their circumstances. Six months had passed since the move.

Tonight, however, seemed different. Ethan had never seen Beth so disillusioned. She was harder on herself than anyone else could dream of being.

"You know," she began, as if reading his mind, "it's hard not to question my own abilities. Scrutiny of my work will be brutal. It's like I've never done anything right."

"Oh, come on," Ethan replied. "It's one client. There'll be others. Shake it off. They know the good work you've done."

It was times like these that Ethan questioned having a family with Beth. It was always about her. If things were not smooth in her world, all was in chaos. He often wondered whether they were compatible. Tonight was hard because Mila had returned.

"It's like I set myself up to fail," Beth said.

Ethan looked back at her, surprised. "I thought you agreed to take on this client."

"I did," she replied, "but that has nothing to do with it. If they knew it was hopeless, they shouldn't have let me take it on. No one wins here." She sighed. "I wish I could stop analyzing everything I do."

Ethan had had a bad day but Beth had again turned it around to be about her. He looked across the table at the woman whose bed he shared. Her cheeks were bright with agitation and her eyes bloodshot from so many late nights over the past few weeks. She was cute and professionally attractive. Her daily workouts kept her fit and trim. At work, he imagined she intimidated most people with her relentless drive and ambition. But beyond her professional acumen, Ethan discovered, was someone as unsure and fragile as any person he'd ever met.

The uncertainties of her work environment and her future with a certain client were a regular subject now, and she was paranoid that she had lost her edge. Ethan was not excluded from her group of oppressors—she often saw him as increasingly difficult to deal with. Some nights, if he so much as touched her, she felt he was over the line.

For Ethan, it was like trying to cross a minefield, picking each move carefully, even strategically, not knowing what would touch off an explosion. When things reached this point, the difficulties were compounded further by Ethan's unhappiness at work. His anger would build with one incident after another, often culminating in Beth's making an offhand comment that he would take to heart. Something would snap inside him, leading to a sudden burst of fury and an unleashed punch at a wall or a door. There was no desire to hurt anyone, only an embarrassed lack of self-control.

Although he loved Beth in many ways, there was too much feeding into a tangled web of self-disappointment. He needed to affect the cause, not simply adjust to the effect.

In bed, lying beside Beth, his thoughts turned to Mila—her soft skin, her kind whispers, and her love. She would have known what to do.

CHAPTER 9

It wasn't long before he saw her again.

Ethan had left the office because he was not feeling well. Sharp stomach pains and chills had plagued him throughout the day. He was heading back to the apartment and decided to stop at the pharmacy for some Gravol. He found the stomach medicine quickly. He exited the aisle while reading the instructions on the box … and that's when he saw her, with a wisp of her brown locks across the center of her lovely face.

He thought his heart might explode, and the brightness suddenly made him lightheaded. She turned to go down the next aisle but stopped. Ethan looked right at her.

"Hello," she said. It was the first time he'd heard her speak—beyond her whispers in his ears—in years.

"Mila?" he gasped. "You're here?"

"Of course," she replied plainly. "Where did you think I was?"

"You went away."

Ignoring his statement, she continued as if only days rather than years had passed since they'd last spoken. "How's Robbie doing?"

A previous life flooded back on hearing Robbie's name. He hadn't talked to Robbie Johnson since graduation three years ago. They'd gone their separate ways when Robbie left for California after being recruited by a major oil company for his engineering brilliance.

"I … don't … know," Ethan replied, his words slow and careful.

"You should call him," she replied, squinting, as if confused by his answer.

Ethan could hardly speak. His worries disappeared like oppression lifted from his shoulders. "It's really good to see you," he said. "I thought you were—"

"Why did you think that?" Mila interjected before he could finish.

"I don't know, I just …" As he searched for the right words, he dropped the box of Gravol in his hand. As he bent down to pick it up, Mila vanished.

"Can I help you, sir?" a young voice asked him from behind.

He turned, startled by the pharmacy clerk.

"No … I'm good, thanks," he replied, moving to the next aisle. He was just quick enough to see the back of Mila's jean jacket disappear behind the next aisle. "Wait!" he shouted. "Mila, wait!" He took another step before breaking into an anxious run.

The comfort of seeing his true love was seeping away but at least he'd talked to her. When he reached the end of the aisle, she was gone. From where he stood, he could see the front door closing but no sign of who had gone through it. But he knew.

For days, he wondered why she had returned but then left so quickly.

When he got back to the apartment, the Gravol did its thing. Even his chills went away. He didn't mention his encounter to Beth but did resolve to give Robbie a call.

That was the first night he had the dream.

He had not told Beth about Mila up to that point. He could not speak about her. There was a hole he couldn't go down surrounding Mila's leaving in university. That night, however, he told Beth he'd seen Mila in the pharmacy. He went on to explain who Mila was and what she had meant to him. Something seemed to clear around him.

Beth became upset; a jealous rage ensued. She told him to stop with his nonsense. She didn't want to hear it anymore.

He said his relationship with Mila was long over, but he knew differently. He'd been so pleased to see Mila again. To know she was alive was simply wondrous.

48

Hearing the familiar voice at the other end of the phone line brought back a lot of memories that Ethan had tucked away. His spirits picked up on hearing the voice of his old friend to whom he hadn't spoken in almost four years.

"It's been a long time, bro," Robbie said after a few minutes of chatting. "What's up with you?"

"Keeping pretty busy these days and keeping my options open," Ethan replied. The words were out of his mouth before he'd even thought about them. "Work's pretty mundane, and life could be better."

"You still with Beth?"

"How do you know about Beth?" Ethan asked, surprised.

"Ah, heard it from someone," Robbie replied quickly. "Don't remember exactly. You know, friend of a friend."

"Yeah, we moved in together about six months ago."

"Hey, that's great."

"So what's California like?"

"Unbelievable, man. You should come down." Ethan didn't say a word. "Nothing like a trip to sunny California to straighten you out," Robbie teased.

"I think you're right," Ethan answered. "Did you have something in mind?"

"Ever think about working stateside, Ethie boy?"

"No," Ethan answered quickly and honestly. It was a bigger move than he'd ever considered seriously. "Can't say I have."

"Well, why don't you?" Robbie asked. "Might be important to your future."

"Yeah, how so?"

"Eth, I might be able to rustle up something, if you're interested. Our suppliers are always looking for engineers with experience, especially those who come highly recommended."

"Really?" Ethan said, surprised by Robbie's quick invitation. "You know … I have to do something, but California really never crossed my mind."

"Doing any acting these days?" Robbie asked.

"No," Ethan replied. "That was in another lifetime." As the words left his mouth, he realized that was why Mila had suggested he contact Robbie. She wanted him to be acting.

"That's a shame, man," Robbie stated. "You could have made it here. You're still the best actor I've ever seen. No one comes close. You made the hairs stand up on the back of my neck." Ethan didn't say a word, but something stirred inside him. "You move down here, and the big screen will be too much to resist."

Ethan heard the words but pushed them away; he wasn't ready yet. "Good try, Robbie," Ethan said, as his heart rate quickened and sparks went off in his head. "Long gone, my friend, long gone." His words could not have been farther from the truth.

"Think about it," Robbie added, "but it'd still be good to see you."

Ethan was already on the what-if scenario. No more NewTec; no more snow and cold. Ethan agreed to send his CV and then hung up, shaking his head and trying to comprehend what had just happened. The idea wouldn't let him go. Two events in the days that followed settled the decision.

CHAPTER 10

Ethan's Timeline
March 1990

As if preordained, the next night was a mixture of slush and freezing rain. Beth suggested they go see a movie. Ethan couldn't remember the last time he'd seen a movie in a theater.

He left work late and knew before he got there that Beth would be pissed. He drove directly to the theater and found Beth standing outside, smoking one of her du Maurier Special Lights.

"You just can't be on time, can you?" she bitched.

"Sorry, Beth," he said, genuinely apologetic. But *sorry* didn't cut it with Beth—he'd abused the word too many times. "David walked in at five-thirty, wanting a test report."

To say Beth was angry would have been an understatement; insanely pissed off was more appropriate. He knew he deserved it. Work was just an excuse. Beth did not tolerate the "doing the best I can" answer. Shaking her head, she said nothing but glared at him as he brushed the winter wetness from his head. Throwing her half-finished cigarette on the ground, she heeled the butt with her salt-stained black pump.

Her smoking didn't bother him as much as the butts on the ground, but he knew she was making a point. Ethan paid their admission as they entered the theater in silence.

The movie, *Scarface*, let them both escape for a while. With a heavy storyline of the drug underworld and Pacino as the ambitious kingpin, Ethan was not disappointed with his first movie in years. Beth said she liked it too, having cooled down during the show.

It was more than just another movie for Ethan, though. It was more

51

like a launching pad. At the midpoint of the movie, he had realized he was kidding himself to think he could exist without the movies. His dream remained an ember, still burning inside him.

It's your time, my sweetness, he heard Mila whisper. He turned to his side, expecting to see her, but the seat was empty.

But it was a moment of pure magic. Tears rolled down his cheeks.

He *could* do it. He *had* to do it.

"You okay, Ethan?" Beth asked as they exited the rear doors of the theater into the cold, damp evening. Wet slush soaked their feet. "You looked upset."

Beth put her arm around his back, but Ethan was miles from the theater exit, thinking of his call to Robbie. He thought of the future and the sacrifices he would have to make.

"Ethan," Beth said, louder this time. "Where are you?"

"Just ... thinking," he replied, turning in her direction but seeing Mila again in the pharmacy.

He *could* do it. Heading to California seemed ludicrous in many ways, but he had a way to get there now. It had been a long time since he'd been excited about where he was going. It was clear. It was time for change.

"Did you like the movie?" Beth asked. Her face was bright but somewhat anxious. Gone was the dark contempt reflected earlier.

He climbed in the driver's side of his three-year-old blue Chevy Cavalier, thinking, *Odd. For a moment, it looked green.* "It was good ... very good," Ethan answered, his mind focused on where he'd put the most recent update of his CV.

"That's all you can say?" Beth groaned. "I can't believe it. That movie was incredible!"

Ethan wondered whether Beth would ever say that on seeing him in a major motion picture but decided not to go there. Instead, he turned right onto the westbound ramp to the 417, different from the usual route home.

"Ethan, this is not the way," Beth said. "Where are you taking us?"

"Nowhere in particular," he replied, pressing the accelerator to the floor. The car surged forward. "We need to talk about a few things."

"We do?" Beth replied. "Like what?"

Ethan paused for a moment to collect his thoughts. The car was moving very fast down the highway. "Beth, what do you want?" he finally asked. It was exactly what he wanted to ask, simple and to the point.

"What do you mean?" she answered, surprised by the question.

"Simply, what do you want? If you could have anything, what would you ask for?"

"You mean like world peace or something?" she asked, screwing up her face.

"No, a little closer to home," Ethan said. "What do *you* want?" He continued looking for something he was sure he wouldn't find.

"I don't know. What do you want?" She looked at him like he was being a goof.

"I want to go to California," he said without hesitation. "Do you want to come?"

"Sure," she answered, smiling. "I've got some vacation time to use up."

"Not a vacation," he said, watching her shift in her seat. "I was thinking of moving there. I want to live in California. What do you think?"

He knew her answer, but he wanted to hear her say it.

"Oh, Ethan," she said with a pained expression on her face. "It's so far away. My career is starting to move forward. Why California? You've never even been there."

He took his foot off the pedal, slowing the car as he looked at her. In that moment, she seemed foreign to him, and he wondered if he knew her at all. "I want to be a movie star," he stated.

Beth started to laugh. "Be serious," she said, covering her mouth with her hands, embarrassed by her own laughter. "Ethan, you're an engineer. Don't be ridiculous."

Ethan stared at the road ahead in silence. *She doesn't know a thing about what burns inside me. But I can't blame her. I shut that part off before we met.* "You asked me what I wanted," he replied, "and I told you."

"But Ethan, that doesn't make any sense!" she cried, leaning forward in her seat until the shoulder strap was taut. "You're playing with me. I'm not going to fall for it … but good try."

Ethan took the exit ramp to head north and then turned into a "Kiss-and-Ride" parking area and stopped the car. "It's no joke, Beth," he said, turning to face her. "I'm going to California. You're welcome to come, but my decision's made."

"Ethan, I'm not falling for this crap, so stop."

"I called an old friend from university," he explained. "He invited me to come visit and check it out. He said they're always looking for good engineers." He paused for a moment and then added, "I could make ends meet with engineering work while I try my hand at acting."

Beth seemed quite taken aback. "Ethan, what are you talking about? Since when have you been interested in acting?"

He'd never mentioned acting, hiding it deep inside so as not to be disturbed. "I did some acting in university," he said, watching her reaction. "I was good. But it was a tragic time, and I've tried to forget. I've blocked it for a while, yet it comes back from time to time, knock-knock- knocking. Usually, I don't answer, but this time … well, this time I did. I don't expect you to understand, but maybe you can forgive me." He could see by the perplexed look on her face that his words were difficult for her to comprehend.

She leaned back in her seat, her head against the backrest. "Let's go home. My head hurts." A few minutes later, once they were back on the highway, he heard her mumble, "I'm not going to California."

For all intents and purposes, that was the end for them.

CHAPTER 11

The next day, Ethan was sitting at his desk, reading a report from the controls group that explained their method for controlling the engine temperature. They wanted his comments before finalizing the report. It was 10 a.m.

An assembly technician from the plant floor approached his desk. Paul had been around the company for years and had an uncanny ability to get under a person's skin by saying only a few words. "How does an engineer with all that expensive education screw up a drawing so badly?" Paul demanded, shoving the drawing in Ethan's face.

Ethan had tolerated the man's comments in the past, but today he had zero patience. He was enraged not only by the intrusion but by Paul's disrespect. "What the fuck is this!" Ethan exclaimed, on his feet before Paul could utter another word. "What the hell gives you the right to come in here and throw your shit on my desk?" If Paul had been any closer, Ethan might have taken a swing at him.

Paul listened to Ethan's outburst and then replied, "I don't know why engineering is allowed to put out this crap. I might as well draw it myself."

Ethan suddenly saw things more clearly than he had in months. In an instant, his decision to go to California was confirmed—it was a decision that would change his life. "Paul," he said, demanding attention, "you're going to get your chance to do exactly that." Ethan stood motionless for a few seconds but then picked up the logbook and pen on his desk and glared at Paul. "I'm tired of your bullshit, Paul.

I'm tired of being your fucking kindergarten teacher. Here." He handed the book and pen to Paul. "Have a good life, but take my advice and at least get one."

With that, he grabbed his gray jacket from the back of his chair and brushed past a flabbergasted Paul.

"Where are you going?"

Ethan turned and looked him square in the eye. "Paul, I hope I never see you again, but believe me, you won't forget me."

Ethan walked into their engineering conference room and closed the door. Robbie's number was written on a Post-it note on the back of his planner. He dialed the number, realizing it was still pretty early on the West Coast. After the third ring, Robbie picked up.

"This is Robbie."

"How you doin' today?" Ethan asked without identifying himself. "Understand you're lookin' for some engineers."

There was a pause at the other end, and then Robbie answered, "Could be true. We're real interested in crazy Canucks right now. Know any?"

Ethan smiled. "As a matter of fact, I do. How goes it, my friend?"

"Pretty fucking excellent, if you really want to know," Robbie replied excitedly. "But don't tell anyone. I wouldn't want them changing the rules." There was a brief pause before he added, "Dreams do come true. So what's up?"

Strange turn of phrase, Ethan thought. He leaned forward, his elbows on the conference room table in front of the speakerphone. "I'm resigning, Robbie. I'm comin' to California."

"No fuckin' way!" Robbie yelled out at the other end.

"Way, dude," Ethan burst out, "so you better find me a fuckin' job!" He felt amazing. The weight of his responsibility at NewTec was slipping off his shoulders as each moment passed. He guessed this was how a person felt when winning the lottery. Next week's production schedule and engineering reviews were fading fast. A wide smile stretched across his face as freedom overcame him.

"Ethan! Ethan!" Robbie screamed at the other end. Robbie had been talking but Ethan had hardly heard. "Are you there or what?"

"Yeah, I'm here. I'm just trying to get used to how crazy this is."

"Yeah, well, get used to it," Robbie said. "We'll talk soon."

Ethan hung up and returned to his desk. He then decided to call Beth.

"I'm not coming to California," she said after he told her he'd resigned. "I don't know who you are anymore, Ethan, or what you're doing."

He wanted Beth to understand, but he couldn't give up on his dream any longer. His vow to Mila haunted him. Hollywood—if he was to make an earnest attempt—was where he had to go. His energy now had to go into fulfilling his dream, not defending why he couldn't.

"The weather!" Beth shouted. "That's the best you can do?"

He wasn't aware he'd said anything, but clearly he had, and Beth was none too happy about it.

"I'll drive you to the airport and wave good-bye!" she cried and hung up.

Ethan looked at his desk. For a place where he'd come to work for as long as he could remember, he had remarkably few things to take with him. Inside his tan leather satchel he loaded his planner, a gold-dipped maple leaf Mila had given him for good luck, and a magazine he'd kept with a Sly Stallone interview because it ended with Mila's favorite quote: "Become a pest to life until it gives you what you want."

He walked out through NewTec's reception area and stood motionless, taking a last look at the leather couch and armchairs, remembering that the hiring of the interior designer had cost more than he and Beth had spent furnishing their entire apartment. He sat down on the cushy leather couch, wondering whether he was doing the right thing or if he had lost his mind. His answer to both questions was the same: maybe.

With that, he stood up and walked to the front door for the last time.

CHAPTER 12

That night Ethan's dream was all white with edges and walls. There was a doctor or someone in a white lab coat. Beth wanted him to talk with the doctor, and she became quite agitated when he at first refused.

"What do you remember?" a doctor he didn't recognize, asked.

"About what?" Ethan replied, confused by the situation.

"Is there something in your past, maybe?" the doctor asked, placing the end of a black-and-white ballpoint pen between his teeth. "Something you don't like to talk about?"

"Let's instead talk about something I do want to talk about," Ethan shot back, annoyed. "Like, why am I here?"

"I think you know why you're here," the doctor replied. "You want to go to California. You want to run away from your life and responsibilities."

"We want what's best for you, honey," Beth insisted, now standing beside a white desk in a white lab coat.

"We've always wanted what's best for you, son." His father stood on the other side of him against a white wall.

"We all love you, Ethan, and want what's best for you," said a woman who looked like his mother as tears rolled down her cheeks. "Why do you have to go to California? That's so far away. It doesn't make any sense."

Ethan was bursting inside. He wanted to be left alone. Why did they care? "Leave me alone!" he screamed. "It's my life! You can't control me!" He tried to stand up but couldn't. He thought he was sitting in a chair, but there were white sheets over his legs. He was sitting upright in a bed. They were standing around the bed. The woman who looked like his mother was crying. His father's face was expressionless. Beth was shaking her head, her eyes wide as if something was frightening her. Another doctor stood at the foot of the bed with a white clipboard. He was wearing glasses with black frames.

Ethan tried to move his arms. They were restrained. He was harnessed to the bed. He screamed. "What the fuck! You can't stop me!"

He looked back at the doctor, craning his neck. The doctor lowered the clipboard he'd been writing on. Ethan recognized the doctor—he wasn't a doctor at all. It was his longtime friend, Robbie.

Ethan screamed out, "California, here I come!"

CHAPTER 13

Beth did as she said she would and drove him to Ottawa's airport. The drive out to Uplands Airport was foggy. The mist had floated in across Bronson Avenue, creating a melancholy dreariness, as if to ask if this was really happening.

When Beth let Ethan off at Departures, the airport looked smaller than he remembered. Beth helped him get his bags out of the trunk of their Cavalier. *Strange how it looked blue again.* They'd agreed to talk of the other things he might need once he arrived in California. She would keep the car. As the entrance doors to the building slid open, Ethan saw very few fellow travelers around. Most of the people were uniformed custodians, security, and other support staff. There was a sterile feeling to the terminal at this hour that he'd not noticed when he'd traveled for business with NewTec, but then he didn't usually travel at 11 p.m.

"Well, take care of yourself, Ethan," Beth said as they approached the customs area. "I'll come and visit. I love you, you know."

She gathered together her long blonde hair as if to form a ponytail and then let it fall to her back. It was something she did when she was weary. He put down his carry-on, put his arms around her, and kissed her forehead. Going to Hollywood was something he had to do, but it didn't take away from the fact that he loved her too.

For a moment he pondered why he was going, but he chased the thought away. He knew why, even if he couldn't explain it.

His wave was quick as he checked in to get his gate pass. As he slung his carry-on bag over his shoulder, he noticed a band on his wrist, like those used in hospitals to identify patients.

"It's the new gate pass," he overheard someone say.

Funny, he thought. *I don't remember anyone putting it on.*

From there, Beth escorted him to customs. A woman in uniform approached with a wheelchair and stopped in front of him. He looked around. Beth was a distance away.

For you, sir, the woman seemed to say without moving her lips.

"But I don't need flight assistance," Ethan said and waved his hand toward Beth, but she was too far away to see him. The woman nodded as he sat down.

There was a man beside her, also wearing uniform. His was white too. "Might as well enjoy the ride," the man said and smiled.

From there they headed to Ethan's gate. He could never remember his gate number and thought the wristband was a great idea. On route, he asked the man and woman to stop at a kiosk. He wanted to buy breath mints and a can of Coke.

It seemed only minutes before he found himself waking up on the red-eye for Los Angeles.

On waking, he recalled his meeting with his father on the previous night, when they'd met at his father's favorite Italian restaurant in the city. They had enjoyed an exquisite dinner of scallops and prawns on fresh linguine, served with a California Pinot Noir and followed by slices of very chocolate Queen of Sheba cake.

Ethan had been pleased that his father, not normally a comfortable man, looked relaxed. When they finished their meal, their waitress brought two snifters of Remy Martin. Ethan then pulled two Davidoff cigars from the inside pocket of his gray jacket.

"Must be some kind of news," his father said, wetting the cigar in his mouth. He rolled the cigar adroitly to get an even light. Ethan followed his father's lead. "I haven't been treated so royally since you told me you were moving in with Beth. Are you still together?"

"Yes and no," Ethan replied, "but it is connected."

His father peered at him through a puff of smoke. He recently had grown a beard, and the sides had grown in silver-gray like his hair. Ethan thought it made him look majestic.

"Dad," Ethan said, "I'm going to California."

His words hung in the air like the swirls of smoke from their cigars. His father's reaction was difficult to discern as Ethan watched him take a draw on his cigar.

"I knew you had something going on," his father said, speaking through a cloud of smoke. He smiled, surprising Ethan. "When?"

"Tomorrow," Ethan stated and then added, "I'm looking at a job with an engineering firm in Los Angeles."

His father rubbed the whiskers of his beard. It reminded Ethan of his mother's comment of a man's need to fondle his facial hair.

Ethan took another draw on his cigar and touched the tip to the ashtray, knocking off a length of silver-gray ash. He hadn't provided the real reason why he was leaving. "Do you remember my roommate from college, Robbie Johnson?"

Ethan's father tried to put a face to the name. "A tall guy with brown hair? Always trying to grow a beard?"

"That's the one," Ethan answered.

In characteristic fashion, his father then switched subjects, a habit that brought him respect in business but did nothing of the sort for those trying to converse with him. "What do you think of the new look?" He rubbed his beard.

"It looks great—majestic, even."

"Your mother would never let me have one—hated the scratchiness. I like *majestic*."

With palms sweating, Ethan brought the conversation back to him and was ready to own up to the real reason for heading south. He wanted his father's acknowledgement, if not his support. But his father surprised him again.

"You're going to Hollywood to be an actor."

Ethan smiled in relief and eased back in his chair. It was what his father said next, however, that had the biggest impact.

"It's okay, Ethan. Go and chase it. You'll never be satisfied if you don't. Believe me—I know."

At a loss for words, Ethan's eyes welled up. He could not recall his father ever speaking so candidly with him.

His father's only question: "What took you so long?"

Ethan reflected on his father's words as the flight attendant made her way down the aisle with water for thirsty passengers.

What took me so long? "Fear and insecurity" was what he would have said if his father had been sitting next to him. Fear had fixed itself in the back of Ethan's head for as long as he could remember—fear of going to school, fear of his teachers, fear of bad grades, and sometimes, even the fear of what would happen just getting out of bed in the morning. He'd convinced himself that if he didn't feel fear, the outcome of anything he did would be a disaster. Until recently, the cloak of fear had controlled almost everything he did.

By his own conventional measures, he'd followed instructions to the letter. In school, he'd been good in math and science, so engineering had been a great fit—except that engineering had never made his heart beat faster, had never made him want to get up early or stay up late, and had never made him do crazy, unthinkable things. It had just *fit*. He loved beautiful buildings and exotic cars, and he loved beautiful design, but the everyday work of an engineer bored him to death. The map he'd followed was simply the wrong one.

"Excuse me ... would you like a beverage, sir?" asked a middle-aged flight attendant.

Although not asleep, Ethan's thoughts had taken him far from his seat in the aircraft. He looked up at the woman with a confused expression on his face. "No ... no, thank you. What ... what did you say?" he stammered.

"A beverage, maybe?" she repeated.

"Just a Coke, please," he responded.

The flight attendant's smile disappeared into a thin line as she poured the Coke. Her lips were carefully traced in a dark burgundy lipstick, and Ethan found it difficult not to stare at them. He wondered what they'd be like to kiss. She poured a tomato juice for the woman beside him. The tomato juice looked good too.

It was then he heard her voice. *Be a pest, Ethan, until life gives you what you want.*

Before he could think, he spoke. "Excuse me," he said, giving the attendant the best smile he could muster. She returned his smile. "On second thought, that tomato juice you just poured looks mighty good. Could I have a glass of that instead?"

He knew he'd inconvenienced her, but that was what he wanted. *Small decisions*, he thought. He would have to make them. No one was going to give the prize away. The flight attendant poured him the tomato juice and left the glass of Coke.

Ethan turned and looked two seats ahead across the aisle. He hadn't noticed the brunette sitting there. He thought of Mila and was reminded of the promise he'd made himself to dedicate his life to acting. His eyes closed as he thought about it. He smiled as he realized his vow to keep her memory alive hadn't died; it simply had been dormant, preparing him for the future he now embraced. His only strategy was to keep persisting until he was on the big screen. At that instant, there wasn't a doubt in his mind that he wouldn't achieve it.

Again, his eyes moved up the aisle. This time the brunette turned. He knew who she was. Yes, the odds were against him but instead of feeling discouraged, he was even more encouraged.

ACT III

If one advances confidently in the direction of his dreams,
And endeavors to live the life which he has imagined,
He will meet with success unexpected in common hours.
                                    —Henry David Thoreau

CHAPTER 14

Sunshine blasted through his eyelids. The whole world seemed lit up, setting his brain on fire. He moved his arm to shield his eyes, only to be struck by pain so intense it felt like a nail was being driven into his right eye. He prayed for relief. What had he done to deserve this? Before he could think to answer, a hand touched his bare back.

"You gotta get out of here!" Her voice was sweet and familiar but with serious urgency. "He will kill you if he finds you here."

Ethan turned over to diminish the harsh brilliance of the sun, only to have his temples attacked by the vengeance of a hangover. Driving his throbbing head further into the pillow, his bloodshot eyes flashed open as the woman leaned over him. He felt the press of her breasts through her T-shirt on his arm. The bed came alive as she shook him. Closing his eyes, he still wanted her—such an erotic brown beauty—but not now. Tylenol and a still bed were all he desired. And darkness. *Fuck the sunshine.*

The woman got out of the bed, picked up Ethan's shoes, and threw them at him. "He will fucking kill you," she screamed in frustration, "if he finds you here!" Her voice had a hard edge that disturbed him and tarnished her beauty.

It was brutal lifting his pounding head off the pillow. He pulled on his worn deck shoes. If there was hell, he'd found it. Even his fingernails hurt.

"For Christ's sake, please get out!" A bang came from somewhere beyond the door of the bedroom. Someone had entered the house. Her boyfriend was back. "Holy shit!" she hissed, redirecting Ethan from the bedroom door. "The window!"

The window opened wide enough for him to slip through. His movements were heavy and slow, despite his trying to go fast. But once outside, he was on green grass and running. He thought he'd put his shoes on but now was running in bare feet. His motion was hard but lethargic and in no particular direction—just away. There was a small backyard and a wooden fence that led to an alley of garbage cans and trash. Several dogs barked from the surrounding yards.

Ethan kept running until he reached a street. His head was swimming, trying to grasp where he was and how he'd gotten there. Nothing was clear; any memory of how he'd arrived was gone. Nothing seemed familiar to his foggy eyes—houses with white siding and white doors with black numbers.

Questions flew through his mind in bits and pieces. Who was she? Was she married? Was he being chased?

He didn't get much farther before his stomach reminded him that the previous night was not to be forgotten. Before he could stop, his stomach unloaded like a fire hose through his mouth, forcing him to the ground. His stomach heaved, locking his entire body in spasm. He ached all over. Rolling onto his side, he lay still, like a man beaten, waiting for another kick to end his misery, not wanting to die but helpless to do much about it.

Calm eventually prevailed as he curled into a ball. Dry scrub grass scraped his face. He could smell the parched earth. The chant of insects was amplified to unbearable levels inside his throbbing head.

What was he doing? He was glad he didn't know anyone here who might recognize him. He must be nuts to think he could actually achieve anything in this crazy town.

A father and son passed on the sidewalk beside where he lay. The little boy spoke. "Is that a homeless man, Dad?"

The father's reply was laconic. "Probably."

Ethan's heart crumbled. Could this really be him? Had he reached bottom? His slight body heaved again in response. Dry. His stomach was attempting to turn itself inside out as if to reject its own emptiness. He tried to remember the woman's name. Ashamed and barely conscious, his last thought was that it started with K.

As he came back to consciousness, an older woman was walking by with a young girl who had a braided ponytail. "Do you have the time?" he asked the woman.

She looked to be in her mid-fifties. Her face had the look of wrinkled leather that years of hard drinking and smoking leave behind. Her gray-streaked hair was cut short and stylishly thinned at the sides. There was a street toughness about her that implied she knew a lot more than she would ever reveal. The woman scrutinized him. "Three thirty-five," she responded, staring him straight in the eye. "You look lost." Her guard came down at that point and the hint of a smile curved her thin lips.

"I've had better days." His voice cracked. His throat was dry from his night of smoke and alcohol, making it difficult to speak.

"Where you from?" she asked, her face softening but keeping hold of the little girl's hand.

"Ottawa, Canada," Ethan coughed, forgetting for the moment about his apartment in California.

"Then you're really lost," she said, grinning.

Ethan didn't know whether she was making fun of him or trying to show some compassion.

"I ... could use a cup of coffee and some Tylenol," he replied, realizing he'd lost his wallet. "And ... where am I?"

The woman handed him a ten-dollar bill from what looked like a white clipboard at her side. Ethan was dumbfounded. "Sorry to see that you're down on your luck. This is a loan to get a coffee and something to eat. May your luck improve soon." The woman started to walk away but then stopped. "By the way, what's your name?"

"Ethan Jones," he said. "Remember it. You'll hear it again someday."

"I'll watch for you," she said, then turned and walked away.

He raised his hand and waved, but no one saw it.

CHAPTER 15

The interior of a taxicab usually reveals some part of the driver's personality; the one Ethan climbed into was no different. He was confronted by Batman, Ironman, and Captain America, all fixed to the passenger-side dashboard in their four-inch superhero splendor.

"Don't you feel safe?" asked the driver, pointing to the figures in front of Ethan. "They protect us from the world's evildoers."

"Yeah, I need some of that," Ethan said.

The driver laughed and turned the banana-yellow taxi onto the roadway. Ethan still didn't quite know where he was.

"So where we going?" queried the driver. He was wearing a white dress shirt with a button-down collar.

"Bank Street in Redondo Beach," Ethan answered. "It's an apartment building."

"Yeah, most are, in that area. What brings you way out here in the late afternoon?" The driver, like most Ethan had experienced, was not short on conversation. It seemed to go with the territory.

"Well," Ethan said, wary of getting too familiar too quickly, "a little misdirection and a lot of indiscretion."

"That sounds kind of heavy, man. Rest assured, Randy's at your service with his crew of superheroes to make your trip safe and worthwhile."

The driver turned his shaved head sideways and proffered his right hand. Ethan shook it, surprised by the man's firm handshake. He was

70

expecting a somewhat limp exchange, considering the plastic company in their midst.

"Good to meet you, Randy," he replied. "Ethan Jones." He sat back in the seat and absorbed the full interior. There were figures and pictures placed everywhere—a shrine to comic-book heroes. It was weird but comfortable.

"I'm an animation artist," Randy announced. "Welcome to the office."

Ethan was still guilt-ridden by his actions of the night before. What was his next move? Would there even be one? Did he believe in himself, or was he just blowing smoke? Maybe he should just pack his bags.

Don't be an asshole, Ethan, came the all-too-familiar voice that had brought him here in the first place. He pushed his doubt aside.

"So what's your gig, man?" Randy asked, shifting himself on the worn black-vinyl seat.

Ethan replied with the same answer he'd used since coming to California. "I used to be an engineer."

"Yeah? Cool. Chemical? Computer?"

"Mechanical."

"A gear-head," Randy stated and went quiet. The rush of passing air around the car became noticeable. He changed lanes, maneuvered the cab around a slow-moving Ford Econoline, and sped up. His confidence behind the wheel in city traffic was evident. Heavily veined hands spun the steering wheel with ease without jostling his passenger. A miniature Superman was mounted on the dash to Randy's right, with his cape outstretched toward the windshield, as if a fierce wind was blowing from somewhere inside the cab.

"Superman's your favorite character, I see," Ethan surmised.

"You got that right, my man," Randy replied, a big grin stretching across his face. "Superman's the leader, mentor, and most powerful of all superheroes."

Ethan smiled too.

A red Ferrari appeared one lane over to their right. "Take a look at that," Randy said breathlessly, pointing to a 308 GTB. Randy moved in beside the exotic machine. "That car beats all. Mark my words—I'm going to have me one of those fine pieces of machinery one day."

Ethan smiled. *There's about as much chance of this guy owning a Ferrari as there is of his dating Farrah Fawcett.*

Randy glared at Ethan. "I know what you're thinking, man, and that's where you're wrong. Mark my words ... as sure as I'm spinning this steering wheel, I'll have a red 308."

Ethan couldn't deny Randy's zeal. There was definitely something different about this guy, and quite suddenly, Ethan's doubt vanished.

Randy glanced at Ethan. "So," he said as the Ferrari zipped away, "you spoke in past tense. You're not working as an engineer now?"

"I'm down here to become a movie star," he blurted. It was the first time he had stated his intentions so directly. He cringed, anticipating the driver's smirk. For a few minutes, they sat in silence, except for Bobby Darin singing "Mack the Knife" on the radio. Ethan was unprepared for Randy's response.

"That's awesome, man. Bets are, you will be too."

"Thanks," Ethan said, not knowing what else to say. He was dumbfounded by the man's optimism.

"I'm serious." Randy's dark eyebrows dropped, nearly touching the bridge of his nose. "If it means anything to you, I get this sixth sense about people. People think I'm crazy, but I get this feeling."

Ethan smiled, not caring where the feeling came from. The man's words were miles from rejection, and that's all he cared about. He felt like he'd been given a shot of Demerol and settled back into the seat to stare at Batman, his favorite superhero. Randy's words were just what he needed. "You know, I've had a pretty shitty twenty-four hours," he started, retracing as much as he could of the previous night. "I met a woman—"

"Fucking always starts with a woman," Randy agreed, nodding his head while he rolled up his sleeves like a workman.

"Well, this was no different," Ethan continued. "I left the crazy bitch earlier today, but don't ask me when. Only thing I know for sure is I won't be seeing her again. Not in this lifetime." He continued with his story of waking up with this woman and his head exploding with a brutal hangover. At this point, a few more things came back to him from the evening. He'd met the woman at an industry party for some producer named Logan. He didn't know Logan but was eager to go to the party, with a chance to make some connections. Then he'd messed up in finding the location. The rest was a blur. "And that's pretty much how I became the shit you're talking to," Ethan wrapped up.

The end of his story coincided with the taxi's pulling up in front of his apartment building. Ethan's heart sank when he read the meter: twenty-eight bucks. He had the ten in his pocket that the kind lady had given him but was sure he'd left his wallet at the woman's house. "Shit!" he hissed. "I've got ten bucks."

Randy stared at him, his expression becoming hard. "Come on, man," he said. "You're shittin' me."

"Listen," Ethan replied, scrambling for a solution, "my apartment's upstairs. Give me five minutes to get the money in my room."

Randy's eyes locked on Ethan's as if trying to confirm a trust between them. "I'll wait, but you'd better not be fuckin' with me."

Randy's hard-ass response didn't sit well with Ethan. The common ground they'd reached was quickly dissipating. "Give me your business card." Ethan took the card and wrote his name and telephone number on the back. "Take this. If I don't come back, call the cops and tell them I stiffed you on the fare." Opening the passenger door, he handed Randy the ten. "I'll be back in a few minutes," he said, looking into Randy's eyes and holding his hand out to shake. "Count on it."

He ran up to his third-floor apartment, grabbed money from a drawer, and ran back down to the street. Randy was leaning against the side of his idling yellow cab with his arms crossed when Ethan came out the glass entrance doors of the apartment building's front foyer. There was a rolled comic book in Randy's hand.

"You are for real!" Randy exclaimed as Ethan walked up to the parked car. A tight grin bent his lips as Ethan approached. "Sorry to be rude. You can't imagine how many people I never see again after they split to get money." He pulled a card from his shirt pocket. "Any time you need a lift, you know who to call."

The card he handed him was different from the one on which

Ethan had written his name and address. A figure with the physique of a superhero was pictured on the front. Randy unrolled the comic book in his hand. Pictured on the front cover was the same muscular figure on his card. Ethan didn't recognize the character but marveled at the artwork. Randy handed him the comic.

"He's mine," Randy said proudly as Ethan paged through it. "The name hasn't stuck yet, and I'm still working on the title. But I'm this close"—Randy held up his hand, showing a space between his thumb and index finger—"to a deal with an animation house."

"This is yours?" Ethan exclaimed, impressed with the colorful graphics. The guy had talent far beyond steering a car through traffic in LA. "This is amazing." Ethan motioned to give it back.

Randy shook his head. "It's yours. Don't lose it. It'll be worth a fortune someday." He stuck out his hand. "Gotta go, man. Got rent to pay, like every other sucker. Give me a call sometime. We'll go for a beer."

"I'd like that," Ethan said, locking hands.

Ethan headed back up to his apartment and browsed through Randy's comic book. The artwork was incredible—vibrant colors and immaculate detail. He might not know much about art but he knew what he liked—and he liked this. He could tell that Randy's days of driving a taxi were numbered.

Ethan paced around the apartment as if for the first time. The living room was white and connected the kitchen, bedroom, bathroom, and balcony. Sliding glass doors separated the balcony from the living room. It was a nice place to sit, late at night when he couldn't sleep, and dream about the movies. He couldn't, however, remember having done so.

A shower was his first order of business. He stripped off his soiled clothes. The scum-like film that clung to every square inch of his body felt disgusting. Once in the shower, he winced at the possible opportunities he had squandered at Logan's party. *You're a piece of work Ethan Jones*, he said to himself as the streaming water from the showerhead began to restore his soul.

After a time, he shut off the water and dried with the only towel on the rack. Refreshed, he searched for a clean shirt. His drawer was empty, so he wrestled something he thought was clean enough from the pile of dirty laundry beside his bed.

After pulling a white T-shirt over his head, he noticed the red light flashing on his answering machine. Funny—that was always the first thing he checked when he came in, but somehow he'd missed it. A tinge of excitement kindled inside him. Messages were rare. Messages were hope. It was that kind of day.

The first message was a familiar voice he didn't want to hear. She hoped he'd made his way home okay. Christa—that was her name—wanted to apologize for the abrupt end to their night. He cringed when she said she wanted to meet again. "I don't think so," he said aloud to the machine and promptly deleted the message. "Once was enough."

The second was from Beth and brought with it a whole mixture of feelings. Beth had surprised him when she said she loved him at Uplands. After almost a year, he found it strange how little he remembered of the flight to California or even of his connection in Toronto. Her message indicated she wanted to know how he was doing. Was he getting the work he wanted? There was more, but he could only handle so much at a time. He would listen to more later ... maybe.

The third message was a male voice with a thick accent, who identified himself as Sven Irons. He wanted to meet with Ethan to discuss the project they'd talked about. Ethan could feel his pulse quicken as the message concluded with Sven leaving his number. Ethan couldn't recall meeting the guy but dialed the number anyway. Sven's answering machine picked up on the first ring. "Sven here. Leave a message." Ethan did so and hung up.

Things were looking up. Randy's business card was on Ethan's white kitchen table. As he slipped it into his pocket, he saw his lizard-skin wallet on the floor. He hadn't left it at the crazy woman's house after all. It must have fallen off the counter. The wallet itself reminded him of when he'd first slid it into the pocket of his shorts under the hot Yucatan sun while vacationing with Beth. It was one of the few possessions he'd kept after leaving Ottawa. The wallet signified something he didn't want to let go of but couldn't quite explain.

It was almost four, by the school-style clock that hung on his wall, so he had an hour before he had to be in front of his computer, drawing lines at Build Industries. It hadn't taken him long to land the job on arriving in California. Build Industries Inc. was an engineering firm that did contract work for oil-rig builders. Ethan's biggest adjustment was working nights. Now, as a result of his vomiting, he needed to get something in his stomach first, so he had to get moving. There was a clean pair of jeans hanging in the closet; he pulled them on, tucked in his T-shirt, and was on his way.

On route, he bought a newspaper. Entertainment and classifieds were all he read these days, looking for work—open auditions, casting calls, anything that got him closer to the movies. His last audition had been for a television commercial that hadn't yielded as much as a call-back. It wasn't enough, and he knew it. "Keep sharpening the saw, or the trees stop falling," his mother was fond of saying. At the time, she was referring to his lack of piano practice, but the phrase had stuck with him and seemed applicable to so many things in life. If he didn't stay tuned up, his chances would dwindle. The only game in town was persistence—gig after gig.

Gonzo's Sub Shop was his next stop. More often than not, he stopped by before or after work to grab a bite. The proprietors were a couple of excitable Mexicans who had befriended him when he first arrived in California. He was a regular and enjoyed the privilege of extra toppings on his choice of submarine sandwich. They were crazy about the movies and Hollywood and always had a trivia question at the ready. When Ethan walked in, Jesse Gonzales was behind the counter in his usual white Gonzo T-shirt, black belt, and white pants. Ethan was there before the dinner crowd, so he didn't have to contend with any lineups. The only other customer was eating at the counter.

"How's Al Pacino today?" Jesse asked after Ethan ordered his favorite pizza sub with extra guacamole.

"He's doing fine. Wanted some advice on how to play a mean son of a bitch," Ethan answered, his face displaying a convincing evil grimace.

His anxieties always weighed less on him at the sub shop, where the brothers not only made the best submarine sandwiches around but also provided Ethan with unintentional counsel. Now, he looked forward to his first bite into a Gonzo sub, as well as what Jesse had to say.

"How about you?" Ethan asked. "Still playing by the rules?"

"Well, boss," Jesse answered, addressing Ethan with his usual sign of respect, "of course not. It's no fun to work that way, 'specially when the deck's stacked against you. Gonzaleses play to win, my friend. Coke?"

Ethan nodded, his feigned grimace changing to a grin. There was something different about Jesse. His mood seemed to weigh him down. Normally, he kept talking about a star's latest movie or his own dream of becoming a millionaire—there'd be a Gonzo's franchise on every corner in the US of A. Like Domino's or Denny's, Gonzo's would be a household name. "You'll see," he'd say. "Big plans." The Gonzales brothers prided themselves on their achievements. They'd come a long way from their roots in a village north of Mexico City.

"So where's Pedro?" Ethan asked.

Jesse halted his sandwich-making activity. His hands clutched the sides of the stainless steel counter, as if straining to keep the counter in place. His arms tensed. The prominent veins in his muscular forearms bulged. Ethan began to wonder what he'd said wrong as he watched Jesse's face darken. Another side of the normally jovial and lighthearted man preparing food behind the counter emerged. It was the face of a man who'd witnessed horrors no human should have to see. His lips were pressed so tightly together, they were white. His eyes were dark and blank. For an instant, Ethan questioned his own safety. Then, as suddenly as the transformation appeared, it was gone, and a tear rolled down Jesse's cheek.

"Pedro got shot out back two days ago when leaving the shop," Jesse said between clenched teeth, his jaw locked in anger as he wrestled with his self-control. "I'll kill them all if he dies."

Ethan watched, frozen, as Jesse's open palm swung down and struck the countertop. The sound reverberated through the shop like a bomb blast and scared the shit out of Ethan. That the counter remained erect was a wonder.

Shaken, Ethan was the first to speak. "Fuck, what the hell was that?"

"Sorry." Jesse's face became flat and expressionless.

"How bad?" Ethan asked, his heart in his throat, realizing he'd never known anyone who'd been shot.

"He's out," Jesse answered. "Unconscious. He's been like that since it happened. Doc said it don't look good." Jesse put Ethan's sub together, but his hands shook noticeably. Tiny beads of sweat broke out on his forehead and upper lip, making them shiny from the reflection of the ceiling lights. "Maybe you heard the sirens. There were cops everywhere. They closed down the street." Jesse pointed outside with one hand. "Couldn't believe it. Police tape is still out back."

Ethan shook his head.

"You sleep with cotton in your ears?" Jesse asked.

Ethan chuckled, expelling air through his nose. There were sirens every night. "No, I was probably working," he replied, trying to remember where he might have been. "Where's Pedro? Which hospital?" He checked his watch, determining whether he might manage a visit before heading to work.

Jesse shook his head as he bagged Ethan's sub. "You can't see him. No one but family—intensive care." Then, after hesitating for a moment, he added, "Are you religious?"

"I believe in God. I don't go to church," Ethan responded.

"Yeah, me too, but could you put in a word for Pedro anyway? He needs all the help he can get. If the man upstairs is listening, I want everybody praying to him." He inserted a couple of napkins in the bag before twisting it closed. "My friend," he said, handing Ethan his dinner and raising his open palm to indicate it was on the house, "have a great night, and say hello to Harrison Ford. Invite him down for a Gonzo sometime. We're always open for a bad dude with a reputation."

"Thanks, Jesse," Ethan said, knowing better than to do anything but accept the gift graciously. "I'll make sure I do."

As Ethan turned to the front door, Jesse disappeared through the back behind the counter. Parked across the street was a black Chevrolet Lumina with someone inside, trying not to be obvious.

CHAPTER 16

As usual, Ethan arrived at Build Industries Inc. about twenty minutes early and went to the cafeteria to eat his dinner and browse the classifieds. The sub tasted great, as always, and really hit the spot. His thoughts drifted to Pedro. Why would someone want him dead? The list was probably long, from guns to drugs. Jesse likely was involved too—Ethan doubted there was much the brothers didn't do together—and worried for his own life. Ethan understood there was another side to the brothers that he knew nothing about—a side Jesse revealed in a momentary lapse behind the counter. Still, they did make awesome sandwiches. Ethan shoved the last bite into his mouth, poured himself a cup of the barely drinkable coffee, and headed to his desk.

After leaving the cafeteria, he meandered through the maze of office desks at Build, thinking about his agent. Sure, Steve Cushman was a friend of Robbie's, but was he working with Ethan's best interests in mind? Cushman rarely called, and half of the acting work Ethan had done since coming to California, he'd found without his agent's help. He made a mental note to call Cushman later. Something had to change. His *Persist or Die* screensaver was scrolling across his monitor as he plopped down in his office chair.

Robbie had helped get Ethan the job at Build, which was a subcontractor to J. Gordon Engineering, the firm where Robbie worked. Build Industries had required a senior engineer with pressure vessel design experience—perfect for Ethan—and so began his association with a new employer. He'd planned to stay at the Holiday Inn Express until he found his own place, but Robbie would have none of it, and so they shared Robbie's apartment.

Time seemed to merge the events for Ethan, from his kissing Beth good-bye at Uplands Airport to landing at LAX and meeting Robbie. Even the time he spent at Robbie's apartment before Build Industries' relocation service found him his small bachelor apartment was a blur, but it didn't matter. He was living the dream.

Three drawing projects awaited his attention when he sat down at his desk. He had to complete them all before he left, but none would take more than a couple of hours. The engineering activity was more demanding than had been explained during his interviews; he was up to the task but preferred to work evenings when the office was quiet. It also allowed him the freedom to focus on the work at hand or on upcoming auditions if he wasn't busy. At seven thirty, he had finished the engineering calculations for his design and was about to start the second project when his phone rang.

"Ethan, how are you?" It was Steve Cushman, for once beating Ethan to the punch. "Where've you been? I've been trying to get you since yesterday."

"That's funny. I didn't have any messages on my machine," Ethan replied sardonically.

"How was the party?" Steve asked, ignoring the comment.

"Wild but disappointing. Different than I expected."

"I know how you feel. Seems like most of life is like that."

"So what's up?" Ethan asked.

Robbie had introduced Steve Cushman to Ethan somewhat by accident a few weeks after Ethan arrived in California.

"Fuck, Steve, at least give him a shot," Ethan had overhead Robbie saying to someone Ethan hadn't seen before. They were in a bar just around the corner from Robbie's apartment.

Before Ethan could interject, the other guy replied, "I need another wannabe actor like I need a bullet hole in my head."

Ethan then stepped in to let his presence be known. "Hey, Robbie, what's going on?" Ethan said, moving up to the bar beside his friend.

"I'm trying hard to get you an agent," Robbie replied, leaning his head in Steve's direction. "Ethan, meet agent extraordinaire Steve Cushman."

Ethan shook Steve's hand and thus started the awkward beginning of their relationship. Steve explained that his clientele were serious actors, trying to make a living. Most were waiting tables or selling consumer electronics to make ends meet, not "white-collar professionals who fancy becoming movie stars because they look like James Dean." It was that comment that gave Ethan a new purpose to his quest: to prove Steve Cushman wrong.

Now, Steve said, "I've got a line on some work, but it's a night job. You'll have to read for it, but that's your forté. You up for it?"

"You better believe it!" Ethan shot back. "No problem. When and where?"

"Tomorrow night at Bronson and Main," Steve added. "It's an old converted church. They'll give you the script there. Knock 'em dead, kid."

"I'll wait," Ethan said, smiling. "If they choose someone else, then I'll kill 'em."

"Yeah, I hear you. Let me know how it goes." Steve then paused before adding, "Be there early. You're on at seven. They don't wait. Miss your place, you're history."

Ethan hung up. In his excitement he had risen to his feet. He wanted to go now. The second project no longer held any interest. Steve had said little about the role, so Ethan started imagining the possibilities. It would be great if he could land a few small parts and get more experience.

Pacing around his desk, he stopped and closed his eyes. With his hands on the back of his chair, he steadied himself and took several deep breaths, expelling the air slowly to relax his muscles. The projects had to be completed. He'd be here all night if he didn't get focused. Opening his eyes, he sat down and began adding line after line to his design on the screen.

Fifty minutes later, he was still fiddling with the same drawing. He was overdue for a break—his mind was full of everything but the task at hand.

Returning to the cafeteria, he bought a Coke and a bag of Fritos from the vending machine. The sports section of the *LA Times* was open on one of the tables. Standing, he flipped through the sports scores, but nothing held his interest for any length of time. He refolded the paper and left it where he'd found it. He headed back to his desk. His time in the office already seemed too long.

At eleven thirty, he plotted his last drawing. As the drawing printed, his trained eyes caught a duplicated dimension. Dimensioning parts—describing the length, width, and height—was always a nightmare for him. Designing was an act of creativity, exciting with its chance at discovering value with new function, but describing the parts that went into the design—dimension after dimension—was painstaking drudgery. No matter how closely he scrutinized his work on the screen, there was always something incorrect or missing. A mistake here cost production dearly. He hated to make mistakes. He shut the plot down, made the correction, and then rechecked the rest of the drawing on his screen before resending it to the plotter. Collecting the three projects, he placed them on his manager's desk with a note about the morning's production run. Then he tidied up and left. It was midnight.

On his walk back to the apartment, he thought of the message Beth had left on his answering machine. He thought of her often. If she was here, he'd take her back out of sheer loneliness. His remedy to block her from his thoughts had failed, as all it took was a phone call, a name, or a face to trigger her back again. His feelings for her were stronger than he liked to admit. His previous night's actions had been more a result of missing her than anything else. Now he felt guilty. Her call played with his heartstrings. At times, he had little power to fight it. It was like the pull of nicotine—despite an awareness of its harm, that didn't stop the intake.

And she knows it, he reminded himself.

On entering the apartment, he grabbed the cordless phone and flopped on his chair. He would call her. But for the moment, he closed his eyes to think, quickly drifted off to sleep, and dreamed.

CHAPTER 17

Men in white coats surrounded the bed. Beth was at his side, dressed in a navy tailored suit, ready for work. He was glad to see her.

"Beth," he said, "why am I here?"

"Because you need to get better."

"Better? I'm not sick." He felt fine.

"Where are you, Ethan?" a person in one of the white coats asked.

Ethan heard the question but paused, sensing a trick. He was in California but couldn't figure how Beth could be there—or why he was in a bed surrounded by people in lab coats. "California?" he replied, attempting a confident response but realizing that it sounded like a question. Then, looking at Beth, he added, "When did you get here?"

Beth shook her head and looked away.

He wondered what he'd said to cause her to react that way. She bent down and kissed his cheek. "What? What's wrong?" he asked but nothing came out. "Beth! Beth!" he screamed, trying to move, but his arms were held tight, restricted in some way. "What the fuck is going on!" He tried to kick his legs free from their bindings.

An alarm sounded—a loud alarm.

He squeezed his eyes closed and then opened them.

CHAPTER 18

The ringing didn't stop. Ethan's eyes opened to his dark apartment. The cordless phone was ringing beside him on the bed. For a moment, he hesitated, trying to determine if he still was in the dream. His room looked real. He picked up the phone.

"Hello?" he said, glancing at his clock radio. It was 1:30 a.m.

"Ethan?" asked a vaguely familiar female voice.

"Yes," he responded, wondering who would be calling him in the middle of the night.

"It's Christa. We met last night."

His mind was still groggy as it tried to register reality from his dream.

"We were together last ..." the female continued.

"Ah, yes," Ethan interrupted. *Oh God, why is she calling me?* "How you doing?" he asked cautiously.

"Oh, just fine," she replied, her voice bright—very different from her tone when he'd left her that morning. "I was wondering whether I could meet you someplace for a coffee. I've got the blazer you left behind yesterday."

Ethan wavered before answering. *My blazer. Fuck.* It suddenly came back to him. "Sure ... I guess. Sorry, I didn't realize I left ... but I'm not surprised. As I remember, I left in a bit of a hurry." *Why am I agreeing to meet with this woman?*

"I'll meet you at Dorian's Coffee Emporium in half an hour, okay? I really need to talk to you. Bye." She hung up.

"Where the fuck's Dorian's Coffee?" he asked, speaking into the dead line. "Like I'm going to meet her at two o'clock in the morning. She's fucking nuts!"

It likely was her boyfriend put her up to it so he could beat the living shit out of Ethan—or kill him. After hearing Jesse's story at Gonzo's, it seemed more than a possibility. People did things like that here; they didn't just *talk*.

Ethan had never been a physical fighter, and he wasn't about to start now, but it was his navy Hugo Boss blazer that made him reconsider their rendezvous. When he'd left for the party, he'd been wearing it. Now, he looked in his closet, even though he knew he wouldn't find it. Fuck. The blazer had cost him a fortune. He was not comfortable, knowing what was sure to follow.

Clicking the buttons on his answering machine, he searched for her earlier message, but it was gone. "Shit, I knew it." He dialed directory assistance.

"For what city, please?" asked the operator.

"Oh, I don't know … Los Angeles."

"For what name?"

"Dorian's Coffee something or other."

There was a short pause and then the operator came back on the line. "You're looking for Dorian's Coffee Emporium?"

"That's right," he said, his patience waning. "Where is it?"

"There are two. Do you know which one you're looking for?"

"Where are they?"

"There's one on Bank Street and the other is—"

"That's the one," Ethan interrupted and hung up the phone.

Instead of leaving, he dropped into his comfy chair and leaned his head back into its softness. He needed his Hugo Boss back, but now his thoughts turned to Beth and his disturbing dream. At the same time, he saw a statuesque figure wrapped in a tight black dress. Dreamy brown eyes looked into his. Christa had caught his eye from across the pool on the dimly lit patio …

His thought was interrupted by the insistent ringing of the cordless beside him. Disoriented again, he fumbled for the phone and glanced at his watch. Shit—he'd fallen back asleep.

"Hello?" he answered, his voice now raspy from sleeping.

"You're standing me up?" Christa said, sounding on the verge of tears.

"Shit, I'm sorry," he apologized. "I dozed off. I'm on my way."

Before he realized what he was doing, he was walking down Somerset Street in front of his apartment building. He ran along Somerset until he reached Bank and swung left. He was out of breath by the time he saw the sign for Dorian's Coffee Emporium on the other side of the street. It was written in three-inch pink neon script, one word above the other, beside the entrance door. If he'd been driving, he likely would have missed it.

Sitting alone near the window farthest from the door was a lone woman. He stopped in his tracks, understanding why the previous evening had happened. She was the most stunning woman he'd ever seen—more beautiful than his pictured recollection. He was struck by how little familiarity he found in her features. If she had not been the lone person in the café—and had not been wearing an oversized navy blazer—he would not have known her. The blazer added a sexy nuance to her stunning beauty. His heart, already pumping hard from running, climbed into his throat as he stared at her through the window. She tucked a strand of her long chestnut-brown hair over her ears, first the left side and then the right—a nervous habit. Her hair then fell quite naturally, covering her cheeks and hiding her anxiety. Her arms dropped to her sides as she stretched them downward, straightening her posture, which in turn adjusted the blazer.

As he moved closer, she crossed her legs under the table and then bit her lower lip, as if she was preparing for an important event. As he continued to stare at her, he had not realized he still was in the street until a passing motorist honked at him. It startled Ethan and caused Christa to turn and, for the first time, see him approaching. Her face brightened as she smiled, revealing immaculate white teeth. After a quick wave, her fingers again traced her hair behind her ears, this time revealing her dangling gold earrings.

He quickly moved to the front entrance. If this was a setup, he no longer cared.

"Hello, Ethan," she said, standing up from behind the small table.

"Hi," Ethan replied, moving toward her across the small café. The strange sense of knowing and not knowing the woman in front of him was quickly forgotten when he saw the bruise below her left cheekbone and a small bandage her hair did a poor job of covering above her eye. Both had been hidden from his view out in the street. Her eyes were bloodshot.

"I'm sorry I look such a mess, but I had to see you."

"It's okay, Christa," Ethan replied, staring at her cheek. It was the first time he could remember using her name. "What happened?"

They sat down at the small table.

"I'm sorry to call you," she began, "but I felt dreadful about what happened this morning and how I treated you. I was out of my head, and I panicked. I didn't want you to get hurt." A forced smile appeared on her face as Ethan nodded. "I wanted to see you again. I wanted to meet the sober Ethan Jones. The wasted one didn't last very long. I wanted to start over."

He continued to listen without commenting.

"Mark found out you were there last night," she said, dropping her head and looking down at the table. "He didn't believe me when I told him it wasn't what he thought." Then abruptly she raised her head and met his eyes. "Just so you know, nothing happened last night between us, despite what it may have looked like. You passed out in your clothes before I got to the room."

Ethan nodded. This wasn't the time to explain how out of character his previous night's actions were.

She winced as she smiled and went on. "He slapped me around and called me all kinds of nasty things. Then he kicked me out. I'm not a slut or a whore, Ethan. Please believe me." Pausing, she took a sip from the white porcelain coffee cup. Her hands were shaking.

Ethan's emotions hardened. One thing he had zero tolerance for was a man who abused women. It was beyond his comprehension and made his blood boil.

"Everything I own ended up in the front yard," she said.

It was then he noticed the large bag against the wall beside her.

She laughed weakly, but her eyes welled up and big tears rolled down each cheek. Her voice cracked when she spoke. "You seemed like a good person, so I called you. I need a place to stay ... for a few nights ... until I make other arrangements."

"But why me? You don't even know me. You must have a friend or family."

"Mark is very possessive. He was jealous of anyone I got to know—girls or guys." She paused to wipe the tears from her face. "My family's in Canada. I wouldn't go there anyway."

Ethan was quiet. He couldn't take his eyes off the bruise and bandage on her face. Those were the wounds he could see—wounds that were there because of him. A hard lump formed in his throat. Although a nagging *What are you doing, bro?* repeated in his head, without hesitating further, he said, "Christa, I don't have a lot of room, but we'll figure something out."

Christa took another sip of coffee, trying to hide the tears rolling down her cheeks. "I was able to rescue your blazer," she said, sitting erect and smoothing the lapel with her fingertips. "It's very nice." She smiled again, showing her white teeth. The tears made her eyes sparkle. She had a beautiful smile. "Thank you, Ethan." She reached her hand forward, shaking noticeably, and touched his hand. "I won't be any trouble. I promise."

Ethan couldn't help but think he would regret hearing those words.

They strolled back to his apartment. A light rain was falling. He carried her possessions, which amounted to a surprisingly heavy khaki bag stuffed full of clothes, as well as a small sports bag. They didn't talk a lot but shared how little Americans seemed to know about Canada.

Back in his apartment, Ethan pulled two cold Bud Lights from his small refrigerator and twisted off the caps. He handed one to Christa.

"I never pictured you as a Bud man," Christa said, her voice coy, her brown eyes a little brighter.

"Well, I never pictured you drinking from a bottle," he shot back with a wink.

"Are you kidding? I'm from Calgary. On the ranch, the bottle is the glass."

They both laughed.

Ethan moved to the side of the room where he stored some of his stuff.

"I have to put down some cushions, as there's only the sofa for a bed, but you can have it." Christa's eyes followed his movements. "I just need to move a few things around." Sliding a box of books to one side, he piled some clothes on top to clear enough space for a makeshift bed of cushions. He then returned to his beer.

"These are some great pictures," Christa commented as she flipped through one of his magazines. "Clint looks awesome, and Stallone ... well ... 'become a pest to life until it relinquishes your dreams.' Isn't that the truth?"

He laid the sofa pillows on the floor. "I'm fascinated by the beliefs of people who've made it," Ethan replied. "I find them such a contradiction to what we're taught. It's almost as if we learn to be ... where we are."

"That's deep, Dr. Jones," she replied, her lips pursed and her face resisting a smile. She held up a multi-page spread that stretched the length of her forearm. "Look at these. I've never seen this one of Marilyn Monroe and Paul Newman. His blue eyes just take me apart." Then, closing the magazine, she concluded, "I'm done for the night."

"Yeah, me too. I've got to work tomorrow—later today."

"Work!" she cried. "God, I forgot all about that. I'd better say good night."

"I'll leave a towel on the vanity." He handed her a blanket and sheet. "You can use these. They're clean."

"Thanks, Ethan," she said and kissed him lightly on the cheek. "You're a saint. I don't know how I'll ever repay you."

"Forget it, and a saint I'm not," he replied, throwing a sheet over the pillows on the floor. "You found that out last night."

By the time he was comfortable on the cushions, his clock read 3:30 a.m. He did his best not to think about the beautiful woman lying close by. Just as he'd manage to contain his thoughts, she'd move or sniffle and rekindle his desire for her. But he couldn't—he just couldn't. She was in need of a friend tonight, someone to provide her stability from the crazed relationship she'd had. He could hear her breath; she seemed so close he could almost feel her breathe against his skin. He forced himself to let it go.

His eyes closed, and he hoped he wasn't making a big mistake in helping this fellow human being. His thoughts drifted to the audition Cushman had arranged, and he prayed the dream wouldn't return that night. It wasn't long before he was in a deep sleep.

CHAPTER 19

Ethan's Timeline
April 1991

The next day dragged on, although he didn't start till noon. He still found his hours strange, so accustomed to daytime hours at NewTec. He tried to relax, refusing to clutter his thoughts with project details. He was best when he knew what he was going to read. Tonight would put his spontaneity to the test. Would the lack of sleep, raw nerves, and no pre-read take him out of contention? He tried to calm himself by repeating little phrases like "you're the best" or "you can do this." To reduce his tension, he resolved that it really didn't matter; there'd be other auditions. It wasn't likely he'd want it anyway, but knew if it involved acting of any form, he'd be a fool not to give it his best shot. Everything mattered—every second, every word. He never knew who might be watching or when opportunity would strike. He wished for a way to hurry his workday along.

Christa also was on his mind for most of the day, but each time he thought of Christa, Beth wasn't far off. Hopeful thoughts of Christa were suffocated by guilty musings of Beth. Christa excited him and made him feel good. His inner voice encouraged him, saying, *It's time to move on, Ethan.*

When dinner break arrived, two fellow engineers invited him to join them, but he declined, using the excuse that he had too much to do. He grabbed a prepackaged sandwich from the vending machine and ate it while looking over the classifieds at his desk. A couple of new casting calls caught his eye. He found Sven Irons's number from the day before in his pocket—he was worth another call. He left the office for a few minutes to call from the pay phone across the street. One thing Ethan had learned while in LA was that no one called you. If you had a number, you'd better call it, because someone else was right behind you, ready to pounce on your squandered opportunity. Competition was ruthless, and the hungriest got fed.

He dialed Sven's number first and after a couple of rings, the answering machine clicked on. He left another message and his number. Curiosity gave way to determination in finding out what Sven Irons was all about. The other two casting call numbers resulted in voice messages to "leave your name and number at the beep."

No farther ahead, Ethan decided to take a little walk along the sidewalk before heading back to the office. He'd bought his Hugo Boss in Tailor's, a small men's clothier on Rivoli Road. After the purchase, he'd promised to treat himself to another trip down Rivoli when he landed his first movie role, no matter how big the part.

Everything from the frivolous to the practical existed on Rivoli, from snakeskin shoes to body piercing and tattoos. It seemed funny to Ethan that it took him away from where he was and closer to where he wanted to go. He needed to find the elusive crack in the Hollywood shell. He returned to his office along the opposite sidewalk. Seeing the front of Build Industries brought him back to his present circumstances.

For the rest of his shift, he alternated between revisions to his current project and discussions on a new one that would take several oxygen reservoirs five hundred feet below the ocean's surface. It was a classified project, on client request. Ethan and another engineer were assigned to the design. At six o'clock, they called it a day. They'd pick it up tomorrow. Ethan packed to leave for his audition.

It was then that Goldsmith, the manager who had hired Ethan, approached his desk. Ethan rarely saw the man, but when he did, it meant there was a problem that needed solving.

Goldsmith was the only person who had asked Ethan anything other than technical questions during his interviews. "What do you like to do besides engineering?" Goldsmith had asked. Ethan had answered truthfully, that acting and movies were his hobbies. Goldsmith seemed to accept Ethan's answer, as he was searching for something more than just a degreed engineer. Ethan got the job.

"How are you, Ethan?" Goldsmith asked, his large outstretched hand swallowing Ethan's. Despite being short, his hands were huge, as were his head and feet—a caricature of himself. Goldsmith always greeted Ethan by name.

"Great," Ethan replied, trying to hide his reluctance. He knew Goldsmith wasn't there for a social visit.

"That's what I like to hear," Goldsmith chortled, nodding his big head. Six days had elapsed since his last visit, which had ended in a twenty-four-hour marathon of drawings and the reason for Ethan's recently messed-up schedule. "They're treating you well?"

"Just fine, sir," Ethan answered, as if responding to a drill officer's question. "There's always something to do."

"Listen ..." Goldsmith pulled three sheets of paper out of his binder. "I need some ideas for this proposal I'm putting together."

For Ethan, the timing couldn't have been worse.

"Have you got a few minutes?" Goldsmith asked, spreading the pages out on top of Ethan's desk. He paused momentarily, his quick eyes measuring Ethan's movements. "If you have to go, I understand." His eyes held Ethan's. There was only one response Ethan could give. The test was on.

"Sure, no problem," Ethan answered, grabbing his notebook and a pencil.

They moved to the conference room. Ethan checked the time on his watch. It was 6:10. The audition was at 7:00.

At 6:40, Goldsmith was finished. He abruptly stood up and said, "Dammit! Look at the time. Sorry I kept you so late. They're no doubt waiting for me now. I need the drawings on my desk by noon tomorrow, Ethan. Have a good evening." He left without another word.

Ethan was right behind him but left sufficient distance between them to avoid any more questions. The only thing on his mind was what chance in hell he had of making his scheduled audition time.

The taxi driver laughed when Ethan told him where he was going and that he had fifteen minutes. But after running a number of red lights and ignoring some of the posted speed limits, Ethan was at the church by seven-fifteen.

He only hoped they were running late.

After giving the cabbie an extra ten for his effort, Ethan ran to the building with no idea of where he was going. No signs indicated auditions or any other event. He ran up a dozen cement stairs that led to a set of glass doors and entered a deserted church foyer. The quiet that confronted him was discomfiting. He traversed the rear alcove that ran the width of the building and found a stairwell that led downstairs. Taking a few steps down, he heard voices and quickly descended the remaining stairs, coming to a small antechamber, where half a dozen people sat on stackable wood chairs with sheets of paper in their hands.

"Is this where the auditions are?" he asked to no one in particular.

"Shhhh! Yes," hissed a heavyset young man wearing a bright pink Ben and Jerry's "I Love Ice Cream" T-shirt. *No shit*, Ethan thought. "The scripts are next door." His pudgy finger pointed at a closed door beside the stairs.

"Sorry. Thanks," Ethan replied, walking in the indicated direction. Posted on a bulletin board beside the door was a schedule for a Bible study group. Inside sat a middle-aged woman with long strawberry-blonde hair tied back with a fluorescent-green scrunchie. Prematurely wrinkled with earthy good looks, the woman immediately smiled as he approached.

"Can I help you?" she asked in a deep, almost masculine voice that surprised Ethan with its loudness.

"Yes, I think you can," he answered. "I'm here to read for the audition."

"Why, of course you are. Your name?"

"Ethan Jones."

"Ethan Jones," she repeated, seeming to reflect on the sound of her voice while shuffling through several sheets of paper on the table in front of her. "I remember seeing your name somewhere here."

Farther to his right was another closed door. He could hear faint voices coming from behind it.

"Here it is," she said with a note of triumph in her voice. "Oh, I'm sorry, Mr. Jones, but you've missed your call time. You were scheduled for seven o'clock. Mr. Jackson won't be able to see you tonight."

"Dammit!" Ethan cursed before realizing where he was. "Sorry." At the same instant, an idea flashed through his head. "Would you mind if I had a look at the script anyway?"

The woman seemed relieved by not having to deal with a confrontation from another irrational actor, and she handed him a small coiled-ringed booklet.

There was no way on this side of hell he was going to waste an audition after coming this far. Quickly, he read through twenty-odd lines of dialogue and was ready to perform.

"You can take it with you if you'd like," the woman offered, rearranging the papers on the table in front of her.

"That's okay," Ethan replied. "I just want to know a little more about the character. Thanks." *I need to know these lines. This is my life,* he thought. He re-read the lines and conjured the character in his head while watching and listening for signs that the closed door was going to open. There was one chance to make this happen—only one. He had to be on his way to the door as soon as he heard the click of the doorknob turning. When the door opened, he had to be through it.

The lines flowed through his head. *The character was nervous and insecure by nature. Holding a roomful of hostages in a bank's vault for most of the night had begun to wear on him. It wouldn't take much to set him off while an undercover cop tried to talk him out of it.*

He heard the click.

Without hesitating, Ethan skimmed past the man leaving and was through the door in a shot. He closed the door behind him as the woman at the table shouted for him to stop.

Fired up, Ethan felt the pressure his character was under as he entered … the bank vault. Whether they liked him or not, they would remember him.

"You guys are making me crazy!" he shouted across the room, holding a semi-automatic that only he could see high in the air. "Listen—I've got three executives behind me, messing their pants. Smells like a shit house. You all look like fuckin' baby lambs, praying for mercy. Wrong day to fuck with me, mister. Keep your shrinks locked up. What's inside my head stays. No fuckin' around."

The manuscript described a pause as the anarchist grabbed a young woman hostage and brutally dragged her across the room by her long blonde hair. They were on the main floor of a Manhattan skyscraper, and he'd just blown out the window with a round of gunfire.

"I want three things," Ethan shouted, miming dragging the woman by her hair to the blown-out window. Ethan visualized the scene in his mind with extreme clarity. Wind, coming through the broken window, blew his hair around. "First, I want the three men in last week's bombing released and flown back to Iran. Second, I want the salaries of these three gentlemen deposited in an unmarked Swiss account today. And third, I want safe transport for me and my escort." He shook the woman he was holding, indicating she was his escort. "To Columbia. You got thirty minutes, or I start getting fuckin' creative with my new associates."

When he finished leaning across the desk he'd used as the open window, he stood up. With his lines delivered, he looked as if he were waking from a trance and seemed surprised that he was in a church basement. It was an inspired performance.

Standing, he took a step back from the desk. The two he'd auditioned for were silent. The woman who had handed him the script was standing in the doorway. Her face showed she was perturbed by his actions, but her dark eyes were alight with what she'd just witnessed. She spoke before anyone else had a chance.

"I'm very sorry," she said to the man and woman sitting behind a foldout table. "He just barged in. I couldn't stop him."

The woman behind the table spoke next. Her bleached-blonde hair was cropped close to her scalp. Prominent black-rimmed glasses were positioned near the tip of her nose, which was pierced with a tiny diamond. Ethan figured she was approaching forty.

"Jason?" she asked tentatively. "That was most ..."

"Entertaining," finished the man sitting by her side. He stood up and towered over Ethan's five-foot-ten frame, extending a long-fingered hand to Ethan. "Good to meet you, Jason."

"Actually," Ethan interrupted, feeling very confident about his audition, "my name is Ethan Jones."

There was a pregnant pause as the man looked at the list before him. "But the list has Jason … next," he said as he scrutinized the sheet he was holding. "Ah, here it is. Yes, Ethan Jones. We waited for you at seven o'clock, didn't we, Bren?"

The woman nodded her head, refusing to raise her eyes from the table.

"Very well," said the man. "We have a number here at which to contact you. Thank you for coming out. Who's next, Shirley?"

"That's it?" Ethan cried out. He'd just poured his living soul into the audition, and all he was getting was a "thanks for coming out." He felt like he'd just been gutted like a slaughtered pig.

"Yes, thank you. We'll call you." The man sat back down and scribbled something on his sheet.

Ethan still couldn't believe it. They were rejecting him because he was late. *Fuck. Life isn't perfect. You have to grab opportunity when it presents itself and not squander it because of some pre-planned procedure that it doesn't quite fit.* He'd done enough of that over the years to recognize it for what it was. He stood there shaking his head. It wasn't right, but he wasn't about to change them. He'd nailed the fucking scene, and he knew it.

Shirley held the door open as he passed. "Just a tip, Ethan," Shirley whispered. "Next time, be *on* time."

"Yeah, right," he huffed and walked by the fat boy on his way to the stairs.

"Ethan!" Shirley called out, moving toward him. "If it means anything to you, that was amazing. Don't quit. Come back again. You've got something we don't see every day."

"Thanks," he replied, still dejected and more than a little pissed off. The part should have been his.

He climbed back up the stairs and pushed open a side door. The warmth of the evening met him full-on. The heat of the day had subsided, but it was warm compared to the air-conditioned coolness of the church basement. It felt good. He had paid little attention to it earlier. Disappointment weighed heavily on his mood.

A long night was in store back at the office. Most of it would be in front of a computer screen, not acting. He was back in half an hour, having walked for a piece before waving down a taxi. When he pulled up in front of Build Industries, he decided to grab a bite from the diner across the street first. He sat quietly and ate a cheeseburger and fries, washing it down with two Budweisers.

Realizing he had to get back to it sooner or later, he walked back to the office and his computer. Before beginning, he dialed into his home phone for messages. After two rings, Christa answered.

"Hello. Ethan Jones's residence," she said.

"Christa? Hi," he said, his voice holding a note of surprise. He hadn't anticipated a live voice answering his phone. "You're there?"

"I think so," she laughed. "Just got in. I thought you would be here too."

"So did I, but some extra work came up—a bullshit job I have to finish before the morning. Found out about it a couple of hours ago." Ahead lay a full night of work, his annoyance exacerbated by thoughts of his fucked-up audition. Adding a further kick to the head was having a beautiful woman in his apartment, someone with whom he wanted to spend time.

"Someone called asking for you," Christa said. "She didn't leave her name but said she'd call back later. How late are you going to be?"

The question sounded vaguely familiar to Ethan but the condescending expectation wasn't there. It was just a question. There was something comforting in it. "I'll be real late."

"Oh." Christa sounded disappointed. "That's okay. I threw a few things together for ... to eat. Hope you don't mind. I'll stick it the fridge."

"That's nice of you," Ethan replied, further inclined to say fuck it all and leave. He had a dinner waiting, something he'd not experienced since moving to California.

"And just so you know," she added, "I'll be out of your way tomorrow.

My friend from work offered to let me stay with her until I can get my shit together."

Fuck, he thought. His disappointment was instantaneous, which surprised him. He didn't want her to leave. "That's great," he lied. He wanted to retract his words as soon as he spoke, but to his own amazement, he added, "But there's no problem if you want to stay longer. It's not like I'm around much anyway."

"You sure?" Her voice brightened as if she might have been hoping he would invite her to stay longer.

"Couldn't be surer," he replied.

"I don't want to be in the way. You've done enough already."

"It's not a problem, Christa. Make yourself at home. It'll be early morning before I'm back anyway."

Suddenly, Ethan had a lot of questions he wanted to ask her. But they'd have to wait. There was work to do, and the sooner he got to it, the sooner he'd be done. Hanging up, he felt better, and his audition, for the most part, was forgotten.

After three hours, he took a break and picked up a couple of pizza slices from the all-night pizzeria down the street. Shortly after one o'clock, he decided he was happy with his design. Another hour, and he'd be on his way.

He was plotting the final drawings, when his phone rang.

"Are you coming back soon?" Christa's voice whispered in his ear. His senses tingled. Just the sound of her voice turned him on. "I'm a little nervous, Ethan, all alone here. How much longer are you going be?"

"Just about done," he told her, thinking he could manage the last few things when he came back later in the day. "Half an hour, tops."

"Okay, but hurry. I don't want to fall asleep without you." She whispered a good-bye and hung up.

I hope you know what you're getting yourself into, buddy, he told himself. *You can't lose this job.*

Of course he didn't know what he was getting into—but did anyone? Besides, he really liked her.

He got to the apartment as soon as he could, unmindful of the time. Excitement overruled his exhaustion as he thought about what awaited him. He wondered what she looked and felt like under her clothes. Just the thought of kissing her lips made his heart beat faster; her soft skin beneath his fingertips; cupping her breasts in his hands; nudging her swollen nipples with his thumb—it all served to pull him over the edge.

When he arrived at the apartment building, he ran up the front steps. He pictured her lying on the couch, waiting for him, wearing only his Hugo Boss blazer. His hands were shaking as he unlocked the door and stepped into a very dark apartment. His hand sought the light switch on the wall, but he couldn't find it. His movements slowed as he swept the darkness with his hands. His right hand brushed against the lampshade. He reached under the shade and pressed the switch.

Nothing happened. His heart came into his throat.

"Christa?" he called. His voice was quiet but broke the silence like a hammer hitting a gong.

In that instant, a numbing explosion split the air. Something rocketed past his head, sending him reeling in the dark space. His cheek burned as if a hot iron was pressed against it. He lost his balance and fell.

"Ethan," slurred a vaguely familiar voice, wet with liquor, "if that's really your fuckin' name. It's quite the habit you have ... moving in on another man's property. Did you like fuckin' her?"

Ethan didn't hear any more and passed out.

CHAPTER 20

Everything seemed white. Or white and black.

He was dreaming again and knew it, because Beth was there beside him. She looked tired. There were wrinkles—crow's feet—dispersing from the corners of her blue eyes.

Again, he was locked to the bed.

"You haven't spoken of Mila for a while," she said to him, adjusting herself to sit on the side of his bed. "Has she not been by to visit?"

"Funny you should ask," he said in a voice not his own—it was like his mouth was full of cotton candy. "But no, I haven't."

The mention of Mila brought a melancholy longing of something he couldn't quite touch. It was a soft feeling, warm and comforting, like warming cold hands in front of a fire.

Beth put her hand on his. Her warmth was nourishing, yet her smile was missing something. *How odd*, he thought. *Is it missing happiness?* A tear rolled down her cheek.

"Mila hasn't been back here to see you?" she asked again. She squeezed his hand.

He didn't like it when she did that and tried to move away, but his wrist was bound by something. He shook his head.

"I don't believe you, Ethan Jones," she said, leaning forward, her face right in his. "You're lying to me." She wasn't angry or even excited. Her voice was flat, as if she was describing how to apply makeup.

"I'm not lying to you," he said, even though he was. "She hasn't been here."

"Where did she go?"

"How would I know?"

"Because she told you. Because she wants you to believe her."

"Believe her? What do you—"

But before he could finish, a doctor—or at least someone who wore a white lab coat—interrupted. "I think that's enough for today," he said in a loud, friendly tone, looking at Beth and putting his hand on her shoulder. "Ethan is ready for some rest."

Ethan looked at the doctor but didn't recognize him. The doctor stepped away. "I don't need any rest," Ethan said, looking at Beth. His words now came out stronger and louder. "Believe her? Believe what?"

Then he saw Mila at the end of the bed. Her pointed index finger was raised to her lips. Mila shook her head. She mouthed the word no.

Beth was standing beside him. Her lips were moving, but he couldn't hear what she was saying. Her cheeks were wet.

He tried to hold on but like most retreating dreams, he was powerless to keep it going.

The white sheets and white coats faded away.

CHAPTER 21

"Ethan? Ethan, oh please, wake up."

Christa was crying as she pleaded with him to open his eyes. Something cool and wet was on his forehead. He could smell her hair.

"Ma'am, he's gonna be just fine," Ethan heard a man say. "He's bumped his head a good one. Lucky the bullet only grazed his cheek. He's one lucky son of a ... gun."

On hearing this, Ethan opened his eyes.

"Ethan!" cried Christa, "Oh God. You're okay." She kissed his face and squeezed him tight. "I'm so sorry." Her slender body shuddered against his chest as emotion seized her.

Disoriented and not knowing where he was, his hand slid across her back. It was the first time he could remember touching her. "Christa, it's okay," he whispered.

As she lifted her head from his chest, he could see her eyes were swollen and red from crying. There was a white bandage above her left eye.

"What the fuck happened?" Ethan asked, concerned. The dream of Beth faded as he tried to figure out what had happened with Christa.

"He's gone, Ethan," Christa whispered, placing her hand on his chest. "He thought you were dead. He's probably halfway to Pasadena by now."

Ethan tried to sit up. "Who's halfway to Pasadena?"

"Hey there, big guy," the paramedic interrupted, putting a firm hand on Ethan's shoulder. "You gotta rest easy for a bit. You're not ready to go anywhere."

Ethan eased back onto his sofa, guided by the paramedic's hand.

"The police have already put a search out for him," Christa said.

"For who?" Ethan asked again, impatient that he was not getting an answer.

"The bastard I used to live with!" Christa hissed.

Ethan caught the movement of a police officer in his peripheral vision as he recognized his apartment. The cop was looking at something in the wall. Ethan's hand moved to the side of his head, and he touched a gauze bandage. He suddenly recalled coming into the dark apartment.

"Was I shot?" he asked. His head was sore.

"Yes," answered the paramedic. "The bullet grazed your cheek, sir, and looks to be in the wall over there."

"But the side of my head is sore," Ethan said.

"You sustained a contusion on the left side of your head when you fell," replied a second paramedic from somewhere behind Ethan.

"You bumped your head a good one," the cop added. "You're a lucky man, Mr. Jones."

Christa was sniffling beside him, with a wet tissue in her hand. Even upset and crying, Ethan thought she looked beautiful and was glad to have her by his side.

"Are you okay?" he asked, seeing a red welt on her already bruised cheek. Anger simmered inside him. How had a woman like Christa become involved with such a piece of shit? He reached up and brushed a tear from her cheek. Her skin was so soft to touch.

She smiled, keeping her lips together. "I'm fine." Her smile faded.

"What happened?" he asked

"Stalked me at work. Followed me to your place. Waited for you to show and when you didn't, decided to give me a visit." She pointed to the bandage. "I knew he was crazy but not psychotic. He's a killer, Ethan. God, I can't believe it."

Then he remembered. "He was here when you called, wasn't he," he said—it wasn't a question; he knew the answer.

"He said if I didn't call you, he'd kill me." She started to cry again but kept talking. "When you dropped to the floor, he said you were dead, and he ran. I dialed 911 as soon as he was out the door. I thought you were dead too. I saw your cheek and the blood … you weren't moving at all." Her voice trailed off, sobbing. Then she added, "But you were breathing. They were here really fast." She stopped and wiped her nose. "Ethan, I thought you were dead. Can you ever forgive me?" Her head fell to his chest again. She cried into his shirt. His hand touched her long brunette hair. Not knowing what to say, he just held her.

"Sir," the paramedic said, "we need to get you to the hospital. It doesn't look like you have a concussion, but we need to run a few tests to be sure."

"I'm going to stay here," Ethan replied. "I'm fine."

There was a pause, and then the paramedic beside him spoke. "We can't make you go, sir, but ma'am, you need to observe him every two hours, waking him up if necessary. If he feels dizzy or starts vomiting, get him to the hospital."

"That's okay," Christa replied, perking up. "I can do that." Then, turning to Ethan, she said, "Shouldn't you go, just to make sure?"

"I'm fine. I bumped my head," he said, not entirely confident himself but having no desire to go to the hospital. "Look, if I start feeling woozy, I promise you can take me in. What worries me more is the psychopath out there. What's to stop him from coming back?"

Ethan watched as the officer approached them. The man looked huge from Ethan's vantage point on the couch. His hair was crew-cut short but flat on top. Ethan guessed he was in his late twenties. Despite his short sleeves he looked warm. He'd not spoken up to this point.

"Mr. Jones," the officer started, "I'm Officer Barnes, LAPD, and to answer your question, nothing. I do need to ask the both of you a few questions, if you're up to it."

The two paramedics packed their bags, their work complete.

"Can I get you anything?" Christa asked, kneeling beside Ethan.

Ethan could see the light of dawn through the window behind her. "Maybe some orange juice."

She smiled. Hers was a beautiful smile—comforting and exciting at the same time. "Sure," she said. As she got to her feet, she leaned forward to kiss him.

The paramedics left as another officer, a near copy of Barnes, came through the door with a plastic Ziploc bag in his hands. What looked like a small black stone was in the bag.

"Say, Rick," he addressed Barnes, "I'm about finished here."

"I've still got a few questions to ask these folks," Barnes replied, "and we need something from the super."

The building's superintendent was at the door. Ethan hadn't seen him yet. He spoke. "Yes, whatever you need."

Barnes came back and sat down on the arm of the gray sofa. "You know, you could use a few more chairs in this place." He smiled and shifted to find a comfortable position.

"Yeah, I know," Ethan replied. "I need a few things, but furniture's down the list a ways."

"Mr. Jones, I need to get a few things straight. Tell me what you remember."

Ethan started with Christa's phone call and ended with coming through the door, unable to turn the lights on in his darkened apartment.

"You didn't see this guy?" Barnes asked without expression.

"No, just heard his voice."

Christa returned with a large glass of orange juice. Slowly sitting up, Ethan took the glass. It was cool compared to the temperature in the room.

"You must be sorry you ever met me," she said, sitting down close to him, while Barnes wrote something in his notepad.

Not knowing quite what to say, he smiled, pleased still to have her beside him.

Before Barnes left, Ethan wanted assurance they would have some protection. "There's no telling what that gun-toting maniac might do or where he might be." It wasn't as if Ethan could walk away from the situation either—and the guy knew his name and where he lived. Christa was afraid, but Ethan was the target.

The option of simply returning to Canada began to eat away at him. Any measure of success had eluded him. Was he ignoring the obvious and just not cut out for this sort of life? His job was shit, his best wasn't good enough at the audition, and he'd nearly taken a bullet for a woman he barely knew—all in a span of twenty-four hours.

Still, he'd made a promise that no matter how bad things became, he wouldn't give in. *Really?* He was really testing that promise. He'd come to LA to star in a major motion picture. *Suck it up.* He forced away the thought. He couldn't afford the luxury of even thinking about running away. Others had found a way; he would find one too.

Barnes spoke, returning Ethan to the matter at hand. "We'll set up extra patrols in the area for the next few days," Barnes stated, peering down at the street from the third-floor window. "Keep a low profile for a couple of days. Stay with a friend. We'll issue a warrant for his arrest in the APB. There's not much to go on outside of Ms. White's description of him. A picture would be real helpful."

Christa shook her head. "I'm sorry. I don't have one."

"Shit!" Ethan cried suddenly, remembering his meeting with Goldsmith. "What time is it?"

"Almost six. Why?" Barnes asked.

"I gotta get back to work," he answered, turning on the couch.

"Ethan!" Christa exclaimed. "You've just been shot!"

"I know," he replied, "but I have to at least let somebody know." He paused for a moment, thinking, and then went on. "Officer Barnes is right—we can't stay here." He looked at Christa. "Who knows where he might be? I'll stay at a friend's. You call the friend you mentioned earlier. You can drop me off before you go over."

"Okay," Christa agreed reluctantly. Ethan didn't know her well but could see she was on the edge of her emotions. The whole situation was wearing them both down. "I'll pack my things."

Ethan dialed Robbie's number. It had been a while since he remembered last talking to him.

"Hello?" answered an unfamiliar, sleep-laden voice.

"Robbie?" Ethan offered.

"No."

"Sorry. I must have dialed the—"

"Just a minute," interrupted the groggy voice.

"Hello?" Robbie answered, his voice rough with sleep.

"Robbie, sorry about the time."

"Eth? What the hell?" Robbie replied, coughing to clear his throat.

"Listen," Ethan continued, "a couple of things have come up. I need a place to hang for a few days. Can you help me out?"

There was a pause at the other end, and then Ethan heard Robbie speaking to someone—but few words were coherent. Then Robbie said, "Yeah, no problem. When?"

"In about half an hour, if that's okay."

"Yeah, sure, Eth. What's up?"

"I'll explain it when I get there." Suddenly, Ethan had second thoughts about Christa's staying with her friend, and added, "I'm bringing someone with me, too. I owe you one." Ethan hung up before Robbie had a chance to say more.

Robbie had a two-bedroom apartment. It wasn't the Waldorf-Astoria, but it would be safe and comfortable.

"I'm going there too?" Christa asked, surprised. "You just said to call my friend."

"It's pretty early, Christa," he said with a smile. "You likely won't impress anyone with a call at this hour. We'll figure something out when we get there. You can meet Robbie. He's the one who got me here."

Christa smiled her agreement with the plan.

"All right, then," Ethan announced. "Let's go."

After some quick packing, Christa raised her bag. "I'm ready when you are," she said.

They were just about out the door when Christa remembered the messages she'd taken during the day. Scooting back, she grabbed a scrap of paper and handed it to Ethan. There were two—Sven Irons and Beth.

Barnes helped them take their bags down to Christa's white Toyota Corolla. "I'll call you with anything we get," he said, giving them both one of his business cards. "If you think of anything that might help—anything at all—please contact me directly."

They both thanked him and shook hands.

Ethan had difficulty keeping his eyes open on the drive through early-morning LA. Twice he dozed off, and Christa had to wake him to ask directions to Robbie's place. Christa was shaking him again as she drove up to the front of the apartment complex. Disoriented, it took Ethan a moment to ground himself. Everything seemed mired in a foggy mist. Getting from the car to the front of the apartment building was akin to moving in a highly viscous fluid. Robbie was up by the time they buzzed his apartment, and he let them in.

He greeted them at his door, his eyes seeming to pop at the sight of their bandaged faces. He helped them inside as Ethan introduced Christa. The smell of hot coffee brewing in the kitchen permeated the air. There was no sign of the other person who had answered Ethan's call earlier.

"It's not every day you get chauffeured across town by a beautiful woman, you know!" Ethan laughed.

Robbie followed with, "And pretty special in head bandages, no doubt. What kind of action have you two been up to, anyway?"

"I might ask you the same thing," Ethan added, thinking of who had answered Robbie's telephone. The exchange between Robbie and another man when Ethan called had occurred quickly, as if they were beside each another. In the same bed? The question of Robbie's sexuality perplexed Ethan. He couldn't remember any of the girls Robbie had dated.

Robbie stared intently at Ethan, all but ignoring Christa. Ethan did his best to describe the events that led to their arrival at Robbie's apartment. Robbie brought them both coffees.

"He fucking fired a gun at you!" Robbie demanded, his eyes bulging.

Ethan pointed to the bandage on his cheek and nodded his head.

"You have no idea where he might be?" Robbie asked in amazement. Now he was wide awake and riveted by Ethan's story. He sat in his frayed armchair, looking from Ethan to Christa.

"No," Christa replied, curling her straight brunette hair back over her ears.

"That's the reason the cop told us to find another place to stay for a couple of days," Ethan added, sipping his coffee. The coffee was good, but his eyelids were heavy. He'd hoped for a second wind from the caffeine, but it wasn't coming. "There's a warrant out for his arrest. They'll catch him."

"He's not that smart," Christa insisted, nodding her head, "but that doesn't say much about me, does it?"

They all chuckled as Robbie stood up and retrieved the coffeepot from his Mr. Coffee machine on the counter. "Listen," Robbie suggested, refilling Ethan's mug, "you both look like you could use a shower and some shut-eye. You can have the room you stayed in, Ethan, when you first arrived. There are sheets in the closet."

"Ah, thanks, Robbie," Ethan said, looking at the time on Robbie's VCR. "One more thing—I need to be up in an hour. I have to call work."

Robbie looked at him with a strange expression. "I think they can make it through one day without you," he stated. "Take the fucking day off. Besides, you look like shit."

"Yeah, but it's important, Robbie."

"Oh, I'm *sure* it is," Robbie snorted, shaking his head. "Some things never change. I'll call them and vouch for you."

Mixed up in his thoughts, Ethan couldn't help but wonder whether another person was in Robbie's bed. He was surprised by his curiosity.

"Robbie," Ethan said as he and Christa headed to the second bedroom, "thanks."

"No problem, mate," Robbie replied as Ethan closed the bedroom door.

Ethan then found himself in bed beside the beautiful Christa for only the second time. It was strange how familiar it felt.

"It's going to be all right," he said, turning his head on the pillow to look at Christa pulling off her socks.

"I think so too," she replied, her smile showing her weariness.

Even though there was a lot wrong with their situation, something somehow felt right.

CHAPTER 22

The alarm buzzer went off like a rocket beside Ethan's head. It seemed as though he had just closed his eyes. He looked across at Christa; her tanned brown legs were curled up almost to her chest. The alarm hadn't disturbed her in the least. The room was warm but not uncomfortable. Christa had shed all but her bikini brief Calvin Klein's and a yellow T-shirt. Wanting to stay, he turned over but could only remain still for a few minutes as the day took shape in his mind. The two of them had slept for most of the previous day, although he couldn't remember much of it. Robbie had called in to work for him, as he'd said he would, and explained the predicament. Christa simply called in sick. Now, he would have to face Goldsmith in a couple of hours and review his project work from two days ago.

Seeing Christa sleeping so peacefully beside him, he refused to disturb her and carefully slid out from under the covers. Only the bandage on her cheek revealed anything of their earlier turbulence. He pressed his hand hard against his arousal, wanting relief from the desire he felt for this woman, silently begging her to awaken. He forced himself to move away and into the small bathroom, where he showered. The water felt good and helped calm him. He replaced the gauze packing on his cheek with a smaller bandage. The bullet had only broken the surface. As quietly as he could, he filled a mug with the hot coffee Robbie had made earlier and sipped it as he dressed. Christa hadn't moved. He looked at her again before closing the bedroom door and leaving.

111

Once on the street, he flagged down a taxi. Fifteen minutes later it pulled up in front of Build Industries. He paid and hustled into the office.

Everyone was in by the time he reached his desk. A few said good morning as he passed, but he could sense he was the talk of the office. No doubt the bandage on his cheek only added to the rumors already started. The drawings were on his desk where he'd left them. It seemed such a long time since he'd last been there. Shuffling through the drawings, he arranged them in the order he would present them to Goldsmith.

A few minutes later, while he was logging on to the network, one of the designers came by his desk. "Hey, man, what happened to your face? Cut yourself shaving?"

There will be a few of these today, he thought. "No, somebody tried to shoot me," he replied matter-of-factly.

"Wow, no way!" the designer exclaimed. "Were you mugged?"

"No, deranged ex-boyfriend," Ethan replied. "Crazy son of a bitch."

"What are you doing here?"

"You know. What else? Goldsmith's project."

"You look like crap. Can I help?" He pointed to the drawings on top of Ethan's desk. "Looks like you could use a little. Goldsmith's supposed to be here in half an hour."

"No shit!" Ethan exclaimed. "Yeah, for sure. You can start by plotting the files I send you." Ethan picked up the work he'd completed and carried it into the engineering conference room. Preparation was key in handling Goldsmith. Ethan wanted to be as organized as possible, despite his turmoil, but he couldn't believe how tired he was. His eyes seemed to close involuntarily, getting smaller by the minute. Every time he sat down, it was an effort to get back up. He needed another coffee.

Goldsmith's whole project seemed strange to him now. It was like the nightmare of taking a school exam and not understanding any of the questions. Back at NewTec, he'd have wanted to do a good job to get promoted to the next rung. Here, he was holding on to keep money coming in. His perspective had changed. He only hoped he'd done enough to keep Goldsmith happy. It wasn't five minutes before the boss walked into the room—he was early.

"Good morning, Ethan," Goldsmith said with a slight smile. "I understand you've been through quite an ordeal since we last met."

Yeah, I'm sure you do, Ethan thought. *Like you care.* "Yes, it's not every day that someone shoots at you," Ethan replied, pulling out the first drawing he wanted to show Goldsmith. He hoped his tired eyes wouldn't betray him.

"You sure you're ready, son?" Goldsmith asked, sitting down beside him. "I've been thinking about this a lot, maybe looking at it from a different perspective." Ethan laid out his drawings. Formulas and calculations were of little interest to Goldsmith. He picked up one of the drawings before Ethan could explain what he'd done. "What's this?" Goldsmith announced, sounding annoyed.

"The accumulator reservoir," Ethan answered, taken aback by the question. He'd followed Goldsmith's instructions meticulously.

"We never talked about a reservoir. Don't need another reservoir."

Ethan was caught off guard by Goldsmith's reaction. He thought Goldsmith would like what he'd done. "Can I explain what I went through to get here?"

"Go ahead and start," Goldsmith retorted, "'cause I can't figure out what the hell you've done."

Ethan was struggling to focus. It was as if he was grasping at something just out of reach, both on the table and in his mind. Goldsmith's curt reaction to his work was completely unexpected.

"Ethan, it appears as though you didn't understand what we talked about the other night," Goldsmith stated. "I know you're tired and you've worked hard, but you've missed the point."

Ethan was aghast. His mind flashed back to his being late for the audition and not getting the part. Why? Because of Goldsmith. Ethan had been through a life-or-death situation, and what had he been thinking about through all of it? Goldsmith. Now, after all that, he was getting a shit-kicking from whom? Goldsmith. It was time to put an end to it. *Stand up, and let the chips fall where they may.* It was quite clear that he and Goldsmith were on different planets. "You know, you're right," Ethan agreed. "I did what I thought you asked and in doing so, I killed an entire night."

"Looks like you did more than kill a night," Goldsmith sniped. "What's the other guy look like?"

"Don't know," Ethan answered, uncertain of how much he should say. "I was shot at when I got back to my apartment."

"I heard something like that." Goldsmith seemed to reconsider something for a moment. Then he pushed his chair away from the conference table, saying, "Ethan, when I hired you, you mentioned your interest in acting and the movies. It's obvious to me you don't understand what we do here. I think your heart lies elsewhere."

Ethan's chin dropped—listening to Goldsmith's words was like taking another bullet, this time in the stomach. There was no way he'd misunderstood what they talked about. Goldsmith had changed his mind; Ethan was certain of it. Goldsmith either was losing it, or his intentions had changed. Regardless, Ethan was through.

"You won't forget me," Ethan said, speaking from his heart.

Goldsmith stood and walked to the door of the conference room. He stopped short and turned to look at Ethan. For an instant, Ethan relaxed, half expecting Goldsmith to tell him he was joking.

"Maybe not, Mr. Jones," Goldsmith stated, "but I'm afraid, under the circumstances, that we no longer need your services. Good luck with your other ventures. Audrey will assist you with your things." At that, he turned and walked out. The door closed behind him.

Ethan, who had risen to his feet, was dumbfounded and dropped back to the conference room chair. *What the fuck did I do to deserve this?* Twenty-four hours ago, he'd been shot, and now he didn't have a job. Too confused to be angry, he sat in the chair and stared blankly at the wall.

Thirty seconds later, Audrey, the engineering receptionist, was at the door, expressionless and very direct. "Ethan, please come with me."

He didn't have time to do as much as stop and collect his thoughts. It was over. He stood up, zombielike, and followed Audrey to the front entrance. No one looked up from their suddenly important tasks or even acknowledged his presence. He'd already become a nonentity.

Audrey held open the front door. She wasn't looking at him either, as much as she was looking through him. "You can pick up your personal effects after five," she said, speaking the words without emotion. "If you don't, we will collect them and forward them to the address we have on file, along with your severance check. If you have any questions, please contact me. You know the number." She then thrust her hand out in a good-bye gesture and added, "Good luck, Ethan."

"You won't forget me," he said, staring at Audrey. "Count on it."

He had come to LA to be an actor, not an engineer. It was time to get on with it.

CHAPTER 23

Ethan walked for nearly an hour before he stopped for anything. He had not headed in any particular direction, nor had he any destination in mind. His feelings left him in a state of suspended disbelief, where he could only observe and not participate in the world around him.

Fired. At first, it seemed a little like being dead. But he'd come close enough to that in his own apartment to last a lifetime. It wasn't like that.

He'd never been fired before. As a kid, he'd been cut from his hockey team and cried for hours, but this—this was something he thought was both undeserved and incredible. As he walked along Somerset Lane, he retraced, again and again, his last meeting with Goldsmith and the moments in the conference room, searching for a clue on what had set Goldsmith so against him. Ethan could have sworn he hadn't misunderstood the intention of the project. Goldsmith had changed it. Tired—yes, even exhausted—but tired or not, the instructions had been clear. He could accept the blame for a misunderstanding but not one that led to his dismissal. He had been routed and was not about to agree with the decision—or, for that matter, accept fault in it. After an hour of aimless walking and self-reflection, he remained bewildered by the situation.

Still trying to make sense of it all, he approached a small café with tables outside. Two waitresses were talking at the front. He assumed they were taking a break before the lunch crowd started. As he pulled out a metal frame chair to sit down, the taller of the two women asked whether he'd like to see a menu.

"No, thanks," he said. "Just a large coffee and Danish. And ... do you have a telephone?"

Her reply was quick and easy. "Yes, sir, there's one in the back, beside the restrooms."

Ethan followed her instructions and found the pay phone opposite the men's room door. All he really wanted to do was go back to Robbie's apartment and sleep the whole mess away. Christa would be there and in fifteen minutes, he could be back and tucked away from this unruly world. But it wouldn't solve anything. On picking up the receiver, his hand pulled out the slip of paper in his pocket. Sven Irons's name and phone number were written on it. He dialed the number, fully anticipating Sven's answering machine again.

"Good morning. Sven Irons's office. Jacqueline speaking. How can I help you?" answered a sexy voice.

"Good morning," replied Ethan. "Could I speak with Sven Irons?"

"Sure can. May I tell him who's calling?" she asked with a smile Ethan could hear over the telephone.

"Yes, it's Ethan Jones. I'm returning his call from yesterday."

"One moment, sir," she said. He was switched to the music of Mozart. A few seconds later, Jacqueline's shining voice interrupted a climbing crescendo. "One moment while I connect you, Mr. Jones."

"Ezan Jonez," announced Sven Irons "Iz about time I get to zpeak viz zee real perzon. Good morning."

"Good morning," replied Ethan. "I could say the same thing."

"Zo howz zee man zat vent home viz zee most beautiful voman in zee room?"

"I'm doing okay. Yourself?"

"I'm doing great and getting better," Sven chuckled. "I'm zo glad you called. Iz a crazy vorld, izn't it? All zeze mezzagez?"

"In more ways than I care to recount," Ethan replied, shaking his head. "I'm returning your call from the party."

"Yez, vell, of courz you are," Sven replied. Ethan could picture him reclined behind a big oak desk with cowboy boots resting on the corner. "I called you zee ozer day regarding a project I'm verking on—zort of a cazting azignment. At zee pa'ty, you fit zee profile ve're looking for. I

117

called you to meet for lunch." Ethan's heart rate sped up. "But late laz night, I believe ve found zee perzon ve vere looking for, so zat pretty much zayz it all. Zome zingz vork, and zome zingz don't. Timing is zee name of zee game."

Ethan's mouth dropped. *Damn.* It was like a fisherman whose line takes a big hit and then goes still. "Isn't that the truth," he shot back, not about to let the man off the line. "But I'd still like to take you up on that lunch." He was about to query Irons on the details but didn't want to sound desperate and bit his tongue. *Less is more*, whispered in his head. When he was excited, he had a tendency to talk too much.

A pause at Sven's end of the line made Ethan realize he was considering it. "Vell, I'm zuppozed—"

"Could I meet you around two today?" Ethan interrupted.

"Vell, I don't zee vy not. I have an early lunch meeting, but I should be done by two."

"Great," Ethan replied, flexing his hand as he realized he'd been crossing his fingers. "I'll see you then." Not waiting for Sven's reply, he hung up.

Excited with the twist to his day, he called Christa. Robbie's answering machine clicked on after four rings. He returned to the table and finished the coffee and pastry he'd ordered, while reading the morning's paper someone had left on the next table. He kept pushing away the lingering thoughts of his morning.

After calling Sven's office a second time for directions, the taxi dropped him in front of a refurbished mid-century home on the west side of town. It was a beautiful piece of renewed architecture, fronted by giant marble columns and extensive stonework. Ethan walked up the front steps to the entrance foyer at five minutes to two. Both sides of the stone sidewalk were lined with manicured gardens full of bright summer flowers spanning the color spectrum. The aroma was refreshing and very alive, relaxing his anxiety as he stepped up to the heavy oak entrance doors. A motion-activated intercom announced his arrival, opening the doors automatically. A woman greeted him as he entered. He assumed she was Irons's assistant. A life-sized Barbie doll—big bust, big blonde hair, and big beautiful tan—she epitomized the California look.

"You must be Ethan," she said, smiling, revealing big bleached-white teeth and ruby-red lips. Ethan found it difficult not to stare. "I'm Jacqueline. I work with Sven. Very nice to meet you. Sven will be just a few minutes. He's on the phone."

"Okay," Ethan answered.

She tilted her head slightly and touched her cheek with long, red, professionally manicured fingernails.

He answered her unasked question with, "Grazed my cheek on the edge of a door. It's almost healed."

"Ah," Jacqueline replied. "Can I get you a coffee or espresso?"

"No, I'm good," he answered.

"I'll bet you are," she said, holding her smile. "You're the one Sven met at the party, aren't you?"

"Yes, we met the other night," Ethan replied, catching himself looking at her chest. "Sven called me, and here I am."

Jacqueline turned, retrieved a clipboard from a mahogany desk, and then turned back to face him. In heels, she was as tall as he was. Her emerald eyes were dangerous in their attractiveness and swallowed him up. She passed the clipboard and pen to Ethan. "Sven likes to have new people fill out their personal history, if you don't mind. You can get started while you wait." Again, she flashed him her full white smile. The hairs on the back of his neck prickled.

Most of the questions were related to his past experience. Also requested were characteristics, like his eye color and hair color, height and weight, and (surprisingly) sexual orientation. His internal warning alarm was sounding, but he went on as instructed. He had nearly completed the form when a gray-haired, middle-aged man opened one of the cherry wood double doors beside the reception desk and approached him.

"Good afternoon, Ezan," Sven greeted him, extending his hand. Ethan had no recollection of the man. His graying hair was long for a businessman and, as Ethan noted a moment later when Sven turned, tied in a ponytail. On his chin, Sven sported a very thin goatee. "Zo glad you could make it."

"I'm glad the timing worked," Ethan said, shaking the man's hand.

Sven leaned forward, noting Ethan's bandaged cheek. "Zat doezn't look good," he said; his disinterest in how it happened was immediately evident.

"It's just a scratch," Ethan said, praying the meeting wouldn't end because his mug was marked up. Christa's ex still was fucking him up. "A couple of days and it'll be gone. I can show you."

Sven raised his hand. "Not nezezzary, young man." He turned to Jacqueline. "Could you bring uz zome café."

Jacqueline smiled. "Certainly, Mr. Irons." She disappeared through a door to the right of her desk.

As Sven ushered Ethan into his office, Ethan's eyes were wide. He had seen private offices before but nothing like this one. It was large and stylishly decorated—and immaculate. Sven moved directly to his desk, angled between two adjoining walls. Above it hung two large, coordinated, multicolored abstracts of blood-red, forest-green, and canary-yellow markings, something both beautiful and gruesome. The furniture was red, black, or chrome. The walls were covered in a gray-print wallpaper. His desk was four cylindrical chrome legs, supporting a red-leather desktop and black blotter. The desk fronted a large red-and-black leather chair with chrome tips. Sven sat down in it after offering a similar but smaller version to Ethan. A matching couch lined the wall to his left, with matching armchairs facing the couch on each side, all surrounding an authentic polar bear rug, whose head faced Ethan. Two matching black-and-chrome wall units were positioned as bookends on each side of the couch, one containing an assortment of books, albums, and videos and the other an extensive audio system. On the opposite wall, three oversized movie posters were hung. Ethan didn't recognize two of them, but one showed a Roman guard and was titled *Caligula*, which seemed familiar. Positioned on the corner of Sven's desk, next to a small black-lacquer box, was a lone book titled *The Catcher in the Rye*.

Ethan sat down, placing his hands on the cold chrome ends of the chair's arms.

"Zo," Sven began, with his hands on his stomach, fingers intertwined. "Do you like my offiz? It vas finished juz a veek ago."

"It's …" Ethan paused a moment for the right word. "Incredible."

"You know, I kind of like it too," Sven said, offering Ethan a cigar from the black lacquer humidor on his desk. "I zink of it az Batman Meetz Daylight." Sven laughed loudly at his own joke.

Ethan smiled, selecting a medium-sized cigar with a Churchill band. A bronze cigar cutter appeared in his hand. He cut the ends. Ethan enjoyed the opulence of the surroundings yet was wary of something he couldn't quite put his finger on.

"You told me zee ozer night you've been in California for a vile. Zat you came 'ere to become a movie ztar."

"That's pretty close to the truth."

"Yer prepared to do votever it takez to get zere, no?" Sven asked, and then he continued before Ethan had a chance to answer. "You appear to be very determined young man, no? Zacrified a lot, haven't you?"

Ethan thought for a moment as he leaned forward and allowed Sven to light his cigar. He had sacrificed a lot—pretty much his entire past. His entire future depended on his success in the movies. "Yes," he replied. "I have."

"Ezan, I know zis iz a perzonal queztion, and you don't have to anzer it, but how old are you?"

"Twenty-eight." Ethan was becoming more comfortable by the second.

"Yer juzt a babe," Sven said, smiling warmly. "And your timing couldn't be better for breaking into zee Hollyvood."

Ethan smiled and blew a large plume of smoke into the air.

"Iz good, no?" Sven said, holding his cigar up as if having won it.

Ethan nodded his head as he took another draw from the end. Strange, he couldn't remember cutting the cigar.

"Vot kind of movie do you hope to ztar in?" Sven asked, standing up and removing his black blazer. "Vot kind of movie actor do you plan to be? You muzt have zomezing in mind, yez?"

Ethan thought for a moment. It had been a long time since he'd had a serious conversation about his movie goals. For a change, he felt in the right place at the right time. This was it. The answers were easy. "Action movies with good stories and strong characters—the underdog type, where good prevails over evil in no-win situations. Something that has an edginess to it. Sylvester Stallone, Bruce Willis style, with Norman Bates edginess. I want it to be good entertainment with a point. Suspend the audience's disbelief."

"An edgy good guy who breakz zee rulez zee right vay?"

"Exactly," Ethan agreed. He was enjoying the conversation. Here he was, finally talking about what was most important to him. He hoped his desire and drive were coming through.

"Ezan, vot have you done zinze arriving in California?" Sven asked, leaning forward with his elbows on his leather desk.

Ethan thought for a moment on how to respond. He didn't want anything to jeopardize his chances, least of all give any indication he might lack experience. "I've worked on several movies and done a few commercials," he replied, doing his best to avoid specifics.

"No," Sven interrupted, "I mean vot are you doing to pay zee billz. You have a day job, no?"

Confused, Ethan answered before even thinking. "I'm an engineer. Since leaving Canada, my engineering experience has paid the bills, but ..." He stopped himself before revealing more than he wanted.

"But vot, Ezan?" Sven prompted him, picking up on Ethan's hesitation.

"Well, it's really not that important," Ethan said, backing off.

"Don't vorry about it zen."

But Ethan was unable to hold back. "I lost my engineering job this morning," he admitted, dropping his eyes in defeat.

"Zaz terrible," Sven stated without emotion. "Zomezing vill vork out."

"Yeah, something always works out."

Jacqueline returned, carrying a tray with a chrome coffee urn and two fire-engine red mugs. Sven looked at the lit end of his cigar and then mashed it into the chrome ashtray on his desk.

"I forgot about zee café. Zankz, Jacquie," Sven said. His face took on a hard, stoic seriousness. His dark eyes stared at Ethan as Jacqueline placed a coffee mug on the edge of the desk for him. "Okay, Ezan," he announced, "zee reazon vy I aczepted ziz appointment viz you vaz to zee vot you can do." Sven stretched back in his chair, holding the hot cup of coffee in both hands. His watchful eyes never left Ethan. Ethan smiled, uncomfortable with being observed so closely and so flagrantly sized up. Sven remained silent, continuing to stare across the desk at Ethan as if he'd asked a question and was waiting for a response.

"What do you want me to do?" Ethan finally asked, finding the silence unbearable.

Sven remained still a moment longer and then leaned forward and placed his cup back on the desk.

"Ezan," he said as he picked up the book on the corner of his desk, "have you ever read zis book?" He was holding the book Ethan had seen earlier, *The Catcher in the Rye*.

Ethan's facial expression gave away his confusion. "Well, yes, everybody who's gone to school has read *The Catcher in the Rye*."

"Exactly," replied Sven, his face alight with excitement. "Vell, ve're adapting it into a movie. You ztrike me az a potential player for Ztradlater. Your cut faze might be a good add to the character."

Ethan laughed. He could hardly believe it. Here was the opportunity he'd longed for.

"Do you know zee ztory?" Sven asked, his tone remained serious.

"Studied it in high school," Ethan replied, hoping Sven wouldn't call his bluff. For the life of him, he couldn't recall what the story was about, outside of sex. He was certain of one thing: if he got an audition, he'd have a copy of the book in his hands that afternoon. He'd read all night if he had to.

"Okay," Sven continued, leaning over his desk. His serious demeanor remained. "I would like you to come back tomorrow afternoon. Four o'clock." Sven pulled a black three-ringed binder from a desk drawer and handed it to Ethan. "Zis iz zee vorking zcript. Zird zcene. Go home and vork it out. I'll zee you here tomorrow."

"Definitely," Ethan replied, taking the binder.

Sven got up and stepped around the side of his desk. Ethan stood and shook his hand. "No more cutz on zee faze," Sven cautioned, pointing to his cheek.

"Not a chance," Ethan replied, all but bounding out of the office.

On his way out, he smiled at Jacqueline. "We'll see you tomorrow," he said, giving her a nervous wave and nod. "Nice to meet you."

Jacqueline returned his smile. "Looking forward to it," she said, giving him a wink and then flitting her long red fingernails in a wave.

Suddenly, a sense of foreboding hovered around him. He shrugged it off as simple paranoia. Once outdoors, he started searching for a pay phone to call Christa. He had to let her know his news. As he walked, he also kept an eye out for a taxi. The taxi came first.

On the ride back, the binder Sven had given him was open on his lap. He started reading the third scene, thinking of ways he could own the audition. He was deep into the scene when the taxi stopped at a red light. When Ethan looked up, the view out the window had changed. The day had turned gray, but it wasn't raining. Where there had been buildings lining the street, he now saw houses and lawns and flower gardens.

She was standing at the curb, all alone.

He blinked. *Can't be,* he told himself. *Not here.*

She was looking the other way but was as beautiful as ever. Her hair was longer, well past her shoulders and blowing a bit in the light breeze.

He moved to wave but his arm was stuck, restricted somehow inside the car. As the cab moved forward, he watched her, unable to look away. She was looking at something in one of the houses that he couldn't see.

"Stop! Stop the car!" he shouted, but his words were drowned in a space silent of sound. He watched as Mila walked away from the cab and toward one of the houses. There was something about the neighborhood that looked familiar, but it wasn't where he thought he was.

He turned away from the window. The door had a small ledge where he would have rested his arm if he could move it. He looked down at his lap, where he'd put what he thought was something to read, but couldn't remember what it was and couldn't find it. As he took in more of his surroundings, he realized he was no longer in a cab but in a bed, with white sheets over his legs. He couldn't remember where he thought he was. As he turned to look at what was preventing him from moving his arm, he noticed a woman standing at his side, wearing a navy blue suit and a light-blue blouse with a frilly collar. It was Beth. Beth was standing beside him wearing a white lab coat over a navy business suit. She wasn't smiling but thankfully wasn't crying either. Beth looked very pretty. Behind her were white walls—white walls that were moving. No, it wasn't the walls; it was the bed he was in with the white sheets. Beth was walking beside the bed. The bed was moving like a boat.

"Did you see her today?" Beth asked. Her lips were red but light in color, a professional red.

Ethan shook his head.

"Are you sure?" Beth asked. "We know when you're not telling the truth, you know."

"Then yes, I saw her," he replied, hoping the truth would set him free from whatever bound his movement. "She was standing on the corner. I saw her from the taxi."

Beth leaned down, her soft face stern and close to his.

"From the taxi?" she asked. "Where were you going in a taxi?"

"Back to Robbie's apartment, of course, to tell Christa the good—"

"Mister! Mister!"

Beth still was talking, but it wasn't her voice he heard. She was bent down in front of him. Her face almost in his.

"Sir, excuse me!"

Someone was shaking him. It wasn't Beth.

The sun shone brightly into the car.

An animated man was glaring at him. His mouth was moving, but Ethan couldn't hear. No. Maybe he could.

"Are you awake? Can you hear me? We're here."

He could move his arms. He *was* in a taxi.

Ethan opened the rear passenger door and stepped out, holding tight to the black binder. His mind was swimming, trying to wake up and make sense of wherever he'd just gone. A dead sleep must have overtaken him in the cab. His mind didn't quite connect to his eyes. He felt drugged and more than a little mixed up. Maybe he was more sleep-deprived than he thought.

Upon leaving the taxi, he sat down on a wooden bench opposite the apartment and attempted to clear his head. He placed the binder flat on his lap and opened it again to the third scene. The story was not familiar, but he hoped to stir his memory on it. Then something clicked, and he was back. Maybe Robbie had a copy of the book. In the binder, he read that there were two male characters, Stradlater and Holden—Stradlater apparently more magnanimous than Holden. He searched for character traits and mannerisms to help him play the scene but needed the background of the book, a foundation to latch onto and build on.

Still dazed and fuzzy, he sat for a while longer and got a second wind. The fifteen-minute sleep in the taxicab seemed to have helped. Midway through the scene, a girl with whom Stradlater professed to have had a relationship returns. Ethan wondered if she would be part of the audition. Reading further, he was seeking the connecting relationship when an ambulance flew past with lights flashing and sirens blaring. The interruption was enough to distract him. He had yet to share the day's developments with Christa.

But five minutes later, he was back in a taxi. Christa was asleep, and he didn't want to wake her. Something else had popped in his mind. Since he'd arrived in California, he'd not been to the location of the Academy Awards. He needed to go. As the taxi approached the Dorothy Chandler Pavilion, he envisioned himself approaching the hall in a limousine on the evening of the awards. ...

People lined both sides of the street, trying to catch a glimpse of their favorite movie star among the many celebrities mingling about. His long, pearl-white stretch limo pulled up to the curb while he sipped on a cool rye and Coke. Christa was beside him on the white leather couch seat, holding his hand, more anxious than he was, calling out the name of each star they passed, many of whom he'd met and worked with. Limousine after limousine arrived, holding the secret of each new arrival behind tinted glass windows. Every limousine was different, delivering celebrity after celebrity to the adoring fans, each trying to guess who the next star would be to emerge from a limousine.

His cabbie stopped outside the entrance and asked if Ethan wanted him to wait. "I could be a while," Ethan replied. "I'll catch another later on."

Ethan's vision continued. ...

Everyone was dressed to the nines, with an incredible assortment of the world's best designers' work on display. His choice was a lightweight, olive Georgio Armani design with a navy mock turtleneck. Christa walked at his side, gripping his arm tightly, her statuesque figure dressed in a hot red gown designed by Versace, with a revealing heart-shaped cutout in the front that dropped to her navel. Her brunette hair was pinned up high in the back in a French braid. A diamond necklace with matching bracelet and earrings completed her ensemble. Ethan thought she was more beautiful than the many actresses present. The crowd parted behind the roped-off access to the building. Flash after flash popped in their eyes, with cameras capturing their every move and gesture. Shouts of excitement blended together to create an enormous buzz from the crowd as fame entered the auditorium—legend and newcomer alike.

Up the carpeted cement steps, they approached the hall in all its glamour and elaborate staging, her hand on the inside of his elbow. Stopping a moment to hold Christa with both hands, he turned and looked out over the huge crowd of adoring fans. The train of limousines extended beyond the block, slowly moving forward, delivering the famous for that moment in the limelight that so many dreamed of one day experiencing.

An instant later, they were inside, seated near the front, his nomination giving them preferential seating. The gala affair was simply fantastic, the glitz and glamour all larger than life. Then, the moment many worked their entire lives for—standing on stage to accept the year's best honor. Sitting rigid as a board, with fingers and toes crossed, he listened to each of the nominations, everything magnified a hundredfold. Cruise, Cage, Travolta, Pacino, and ... Ethan Jones, for his role as ...

Christa was twisting and squeezing his arm off.

"And the winner is ..." last year's best actress said, fumbling with the envelope. With feigned impatience, she ripped open the gold-edged envelope and announced, "Ethan Jones."

The glamorous audience was on its feet before he was able to move. Christa, already in tears, was clapping uncontrollably. Rising to his feet,

Ethan shook the hands thrust in front of him and kissed the lips rising to his, all offering congratulations as he made his way to the lighted stage. His prepared speech was in his pocket, all but forgotten. "Ladies and gentlemen ..." he began.

"Excuse me, sir," asked a young man, suddenly standing beside Ethan. "Are you okay?"

Ethan hadn't noticed the gathering crowd he'd attracted. Several people were watching him as he prepared to address the audience. Agitated by the interruption, he realized what was happening and said without missing a beat, "I'm practicing." At that, he stopped. His spell was broken. He headed back toward the taxi stand where the cab had dropped him earlier.

"Ah, come on," shouted a rough, unshaven man with his shirt buttoned incorrectly. "We were just getting interested."

Ethan didn't respond and kept walking, bothered by the depth of his imagination and how real he was able to make the experience of the awards ceremony. He still felt great but perturbed. He'd be there again. One day it would be real. He would stand on the podium and accept the golden statue.

As he crossed the sidewalk in front of the taxi stop, he wondered what he would say in the real situation. Whom would he thank? Would Cushman and Christa still be part of his world? His father would be so proud and his mother, God rest her soul, would be beaming. It was then he knew. His was the story of an average man with an average life and an unquenchable persistence to pursue a dream to be in the movies. Risk and sacrifice were the price he'd have to pay. The picture was clear as he waved down the next cab.

Since arriving in California, he could not remember being as clear with where he needed to go as he was now. Fear and anxiety remained but were losing their corrosive influence. Being fired was the kick in the ass he needed to get on with why he'd come to Hollywood in the first place. If he truly wanted the silver screen, he had to find a way to distance himself from everything else and focus full-time on getting in the movies. He had to do more—much more—and Steve Cushman was his catalyst to making that happen. His full-time attention would get Cushman engaged.

Back at the apartment, still pumped from his trip to the Dorothy Chandler Pavilion, he found Christa asleep in the bedroom. Quietly closing the door, he whispered a silent prayer of thanks for more time on the planet. Only a few inches had separated him from this life and the next, and now he wanted to make sure he didn't waste it.

Not wanting to disturb her but anxious to talk to someone, he dialed Cushman's number, only to reach his answering machine. He left a message to call back as soon as possible—it was important. His mind was going in a million different directions, mostly attributable to his lack of sleep and the changing events in his day. He stared at the script on the couch but wanted Christa.

As if summoned by his thoughts, the bedroom door opened and Christa peeked her sleepy head out.

"It looks like you've been up to some serious sleep," Ethan said as she came into the living room, tying her hair back. "You won't believe what happened to me today, even after I tell you."

Christa sat on the couch, rubbing her eyes. She looked like she'd slept for most of the day. "Like the last couple of days haven't been evidence enough," she replied. "Come on; try me."

"Okay, first the good news," Ethan began, watching for her reaction. "I'll wait until Robbie gets here for the bad news, as it impacts him."

"Okay, whatever," Christa replied, leaning her head against the back of the sofa.

"I've an audition tomorrow afternoon," Ethan exploded. "I brought part of the script back to practice tonight."

"Ethan!" Christa almost screamed, sitting straight and pumping her fist. "Woo-hoo!"

At nearly the same moment, Robbie came through the door. "Hey, kids," Robbie greeted them, removing his jacket and tossing it on a chair. "I see you found your way back to the ranch."

"Ethan got an audition!" Christa shouted, her arms now around Ethan's neck.

It felt good having her there. "That's the good news," Ethan said, watching both of their reactions. "And the bad news is … I lost my job at Build this morning."

Christa stretched her head back away from him, giving him a look. "Oh, Ethan," she sighed, "that's not so good. What happened? You work so hard. Didn't that …" She paused momentarily and then stepped it up a notch, realizing what he had said. "What the fuck's their problem? God! Did you tell them you were shot? And what you've been through? Fucking assholes."

"Christa, it's okay," he said. He knew she was blaming herself, but that wasn't his intention. He just wanted her to see how things had worked out. "It'll be fine. I'm here to act in the movies. It's time to get serious."

Robbie didn't say a word as he went to his room. Ethan was showing Christa the script when Robbie returned in shorts and a T-shirt with the message "Go Ahead. Make My Day" and a picture of the enlarged business end of a .44 Magnum.

"So what do you think?" Ethan asked.

Robbie smiled. "I think it's bullshit. I've never heard anything but good stuff about you. I'll be calling them first thing in the morning."

"Don't bother," Ethan replied, deciding as he spoke. "I'm not going back, even if they'd take me. I came here to get in the movies, and that's where I need to work." He pointed to the black three-ringed binder he'd been showing Christa. "I needed a fucking kick in the ass, and today I got it." Ethan's facial expression tightened in seriousness. "How do you feel about having another roommate?" He looked at Christa and added, "Or two?"

There was no hesitation in Robbie's response. "Sure, that we can make happen. Fuck, I invited you down here." Robbie shrugged his shoulders.

"Great," Ethan replied, relieved that Robbie was okay with the arrangement. Looking at Christa, he said, "We'll see how things work out, if that's okay with you."

Christa smiled her agreement but didn't say anything.

Before Robbie had answered, Ethan thought he saw something shift in Robbie's facial expression. It was subtle. His brow wrinkled or his lips pursed, like he'd tasted something that didn't quite agree with him. Robbie's quick answer, however, made any concern Ethan had evaporate.

The apartment buzzer rang, and Robbie smiled. He stepped forward and pressed the button that opened the door to the apartment building. Turning, he then answered Ethan's suspicion from the night before. "I've a little something to tell you as well," Robbie said, looking directly at Ethan. "That's David. This may come as something of a shock, but he's my … my good friend." And then, seemingly unable to find another way to explain it, Robbie said, "I'm gay."

Despite his anticipation of Robbie's news, Ethan had not thought about how he might respond to it. The right words seemed to evade him. "Great, Robbie," he said, without a clue on what to add.

After a few awkward moments, it was Christa who broke the silence. "Hey, I've got an idea," she suggested. "I was going to order take-out tonight. Robbie, why don't you and David join us?"

"Sure, if you don't mind," Robbie agreed. "You two can get to know David"—he looked at Christa—"and I can get to know you."

"I'm in," Ethan agreed.

Christa's smile lit up the room. Ethan sat down beside her on the sofa. Robbie unlocked the door, where moments later, David appeared.

"Come on in, David," Robbie said, moving to greet David with a hug. "I'd like you to meet a couple of my friends—one new, one old."

They all exchanged hellos while Robbie pulled four Heinekens out of the refrigerator.

"All right," Ethan said as Robbie returned with the beer, "I need an hour's sleep. You can pick the food. It's on me tonight, as it might be a while before I can treat again."

Without another word, he gulped down half his beer, which he couldn't really taste for some reason, and headed to bed. "If I'm not up in an hour, wake me."

"Okay," Christa said, raising her green bottle toward him. "I will."

As soon as Ethan lay down, his mind started buzzing with what his next day might bring. It was an opportunity he couldn't afford to screw up. He had nothing to fall back on now. He still found it incredible that he'd been fired. *You didn't come here for a job, Ethan,* came Mila's voice, pushing him back into the ring. *Don't go there anymore.*

He rolled on his side and thought of Randy Baseman and his superheroes. How was he making out? And his stuff at Build—maybe he'd just leave it there. If they kept it, it might someday be worth something. He could see it now—*This was Ethan Jones's stapler.* He smiled. Then Jacqueline's image came to mind. He pictured the audition in a small room with a watercooler.

His next thought took him to another place …

There were white coats again, standing at the end of his bed.

Beth was sitting in a chair by his bedside. Her eyes were closed.

A white sheet covered his legs, and only the outline of his legs was visible.

CHAPTER 24

After what seemed like only moments later, Ethan awoke. Christa was massaging his back.

"Ethan, do you still want to get up?" she whispered. He rolled over and stared into her tanned face. "You've been sleeping for almost two hours."

"Shit!" he spat out between parched lips. He stretched, but his body was more than willing to remain at rest. He rubbed dried saliva off his chin.

"Robbie and David went on ahead to let you sleep," she whispered, close to his face. "We can catch dinner later. You need the sleep."

Looking into Christa's big brown eyes didn't take long to revive him. He was pleased she was there. "No," he said, lifting up off the bed, "I need to get up."

His hand touched her face. He wanted to run his fingers through her long, dark hair. She touched his cheek with her fingertips where the bullet had grazed him. They kissed. Her lips were supple—moist, like a dream. Raising the sheet, she slipped in beside him.

God, he wanted her, to become part of her.

"It's okay," she whispered. Her lips parted as he kissed her again.

At that moment, she meant everything to him.

An hour later, Ethan awoke to a dim room, with Christa asleep beside him. The smoothness of her leg on the back his own was heaven. He felt incredible but hungry.

Rolling sideways, he wrapped his arm around her and cupped her breast gently in his hand. She stirred and settled back against him, like one spoon against another. Together, they were motionless, enjoying each other's closeness.

Christa turned her head and rolled on her back to look at Ethan. Her beauty was mesmerizing. She looked happy. "Hungry?" she asked, a hint of laughter in her voice.

"Absolutely starving," he replied, moving his arm from behind her head. "What about you?"

"I could eat something, for sure," Christa replied, rubbing his arm. "What were you thinking?"

"Pizza?"

"No, let's have Chinese with chopsticks. It'll be fun."

Ethan stretched as Christa got up and slipped on her white nightshirt. For Ethan, watching her move was like simplicity, beauty, and genius wrapped together; he could not take his eyes off her.

"I'm going to clean up a bit," she said. "It'll only take a few minutes."

Ethan didn't really care; he just wanted to be with her.

Now, however, as he lay still, staring at the ceiling, his thoughts returned to his visit to the Dorothy Chandler Pavilion and the enormity of being on the screen. Everything he did needed to influence his drive toward the movies. It would take all of his dedication and still more. Rolling on his side, he pulled open the drawer of the chipped and scratched night table. Scrounging around inside, he found an old transparent Bic pen and a pad of yellow Post-its. He wrote down three letters—A, C, and T—and stuck the paper on the wall. Then he crumpled the paper in his fist and rewrote the three letters on the wall, staking claim to the room and—more important—his future.

Swinging his legs over the side of the bed, he grabbed his day-old underwear and pulled them on. He couldn't pull his eyes away from the letters on the wall. It would serve him both in inspiration and heartache in the days and months to come. He couldn't recall being as happy or as discontent at the same time as he was at that moment. The mixture of feelings was discomfiting. He pulled on his wrinkled khaki shorts and stood up as Christa opened the bedroom door.

"Ethan," Christa said, a forced smile on her face, "I'm so afraid and so happy. What are we doing?" He smiled at her. "I'm so afraid of my feelings right now. I don't want to say anything." She sat back down on the bed.

"Well, don't then," he replied. "It's okay."

"But I want to. I need to."

"I kind of feel the same way," he said, rubbing her back. "Let's go find something to eat."

Robbie and David were gone, so they were on their own. An hour later, Ethan and Christa were cracking open their fortune cookies, having finished the last of the boxed lo mein and chop suey with a bottle of cheap California merlot.

"What's your fortune?" Ethan asked.

"You first," Christa replied.

"'Things are not always as they appear,'" he read, raising an eyebrow.

"Really," Christa responded. "Not bad." Then she read, "'A flower is about to bloom.'"

Ethan smiled and decided to retrace a topic they'd previously touched on. "So you left Calgary to get away from your parents," he said. "Why California?"

Christa set down her wineglass. "I was eighteen and knew everything. Ma's sister lived here and was closer to my age than Ma's. We got on fine. She was doing well for herself, so my holiday turned into staying." She put a piece of the sweet Chinese cookie in her mouth and ate it. "I left Calgary with few expectations and came to California with no intentions. Cindy, my aunt, found me a job as a receptionist at the advertising company where she worked. That was three years ago. I made enough to buy a car."

Ethan, still curious, was surprised. "You've never worked as a model?"

"I worked two sessions as a model. I'm thin, thank God, but I was told at my second session not to waste my time unless I had my boobs done. I didn't have the stomach for it. This is the body God gave me. Who am I to change it? I've been asked twice to pose naked, but that's not my thing. *Playboy* is the only one I would even consider, and they've never asked. The company's done some work with them. They seem to be very professional." She laughed and added, "Besides, it would still cost them a ton of dough." She leaned forward with her elbows on the table and her chin in her hands. "So I've showed you mine. It's your turn." Her face was bright and glowing.

Ethan spoke briefly on becoming an engineer and growing up in Toronto. "My father wanted me to play hockey," he said. "He encouraged me quietly without the pressure a lot of kids get. I later learned how he struggled with this. He is an intense competitor himself—hates to lose. He still says I could have made it if I'd stayed with the game, but at seventeen, I quit and started a band. Dad traveled all the time as a sales VP for a software company. And my mom died of a brain tumor."

"I'm sorry, Ethan," Christa interjected, her hand moving across the table to touch his.

"It was years ago," he replied, squeezing her fingers. He missed his mother but his feelings were now well below the surface. "Her illness was long and drawn out—an awful thing to watch a once-strong woman wither away. No kid should have to see a parent go through that. God rest her soul." He stopped. He didn't want to go any further talking about his mother. "My father didn't care so much what I did after that. He just wanted me to chase something."

He hesitated and offered a weak smile, his eyes glassy. His mother was still there. "I loved Mom," he said, surprising himself with his candor. "She gave me the belief that I could do anything I chose. She was sick long before she let us know she was ill. I stay in touch with Dad; he gave me my work ethic and still works eighty hours a week, running his own company." Ethan took a sip from his wineglass. He hadn't touched his cookie. "I just want to make my father proud. He is already, but I want to do something special—something great. It's like giving that special gift to somebody because of how it makes you feel." Ethan stopped. How did this woman get him talking about his life? There was only one other who could. "Are you in touch with your folks at all?" he asked.

"No, not so much," Christa replied uneasily. "You probably guessed I didn't leave under good terms. It's kind of a long story. I haven't talked to Ma since I left. And my father ..." Her voice trailed off, and then she said, "My younger brother writes once in a while."

Ethan put his hand on hers as a tear rolled down her cheek. "It's okay. Forget it. It doesn't matter."

Her long, slender fingers tightened in his hand. She cocked her head sideways, to see the time on his watch. "Ethan, it's eleven thirty," she said, surprised. "Don't you have lines to rehearse?"

"As a matter of fact, I do," he replied, surprised at the time himself. "Tell me something: did you ever read the book *The Catcher in the Rye*?"

"The title sounds familiar," she said after a moment, "but I don't think so. Why?"

"The part I'm reading for tomorrow is based on that book," he replied. "I think it has something to do with teenagers coming of age. I'm to play a character named Stradlater."

"I'd like to be more helpful," Christa stated, giving him a kiss and turning toward the bedroom, "but I haven't a clue."

Ethan grabbed his script.

"You know," Christa added, standing at the bedroom door, "I think I saw a used bookstore around the corner."

Ethan smiled, already focused on Stradlater's lines in the script. "I'll check it out," he answered. "Thanks."

"Good night," she said, smiling, and closed the bedroom door.

It took Ethan all of his resolve not to join her right then, but the word he'd written on the wall earlier reinforced his strength of will. Going to bed with Christa was the wrong thing to do. He sat on the couch, noticing the apartment still was warm from the day's heat. He'd started to read when Christa opened the bedroom door again.

"Thanks, Ethan," she whispered. "I'm not sure I'm worthy of someone like you, but thanks."

"Right back at you, kid," he replied in a poor Bogart impression, not knowing quite what to say. "Thanks. Sleep well."

Quietly, she closed the door. He picked up the script and flipped through several of the pages he'd looked at earlier in the day. Stradlater didn't have as many lines as he first thought, and as he read it more closely, the story seemed to lead up to a larger event left out of the section he'd been given. There was a relationship developing between two characters that confused him. Maybe he was tired. He read and reread the lines, shaping how he wanted to approach the audition. By whispering his memorized lines aloud, he began to sense a certain protected toughness in the character. Stradlater crystallized in his head. Another half hour passed before he'd finished learning all his lines. First thing in the morning, he would buy a copy of the book.

He was about to join Christa when he heard a commotion outside the apartment in the hallway. His body tensed and broke out in a sweat; his heart pounded loudly in his ears. Without a second thought, he sought a weapon … and then the door swung wide and Robbie burst into the apartment. David was right behind him.

"Eth, yerrup," Robbie said in a loud, drunk voice. "Whas goin' on?"

"Rehearsing," Ethan replied, raising his index finger to his lips. "Shh. Christa's sleeping."

Ethan relaxed and his heart rate slowed. On hearing the movement in the hall, he'd started to think Christa's ex had found them again. It would be a while before he reacted otherwise.

"Little distracted tonight, eh, buddy?" Robbie chided him with a stupid drunk grin on his face. "Dinit wanna in'errupt."

"Thanks," Ethan replied. "I was just heading to bed myself."

"Don't let us hold ya up. Sleep well."

"Nice to meet you, David," Ethan said, extending his hand. "Sorry about standing you up. Another time."

"You're on," David answered, his handshake firm.

"Thanks again, Robbie, for helping us out," Ethan added. "I don't know where I'd be if not for you."

Ethan went in the bedroom and lay down beside Christa. He was asleep before his head settled into the pillow.

CHAPTER 25

Ethan's Timeline
April 1991

Ethan awoke the next morning to find Christa's place in the bed unoccupied. *She must have left for work,* he reasoned. He didn't feel much like getting up but as usual when he awoke, the day's activities filled his head. Today was no different: he had to practice his lines for his audition with Sven and find a copy of *The Catcher in the Rye*.

He rested for a few more minutes with his forearm on his brow, shading the brightness. His eyes were closed when the door opened and Christa walked in, wearing only her bra and panties.

"Good morning," she said, her voice cheery.

"Hi," Ethan mumbled, wondering how someone could even suggest the word "good." Mornings were not his high point.

"Did you sleep well?" she asked, pulling a bright yellow dress with an array of printed flowers from the closet. "Ready for your audition?"

"I think so," he replied in a rough voice, coughing to clear this throat.

"You know what I think?" she asked, smiling as she slipped the dress over her head and down over her hips.

"No. What do you think?" he asked with a hint of sarcasm.

"I think you're going to do great," she announced. "The world is waiting for Ethan Jones to step forward."

In one sentence, Christa made him feel like he could do anything. It was the impetus he needed to get up. He gave her a quick kiss and headed to the shower.

Christa was gone by the time he'd finished; Robbie too. Still early, he spent an hour practicing with the script but needed the book to better understand Salinger's intent with the character. He followed Christa's suggestion to a small shop that sold used books. They had a copy displayed in the front window. In four hours, he'd read through three-quarters of the book and was headed to his four o'clock appointment with Sven.

Again, he arrived five minutes early, only to find the reception desk empty. The whole place seemed deserted. *Have I screwed up another audition?* he wondered. He took a seat and tried to be patient, certain he had the time correct. He read more of the book.

Shortly after four, the large wood door beside the front desk opened, and Jacqueline stepped out. She was dressed more casually than the day before, in a wrap-around blue-silk gown and fishnet stockings.

"Hi, Ethan!" she greeted him enthusiastically as she slid behind her desk. "I was sure I'd put it here. Sorry, Ethan, we're running a little behind. Hope you haven't been waiting long. We should be done in another couple of minutes."

"That's okay. Lots of auditions, I'm sure," Ethan replied.

"Ah, yeah, lots," Jacqueline responded somewhat absently as she rustled through something in a drawer. "Ah, here it is!" she cried, holding up a manila file folder. "I knew I'd put it here." She was all smiles as she rose to her feet, adjusting the front of her wrap. "Make yourself comfortable. Can I get you a coffee or something?"

"No, I'm okay, thanks," he replied and returned to his book. Jacqueline popped back through the door and moments later returned without the folder. In her haste to sit down, she pushed a folder of papers off the edge of her desk. Ethan was quick to pick them up and noticed that her feet were bare. "Jacqueline, if this is a bad time, I can come back," he proposed, his enthusiasm for the audition beginning to wane. Things weren't happening as he had anticipated. His confidence was slipping away, edging toward the crack under the front door.

"No, no," Jacqueline was quick to answer. "Everything's cool. We're just trying to get a few things arranged. Sven doesn't like to hurry his work. Give it another couple of minutes."

"What's he arranging?" Ethan asked without thinking.

"Your audition, of course," replied Jacqueline. "He likes things to be exact. He's very detailed."

Ethan's discomfort increased. He was more than a little confused. Most auditions were bare-bones, shoestring-budget affairs with little more than a few stackable wooden chairs to sit on. Why this should be any different made him question what he was getting himself into.

Jacqueline disappeared behind the doors again but this time was back in less than a minute. "Okay, Ethan," she announced, opening the door wide enough to allow him to pass.

Entering Sven's office this time—the same one he'd visited the day before—was a whole new experience. Sven's desk had been replaced by a large bed. Before Ethan could say a word, Sven came into the room through another door. Sven's hand was extended as he approached Ethan.

"Good to zee you again, Ezan," Sven announced in a loud voice. "I'm zo glad you vere able to make it. How'd you make out viz zee zcript laz night?"

"Just great," Ethan answered, holding up his copy of Salinger's book. "I even got a copy of the book—you know, to get a feel for the story again. How is it you came to the conclusion I would make a good Stradlater?"

"Hunch, really. Zere iz zumzing about you," Sven replied. "I veel it in my gut." Sven proceeded to walk across the room and grab a couple of chairs. He placed one chair directly in front of Ethan and sat down in the other. "Okay, lez zee vat you've got!"

Ethan sat down in the chair opposite Sven. His reluctance had grown to the point of near muteness.

"Begin on page four," Sven stated, "and I'll do zee ozer part."

Ethan turned to page four and coughed to clear his throat. His anxiety had grown beyond anything he'd experienced previously. He was about to speak when he heard someone say "Action" from behind the door where Sven had entered the room. Sven made no indication that he'd heard anything. Ethan again cleared his throat, closed his eyes, lifted his head, and began.

In seconds, he transformed himself into character and for the next three pages became Stradlater. At that point, Ethan had moved to a position beside a car—a car that wasn't there, but he and Sven both believed it was. There was no doubt in his abilities, and Sven smiled, seeming to recognize this at once. Like the night at the church, Ethan thought he nailed Stradlater's character right from the start.

Ethan sat back down. The silence was deafening until he heard women's voices coming from behind the door.

"Ezan," Sven said, "you are a gifted actor. Zee parz yourz if you vant it."

Ethan couldn't believe his ears. The moment he'd dreamed of was happening. He was getting a chance. Excited, he stood up and grabbed Sven's hand, shaking it vigorously. His reservations had vanished like water vapor into the air. "Thank you," he said, finding it difficult to contain his emotions. "You can't imagine how long I've waited to hear those words."

"Lizen, vile you're here, vy don't you take a look next door. Ve're shooting a zene for the film right now. It might give you a veel for vat ve're doing. Oh, and by zee vay, you'll be paid a flat rate of two hundred dollarz a day."

"Great," Ethan replied—he hadn't thought about compensation.

Sven put an arm around Ethan's shoulder, welcoming him aboard as he pulled open the door. "Lookz like zey vinished zee zene," he said, allowing Ethan to pass ahead of him. "I'll introduz you to zum of zee caz."

Upon entering the next room, Ethan was overwhelmed by the goings-on of a film in production. Bright white lights and umbrellas were positioned around a large set that was otherwise flat black. A dozen people were milling around, adjusting stands, moving lights, or talking. Two long-haired, stubble-faced men in T-shirts and jeans were moving two big black-bulb microphones on extensions around a rather large Victorian bed with a fancy lace bedspread and pillow slips. Ethan counted three cameras but saw only one person behind one.

A woman with bright red hair, wearing track pants and a Van Halen T-shirt, was sitting in a black cloth chair, writing something on a marker board. "Let's run the second scene again," she said, holding up the board to the camera beside her. "Jacqueline, Carla, we're ready."

On hearing Jacqueline's name, Ethan scanned the room, curious to find her. The signs of what was going on were all there. If he'd really wanted to know about Sven, he could have asked Steve. But curiosity ruled here, taking Ethan further and further into this unconventional world and its underbelly. He remained still, watching the action and looking for something that would confirm his suspicions on the type of films they were making.

Three paneled screens displaying Oriental artwork were to the right of where Ethan stood, adjacent to the bed. His mouth dropped as a big-breasted woman with long dark hair walked out from behind the blind, wearing only black patent-leather stilettos and giant gold hoop earrings. She strutted out, displaying her magnificent body—chest out, stomach flat, and back arched—like she owned not only the studio but the entire world. Her demeanor was one of calm silence, without any qualms about her brazenness. Ethan's feelings were simultaneously excitement, concern, and disbelief; he could only stand and gawk. Without any noticeable inhibition, the woman approached the bed as if she were wearing a costume instead of nothing at all. A moment later, Jacqueline stepped out from behind the blind with no less aplomb. Smiling, she winked as she passed Ethan. Carla, the first woman, lay on the bed with her long golden legs spread wide in an ostentatious display of genitalia from which Ethan could not turn away. A moment later, a technician approached Carla and sprayed a solution on her open thighs, making her vagina glisten in the bright lights. Ethan could barely contain himself, turned on beyond control. The tiny hairs on the backs of his legs and neck stood on end. His testicles tingled. Another woman, whom Ethan hadn't seen, held a tiny black brush and brushed a dark powder across Jacqueline's nipples. He couldn't help himself; the eroticism blew his mind.

"You're in zene zree," Sven whispered, grabbing Ethan by the arm and pulling him back toward the door. "Vot do you zink?"

As they stepped back into Sven's office, Ethan's first reaction was *All right! Let's fucking get started!* But at the same time, he became desperately uncomfortable. The action between his legs pained him. What came out of his mouth next surprised him. "Sven," he said directly, "what is this? I thought you were making a movie based on *The Catcher in the Rye*."

"Vell, it iz," Sven replied, smiling and signaling Ethan to sit in a chair.

Ethan saw a sly, dirty-old-man look in Sven's eyes that he hadn't noticed before. He didn't like it. "Oh, come on, you're making fucking porn," Ethan stated. He didn't like being misled, even if all the signs were there. "Let's call a spade a spade."

"It'z zee ztory of a young man coming of age," Sven continued, unperturbed by Ethan's comments, "in todaze vorld."

"Sure it is," Ethan said, realizing their discussion was going nowhere. He should have known better. "Well, Sven, you've got the wrong guy," he stated emphatically. "I'm not interested. This isn't what I came to California for. I can't do this."

"Oh, come," Sven countered, not ready to settle for Ethan's rejection. "You vant to fuck zose bitchez. I know. I zaw it in your faze. Jacqueline vants you. She told me zo. You'll be rich beyond your vildest dreamz. Vuck whoever you like."

"Maybe, but I wouldn't be able to look at myself in the mirror," Ethan replied.

"Come on, boy zcout," Sven continued as if Ethan had never spoken. "You vant to zuck Jacqueline's big nipplez, no?"

Sven's words flowed around inside Ethan's head. *Is it right? Is it wrong? Who knows?* The frustration and temptation fueled his disappointment and burned in his gut like a bad stomach ulcer. He rose to his feet to leave before anger took him too far and he said things he'd regret.

Sven continued to talk about fucking and sucking. "Fuck, ziz iz zee chanz of a lifetime, my boy," Sven said, smiling, but his brow furrowed in exasperation. "Rich and all zee vucking you can take. Every manz dream."

"Not every man's, Sven," Ethan shot back, biting his lower lip. Reluctantly, he extended his hand to Sven, despite his growing dislike for the silver-haired swine.

"You'll be back," Sven said condescendingly.

With that, Ethan turned and walked out. Furious, he hurried through the foyer and out the front entrance. He was hurt and disappointed about his own self-deception. Desperate hope had made him ignore the obvious, to get that break he so desired. He asked himself again, *Am I really cut out for this life?* There was so much bullshit to go through and still not get anywhere.

Walking fast, without any destination, Ethan was several blocks from Sven's office before his anger subsided and his pace slowed. Walking on the fringe of a small park, he found an empty bench and sat down to take account of what had happened. Strangely, with no one else around, he started to chuckle and then laughed out loud. How things had changed. He laughed as he recalled the events of the past hour. He had walked out on a chance to be with two beautiful, uninhibited women, a chance he would have died for as a teenager—or for that matter, some nights still. *Am I nuts?* His laugh turned to tears as he struggled with his emotions of anger, frustration, hurt, and anxiety, each falling away like chunks of stone from a sculptor's chisel.

Maybe I'm just not cut out to be an actor, he thought, but then he stopped the thought almost instantly, remembering what he'd written on the wall bedside his bed. He had to *act*. He had to find a way. What had Christa said? *"The world is waiting for Ethan Jones to step forward."* There had to be a way.

As he stood up from the bench, a ruddy-faced man ran toward him, huffing and puffing. The man, overweight and prematurely balding, signaled Ethan with his hand to wait a minute. "S'cuse me," he gasped between breaths, his face taking on a deep crimson color, "but I would like"—he gasped again—"to talk to you"—another gasp—"for a minute." The man crouched forward with his hands on his knees, sucking air for each breath. Dark stains grew under his armpits and down the front of his brown shirt, which stretched across his extended belly. A pack of Lucky Strikes protruded from his left breast pocket. His baggy, tan shorts were in need of a good wash, as were his beige nylon mesh shoes. The hair on his legs and forearms was so thick, he resembled a small Ewok from *Star Wars*. What was left of his dark hair extended in different directions. "I'm sorry," the man began again, trying his best to get his breathing under control. "I have ... asthma ... and it catches up with me ... when I run."

Sure, Ethan thought, *it's a little more than asthma, bud.* Ethan directed him to sit on the bench and relax, at the same time keeping his distance. "Slow down and take it easy," he said.

A moment later, the man pulled an inhaler from his pocket and took several long inhalations.

"I'm sorry ... I don't know your name," the man said, looking directly at Ethan, his eyes wide and bulging, his breathing still strained. "Jamie Scott's my name ... and I saw your audition back there. It was incredible. I know the story. You hit Stradlater dead-on."

"Thank you," Ethan replied, shaking hands and wondering how anyone else had seen the audition. He thought he'd been alone with Sven. "Ethan Jones."

"You know," Jamie continued, his breathing slowing, although he still spoke rapidly, "something magical happened in there. You connected or something. I can't always explain it, but I know when I see it. It's a gift, you know—you become the character through the words. It's rare but magnificent to watch. You know what I mean?"

Ethan just stared at the man, who seemed harmless enough but very off the wall. "Kind of," Ethan replied, looking for a polite way to move on before he got too involved.

"I'm sorry. It's just that you have it. You know—the gift."

"Thanks. This just isn't my thing."

"No, maybe not. But you got the presence. You transform yourself. You're not acting. You live the part."

This is crazy, Ethan thought. "Listen, Jamie, it was nice to meet you," he said, standing up, "but I have to go."

"You gotta act, man!" Jamie shouted, stopping Ethan in his tracks. "You can *act!*" he repeated, continuing as if talking to himself. "You got it. You can't waste it. Damn, what a sight."

Hearing the word said aloud by someone he'd never met creeped Ethan out and sent a strip of electricity straight up his spine. The serendipity of the moment was not lost on him. This strange little man had somehow connected with his thoughts and the word he'd written on the bedroom wall. He turned around as if a rock had been thrown at him.

"What did you say?" Ethan asked, sitting back down, increasingly intrigued by Jamie Scott.

"You can act." Jamie frowned. Ethan saw age in the man's face; he wasn't a kid. There was something about his eyes. He could be forty, maybe even fifty. "Why are you auditioning for a porn flick?"

"I wasn't auditioning for porn." Ethan sighed, finding it strange to talk to this little man. "I was auditioning for a part in the remake of the book *The Catcher in the Rye*."

"And you done good," Jamie added, "but make no mistake. Sven Irons makes porn, and that's exactly what he was making in there. So why audition for Sven Irons?"

"Because he asked me to," Ethan cried, a little exasperated by this bald man asking questions that seemed to challenge his decision. "Why are you so interested in why I auditioned?"

"You haven't been in a movie yet, have you?" Jamie asked, ignoring Ethan's question.

"What? Why do you say that?"

"That's what I thought." Jamie grimaced and shook his head. "Have you done any commercials?"

Ethan looked at the ground.

"Okay, here we go." Jamie shook his head and spoke as if to himself. "Incredible. You are naive. You don't know your gift. Not a surprise; the best usually don't. But Sven Irons does. You'll make him richer, you know."

"Ah, now I get it." Ethan stood up to leave. He knew what was going on. Jamie worked for Sven. Sven had sent Jamie to convince him to come back. "I won't be changing my mind, Jamie. You can tell your boss to stop wasting his time. I'm done." He turned and walked away.

"Ethan! I know you can act!" shouted Jamie after him. Ethan kept walking. "I can help you!" Jamie shouted. "You're kidding yourself if you think you can do it alone!"

"Just watch me!" Ethan shouted back, unable to remain quiet.

"I can help you!" shouted Jamie, coming off the bench and following.

Ethan stopped and turned. "How the fuck can you help me?" he demanded as Jamie approached him again. It was enough to have bullshit shoved in his face by some porn king, but having some half-wit chase after him was taking it to another level. Why did he let the little shit get under his skin? Christ, he didn't even know the guy. "Stop jerking my fucking chain and tell me, or fuck off."

"I've worked with Sven for fifteen years—"

"I don't want to hear about fucking Sven. I'm not interested in porn—no way, no how! Got it?"

Jamie ignored Ethan's outburst and continued. "As I said, I've worked with Sven for fifteen years, and he has an uncanny ability to find talent. It's like he can smell it or something. He found you, didn't he?"

Ethan didn't move or say a word. He just glared down at the man.

"I have a friend who's in casting and contracted to Paramount. He's always looking to make a mark for himself, finding the next Harrison Ford or Tom Cruise, like everybody else. Every once in a while I see someone I think is worth passing on. It sets his ears a-flapping when I get one. His motto: all you need is one."

Ethan stood there, perplexed. He was becoming so suspicious of everyone. Was this real or more bullshit? Against his better judgment, he said, "Okay, say that I believe you—which, by the way, I have no reason to. What are you proposing? You'll give my name to this friend of yours at Paramount, and he'll make me a star?"

Jamie didn't answer immediately. Instead, he pulled the packet of Lucky Strikes from his shirt pocket and popped a cigarette between his lips. He tilted the pack to Ethan, and Ethan accepted—anything that might help him relax. Jamie lit both cigarettes by flicking his thumbnail across the end of a wood match.

"Thanks," said Ethan, taking his first drag. He hardly smoked at all but needed the distraction.

"Yes. In a nutshell, that's exactly it," Jamie finally answered after inhaling a deep draw from his cigarette. "I'll arrange a time when the two of you can meet. I'll take your number and be in touch."

"Just a minute," Ethan interjected. "I've been down this road too many times. I'll take your number and your friend's, and I'll call. I'll use your name."

Jamie seemed to hesitate at Ethan's suggestion but jotted a second number on the back of his card and handed the card to Ethan.

"You'll save me some time. Thanks," Ethan added.

Frederick Northum was the name Jamie printed on the reverse side of the card. Jamie looked up at Ethan, his eyes sharp and focused. "How bad do you want to be an actor?"

Ethan was quick to answer. "I left everything I had to come down here. I *will* be an actor—a movie star. Count on it."

Jamie smiled, seemingly satisfied with the answer. It was his turn to speak up. "Then you better get going. Time's ticking—tick-tock, tick-tock. Have a good one."

CHAPTER 26

An hour later, Ethan was back at Robbie's apartment, still wondering what to do next.

Christa was at the door as he opened it, having arrived moments earlier. She was smiling, having had a good day. "So how did it go?" she asked excitedly. "Did you get it? Tell me! Tell me!"

"Well, sort of," he answered. He went to put his arms around her, but she pushed him away.

"Sort of? What does that mean?"

"It means I was offered the part, but I didn't accept it."

"What?" she cried. "You didn't take it? Why?"

"It wasn't my style," he said, skirting around the main reason. "I wasn't comfortable with what the role involved."

"Oh," Christa replied with a sigh, her excitement flattened. "I was thinking about you all day today, wondering how you were doing. I thought for sure this was the one. What happened?"

Ethan thought for a moment on how he would explain it but decided just to tell her. "I don't like acting without my clothes on," he said, staring into her eyes.

"You were auditioning for a nude scene!" she exclaimed, her dark brown eyes seeming to lighten with amazement.

"A little more than that," he added.

"Porn?"

"As it turned out, yes. I read for the scene, which went really well. I was then taken into a studio out back, where they were shooting a scene with two women, and discovered I was to be in the next scene. I left."

Christa was speechless. Ethan watched as she checked him out to make sure he was serious. "Wow," she said, "I guess it's hard for me to encourage you on that one."

He nodded and pulled off his worn-out deck shoes and headed to the kitchen.

She put her arm up against the wall and blocked his way. "Look at me," she said, grabbing his chin. "Tomorrow's another day. You'll find something. I just know you will." She put her arms around him. He followed her lead. "I like you without your clothes on too," she whispered in his ear, "but I don't like the idea of sharing you. Let's get something to eat—my treat."

"You're on," he replied, "but I have to make a couple of phone calls first." He intentionally didn't say a word about his meeting with Jamie Scott. There would be no mention of the name unless something came of it. He didn't want to jinx himself.

There were three people he had to call.

In the bedroom, he searched through his pants and the night table drawer until he found Randy Baseman's card. Randy had told him to call. Cushman would be next. Ethan wanted a commitment that Steve would find him more work. Finally, he would call the name on the back of Jamie Scott's card.

When he re-emerged from the bedroom, Christa was flipping through a fashion magazine on the couch. Ethan checked Robbie's answering machine for messages. His only message was from Cushman. Ethan's heart quickened a few beats at the sound of Steve's voice and the prospects he might have lined up. He dialed Steve's number. Christa got up and went into their bedroom.

Steve answered on the first ring.

"Steve. Ethan. What's going on?"

"A ton my friend. I'm glad you called. Where you been hiding? I've been trying to reach you. Things are cooking. Sorry about your job. The receptionist told me you didn't work there anymore. What the fuck?"

Steve was the fastest talker Ethan knew, especially when Steve was excited. Ethan caught himself taking breaths for Steve. It was futile to try to fit a word in.

"Yeah," was the best he could muster in response.

"Hey, that's great! Now you can focus on acting."

Ethan was surprised by his comment. He didn't think his job had anything to do with his acting work. "I'm ready for whatever you got."

"Well, I got two things. Both in LA. Got a pen?"

"Steve, I have to tell you something."

"In a minute, bud. These are commercials. Both paying gigs. One has dialogue, so some extra bucks there. The other just has you showing up." Steve gave him the details and said he had a line on some TV work as well, but it was too soon to tell where it was going. "What happened the other night?" Steve asked abruptly. "At the church. I never heard from you."

"Jesus, Steve, slow down," Ethan answered, trying to catch his own breath. "Yeah, at the church. I was late getting there. Missed my time but went for it anyway. I forced myself in and did a great job. I really think it was good. They liked it too, until they found I wasn't who they thought I was. They went from really excited to good-bye. It went from bad to worse when I lost my fucking job."

Steve empathized for a second and then summed it up with "Shit happens, dude," and said he'd keep in touch.

Ethan hung up, energized that at least something was happening. Two days of work in the next week was good—great by his recent standards. Looking at the two cards, he vacillated on which number to call next. He thought about Randy first, so he dialed the number and reached the comic book man's answering machine. In the message, he identified himself as the guy who'd stiffed him and came back. He left Robbie's number to call. Then he reluctantly dialed the number Jamie had given him. After three rings, he was ready to hang up when a bothered voice answered sharply, "Hello. Who's calling?"

Ethan was surprised by the terseness. "My name's Ethan Jones, and I'm looking for Frederick Northum," he said, hoping his nervousness didn't come through.

"You're talking to him," replied Frederick. After a long pause, he added, "Well, what do you want?"

Ethan already was uncomfortable but he said, "I'm a friend of Jamie Scott's and—"

"Well, why didn't you say so?" Frederick's voice was suddenly jovial, nearly unrecognizable from the first. "How's Jamie doing?"

"Fine. A little out of breath when I saw him," Ethan replied warily and more than a little confused.

"Is Jamie working out?"

"No, it wasn't quite like that. He was catching up to me."

"What can I do for you? What did you say your name was again?"

"Ethan Jones," Ethan replied. "I'm an actor, and Jamie thought you might have some work for me at Paramount."

"He did, did he?" Frederick mused. Ethan pictured a fat man with a graying white dress shirt, buttons pulled to the limit to cover a bulging gut, sitting in front of a paper-strewn desk. "You must have impressed him."

"He said he liked my work and suggested I meet you. Is there any time that's good for you?" Ethan could hardly believe what he was saying.

"This week's shot but …" Frederick paused for a moment before saying, "How about dinner next Tuesday night?"

"Works for me. How about Aspinwood's, downtown, say around 7:30?"

"No, I'd rather meet closer to the airport. Do you know Smalton's?" Frederick suggested.

"No, I don't," Ethan responded, "but I'm sure I can find it."

"Good stuff. Eight o'clock okay?"

"Yes," he agreed, grinning in victory with his fist clenched.

"I'll make the reservations and look forward to meeting you," Frederick summarized. "See you then."

Ethan's face was wet with perspiration as he pressed the button to hang up the cordless. He pumped his arm in the air and danced in a circle, shouting to the room, "Yes, sir! Thank you, sir! Have no fear; the master's here! I'm a walkin', talkin' acting machine!"

"Looks like somebody's happy," Christa said, opening the bedroom door a crack. "What happened?"

"Everything," he replied, strutting toward her. "I have two commercials and a meeting with a casting director at Paramount next week."

"No way!" she cried, opening the door further. All she was wearing was a pair of purple bikini briefs.

"Yes, ma'am. Yes, way!" He put his arms around her and swung her into the air, her bare breasts pressed hard against his chest. "Can you believe it?" he remarked after kissing her full on the lips. "My mother used to say, 'it never rains but it pours.'"

"Well, it's definitely doing that," Christa added, giving him a squeeze and turning back to the bedroom. "Let's get going. I'm starved, and I'm sure you are too."

Ethan had other things in mind as he watched her perfect figure move into the room. Her smooth, tan skin against the tight purple panties made him crazy with desire. At the same time, the apartment door opened and in walked Robbie. Christa made an imperceptible remark and closed the bedroom door.

"Hey, how's tricks?" Robbie announced, letting the door close behind him.

"Depends on who's asking," Ethan replied, mildly ticked at Robbie's timing.

"Always a condition, isn't there?" Robbie chided. "So what's up?"

"We're going out to grab a bite," Ethan replied, placing the phone on the kitchen counter. "You're welcome to join us."

Robbie needed five minutes. While Ethan waited for Christa and Robbie, David came by, and their foursome ended up eating pizza across the street from their apartment building.

Robbie sat beside Ethan in the booth; Christa was next to David. As the wine flowed, their conversation followed, lively and sporadic.

"Have you heard anything from the police?" Robbie asked abruptly.

"No," Ethan answered. Strange—he hadn't even thought about the police that day. He touched the scab on his cheek and turned to Christa. "Have you?"

She shook her head, frowning. Ethan didn't know whether the frown was because Robbie had asked or because of the reminder of the incident. Still, it was the most relaxed he'd seen her since the shooting. She was not about to dwell on the subject.

"How did you get interested in acting?" Christa laughed as she asked the question. "Did you watch a couple of movies?" She reached across the table and squeezed Ethan's hand.

"It was more than a few," Robbie replied for Ethan, his smile turning aggressive for an instant. "He was in love with a gorgeous cunt." Robbie cackled like the Wicked Witch of the West as the words flew out of his mouth. The effect was uncomfortable and disquieting.

"What the fuck!" Ethan fired back, anger lighting him up.

Robbie rubbed Ethan's arm as Beth might have, aware of the line she'd crossed, wanting him to know her intention was naughty, not mean. Mila flashed through his head. She might have done the same thing. But Ethan had never experienced such a thing coming from another man. He looked across at David, whose expression flashed a lover's disdain for his partner's indiscretion. The display, though short, seemed brazen in the intimacy of the booth where they were seated. Robbie's hand lingered too long on Ethan's arm to be friendly or inadvertent. His thigh then pressed against Ethan's, and his proximity moved from awkwardness to repulsive. Ethan looked at Christa, whose facial expression confirmed her knowledge of Robbie's inappropriate behavior.

Robbie was quick to retract. "Ah, Ethan, I'm sorry," Robbie said, shifting his demeanor. "I'm way out of line. I should never drink. My bad." He quickly moved back and extended his hand. "She was beautiful, Eth. God rest her ... wherever she might be."

Ethan shook Robbie's hand as a truce, but it still didn't sit well with him. The word Robbie had used was unacceptable in mixed company but worse was how genuinely he spoke his comment.

David broke the silence by asking Robbie about work, and then conversation switched to learning more about David. A native Californian, he'd dropped out of high school at sixteen to pursue a modeling career that lasted all of a week. The big city, however, snatched his untamed heart. That was ten years ago. Now he was working as a bartender where he and Robbie met.

"You know, I'd kill him," Robbie interjected, unexpectedly returning to their earlier conversation. "I wouldn't just pull a gun and shoot 'im. I'd plan it."

Ethan thought the booze was speaking. "Well, I'll leave this one to the cops," Ethan said, trying to avoid Robbie's offering more description.

"Yeah, well, sometimes you can't depend on someone else to do what needs to be done." Robbie was shaking his head; his eyes were somewhere else. "Sometimes you have to practice these things." He paused, not seeming to notice everyone else had gone silent. "Take, for instance, a cat," he said, withdrawing to the point of talking to himself. "Practice on a cat."

Christa squeezed Ethan's hand. Her eyes told him all he needed. She was creeped out by Robbie's talk, booze or not.

"We're about ready to call it quits," Ethan interrupted, taking Christa's lead to get out of there.

Robbie and David weren't ready, so Ethan and Christa headed back by themselves, which suited them just fine.

As they walked along the sidewalk in the dimness of the streetlights, Ethan couldn't keep his hands off Christa's bottom. "Ethan, please," Christa said. "We're almost there."

Back in their bedroom, Christa's clothes fell away like petals from a flower. His shirt came off as she pulled it over his head. They fell together onto the bed, Ethan on top of Christa. Her hot, smooth skin was electric to his touch as she moved to accept him eagerly. He was taken to another place and time as they coupled and recoupled until the pleasure exhausted them both. Eventually, they collapsed in each other's arms.

Ethan awoke a short while later with Christa's head resting on his chest and his arm on her smooth back. Her silky brown hair fell across his arm. The clock radio on the nightstand read 4:35 a.m., yet he felt rested. Lying on his back, her hair tickled his chin as he stroked the back of her head. *Amazing*, he thought, staring at the ceiling in the darkness, *how things seemed to work themselves out.* The night had turned out great—except for Robbie's drunken antics—after Ethan's afternoon's disappointment. From one moment to the next, it was so hard to tell where he was. The only thing he knew for sure was that each moment was temporary. He had to stay focused on direction and ignore all the other shit that distracted him from getting it done; he would get there. He must never stop trying. The maze of mirrors was unending—he'd bounce off one of doubt and into another of rejection and hurt, until he found a way through. There was a way, no doubt, as others had found it. The unknown was all part of the journey, as difficult as that was to accept. *Funny weird and funny ha-ha*, he thought, which was more appropriate. One minute things looked desperate and so close to the edge that disaster was imminent. The next saw brightness on the horizon and a path through the chaos, if only for a second.

Moments later, his thoughts carried him off to sleep.

CHAPTER 27

The rest of the week and start of the next week flew by. Ethan called to have his personal items from Build sent to Robbie's address. They paid him four weeks' worth of severance, which was more than he expected. He was tempted to find another job, despite all he'd told himself.

On Monday, he worked on the first commercial Steve had mentioned. Dressed as a chicken for the better part of the day, Ethan walked around giving people information about California Free-Range Chicken ("For those who want chicken, not chemicals"). The costume was a mobile sauna unit with painted-yellow feathers stuck to the outside. He'd lost five pounds by time he took it off, half due to sweat and half to losing his lunch in the sweltering midafternoon sun. At the end of the day, they paid him a hundred bucks and gave him a book full of coupons for free chicken. It was shit, but it was paying shit.

The meeting with Frederick Northum never left his mind. Nervous and anxious, he was on his way out the door the following Tuesday when Officer Barnes called from the police station to tell them they had located a blue '82 Chevy pickup owned by the accused. Christa knew the truck well. They'd been unable to locate the owner. "Left the state, more than likely," Barnes imagined. "Knowing a warrant's out for his arrest, he's not likely to come back anytime soon." He would let them know if anything else turned up. Ethan told him they would not be returning to his old apartment.

As it turned out, Frederick was late—about ten minutes—and

did not look at all like the person Ethan had pictured on the phone. His expectation might well have come from the sort of person with whom he expected Jamie would associate. Frederick was quite the opposite. Dressed casually, his clothes were expensive designer brands—Ralph Lauren polo shirt, Armani cardigan, and Perry Ellis slacks. An immediate rapport developed between the two men as they ate steak and exchanged stories. Ethan had hoped to come away with work. Frederick was reluctant to move further until he saw Ethan in action.

"Where can I see you perform?" Frederick asked as they sipped espressos.

"I'm between jobs right now," Ethan admitted. "I'll know in a couple of weeks where I'll be after the next few auditions. I'm doing a commercial—"

"Ethan, I don't know you well but here's a little advice," Frederick interrupted. Then he paused to ensure that Ethan was listening before adding, "Don't do commercials. Find a day job to pay the rent. It takes such a short time to be pegged as an advertising actor, and it's extremely difficult to break away from. It takes years to overcome."

"When I start the play, I'll contact you right away," Ethan said, thinking about Frederick's advice.

"Yes, that would be best," Frederick agreed, and then almost apologetically, he added, "I won't do anything without seeing you in character. Just call. I'll fit it in."

With that, they got up and shook hands.

"Thanks, Frederick," Ethan said, stopping to acknowledge the moment. "You won't regret this meeting."

Ethan took a cab back to the apartment, bouncing around on the worn and cracked seat that pinched the backs of his legs. He wondered why someone like Frederick would give him a chance. That thought was followed quickly by the "holy shit" moment of landing a part in two weeks. He'd been in LA for two years and hadn't had a part like that. But if there was a play to be had, he'd find it.

The cabbie dropped him in front of a 7-Eleven two blocks from the apartment, where he picked up the day's newspapers to begin his search.

Christa still was up when he walked in just before eleven. His number-one fan looked tired but was eager to hear how things had gone.

"He wants to see me perform," Ethan said, pulling off his dress shirt and tossing it on the couch. He held up the three newspapers. "So welcome to live theater, Ethan Jones. Find your curtain call."

"You'll find it," she said with a tired smile. Her eyelids looked heavy. "I know you will."

Ethan walked over and wrapped his arms around her as he looked into the brown eyes he found so attractive. He wasn't falling in love—he was there; the falling was over.

"Ethan, I'm really tired. Come to bed," she said, knowing what his response would be before he said it.

"Soon," he replied, feeling the hurt of his own willpower. He would have liked nothing more than to make love to Christa right then and there, with her eyes looking into his own and her breasts pressed against his chest. "I've got a few papers to go through. I want to get rolling first thing in the morning."

"Okay, but I can't keep my eyes open. Don't stay up too late. You need your beauty sleep."

"That's why there's makeup and special effects," he replied.

They both laughed. She kissed him full on the lips, testing his resolve, and then turned and headed to the bedroom. Every bone in his body yearned to follow her, if only to touch her long, smooth thighs and watch her fall asleep. But he held his place.

Over the next hour, he scoured the newspaper classifieds and circled thirty-four theater productions that were holding auditions. With that kind of demand, he began to think finding theater work might not be as difficult as he first imagined. Why hadn't he done this before? Relieved and confident that he had a good list for the morning, he decided to turn in. The luminescent numbers of the clock radio showed 3:35 a.m. when he entered the bedroom. He undressed, crawled under the sheet Christa had covered herself with, and slid in against her back, his arm on hers. The last thing he thought about was the word he'd written on the wall. *Act* was what he had to do.

His eyes closed with the confidence of finding his way.

CHAPTER 28

The commercial was a big success, despite Ethan's arriving on the set with a cold. It was the first cold he could remember succumbing to since arriving in California. The commercial, sponsored by the state, promoted healthy eating and pictured Ethan eating green vegetables with a smile on his face. By the end of the shoot, his eyes and throat were scratchy and dry, as if sand had blown into them. The irony wasn't lost on Ethan. His efforts were rewarded with a cast party hosted by the sponsoring tourism group, where he proceeded to cure himself with ample amounts of liquor. He returned to the apartment in the small hours of the morning. Stuffed-up, achy, and hungover, he forced himself up by midmorning and started calling each of the numbers he'd been unable to reach.

By mid-May, he still hadn't landed work with a theater show production and was starting to suffer a few chinks in his armor of confidence. *I have to be able to find one show*, he thought, blowing his nose into a wad of toilet paper. His cold was breaking up, and his nose was dripping like a melting icicle. Desperation was beginning to set in. He didn't care what the part was—in dinner theater, repertoire, nightclub—as long as he was performing. His standards dropped as his list dwindled. Almost everyone had either filled their casts or couldn't be reached. As he got to the last few numbers, he began to lose all hope. One ad read, "Need an actor. If interested, call …" The woman who answered the phone asked him two questions: "What's your name, and do you have any experience?" After that, she gave him a place and time to meet the following Sunday and hung up abruptly. Ethan was ecstatic. With the phone in his hand, his arms shot into the air as if he'd scored a game-winning goal.

Placing the phone on the counter, he stared at the list of numbers he'd contacted. He'd doubled his starting list of thirty-four and only two of the first group of prospective ads remained. *One for thirty-two.* He shook his head. Discouraging odds at best, but he had his audition. He decided to call the last two numbers from the first list. Maybe his luck was changing. The first number gave a popular message he'd heard over and over again—"Sorry, we're no longer looking"—but the other was answered by an elderly sounding man who was in charge of directing a small production company. He wanted Ethan's name and asked when he could meet. Though wary, Ethan agreed to meet on Saturday afternoon.

Ethan hadn't done any live theater since his university days. He'd learned voice projection and stage movement from the director, but it was Mila who had taught him most of what he knew. It was the vow he'd made her and let slide that pushed him even further now—the vow to take his gift and her dream to the end of the earth.

Ethan met Edwin, the old man on the phone, at a small greasy spoon not far from the Build Industries building where he'd worked. Edwin was a short man in his mid to late sixties with a full head of shiny gray hair. After ten minutes of discussion, Edwin suggested that Ethan follow him to an empty warehouse and audition for the lead in his play, *A Baker Makes Three.* Despite what Ethan thought was another unorthodox introduction to theater, he went along with it, determined to perform. His father would have said, *"You have to work with what you've got."* So on that Saturday afternoon, Ethan found himself in an empty warehouse, auditioning for a play he'd never heard of.

"Here's the script," Edwin said, handing Ethan a coil-ringed booklet. "Take a few minutes and go through scene two. I'm going to call over my partners to meet you. It won't take them but a minute to get here." He left Ethan alone to prepare for the audition.

The script itself was neatly typed—probably on a Corona typewriter—and double-spaced. Scene two had a lonely old baker, the lead character and the role Ethan was to read for, planning a bank robbery around a table in front of two stuffed animals. Ethan chuckled as he scanned through the scene; the story was humorous in a goofy way. Ethan kept trying to picture how the scene would look on the stage. As the baker walked through the strategy of robbing the bank, he asked questions of each stuffed toy, and then his character answered for each toy using a different voice. Ethan kept repeating to himself that it was better than nothing, but he really wasn't convinced. The play was poorly written, very disjointed, and hardly ready for public consumption, but given the chance, he could work with the material. He skimmed through the rest, shaking his head. Edwin reappeared with his two elderly cronies.

"Ethan, I would like to introduce my playwright partners," Edwin said, motioning with his outstretched arm. "Bob and Henry."

"Good to meet you," Ethan replied, shaking their extended hands; it was like grabbing cold, limp fish.

Ethan stared into the space between the two men as they sat down behind Edwin. He was beginning to question whether the three men were senile and this was a little sojourn from their daily activities at the seniors home. Rather than playing gin rummy or pinochle, they'd written a play and this time had gone outside their in-house realm by placing an ad in the *Times*. Ethan wondered if he was wasting his time.

Edwin motioned Ethan to a chair in front of them. "We'd like to have you read scene two as an audition," Edwin stated as he sat back, crossing his legs, ready to watch and listen. "You can start whenever you're ready."

Ethan stared out at three pairs of wide, eager eyes awaiting his first words. The arrangement was awkward, but he went along with it, thinking he wasn't much of an actor if he couldn't perform in front of three old fogies. The lines were easy, and it didn't take him long to transform into a hunched-over old man, talking to imaginary toys. He was making something real from the unreal lines of the script, and he had an attentive audience. They became so involved with his magic that he ran out of scene before they stopped him.

"Excellent! Bravo!" cried Bob, clapping. "That was terrific, young man."

Henry was more reserved but later complimented Ethan on his ability to create atmosphere. "I don't know how you do it, son, but it captures something in your heart."

"Totally rad," added Edwin, using language two generations his junior.

Then, without hesitation, Edwin offered him the role. They would have a full rehearsal on Monday night, at which time Ethan would meet the rest of the cast. *Rest of what cast*, Ethan thought, but then Edwin explained that the role Ethan was to play had been filled long ago by another man. The play had performed to sold-out houses for several weeks before losing the main actor to a motorcycle accident. The cast was devastated but had agreed that the show must go on.

Ethan was amazed and more than a little embarrassed about his previous thoughts. He was delighted and left with a copy of the script in his hands. It was the best news he'd had in a while.

An hour later, he was back at the apartment, his feet hardly touching the ground, but no one was there with whom he could share his good news. For the first time since arriving in California, he would finally have steady industry work and a venue where Frederick and others could see him perform.

There was a lot of work ahead of him to get ready. In each act, his character carried nearly half the lines, and learning it would all but consume him. With no one else in the apartment, he immersed himself in memorizing. Once he was through the script, he was ready for a break, but there still was no sign of Christa. Her return would be a diversion, so he opened a can of Heineken and went back to the start. Many hours of work lay ahead but he could only pack so much in at a time. He needed some "simmer" time to process all he'd taken in.

His thoughts turned to Christa and where he might find her. He would have liked to meet for dinner, but they'd made no prior arrangements. He was on his own, with little idea of where she was or when she'd return. After checking his wallet, he was about to head out for a couple of pizza slices when the phone rang.

"Hello," he answered, anxious to hear Christa's voice.

"Hello," replied a male caller. "Is Ethan Jones there?"

"This is he."

"Ethan, Randy Baseman. How the hell are ya?"

"Hey, I'm doing great. You?" Ethan answered, pleased to hear from the animator/cabbie.

"You won't believe it," Randy said, "but I just got back from Japan."

"Japan? What's in Japan?"

"Well, right after I met you, I got this call from a guy about my character. You know, the one I gave you a copy of."

"Yeah?"

"I'd sent it to a local house, Dresden Comics," Randy went on, barely catching his breath. "This guy liked it and sent it to Japan for review. I didn't know any of this. Now, it's catching on. Listen, why don't we get together? I'll tell you all about it. What are doing for dinner?"

"No plans," Ethan answered. "I was heading out for pizza."

"I'll join you. Name the place, and I'll be there."

Instead of pizza, they agreed on a burger joint a block away from Ethan's apartment.

"Also got some news that might interest you," Randy added and hung up.

Not a minute later, Christa walked through the door sporting a new, daring look. Her hair was cropped short just below her earlobes. Her full lips and eyelids were painted with a dark rouge. Like a statuesque model having just left a Paris runway, she sauntered into the living room wearing spiked purple heels. Ethan stared, transfixed.

"I guess it's your turn to meet me at the door," she said, leaning forward to give him a kiss. "To what do I owe this pleasure?"

"Truth or fiction?" he replied, mesmerized by her transformation.

The expression on Ethan's face was the best mirror Christa could use to judge her new look. His eyes said it all. "I think truth."

"Okay, I've been waiting all afternoon for your bodaciousness to come through the door," he replied, breaking into a big smile. "Wow!"

She stepped forward and threw her arms around him. "I love you."

"I know," he whispered into her ear. "I'm in love with you too." He took a step backward and looked at her again. Christa did a full three-sixty spin. "What inspired this?" he asked, still enjoying the results.

"You and just needing a change," she replied. "I was tired of my hair and all the maintenance."

"Well, you look amazing," he added, unable avert his eyes.

"That," she said emphatically, "is the right answer."

"Right on!" He reached forward, took her hand in his, and brought it up to his lips. "Could I have the pleasure of taking this fairest beauty to dinner?"

Christa curtsied elegantly and acquiesced. "Of course you may. And where might you be taking her?"

"How about out for about a burger?"

"Just around the corner?"

"Yeah," he said, staring at her new face. "I just got a call from the cab driver who brought me back from our first party together."

"Yeah?"

"I left him a message the other day, but he was out of town. We're going to meet and have a bite to eat. He's got quite a story and something he wants to talk to me about."

"I don't want to intrude on your meeting," Christa protested, but Ethan assured her that wasn't the case. A few minutes later, as he held the door open to leave, the phone rang again.

"Forget it," he said. "They'll leave a message."

Christa frowned and stepped back in to answer it. Ethan continued to stand at the opened door.

"Hello," Christa answered sweetly. Her eyes brightened as she listened to the caller. Then she said, "Yes, he's right beside me. Just a moment." Waving her hand, she motioned Ethan back in, handing him the phone with an I-told-you-so look on her face.

He grabbed the cordless. "Hello?"

"Hello, Ethan Jones?" asked a strong, unfamiliar female voice.

"Yes, this is he," he responded, his mind spinning through his internal Rolodex of names and voices but coming up empty.

"Ethan. This is Wiggy Jamison," said the woman. "You called and left a message the other day."

"Yes," Ethan answered, trying his best to remember a Wiggy Jamison as his heart rate sped up.

"We're conducting auditions tomorrow afternoon if you're interested."

"Yes, yes of course I am," he replied, feeling clueless and confused at the same time. "Yes, I'm very much interested. Where, Wiggy?"

Wiggy supplied the address and some quick directions that Ethan scribbled down on the back of the newspaper Christa handed him.

When he hung up, Christa mimicked him with a smirk. "*Forget it. They'll leave a message.* Those famous words, if followed, may well have been your last."

"Fuck, how do I know who's calling?" he retorted, hopping around the room like an excited fool. "Cool. I've got another audition. But I haven't a clue which production it is. I've left a lot of messages."

"You'll find out tomorrow, sweetness." Christa was as excited as he was and wrapped her arms around his neck.

"Hey, we better go," he said. "Randy's probably already there."

Ten minutes later, the two of them were sitting in a booth at Burger Fair, sipping New England iced teas while Ethan tried to describe Edwin between fits of laughter. Randy arrived as Ethan was imitating Edwin's two partners shuffling into the deserted warehouse. Still laughing, he shook Randy's hand and introduced Christa as the woman behind his fateful taxi ride home.

"He looks a might better than he did then," Randy chuckled, shaking Christa's hand. "I'd have kicked him out too."

Dinner was a bizarre combination of gourmet burgers and incredible stories from the creative graphic artist driving a cab in downtown LA. Randy talked almost non-stop. At one point, he paused and pulled a business card out of his pocket. He handed it to Ethan. The name Ben Lui was printed in black script in the bottom right corner.

"Before I forget, I met Ben on the plane from Japan," Randy said, switching from a story of eating sheep's eyeballs that was destroying Christa's appetite. "He's a talent scout for the movies. He was on a recruiting mission in Japan." Randy shrugged his shoulders. "Figure that, huh? What's Japan got that America hasn't? Asian women? Don't know why I thought of you. Most of my pickups, I never see again. He gave me his card and told me to get my friend to give him a call. 'Never leave a stone unturned,' he said."

Ethan took the card, hardly believing his ears. Here was another guy he barely knew, helping him out.

They finished dinner, after feeding on wild bison and Cajun shrimp burgers. Randy had to go. His shift was about to start; there were paying customers out there still looking for a way home. He had to make up for his time in Asia. They would keep in touch and planned another get together in a month. Randy promised to bring along his latest character the next time.

On returning to the apartment, Ethan went straight back to the script for *A Baker Makes Three*, while Christa went to visit one of her girlfriends. Two hours later, his stomach began to cramp up. He broke into a heavy sweat as sharp pains shot across his abdomen, doubling him over. The nausea was so aggressive, he hardly had time to make the short distance to the bathroom before vomiting his dinner into the toilet bowl. His head pounded as he leaned over the chipped bathroom sink and looked in the mirror. Beads of sweat dotted his forehead. His stomach knotted, draining his strength. After another half hour, he was too weak to stand upright, so he went to bed, shivering uncontrollably as a fever took hold. He was unable to get warm, no matter how many blankets he covered himself with.

Just before midnight, Christa returned to find him buried in layers of blankets, with a stinking wastebasket of vomit beside him. She gave him some Tylenol and sponged his forehead. He was burning up. An hour later, the Tylenol seemed to stabilize his temperature, but another wave of nausea sent him to the toilet. Death crossed Ethan's mind, but he felt too awful to be scared. Sitting on the edge of the bathtub, waiting for his stomach spasms to subside, Christa wrapped a blanket around his shivering shoulders. Despite throwing up, his stomach continued to cramp. By 3 a.m., he dragged himself back to the bedroom. He was so weak, he could barely stand up. Sleep was all but impossible with his stomach in agony.

"I think you need a doctor, Ethan," Christa whispered at some point, her face strained with concern.

Ethan could not remember ever feeling so sick. "Maybe," he mumbled, not wanting to talk, move, or do anything. "I just want to sleep." He lay still under the blankets, hoping to warm himself and stop shivering. Closing his eyes, he prayed for sleep to come, but his body had different ideas. Minutes later, he was back in the bathroom, dry heaving.

Using what little strength he had left, he rose to his feet, shivering uncontrollably. A blurry haze flooded his vision. Too weak to hold himself upright, he lost his balance as his hands scrambled to grab hold of the sink. In slow motion, everything went dark. He fell to the parquet-tiled bathroom floor like a falling tree trunk.

CHAPTER 29

"Please, Ethan, wake up," Christa cried. "You have to wake up."

Ethan opened his eyes and looked into Christa's horrified face.

"Ethan," she whispered, tears running down her tired, grief-stricken face as she cradled his head in her hands. "You're okay? Can you hear me?"

He felt lousy. His body ached. As his eyes focused, he noticed he was in unfamiliar surroundings. Then he heard Robbie's voice.

"You're in the hospital, buddy," Robbie said, his face moving into Ethan's field of sight. "You fell and knocked yourself out. It's been a while."

His clothes felt wet. Christa was holding his hand. "Can I have some water?" Ethan whispered, his voice cracking. His mouth was parched.

"Sure," Christa said from somewhere close by. "Here—take some of this."

A large glass of ice water with a bent straw came into view. Christa helped him insert the straw between his lips. Cool water flowed into his mouth. It was the best-tasting water that had ever passed his lips.

"Hey, bud, slow down," Robbie said, patting his right arm. "There's lots where that came from."

Christa pulled the straw and glass away. "That's enough for a minute, babe."

"We thought we'd lost you there, Eth," Robbie said.

"You gave me a real scare," Christa said. She was close to tears. "You weren't moving, and your body was burning up." She reinserted the straw in his mouth before he was able to reply.

Again, he took a long draw from the straw. The water tasted glorious as it trickled down his throat. An intravenous tube was fastened to his arm. "Where am I?" he asked, pulling away from the straw. His voice was rough and scarcely above a whisper.

"You're at the medical center," answered an authoritative voice. Ethan turned his head to see who had spoken.

Ethan watched as a doctor approached him from the right side of the bed.

"Relax, Mr. Jones," the doctor said in a direct, professional manner. "How are you feeling?"

"I've been better," Ethan croaked, the sudden coldness of the water in his throat making it difficult to speak clearly. He hacked up some phlegm.

"I would agree with you, but if it's any consolation, I think you're through the worst of it." The doctor paused for a moment and lifted Ethan's right arm to take his pulse. He placed his open palm on Ethan's forehead. "You're still warm, but you're looking a sight better than you did when you came in. Can you turn your head a bit? I need to take another look at that cut." Ethan winced as the doctor examined the side of his head. "I know this won't make you feel any better, but I think it's a good thing you fell and hit your head." He jotted something in the chart.

"Why?" Ethan asked.

"You've an acute case of food poisoning," the doctor answered, peering at something in Ethan's report. "Likely a bad case of salmonella. I understand you were out and had shrimp for dinner."

"Yes, in a burger."

"Well, that's likely where you picked it up. You were quite dehydrated when you arrived, so we've been pumping fluids into you to get your levels back to normal." He pointed to the intravenous bag. "You seem to be doing much better this morning. Nothing a little rest won't fix. You've got some great friends here. They've been here all night."

Ethan looked over at both Christa and Robbie. They looked tired. "Thanks, guys," he croaked, coughing up more phlegm.

The doctor walked to the end of Ethan's bed and hooked the metal clipboard to the bed frame. He looked over at Christa and Robbie, saying, "You two look like you could use some sleep. He's going to be fine, thanks to you. Go get some rest."

With the doctor's exit, Christa came to Ethan's bedside and assisted him with the glass of water. He pushed it away, his memory returning.

"This is Sunday, isn't it?" he rasped, his voice stronger.

"Yes," Christa replied.

"What time is it?"

"Quarter to twelve. Why?" Christa asked, knowing the answer as she spoke. A look of shock shot through her eyes. "No way, Ethan."

Without a second thought, Ethan threw his bedclothes aside and sat up. Though light-headed and weak, he slid his feet to the floor and stood beside the bed. His legs felt rubbery and not altogether stable. His body seemed heavy, disconnected, and not entirely his. Christa shook her head. He raised his arm sideways—the one not connected to the intravenous; he would have to lose the IV—and then lifted his head as if to look at the ceiling. "See, I feel okay?"

"Ethan, you shouldn't be out of bed," Christa pleaded, her hands on her hips. "You need to rest. Come on. Don't fool around."

The white tile under his feet seemed to move sideways. He grabbed the bed frame. Robbie immediately had hold of his arm. Ethan's strength wasn't there. He leaned against the bed. "Okay," he mumbled, disappointed by his weakness. "Looks like you win."

"This is not about winning, Ethan," Christa replied. "It's about your health."

There was nothing to say. She was right, but his auditions were all he could think about. He wasn't about to miss one on account of a little food poisoning and a bump on his head. Keeping himself upright was difficult enough, without the added effort of convincing his friends he was well enough to leave. The sun was coming in the window beside his bed. The room was cool. The place was comfortable. But if he stayed here, he wouldn't be able to live with himself. "Why don't both of you go back to the apartment and get some sleep?" he queried, his face a little brighter than the plan he was forming in his head. They looked at each other as Ethan slipped back into the bed. Before they answered, he added, "I'll be fine. Some of that hospital food will fix me up real good. I'll see you later and catch a little more sleep in the meantime."

"Are you sure?" Christa asked, rubbing his arm. Her eyes looked heavy and bloodshot.

He nodded. "Yes. I can't believe you're still here."

"I can't either," echoed Robbie from the end of the metal-framed hospital bed. Gray bags were under his eyes. "Let's give the man some space. Besides, I'm hungry."

"Okay," Christa agreed, leaning over his bed and planting a full kiss on his lips. "We're out." She turned to pick up her black leather handbag while scrutinizing him closely. "You're sure you're okay? You're not going to do something stupid, right?"

"I'll enjoy the peace and quiet," Ethan lied. He wondered how convincing he sounded. "And I'll get some sleep."

"You might as well," she added, squeezing his hand.

"Thanks, Christa," he said, feeling a little guilty about the plan taking shape in his head but no less committed.

"What else am I going to do?" she replied, a smile showing her relief. "Someone has to look after you."

"Yeah, right."

"Anything you want me to bring you later?"

"My script for tomorrow night. I still have a lot of work to do."

"Sure," she replied, her eyes rolling in their sockets as she moved to the door that Robbie was holding open. "See you later."

"Get some sleep," Robbie said, nodding as they left the room.

The hospital bed was comfortable. Ethan lay still for a few minutes, undecided about what to do next. He knew he'd been pretty sick, but his strength was returning. Sleep was the last thing on his mind. He wasn't about to miss Wiggy Jamison's audition. It meant too much. Otherwise, tomorrow he'd be back to normal and kicking himself.

The intravenous needle still dripped. The tape holding the needle in place in his arm hurt coming off. The needle itself slid out of his arm easily. Fluid dripped onto the bed sheets. He turned the small knob to shut off the drip, tossed it aside, and then slid his legs over the side of the bed.

His bare feet touched the cool floor as he stood up and slowly adjusted to his full weight. It felt much better this time. Light-headedness caused him to pause, catch his breath, and balance against the side of the bed. Once stable in his balance, he started to walk around, using the walls for support.

No question—he was weak. His legs were stiff, especially his calves, and his joints throbbed. His hands and feet felt swollen. It would not be an easy time, but he couldn't let opportunity pass him by. A pair of jeans—with his wallet still in the pocket where'd he left it—and a T-shirt were in the duffel bag Christa had brought. He slipped his left leg into the jeans. It took more effort than he'd anticipated. He lost his balance and fell against the bed. He then used the bed for support and finished pulling on his pants. Standing upright, he was glad that he was alone.

He pulled his favorite T-shirt over his head. A photo of Winston Churchill was on the front, with the words "Never Give Up." It fit the moment. He opened the door slightly and looked out. His room, fortunately, was near the elevators, as taking the stairs wasn't a likely option, given his weakened condition. Without hesitation, he left the room and walked the short distance along the white hallway to the elevator. Acting like any visitor to the hospital, he pressed the elevator button and waited with his arms crossed. The elevator seemed to take an inordinate amount of time, but finally, the door opened. He stepped in, almost colliding with a doctor already inside. He turned, noticed the main floor lobby was selected, and stepped back against the rear wall. Silence reigned as the elevator continued to the ground floor. Ethan wasn't about to speak, keeping to himself as if nothing out of the ordinary was happening. Upon exiting, the pressure in his head was beginning to build behind his right eye. Fatigue quickly was catching up with him as he passed the hospital's gift shop. He detoured to buy some Tylenol.

Holding the money to pay, his dwindling financial position surfaced but was short lived, as the oncoming head-banger took over. He searched for a water fountain without success. Working up some saliva, he dry-swallowed two pills, hoping they wouldn't get stuck in his throat on the way down.

No one confronted him or even took notice of his leaving.

As he walked out the automatic front doors, the midday heat hit like walking into an oven. It made his head swim. Feeling wilted, he raised his hand, which required surprising effort, and signaled a brown Chrysler cab parked at the curb, opposite the hospital entrance. The cabbie nodded acceptance and then drove up in front of him.

"Where to?" asked the dark-skinned, curly-haired driver in an accent Ethan didn't recognize.

Ethan remembered the address he'd written down the night before.

"That's ten, maybe fifteen minutes away," replied the cabbie.

Ethan didn't feel like talking. His head fell back against the top of the seat as his headache gathered steam. His attempt to extinguish the pain by visualizing a ball growing smaller was little help. But it didn't stop his drive to get to the audition either. Willpower and the Tylenol would take him through a fifteen-minute audition.

Ethan paid little attention to the motion of the car or where they were going. He just wanted to be delivered to the front door and prayed for enough strength to get through the audition.

"I think we close, mister," said the young driver.

Ethan opened his eyes. Pain surged through his head as he lifted it from the seat back to face the brightness of the afternoon. The hot sun had scorched everything in sight, leaving little but dust, weeds, and parched cement. His apparent destination was a desolate area of empty warehouses and parking lots. Dry, untended grass grew along the sides of the buildings and up through cracks in the asphalt. A late-model Ford was parked in front of the building where the taxi pulled up. The pain throbbed mercilessly above and behind his eyes, making it hard to focus on anything. The Tylenol had taken some of the edge off but that was all. He felt like a bag of bones but wasn't about to admit it.

"Nothing here, sir," said the cabbie, bringing the car to a full stop. He turned and looked at Ethan. "You sure this is the place?"

"We'll have to see," Ethan answered, every syllable like a hammer striking the inside of his skull. Despite air conditioning, the air inside the cab had become stagnant and nauseating. Ethan pushed the door open and was again greeted by the stifling midafternoon California heat. He was amazed at its oven-like intensity. It sucked what little energy he had right out of him. "I'd better check it out," he said, as confident about finding someone as the cabbie was with his English.

Ethan gripped each side of the doorframe and pulled. It took everything he had to lift himself up to a standing position beside the taxi. Every movement was an effort. He hoped he'd get a second wind to resurrect him in time for the audition.

"Excuse me, sir!" cried the driver. Ethan could hear him coming from the rear of the car. "Fare, sir."

Ethan stopped, reached into his pocket, and pulled out a single bill. Five bucks was all he had left. "How much?" he asked, knowing a five might only cover the tip.

"Twenty-two dollars, sir."

Ethan held out his only bill.

The cabbie's face changed to something between disgust and anger. "No sir, two-two." He held up both hands with index and middle fingers indicating twenty-two.

"I have five," Ethan replied, trying to think his way out. There was no chance in hell he could outrun this guy. The driver went to the front of the car and opened the passenger-side door. He reached under the seat.

Ethan hobbled back toward him and undid his wristwatch. The gold Seiko his parents had given him years before was the only thing he had of any value. "Take my watch!" he shouted as the kid turned around. Ethan thought he saw something that looked like a knife but it never appeared. He extended his open hand, with the watch glistening in the sunlight.

The driver's expression changed as he stood up and walked back to Ethan. He took the watch and rolled it over in his hands to inspect it. He compared it to the rough-looking Swatch on his wrist.

"Thank you, sir," he said politely.

Ethan didn't say a word. He backed away and shuffled toward the nondescript building. His head continued to pound like a post-hole driver. His watch was gone, but the old Seiko had probably saved him from a mean beating, if not his life.

Every step he took landed either on a crack in the sidewalk, crumbled asphalt, or dirt. *Step on a crack; break your mother's back* hummed through his head. Ethan could only imagine who might live down here and wasn't eager to meet any of them. The sun's brilliance burned into his head, intent on melting his skull and brain into a single mass. God help him; he felt awful. He shook two more Tylenol out of the plastic white container and swallowed them both. Physical movement that normally was involuntary became an arduous task—he had to push aside his pain and force his legs forward.

Walking between the weeds and broken glass, he came to stairs and a side door. At the same time, he heard footfalls approaching from behind. His heart beat faster. He didn't dare turn around and show weakness. It likely was someone else coming to audition, but he couldn't help think of a drug-dealing thug, out for a laugh, or the cabbie coming back for more money. As the sound of the steps came closer, Ethan reached for the handle of the steel door, praying for it to open. A hand touched his shoulder, and his heart flew to his throat.

"Enjoying the peace and quiet, I see," Christa announced loudly in his left ear.

At once relieved and shocked, Ethan had to hold the door handle tightly to remain standing. Upon seeing his unsteadiness, Christa instantly moved to support him.

"Well, you know …" he replied weakly. Though up to his elbow in the cookie jar, he couldn't have been more pleased that she was there. Her timing was perfect.

"Yeah, I know," she sighed. It was impossible for her to be angry, seeing him in his current state. "When Ethan Jones tells me he's ready to enjoy 'peace and quiet,' I know enough to be wary. But I have no idea how you expect to get through your audition."

Ethan didn't know either, but he didn't say a word.

Christa followed him through the doorway and into blinding

darkness. Other than the wedge of light coming through the partially open door, nothing was visible. Several seconds passed before his eyes adjusted enough to make out the surfaces of the hallway. Thankfully, the throbbing behind his eyes began to relent as they moved forward in the dark. After several steps, he called out "Hello?"

"Ethan, what the fuck are we doing?" Christa said, her voice filled with concern as she gripped his arm tighter. "I should be taking you back to the hospital."

He didn't answer.

"Ethan," Christa whispered. He could hear the disquiet in her voice. "Is this really worth it?"

"Hard to tell yet," he replied, feeling much the same way, "but it will be." They walked a little farther before Ethan saw a crack of light coming from the bottom of a closed door in front of them. "This must be it," he said.

"I sure hope so," Christa said tersely as her nails dug into his skin.

When they reached the door, Ethan knocked—and even that hurt. His aches were returning, despite the temporary respite from the Tylenol.

Footsteps were audible on the other side of the door as someone approached. "Who's there?" asked a raspy female voice. Ethan couldn't tell whether it was Wiggy he'd spoken to on the phone or not.

"Ethan Jones," he replied.

Metal scraped on metal as the door opened, sending blinding white light into their eyes. It was impossible to see who opened the door.

"Hi," Ethan said, tentatively raising his hand to shield his eyes from the piercing light.

"Hi, yourself," said a young earthy woman in torn jeans and a tank top.

"Is this where the auditions are being held?" He wondered if he sounded as stupid to the person at the door as he sounded in his own ears.

"It sure is," replied the woman, thrusting her hand forward in a friendly gesture. "Wiggy Jamison. Glad to meet you, Ethan."

"Nice to meet you too," Ethan said, stepping forward. "This is my friend Christa."

Wiggy was just as friendly with Christa, introducing herself again. Christa followed Ethan into the room. There were two other people inside, sitting at a makeshift table made of plywood. A gun was placed in the middle of the table.

"You're just in time. We're just starting," Wiggy stated.

The walls were cinder block construction painted beige. The floor was smooth concrete in the same color. The ceiling was unfinished, with plumbing and wiring in full view. Ethan thought the room resembled the inside of a garage.

Wiggy introduced the others. "This is Dale and Lynx," she said, pointing to the man and woman sitting at the table. Wiggy motioned for Ethan and Christa to take a seat as she pulled out and unfolded a brown bridge chair leaning against the wall. "Sorry about the location," she said, "but I needed to find a place away from our present locale. We're making changes to the cast, and I don't want to be interrupted by those not selected. Two of our members were arrested and charged with drug offenses last week."

Wiggy was candid, as if they were all old friends. She appeared to hide nothing and spoke without pretense. "Our on-stage chemistry has deteriorated as of late and is reflected in our ticket sales. We feel the show's in trouble. A friend of mine owns this space. Said we could use it to find replacements and rebuild what we had. Dale and Lynx are helping and are the co-producers." Wiggy paused, taking a breath before continuing. "I know this is very unorthodox, but we're the only ones who can bring it together or lose the show entirely. I'm not yet prepared to give it up." Her smile was joined by nods from the others.

As Ethan listened, the pain in his head continued to build. He had to get moving and do something. Sitting and listening only exacerbated the situation and made it increasingly difficult to concentrate. "Can you tell me what the play's about?" Ethan asked, barely above a whisper, anxious to get on with his audition and back to bed.

"Of course," Wiggy replied, turning her chair around and straddling the seat, her forearms crossing on the backrest. "It's a whodunit story with a twist. The young doctor, who appears professional and caring throughout the play, turns out to be the killer. The doctor's one of the characters we're looking to replace. The other is the police officer assigned to solve the murder." Wiggy paused to take a sip of coffee from the white Styrofoam cup she was holding.

"Which one am I to audition for?" Ethan asked, rubbing his forehead with his fingers for relief. The young doctor was the role he wanted, despite his limited knowledge of the script. "I like your description of the doctor's character."

"Great, let's go with it then," Wiggy responded, her face alight with intensity. "That's what I like—direct and to the point. Dale, let's get another script. We'll use the first scene in the second act as a first go."

Dale handed a script to Ethan.

"I'd like to take a few minutes to run through it, if you don't mind," Ethan requested, again rubbing his forehead with his fingertips as if pressing the skin would make the pain go away.

"Sure," Wiggy agreed. "Take your time. Would either of you like a coffee?"

Ethan shook his head. "No thanks." Caffeine would only mess with his head at this point.

Christa nodded her head. "Sure."

Wiggy then asked Ethan, "Are you feeling okay? I don't want to be impolite, but you don't look well."

"A little under the weather is all," Ethan replied, taking the script and pulling a folding chair into a corner of the room where the light was less intrusive. He opened the script as Christa continued to converse with Wiggy and the others. The first scene of the second act was only a few pages long. Reading quickly through the doctor's lines, he knew at once where he wanted to go with the character. No longer focused on the pain behind his eyes, the scripted words transferred him into another world. He became entranced with imagining the doctor's disposition, going deeper to find more. In five minutes, he was ready to go.

"Okay," he said, standing up and returning to the plywood table. "Let's give it a go."

"Great," Wiggy said and then directed the others. "Dale, you read the constable's lines. I'll take the wife's."

They exchanged pages of the script so they all had the second act in front of them.

"Dale, start," Wiggy said, pointing her index finger in his direction.

With that, Ethan's audition for the doctor was underway. There was no ceremony or elaborate flourishes, just a raw reading of the script. As the audition continued, Ethan's headache became less invasive as he concentrated on the doctor's lines. He tried to shape the character by realizing why he said what he did. The words had to become his own as a different person. His delivery was extraordinary. The reading went on for about ten minutes, leaving Ethan drained both mentally and physically. After the doctor's final words in scene two, he glanced at Christa. Her eyes were wide, her face expressionless.

"Wow, that was great, Ethan," Wiggy said as she put the script down on the table. "You're certainly animated. Listen, I don't mean to hurry you, but we have several other people to audition today. Can I get your address and phone number again?"

The air in the room was stiff, almost suffocating. His eyes watered and dropped to the gun still in the center of the table. Something seemed wrong, but he couldn't put his finger on what it was. Maybe he'd gone too far with the character. Or maybe the gun on the table just bothered him. He knew he'd done well. The look on Christa's face indicated she did too. *Was it too good?* he wondered.

Ethan wrote out Robbie's apartment address and phone number in Wiggy's small notebook. As he wrote, he could feel the slow ache gaining momentum behind his eyes. Still, he was glad for the temporary reprieve from the pain.

"Tell me, Wiggy, did I give you the interpretation of the doctor you envisioned?" Ethan asked, squeezing Christa's hand in his own.

"To be honest, Ethan," Wiggy replied, her vibrant eyes glancing at the ceiling, "we're looking for more subtlety. The character is a doctor, not an entertainer. I see a doctor as a quiet professional. You sounded quite animated. But it worked just the same."

Ethan smiled. "Thank you."

"We'll be in touch," Wiggy said, standing and shaking his hand, indicating the audition was over. Dale and Lynx both said polite good-byes. Wiggy walked Ethan and Christa to the door. They left and headed back down the dark hallway. Christa remained silent until they were outside in the bright heat. They shielded their eyes from the sun, which set off another bomb blast behind Ethan's hazel eyes.

"Ethan!" Christa cried joyously, enfolding him in a tight embrace and giving him a kiss. "That was incredible. I believed you were a doctor. You transformed yourself. It was remarkable. I've never seen anything like it."

The volume of Ethan's headache rose. "Thanks, but I didn't get the part." He pressed his fingertips against his forehead. He checked for the time, only to be reminded of giving up his watch for taxi fare. A brief spell of melancholy overtook him, having given up his prized gift for nothing. "Where are you parked?"

"What do you mean, you didn't get the part?" Christa asked, ignoring the question. Her brow furrowed. "That's pretty negative."

"Wiggy didn't set up a follow-up time," he replied matter-of-factly, blocking the sun with his hand. He searched for a spot of shade where they could stand, but trees were not a part of the landscape.

"Wait just a minute," Christa replied and walked back to the door they had just exited.

"Christa, wait," Ethan called, his voice vibrating the nerve endings above his eyes, but she disappeared inside the building. He struggled to open the heavy door and then stepped inside to stop her. His eyes took time to adjust. He heard the door open at the other end of the hall. Realizing he did not have the energy or the inclination to chase after Christa, he sat down against the cool cement wall for relief.

Christa was in the room longer than he expected. She did seem to have a way with people. Maybe his luck was about to change, but thinking about it required energy—energy he didn't have. All he wanted now was a bed to lie down on. His head continued to pound, and his joints ached. His head hung down, with his chin on his chest, as he prayed for his misery to go away.

"Thanks, Wiggy," he heard Christa say from the other end of the hall. His eyes were closed. "We'll see you Thursday. I'm sure he'll be feeling up to it by then."

Christa was at his side a moment later. She squatted down and put her arm around his slumped shoulders. "You're not doing well, are you?"

"I'm okay," he lied, raising his head. "Can we go?"

"Yes, as a matter of fact, we can." She kissed the side of his warm head. "You're shivering. Your fever's back, isn't it?"

Ethan nodded and leaned against her. He'd used up all he had in the audition. As Christa held him, memories came to mind of his mother sitting with him one cold winter night. The power had been out for hours. She'd brought him to the downstairs den in front of the fireplace. He was six years old, suffering from bronchial pneumonia. For hours, she'd cuddled him in his father's big La-Z-Boy. He'd asked her if he would ever get better. She assured him he would, and that gave him hope he'd not known before. Everything would be okay. She made him feel invincible, although through her sickness, he'd learned invincible was not a human trait.

"Listen, Ethan," Christa said, whispering close to his ear, her breath passing lightly over his skin. "The car's close. We're going back to the apartment and put you to bed. Promise you'll stay there until your fever breaks. You're going to be fine." She crouched beside him for another minute and then whispered, "Wiggy was mesmerized by what you did in there. You have something—a connection. It makes people want to watch you."

A smile crossed his lips. Christa kissed him. Although he physically felt like death, there was a peace inside him. Sleep and rest would help resuscitate him.

"Charisma!" Christa said all of sudden. Her body moved. "That's the word. You've got it!"

He managed a grin but didn't reply.

They shuffled off to her car.

He was in bed at the apartment less than half an hour later, shivering again but not extreme like the night before. With a couple of Tylenol and Christa caressing his forehead, he fell asleep—sick but ever hopeful.

CHAPTER 30

Late the next morning, Ethan woke up feeling like a different man. His fever had broken during the night and left him weak and lethargic, but the shivers were gone. Christa had taken the day off and brewed up some of her grandmother's chicken soup, guaranteed to cure anything—a miracle potion. By midafternoon his strength was beginning to return. He asked Christa to bring in the script for Edwin's production. He was way behind schedule in getting ready for his evening debut rehearsal, but he would be ready.

Christa did not accompany Ethan to the rehearsal. Despite a number of miscues and forgotten lines, Edwin still appeared to be happy with Ethan's overall performance and remarked the same to Ethan. By the end of the night, however, Ethan was exhausted. His performance level was not where he wanted it to be, but he had nothing left to give. There was a lot of work ahead of him, but he'd never shied away from work.

Christa was asleep on the couch when he returned to the apartment early the next morning. He sat on the edge of the coffee table and watched her sleep. He was first drawn to her face and then the open Bible facedown on her chest. Carefully, he lifted it from her grasp and was about to set it aside when he noticed the line, "Now faith is being sure of what we hope for and certain of what we do not see." The words seemed to jump off the page. Funny, he'd never taken much notice of the big book before. He set it down on the table and covered Christa with the blanket from the end of the couch. So as not to wake her, he picked up his script, found a beer in the refrigerator, and retreated to the bedroom.

He wasn't about to go to bed with everything bubbling inside his head. He pictured himself on stage, delivering his lines to a sold-out audience. Concerns about delivering his lines plagued his thoughts. He'd speak a line from memory as quietly as he could so as to avoid waking anyone, but he found it difficult to really get the feel of the words without their aural impact. He decided to focus on memorizing, leaving the full expression of his words until he could manage it without disturbing the others. Sitting on the side of the bed, he could feel the drag of his body demanding sleep. Try as he might, he caught himself nodding off with the script on his lap or having fallen to the floor.

At four o'clock, Christa dragged herself into the room. He was pacing back and forth at the end of the bed, working his lines from scene three. "How's it going?" she croaked. "I'll bet you knocked their socks off."

"Edwin seemed pleased," he whispered as he watched her climb under the sheets, "but I have to get better at my lines."

Christa fell back asleep almost before he finished his reply. Longingly, he watched her sleep for a few minutes, craving to lie by her side and feel her skin next to his own, to cup and hold her breasts and make love to her. He sat down on the edge of the bed and lightly rubbed her back. Her smooth, silky skin was like the taste of dark chocolate truffles on his tongue—exquisite. With the script in his other hand, he forced himself to stand up and leave her alone. He left the room, thumbing through the rest of the script he hadn't yet mastered.

Doubt dropped into the pit of his stomach. Was he facing the impossible? Did he really stand a chance? The mistrust caused by early morning sleep deprivation crept in. What had he just read? "Faith is being sure of what we hope for and certain of what we do not see." *You better start having some faith, Ethan, my boy.* If he didn't, no one else would.

Before the next hour was over, he finished the rest of his lines. Still in the living room, sitting in the center of the couch, sleep overcame him.

CHAPTER 31

Ethan was up just after eleven. Christa had left for work, and Robbie was nowhere to be found. The apartment was hot, and after taking a long pee, Ethan threw some cool water on his face. He longed for air conditioning. The script was on the floor beside the couch where he'd fallen asleep. It wasn't long before he was right back in it, memorizing his lines, amazed at how arduous the task of stuffing words in his head had become. After two hours, it was like trying to squeeze one more shirt into an already full suitcase. He had reached the point where he could manage no more and decided to take a shower. Shortly after finishing, he was off to his favorite place—a place where he could see and feel why he was doing what he was doing.

Outside the apartment, he directed a cabbie to take him to the Dorothy Chandler Pavilion. He left the yellow taxi as if he was exiting a white stretch Durango limousine, with Christa dressed in a tight red gown at his side. The faces that followed him lit up as he walked past, holding her hand. The autograph-seekers stuck magazines and photos in front of him to sign, which he did with a flourish, in between photos with the excited fans who were intoxicated by the celebrity in their midst. The time was his. He could feel it—almost taste it; his vision was so real. On reaching the top step near the entrance, he turned and waved to the people watching. Fame and celebrity took his breath away.

After twenty minutes of dreaming, in an attempt to touch what he was chasing, he headed back to the apartment, charged and ready to work again. For the next twelve hours, Ethan focused on memorizing the rest of *A Baker Makes Three*. It was the early morning again when he finished. To celebrate, he ordered a pizza. Christa got up while he was paying for it and joined him.

"I can't believe your drive," she said, pulling a slice of the steaming pizza from the box. The cheese stretched the length of her arm. "It's remarkable. You don't get tired?"

"Don't be fooled," he replied after swallowing a bite of his pepperoni-and-mushroom slice. "I'm plenty tired."

Christa grabbed another slice and then set it down. Ethan gave her the eye, as if to say, *Two pieces at this time of the night?* She looked across at him and asked, "What is this acting thing all about for you?"

Ethan thought for a moment. Only one other person would have asked him that question. He wasn't sure he even knew the answer. It made him feel good about himself. It felt right. But those answers didn't seem quite adequate.

"Fame and celebrity," he blurted out, laughing, without thinking further, "are high on the list." He thought for a moment and went on. "I have an inherent need to know that I can. I have this gift that I've played around with for years. I need to know. I have a chance to figure it out." He paused, reflecting on his past. Some of what he said surprised him. "There's nothing else I've ever done that gives me this satisfaction. I love being someone else. I'm not that person; he does things I would never do. Yet I get to connect him. If I can believe, I can get there. I want to live—fully. I want to live the saying, 'Two roads diverged in a wood, and I … I took the one less traveled by, and that has made all the difference.' Only it's not that simple. I traveled down the road *most traveled*, only to backtrack and realize I have to take the other one."

He watched as Christa listened to his answer. Every once in a while—and this was one of them—he had to kick himself to believe he had the company, love, and friendship of such a wonderful woman. Her rose-silk nightgown did little to hide her statuesque beauty.

"Thanks, Ethan," she said, sleepily melting into the couch. "I get it."

"The clock is ticking, Christa," he added, pointing to the script. "I'm scared to death that I might be locked in this mediocrity forever, and it's all I will achieve, despite refusing to accept it. Now I'm chasing it, even if it means losing everything." He smiled, thinking he was closer to the truth than he would have admitted. Christa didn't say anything. Ethan picked up the script. "This could be the play that gives me my 'in,'" he said, fanning the pages with his thumb. "It's not award-winning material, but it has enough to let me perform. It's all I have at this point."

Ethan reached beside the couch and pulled two cold cans of Coke out of the brown paper bag that had accompanied the pizza. He handed one to Christa. She took it but set it back on the floor. "I know most of this seems crazy," he said, rubbing his head where he'd banged it in the bathroom. It was still sensitive. "To most, it probably is. But I've played myself—and I want redemption. I'm not happy living that way. I can't let myself slip away any longer." He got up and went to the refrigerator. He replaced his Coke with a Heineken. "In case you haven't noticed," he added, sitting back down, his hazel eyes bright with intensity, "I'm going for it. I will get there. I will find a way."

The second slice of pizza Christa had taken was still on the table. Ethan pointed to it with his open hand. She shook her head and said, "I'll have nightmares from the first one. It's yours, Ethan Jones." He took it and downed a mouthful. "You know," Christa said as she watched him stuff himself, "there's no doubt in my mind that you won't be a movie star. I know you'll be on the big screen and one day accept an Oscar for your work. I know it like I know where I work." She paused for a moment and then rose to her feet. "And speaking of work, I have to get up in a few hours. I don't have an actor's schedule." She laughed. "I hope you finish soon."

"Well, as a matter of fact," he said, extending his smile, "I'm finished for the night. The pizza was my reward. I would be honored to join you, if you'll have me?"

Christa paused, feigning the act of making a difficult decision. "On one condition," she replied, looking to the floor, playing coy. "I get to make love to a movie star."

"Condition accepted," Ethan answered and followed her into the bedroom. His desire for her was overwhelming.

"Ethan, promise me one thing," Christa said, after they'd made love. Their faces glistened with perspiration. His arms were wrapped around her from behind. "Don't forget me when you succeed. I don't think I could bear it."

Ethan tightened his embrace, feeling her breasts against his forearms. "Christa, I'll never forget you. You're with me forever."

CHAPTER 32

Over the next few months, Ethan rehearsed with both Wiggy's small group and Edwin's codgers, becoming ever more comfortable with his lines and the cast. A Juilliard graduate had landed the second role that Wiggy was after, someone who wanted to try live theater. The man wouldn't have been Ethan's choice, but he wasn't consulted.

His finances ate at him constantly, despite attempts to the contrary. All his time was going into acting. He couldn't fit in a day job. Yet it wasn't like rent was an option. His lack of money added to the constant stress of performing.

Learning his lines took more time than he ever expected. Memorizing was usually quick but maintaining character took a lot of energy and concentration. Auditioning lines on the first go-round was exciting and stimulating, but duplicating the performance often seemed nearly impossible on a consistent basis. His focus often was diverted in rehearsals, where he worried about his future and the money he needed to live on. There were days he didn't get through a midday rehearsal without prompting.

His most recent rehearsal with Wiggy's group had been rough. The group had found a new, larger rehearsal space on the east side of the city. Ethan got lost on route. The group had gone ahead without him and nearly completed the first scene before he arrived. Flustered and angry at his own delinquency, he proceeded to screw up throughout the next scene. His lines showed up on his internal teleprompter, but his delivery was flat. Scene two was better, but the third scene was abysmal. The strength of the other players and his lapses in attention denigrated his best efforts. Most stomach-wrenching of all was that his Juilliard pal delivered his lines flawlessly throughout the rehearsal. That same night he learned that Mr. Juilliard was Wiggy's nephew. He knew he was in trouble before Wiggy's phone call came two days later while he was out doing laundry.

She left a message on the machine: "It's not working, Ethan babe," Wiggy said, adding salt to his already bleeding wounds. "Nathan knows the lines. He fits better. I'm sure you agree. I'm sorry. Good luck. Love ya."

Christa was first to hear the message and was at the door when he returned. He knew something was up before she said a word. Down but not out, Ethan had Edwin's rehearsal to prepare for that night. Maybe full concentration on one script would help. He had to ask Christa for cab fare—he'd used the last of his money on laundry. Christa obliged without comment, pleased she could help him. She treated his heavy heart to Chinese food before he left.

They took their usual place beside the front window of the Chinese buffet, two blocks from the apartment. They ordered chow mein, rice, and chicken balls. Ethan was quiet, trying to stay relaxed before the rehearsal. The more he tried to forget about his money situation, however, the more it seemed to dominate his thoughts. Christa didn't know quite what to say, so the two of them ate in silence.

At six o'clock, Ethan kissed her good-bye and left. He told her not to wait up; he'd likely be late. Tonight was the last night before final rehearsal, and Edwin was a stickler for detail. It had to be perfect, or they'd stay until it was.

Christa waved to hail a taxi. Ethan climbed in and blew her a kiss.

On the ride over, he thought about asking Robbie if he knew of any potential jobs. He was uncomfortable pushing the point too far, as Robbie had set him up for the job at Build. Robbie likely had lost ground as a credible source of competent talent, yet he hadn't acknowledged anything of the sort to Ethan. A strange recollection suddenly occurred to him—it was an off-hand comment Robbie had made about Build, something that seemed rather odd in retrospect. *"I've never heard anything but good stuff about you."* Robbie must have been talking to them and had to have known Ethan was going to be fired. Why hadn't he said anything?

Whether Ethan was making more out of it than it deserved, the fact remained he was broke and needed money. Like it or not, Robbie was a means to a paying job. The last thing in the world Ethan wanted to do was wire his father for money. It would be his ultimate failure, admitting that he couldn't take care of himself. *Dad, could you send some money to your useless son?* It simply was out of the question. He'd sleep on the street before taking that route. There had to be another way.

That was when that obnoxious voice returned.

There is a way, my friend, and you know how ...

Ethan shut it down before it finished. He knew what was coming.

Well, where's it going to come from then, buddy boy?

Ethan forced the thought out of his mind.

The cab was getting close to the address. He lifted his arm to check the time that was still a habit after weeks without his watch. A clock on the dashboard showed he was early. It was a good start. He checked the meter. The twenty Christa had given him would cover it, but he wondered why he hadn't asked her to drive him. Strange, really. Things had to go well tonight. He calculated if the show started on Friday, their first pay would come in a week. He could borrow a little from Christa to tide him over. It was tight but workable.

Why not make it easy on yourself? The voice slipped in again. *Just once—it would give you some room.*

Ethan closed his eyes and switched to silently reciting his first lines of the play. *"We can't go on like this, you and me; it hardly seems worth it. Something has to change."* Soon his lines were flowing. The words appeared before his eyes as if someone was holding the pages in front of him. He felt the words as if he was the person they represented. He was ready. This would be a great night.

"This is it, chief," said the butch woman cabbie, turning to look back at him for the first time. "Seventeen-fifty."

His hand was in motion with the twenty, but he was looking elsewhere. The place looked deserted. He was really early.

The building he approached was dark and unoccupied. Things looked different when he was the first to arrive. The front door opened into a darkened foyer, where his hand searched for a light switch. He had to hold the outside door open to see anything in the small space. The door to the lower entrance of the small converted theater was closed. As his eyes adjusted, he noticed a white sheet of paper stuck to the door. The left side of the page indicated it had been ripped from a binder—*Edwin's binder?*

There was just enough light to read the note, but Ethan didn't need to read it to know what it conveyed:

Thanks to all of you who participated over the past weeks in *A Baker Makes Three.* You've helped fulfill a dream held for fifty years. Unfortunately, my partner pulled out. We've decided to close the show.

Best of luck,
Edwin

Ethan's heart sank as the air in his lungs expired, and he stood on legs that didn't seem his own. He tried the door. Locked. His hand gripped the doorknob tighter and turned. It rotated fractionally. He shook the doorknob. He then tugged at it, a little at first and then harder. With suddenness he didn't expect, he slammed his fist into the door, breaking a panel and splitting the skin on his knuckles.

"You can't fucking lock me out!" he screamed, breaking the silence of the quiet night around him. "No fucking way! You just can't!" He hammered the door with the sides of his fists, again and again. He turned and kicked a hole through the drywall of the foyer. He continued to kick and hit the walls and door, his self-control gone. He slammed his open palm against the wall, not seeing a protruding nail. He couldn't see what he'd done, but the pain was staggering. He couldn't pull his hand off the wall. In sudden madness, he jerked it back like he was yanking a stubborn branch from a tree, pulling the head of the nail back through his hand. The instant agony dropped him to his knees.

"Shit!" he screamed, his hand engulfed in searing pain as blood pumped out of the wound like oil. "Fuck me!" he cried. "Fuck! Fuck! Fuck!"

Adrenaline pumped through him like a speeding locomotive as he stumbled up the steps and outside. A mixture of pain, shock, and madness descended on him. He slipped and fell to the sidewalk, his energy dissipating as shock took over. Deep sobs wracked his body as he held his face in his bloodied hands, ignorant of his surroundings.

Warm liquid trickled down his forearm and brought him back. He knew it was blood and scrambled for something to wrap around his hand. He pulled off a shoe and removed his sock and wrapped his hand. He stayed on the ground—five minutes, ten minutes. He didn't know for how long. He didn't hear anything, and no one came.

Even in the dim light of the evening, one look at his sock-wrapped hand let him know he was hurt. He got to his knees unsteadily. Blood had soaked through the white sock wrapped around his hand. Numbness and shock masked the injury and the pain.

Ethan wiped away the tears that ran down his cheeks with the back of his injured hand, smearing blood across his face. Edwin had given up and left them all hanging.

He needed a drink and to think. How could he put so much effort into something and see so little come of it—and still keep going? He thought of a joke he'd heard once that now seemed more real than comic: *Those who never quit, win, but those who never win and never quit ... are stupid.*

The nagging voice piped up again. *There is a way, my friend. Why are you fighting it? You can solve all this nonsense by making one phone call.*

His fight was gone. He found the nearest phone booth and called Christa to come and pick him up.

She was freaked out by his hand, pleading with him to go to the hospital. He'd need a tetanus shot and stitches. He said it just needed to be cleaned and would go tomorrow, if need be. He just wanted to go back to the apartment and sleep. On seeing his distress, Christa acquiesced. He didn't want to talk about it; she complied. Once back in the apartment, she helped him clean the wound and bandage it. It wasn't long before she crashed. Despite trying, Ethan couldn't sleep.

Instead, he searched for the card. He was like a drunk, rummaging around for hidden liquor bottles. He found the dreaded business card at the bottom of his closet.

The voice was right there with him—*Just make the call, Eth, old buddy*—as benign as a lover's.

Unmindful of the time, he left Christa in the bedroom and punched the numbers from the card into the keypad on the cordless. His hands shook as he held the receiver to his ear. Whether it was from what he was about to do or the injury, he didn't know. It didn't matter. Beads of sweat broke out across his forehead. The phrase "You'll be back" repeated itself in his head as he listened to the ring of the telephone at the other end.

What the hell are you doing? he asked himself, drumming his fingers on the arm of the couch. *I'm paying my dues*, he answered as the phone rang for the third time. It was too late. The tightness in his stomach began to relax. He'd try again tomorrow.

"Hello," answered a gruff voice, the accent unmistakable. Sven was out of breath. Ethan imagined he'd interrupted a session with Jacqueline or some other honey from his harem of hard bodies.

"Sven?" Ethan asked, knowing full well who it was. He didn't want to sound too familiar.

"You've got him. Who iz ziz?" Sven replied sharply, impatient with the interruption.

"Ethan Jones. I would like to meet with you tomorrow."

There was a slight hesitation at the other end of the line, and his words seemed to hang in the air.

Then Sven became all business. "Ezan Jonez," he repeated, as if savoring the name like he might a fine cigar. "Iz been a vile. Great to hear from you."

Yes, I'm sure it is, asshole, Ethan thought. He was sure he could hear victory in Sven's voice. His stomach tightened in his act of subservience. He had to concentrate to hold back his true feelings. "Sven, I'd like to reconsider your offer for work," he said, hating himself as the words passed his lips.

"I zee," Sven said. Ethan was sure Sven had a big Joker-like grin on his face, already savoring his victory over another naïve actor. "You'd like to meet tomorrow?"

"Yes, so we can reach a kind of mutual agreement."

"Zo you've run out of money, Ezan. Dezided old Zven's ovver vazn't zo bad."

Ethan cringed as he listened to the man exploiting his power over the phone. He refused to acknowledge any of it. "Can we meet tomorrow or not?" Ethan interrupted. All he wanted was work and an agreed-upon amount of money for the work. "Two thirty at your office?" Ethan said, trying to take control of the conversation.

"Make it zree," Sven said, regaining control. "And don't be late."

Ethan hung up. Sven was still interested. Ethan knew he could use that to his advantage. If he agreed to the work, he wanted to get paid for it.

The thought crossed his mind to bring Cushman with him but decided otherwise. Steve, he was certain, would advise him against it.

The voice from earlier returned. *Wake up! You've got it made in the shade. Most men would die for the opportunity.*

He shut down the voice. He wanted to do serious movie work. Taking his clothes off and fucking unknown women in front of the world was not part of it.

CHAPTER 33

Ethan's Timeline
August 1991

"Camera's ready!" cried the red-headed director wearing a Grateful Dead T-shirt. "Jacqueline—position."

Jacqueline did as directed and bent down, stumbling slightly in her shiny patent-leather cherry-red stilettos. She caught herself on an unknown woman's thigh.

"You're in zee next zcene," Sven whispered in Ethan's ear, touching his arm and motioning him toward another door. "Zay'll get you ready."

"Sure," Ethan replied, not quite knowing what to expect.

A woman led him to the side of the room. He'd had fantasies of being with naked women but the reality was a mixture of vulnerability, revulsion, and inhibition. He was unprepared for what would happen next.

"Shower's through that door. Get undressed and come back," the woman said as if asking for the time.

He followed her instructions, removed his clothes, showered quickly, and with his hair still wet returned with a towel around his waist.

"This your first movie?" she asked as she brushed something on his cheek.

"Yes," he replied, thinking of the three hundred bucks he'd agreed to.

"Ezan, relax," Sven said, staring at him through his reflection in the mirror. "You are a natural. Nozing to vorry about."

Ethan, still shaky on his decision to be there, watched as the woman worked on his face. It was all about survival. "Ah," he uttered as the woman brushed against his injured hand.

"Sorry," she replied and kept working.

He stared at his reflection as she parted his hair opposite to the way he did and brushed it back. The makeup sharpened his nose, chin, and cheekbones.

She massaged his neck and shoulders and then asked him to stand up and remove the towel.

"Why?" he asked, but her hands were squeezing his flaccid penis and testicles before he could move. "Hey!"

"It's okay," she whispered, her hands surprisingly warm and gentle after massaging his neck. "Just part of the job. You have to be erect. Your dick's got to be picture-perfect."

After a few minutes of vigorous motion, he still had not responded; his penis was limp. She pulled out a tube of cream. "We need a little help," she said, squeezing some white gel into her hand. "This'll do the trick."

The cream tingled but after a minute or so, a strange sensation came over him as his penis stiffened without being sexually excited. He didn't know whether to fall down and cry or simply scream. He wasn't where he wanted to be and felt like the victim of a cruel joke, with his dream crumbling before his eyes.

They returned to the room where they were shooting. Jacqueline was with the woman he'd watched earlier. The two women, lying on the large bed, detached themselves from each other like they were removing costumes.

The director approached Ethan with her hand extended. "Joyce," she introduced herself. "You must be Ethan."

Ethan shook her hand while trying to keep his white robe closed. His penis stuck out like a steel rod between his legs. "Yes," Ethan replied, feeling uncomfortable.

"Relax and let things happen," she said. "Let the girls lead. We'll see how it goes." She turned and shouted instructions to one of the technicians. Turning back to Ethan, without missing a beat, she started directing. "The scene starts by you interrupting the girls," she told him, placing her hand on his shoulder and pointing with her other hand. "They giggle as you approach the bed. Let Jacqueline—Jack, come here for a minute," she called to Jacqueline.

Jacqueline hurried over to where they were standing, wearing only the cherry-red stilettos. Ethan felt himself get excited in Jacqueline's presence. Her body was perfect. Her closeness made everything real.

"You lead Ethan onto the bed, and then you and Silk do your stuff. Ethan, just do what they tell you." Joyce turned and called to nobody in particular, "Can I get a coffee—black?" She turned back to them. "Okay, kids, let's go. Get rid of the robe."

Ethan opened his robe.

"Just as I thought," Joyce said, looking down at Ethan's drooping penis.

Ethan felt his face flush, not knowing quite what to do.

"Fluffer!" Joyce cried. "Need a fluffer—now!"

Before Ethan could move, another female was on him. First her tongue was running up and down his neck as her hands worked his penis. She whispered dirty things about fucking. His penis hardened. As quickly as she'd appeared, she disappeared.

"Positions!" Joyce shouted. "Ready!"

Everyone hustled into place. Ethan stood beside the bed. Joyce moved him slightly to the right and stepped away. Jacqueline returned to the center of the bed, wrapping her arms around the other woman.

"Three, two, one, action!" counted Joyce.

The women rolled into action with each other. Ethan watched, his eyes wide at being so close to such beautiful women caressing each other.

Moments later, he heard Joyce calling from a distance. "Cut, cut, cut!" she shouted. "Ethan, glad you're enjoyin' the fuck show, but you're supposed to be in it! Watch my cues."

"Sorry," Ethan replied, refocusing. "Won't happen again."

"Okay, everyone, positions," Joyce called, pausing momentarily as everyone prepared. "Action!"

Again, the women embraced. This time, however, Ethan turned and watched Joyce. Fifteen seconds later, she gave him the thumbs-up sign.

Ethan spoke his first words in film. "May I interrupt?"

When Ethan arrived back at the apartment, the clock on the nightstand read 3:15 a.m.

He'd been disillusioned before but not to the degree he was now. He'd participated in an act of which he was not proud and recorded it in front of a camera for the whole world to see—forever. Three hundred dollars or not, he was disgusted with himself and his actions. Still, he'd done what he had to do; he had to survive.

Exhausted, his clothes fell to the floor beside the bed. In the shadows, he could see Christa lying on her side. Her long, bare leg was pulled up over the top of the blankets on his side of the bed. Her hand was on his empty pillow. His heart was in his throat. Bless her golden heart. She deserved better.

As quietly as he could, he started to lie down beside her but couldn't. He backed out of the room and went to the couch. Slightly off balance due to his exhaustion, he leaned against the arm of the sofa for support and slipped, his injured hand taking his full weight. Excruciating pain shot through his hand and up his arm. He nearly blacked out and did all he could to suppress a cry of agony. Finally, with his entire body soaked in sweat, the pain eased. He lay exhausted.

Tylenol would take the edge off the ache, but he didn't have the energy or any inclination to get up. He expected sleep to take him down. He'd refused it several times throughout the evening but now was ready for it to take him away. He thought of Jacqueline and the other woman, Silk. Their images were indelibly stamped on his brain—their bodies so full and perfect, as if shaped by a master sculptor. God help him—so much confusion, temptation, and mixed desire. What had he done?

He forced the confusion away, thinking of Christa. The last thing in the world he wanted to do was hurt her. *The deed is done, my friend. Stop it and grow up.*

A paying job was the only answer. He'd been given a temporary reprieve for his cash-flow problems, but now he had to find an income. His tired, scratchy eyes closed. Sleep would come.

What seemed like moments later, he heard Christa's hoarse whisper. "Ethan?"

It can't possibly be time to get up, he thought. His eyes opened to stare directly into Christa's face.

"You were gone for a long time today," she whispered. She seemed barely awake as she placed her hand on his chest. "You never phoned."

"I'm sorry, honey, so sorry," he repeated, hardly conscious but already asking for a forgiveness unknown to her.

"It's okay, Ethan," she murmured, kissing his face tenderly with her soft, moist lips. She leaned in closer, her breast pressing against his chest. "Randy called," she said, her voice crackling in the whisper. "Said something about a guy on a plane … wanted to meet you?" She paused and pulled in closer, her warm cheek touching his. "He left a number. Said to call."

Ethan's exhausted mind was all but asleep. He smiled upon hearing the news but sleep recaptured him moments later.

CHAPTER 34

Ethan's Timeline
August 1991

The sun's rays penetrated the blinds covering the single window in their bedroom. Warm and already muggy, Ethan awoke, vaguely remembering Christa's kissing him before she left for work. He lazily turned onto his back and faced the ceiling, a position he'd assumed many mornings since arriving at Robbie's apartment. Getting up was always difficult, it seemed. His head was in the middle of the pillow as his brain ran through everything going on that day. He was often overwhelmed when he first awoke by a myriad of questions that encircled his life. This morning's list was topped by his actions of the previous day and a half.

It's over, Ethan, came the incessant voice from the back of his head. *Get over it, my friend.*

Still numb from the experience, he tried to reassure himself that his actions were justified and that without the money, he'd not survive. But something else kept hounding him. *Face it, Eth. There's always another way. You were curious; the women were gorgeous. Sure, you need the money, but that's not the only reason. Besides, you'd take the two of them right now.* It was hard to fight that truth as he stared down at the tented sheet below his waist.

His stare returned to the ceiling, the cracked, colorless ceiling that needed painting. He had stared at it too many times, searching for answers that rarely came. Where was he going? Was he doing anything right? It sure didn't seem like it.

The three hundred dollars in the pocket of his jeans wouldn't last long. Somehow he had to find another source of income. If he was careful, the money would get him through a month, but that was it. He'd be broke again as his history repeated itself.

"Anytime, Ezan," Sven had said as he handed Ethan his payment. Ethan had remained quiet, picking at the scab on his palm. He'd done his duty, like a stallion on a stud farm, and collected the fee. Exhausted and disgusted, he couldn't get out fast enough. "You von't vind anyzing zat vill pay you zis for a daze vork," Sven had added.

Ethan had turned and glared at Sven in reply. Closing the door, he vowed never to work for Sven Irons again.

Ethan, you have to think of something else, he told himself. His sense of outrage churned his stomach. Somehow, he had to find a way to let it go.

His thoughts again turned to Christa. Wishing she was by his side, he closed his sleep-swollen eyes. He had to tell her. He would explain the situation and pray she'd understand. He couldn't help imagining the press of her breasts against his chest or touching the smoothness of her thighs; even the sharpness of her nails against his skin. The bed sheets tightened. He opened his eyes, hoping for the miracle of her presence, only to stare at the blank ceiling again.

The room was hot. He rolled onto his side, doubling up the pillows under his head. His eyes lined up with the word he'd written on the wall. *Act.* Such a simple word. It should be easy. The word resonated inside him. The reminder wouldn't let him rest. He threw the sheets aside and sat upright. He stared at the word as if his eyes were attached to it by some unseen force. As he stood up, his legs locked in a stretch, his muscles eager to get moving. Turning his torso slightly, his back stiff from the bed, he noticed a paper on the floor. He reached for it, feeling his hamstrings stretch uncomfortably as he did so. Christa had left a note before leaving. It was short: "Call Randy, Love, Christa." A big heart dotted the *i* in her name. Randy's number was at the bottom.

Ethan didn't recognize the number but wasted no time in getting to the phone. He was alone in the apartment and walked to the kitchen without bothering to put on a pair of underwear. The heat of the day was intensifying. It seemed even warmer outside the bedroom. The cordless was on the kitchen counter. He grabbed it and flopped on the sofa, where he dialed Randy's number.

"Hello," Randy answered after the second ring.

"Randy," Ethan replied. "How you doin'?"

"I'm doing just fine but busy," Randy answered.

"Great." Ethan wished he could say the same thing and then he did. "Me too."

"Sounds like it. Leaving that pretty lady to fend for herself. I don't know, but I'd be keeping real close to that one."

"I am, but ya gotta work when work's working. Christa left me your message. What's up?"

"Give me a second," Randy said to background sounds of moving chairs and papers.

Ethan walked to the refrigerator and scrounged some cream cheese and a bagel.

"Okay, I'm back," Randy announced. "Remember I told you about a guy I met going to Japan, Ben Lui?"

"Yes," Ethan answered, spreading the cheese on the side of the bagel. He hadn't bothered to cut it in half. "Why?"

"Well, you may not believe this," Randy said excitedly, "but I ran into Ben about a week ago. He asked me about my acting friend."

Ethan stopped spreading the cheese, remembering the card Randy had given him before the bout with food poisoning. "Go on."

"Well, you need to call him. I don't really know what's up, but he's looking for something. As far as I know, you fit the bill."

Ethan already was headed to the bedroom for Ben's card but couldn't find it. *Why didn't I call Ben after seeing Randy?* "Okay, what's his number?" he asked, taking a pen from his nightstand and the back page of Wiggy's script. There still was a lot of rustling going on in the background at the other end. *Randy must be searching for something.* Before the noise stopped, however, he gave Ethan a number. "I owe you one," Ethan said, after repeating the number back.

"No problem, Ethan. Gotta go. Talk soon."

"Thanks again." Ethan hung up and immediately dialed Ben Lui's number. He hoped Ben was still looking.

"Good afternoon," answered a soft-spoken woman after the third ring. "Ben Lui's office. Can you hold?"

"Sure," replied Ethan as background music began to play in his ear. He detested being put on hold and often just hung up, but that wasn't his protocol today. As the tune ended and the radio announcer came on, Ethan returned to the kitchen counter to spread more cheese on his bagel. He hoped he wasn't heading toward another dead end, but after his previous day's antics, he deserved it.

You better get that shit out of your head, said the voice. *You did what you did. It's done. History.*

Elton John started to sing "Daniel" in his ear and got through the first verse before the soft-spoken receptionist interrupted.

"Hello," she said quickly. Ethan could hear another line buzzing in the background. "How may I help you?"

"Ben Lui, please?" Ethan replied, hesitant to take a bite of his bagel. He didn't want his mouth full of cheese when Ben Lui came on the line.

"One minute, please."

He rejoined Elton who was into the chorus. Ethan couldn't wait, and no sooner filled his mouth with bagel than a quiet man's voice spoke.

"Ben Lui. How can I help you?"

"Hawwo," Ethan mumbled into the mouthpiece, before rejecting the contents of his mouth into the sink. He coughed to clear his throat. "Ahem, Mr. Lui?"

The line was quiet at the other end.

"Mr. Lui?" he said, trying to find a verbal foothold. "My name is Ethan Jones." He paused for a moment to let Ben Lui respond. Still nothing. "I'm a friend of Randy Baseman," he added, trying to stay upbeat, although a sinking feeling filled his stomach in response to the silence at the other end of the line. "He gave me your number to call regarding a project."

There was no pause this time. "Ah, Randy!" Mr. Lui exclaimed, his voice louder and more jovial. "Comic book Randy?"

"That's right," Ethan replied, his confidence restored for the moment. "I was just talking to him."

"Say hello for me," Mr. Lui requested.

"I will."

"So, Ethan, what is this about?"

"Randy told me you were working on a project and looking for an actor." It sounded strange, hearing himself say it.

"Well, I was, but I'm afraid I've filled the role."

Ethan's heart dropped. Randy sounded so optimistic about this guy. "Oh," was the only thing he could think to say, his sins of yesterday coming for retribution. If he hadn't done the fuck movie, he would have been home when Randy called. This was punishment for his act of fornication.

"But you're a friend of Randy Baseman's," Ben Lui said suddenly, his voice rising, enunciating each word with precision.

"Yes, I am," Ethan responded, not knowing whether it was a question or a statement. "Would you reconsider? Randy told me you were still looking."

Ben's next words changed everything. "Listen, come down and we'll talk. A friend of Randy's deserves at least that. Can you get here later today?" Ethan didn't say a word. He couldn't. It was a miracle. His heart was pumping so fast he couldn't think. "How about six o'clock? Meet me here."

Ethan agreed quickly. He didn't want to reveal his desperation or oversell himself. He had what he wanted. He had to shut up and get off the phone.

Ben proceeded to give him his office address and then hung up.

Another step forward after two steps back.

CHAPTER 35

It didn't take Ethan long to get his things together after his phone conversation with Ben Lui. Another chance was all he cared about.

By two o'clock, he was ready to go and still had a couple of hours to kill. To pass the time, he headed out and picked up a paper and some fruit from the small grocery around the corner. When he returned, he paged through the classifieds and came upon a small ad with the name J. Scott at the bottom. His mind struggled to recall why that name seemed familiar, and then he remembered the little man who sent him to Paramount. It had been some time since meeting Jamie. He'd never thanked him for the contact. He must have known he'd come back to work for Sven.

Ethan decided to call the number in the ad. After two rings, he got Jamie's voice mail. He left a message and his number. After leaving the message for Jamie, he realized he hadn't talked to Cushman in a while either. Before putting down the phone, he dialed Steve's number. Cushman never answered his phone, so Ethan didn't expect it to be any different this time. He was ready to leave a message when Steve came on the line.

"Cushman here," he answered, quick and ready.

"Hey, Steve, Ethan here."

"Ethan, how you doing?"

"Is that really you?" Ethan joked, "or am I talking to advanced technology."

"Yeah, it's me," Steve replied. Ethan could hear what sounded like shutters banging in the background. "Every once in a while I decide to answer my phone when important clients call. What's up?"

"I was going to ask you the same question. Haven't heard from you in a while. With you being my agent and all, I thought there might be … you know … something going on."

"Well …" Steve hesitated, and Ethan heard more rustling in the background. "There are two commercials I've got a line on, filming in two weeks. They're both speaking parts. They want someone with a good tan. Are you still as white as Casper?"

"Yep, and not any closer to a beach bodybuilder either. I don't want any more commercials, Steve. I'm not your most popular client, but I need work."

"Listen, Ethan, I know we can do better."

Ethan hadn't expected to get angry, but he could feel his rage building. He liked Steve, but this was business and his life. If he'd had more work, he wouldn't have had to succumb to the skin flick. "Your fucking right we can do better, Steve," Ethan replied, his emotions surprising him. "I just spent yesterday—nearly four hours—fucking two bimbos to put bread on my table, and you're telling me we can do better. Fuck, we can do better, Steve. You better believe it. I'm going to do better." In ten seconds, Ethan realized he'd told Steve everything he'd promised himself he wouldn't, to the point of wanting to retract what he'd said. There was no going back now. "I want to work with you, Steve, but you have to play me. I'm tired of sitting on the bench." The background banging at Steve's end stopped. Maybe he was listening. Ethan went on. "Steve, whether you believe it or not, I'm going to make it. I got nothing to show right now, but mark my words. I will have major roles in feature films. I will be somebody's biggest client. But I need baby steps right now. You got to show me some. You got to believe in me."

Steve weighed in. "Ethan, I believe you!" For the first time, Ethan heard Steve commit himself. "Things take time, but that time is over. I'll get you work. Work every night. I guarantee it. If I don't, fire me, but I'll get you your chance."

"Okay. Here's the deal," Ethan continued, surprised Steve didn't ask him more about his antics the night before. Maybe Steve was hearing what was more important. "Two weeks. You follow through with what you just said. We're a team. Otherwise, two weeks and we're done."

"You're on, my man!" Steve exclaimed, his voice carrying both excitement and an urgency Ethan hadn't noticed before. It was almost as if Steve had been lying in wait for some kind of start-me-up, and Ethan had hit the mark.

Ethan hung up. The negotiation with Steve made him hungry. He had a sudden craving for a submarine sandwich, and the Gonzales brothers came to mind. He hadn't been there since leaving his old apartment. With the same spontaneity as his call to Cushman, he decided to head across town to his old haunt for a Gonzo special.

Considering the distance and the three hundred dollars he had in his pocket, he decided a taxi was in order. His appointment with Ben Lui was at six, so he had more than enough time. The taxi was waiting out front by the time he got downstairs. He gave the driver his old apartment address and was off. A short while later, he recognized some of the first places he'd visited when arriving in sunny California. The taxi came to a stop outside his previous place of residence. He paid the cabbie and stepped out.

It had been a while since he'd been in the area. There was a comfort in seeing the old neighborhood, but it ended abruptly when he remembered the events of that early morning attack. He turned and walked in the direction of the sub shop.

At the corner of Bank and Somerset, he saw that something had changed. The Gonzo's Sub Shop sign was gone. Only remnants of the place remained. Ethan continued down Bank Street, his eyes fixed on the spot across from where the sub shop had existed. The windows were covered with old newspaper, and a large sign was in the window—"For Rent or Lease"—with a number to call. He stood on the edge of the curb, staring at the sign, disappointed that the boys had closed. They'd had such big dreams. "Gonzo franchises across the almighty US of A," Jesse had said. Things must have gone bad. Maybe Pedro had never recovered. It troubled Ethan that he'd left that part of his life behind. His stomach rumbled its emptiness, with a Gonzo sub no longer one of his choices. Ethan decided to cross the street anyway and have a closer look at what was left. He'd grab a burger next door.

Approaching the vacant storefront, he found the newspapers blocked everything from passersby. He wondered what had happened and could almost hear Jesse and Pedro's jibing him on the actors he knew. "Say hello to Bobby D. for me," Pedro would shout across the store. "Tell him he needs to pass on the Italian sausage once in a while." Pedro seemed so harmless. It saddened Ethan that he'd not said good-bye to either brother.

He decided to pass on the burger and walk farther down the street to get a coffee and sandwich.

Coffee-to-Go was a not quite a block away. It was a small shop with a few tables and a standup counter at the window. Ethan occasionally had stopped to pick up coffee on his way to work. A lot had changed since then, but the shop hadn't. Even the same big-boned waitress dressed in white was pouring coffee. It seemed as if the same coffee stains graced her white apron.

The shop was cool relief from the heat of the afternoon.

"What'll it be, sir?" she asked in a sharp voice. There was no indication that she recognized him.

"Small regular coffee and tuna fish on rye."

"Toasted?"

"Sure," Ethan replied, pulling a twenty from his pocket. It was great to have some money. He refused to let its source enter his head.

"Three twenty-five," the woman said, pouring his coffee into a small paper cup.

He handed her the twenty and collected his change. At the same time, he turned as a tall, slender man entered the shop. Ethan recognized the oiled, curly black hair but couldn't put the hair and face together. The man was wearing a wrinkled black business suit and dark sunglasses. As he approached the counter, he pushed his shades to his forehead and revealed Jesse Gonzales's tired, bloodshot eyes. There was no indication that he recognized Ethan at all, but Ethan wasn't about to let the man go unnoticed.

"So how's Al Pacino, my friend?" Ethan asked, catching Jesse's eye.

Jesse looked back at him. Ethan watched as recognition came into the man's eyes. The Gonzales brother he was looking at had lost a lot of weight since their last meeting. His face was gaunt, his eye sockets were gray and sunken, and his cheeks were thin and drawn.

Ethan stuck out his hand, only to have it ignored as Jesse stepped forward and gave him a giant bear hug. Ethan hugged back, shocked by the transformation in the once big, strapping man. He hoped his amazement wasn't too evident.

"It's been a while," Ethan said after Jesse released him. "It's been months since I've been back here."

"I remember you comin' by the shop. Was the day after Pedro was shot," Jesse said as they sat down at a table. "I remember 'cause I kinda lost it. I never talk with nobody after that. I remember the feelin'. Kinda like a giant ball of fire sittin' way down in my guts." He motioned like he was holding a basketball in front of him. "You said somethin' that set me off. Like a dragon, I spat it right back atchya. I never seen you again after that."

"Well, stuff's gone on since then," Ethan replied not quite knowing where to start and not really wanting to get into it. He took a bite of his sandwich and grabbed a napkin from the chrome dispenser between them as some of his tuna fish squished into his hand. "I came down today to get a Gonzo sub and found the shop shut down. What's up?" Ethan wanted to ask about Pedro but hesitated, unsure of how to bring up the subject.

"Things dinit get no better after you was in. We buried Pedro a week later. Not the same after Pedro not there, you know. Dinit open up regular no more. Dinit feel like it. Just gave it up. The Gonzales brothers no more." He pushed his open hands facedown across the tabletop toward Ethan to show the sub shop was finished. His eyes never met Ethan's.

"I'm real sorry, Jesse. Is it getting any better?"

"I have my up days but no so many." Jesse changed the subject and focused on Ethan. He didn't want to talk about Pedro or his future. "So how's the movies, Mr. Actor? Know any big-shot movie stars? Hanging with anybody I know?" This brought the first hint of a smile to Jesse's face.

Not knowing what to say, Ethan realized the man had lost more than a brother; he'd lost his whole world. "Well," Ethan started, realizing he could now add a line to his résumé, "I've done a movie and am working on a part in another one."

Jesse's eyebrows rose as his smile grew larger. "Really. That's great. I'm gonna know a real celebrity. Who's in the movie?"

Ethan didn't go into the details, although Jesse might well know more about Jacqueline and the other woman than he did. So he made it up. "Your buddy, of course, Mr. Pacino."

"No way!" Jesse exclaimed, leaning forward, more interested than before. "What's it called?"

"Afraid I can't tell you," Ethan continued. "I'm sworn to secrecy, but it's coming to a theater near you."

Jesse leaned back and gripped the chair beside him, stretching his arm. Ethan sipped his coffee and took another bite of his tuna fish sandwich without squeezing any on his hands.

"You know, come to think of it, I remember something else," Jesse said, leaning forward with his elbows on the table. "A man stopped by one day after I seen you. Looked pretty uptight—you know, all nervous like. Asked if I know an Ethan Jones. 'Never heard of him,' I said. I never say, even if I know. Couldn't remember your last name but didn't know any other Ethans before you. Was pretty sure who he was talkin' about."

Ethan nodded. His mind was alert to what Jesse had to say about his visitor. He was pretty sure he knew who it was. Christa's ex had asked questions on their whereabouts.

"How long ago was this?" Ethan asked, trying to remain casual. If the guy was around, why hadn't the cops tracked him down? It scared him because he didn't know what Christa's ex even looked like. Strangely, Christa had no photos. Her ex could walk right up to him, stick a six-inch blade in his stomach, and Ethan would be defenseless.

"Hard to say," Jesse replied, leaning back in his chair, causing the front legs to rise off the worn wood floor. His face lifted as his dark eyes looked toward the ceiling. "Maybe a couple of days, a week after I last saw you, but I never saw him again." He then dropped forward and looked directly at Ethan. "Yer in trouble too?" he asked, his tone indicating concern.

"Well, not with the law but with a disenchanted lover," Ethan replied, trying to laugh it off, but his eyes failed to hide his anxiety. Another customer entered the coffee shop. Ethan's eyes darted to the man. All of a sudden, he felt like a carnival duck, popping up for paying customers to shoot at.

Jesse smiled back at him. "Another Hollywood playboy," he laughed. "Well, you in the right town."

Ethan laughed. He'd never thought of it quite like that, but Jesse was on the mark. He took a last bite of his sandwich. "It's real good to see you again, Jesse, but I must be moving on," he said, hearing the words to the old Supertramp song come out of his mouth. "I've an appointment across town this afternoon."

Their chairs scraped the floor as they stood up. Ethan took his half-finished coffee and left the rest of his sandwich.

Outside, they shook hands.

"Make sure you come out to see my movies," Ethan said, holding Jesse's hand for an instant longer. "I'm sure things will work out for you."

"No probs, man," Jesse replied. "I'll be lookin' for your movie with big Al." As they stepped away from each other, Jesse added, "Say hello to Jessica for me too."

Ethan didn't know a Jessica but figured he was referring to Jessica Lange. "I will, my friend," Ethan said, nodding his head as they turned and went their separate ways.

CHAPTER 36

Ethan's Timeline
August 1991

After leaving Jesse, Ethan continued down Bank Street en route to Ben Lui's office. He found it quite amazing—even disturbing—that he'd run into Jesse, considering that Jesse's business was closed down and Ethan had been away for so long. Jesse obviously was devastated over losing Pedro. Ethan hoped Jesse would get back on his feet. What raised the hairs on the back of his warm neck, however, was the idea that if he could run into Jesse on this street, he could very well run into Christa's ex too. Was he being watched now, his attacker lying in wait for the right moment? He kept seeing a blood-streaked knife blade in front of his stomach, a fatal wound inflicted before he could defend himself. Each male passerby was a potential foe. Where were their hands? Were they watching him? *Paranoia will destroy you*, he told himself. Was he really paranoid?

As he stopped for a red light at an intersection, he wavered on whether to return to the apartment. It still was early, and he wanted to get out of his current locale. There was no real reason for him to be here. The feeling of being watched was bothersome and a distraction from what he should be thinking about—acting and work. A lunatic who wanted him dead was unnecessary baggage. He decided to head directly to Ben's office. His hand rose to wave down a taxi as he crossed the street.

Things were about to change for Ethan Jones.

CHAPTER 37

The building sparkled, encased as it was in glass and mirrors. Ethan felt good, even excited, just walking into the cathedral-like lobby. He loved modern architecture and became disoriented looking up into the overhead structure of the seventy-foot sparkling-silver ceiling. Glistening chrome pillars stood fortresslike around the periphery, as if the building was chiseled into the side of an ice mountain. Even the coolness of the air inside—so unlike the afternoon's heat—added to the illusion. Giant pieces of sculpture—art forms of pseudo-dinosaurs—hung from the ceiling, creating the foreboding that precedes one of nature's violent tempests. The power of size and form was inspiring while at the same time intimidating, much as life could be.

Big-business money had built the edifice. It was at once beautiful and dominating. The building breathed new life into Ethan. He couldn't help feeling he was there by purpose.

It was just past four o'clock, according to the giant rectangular-shaped clock hanging on the wall behind the multi-door front entrance. The clock, like most of the décor in this cathedral-size concourse, was colossal and extravagant. A huge Roman numeral marked each of the twelve numbers and followed the outside frame into each corner of the rectangle. It was designed for its location, but Ethan could picture it mounted to the side of a snow-covered mountain. The leviathan-sized heads of Washington, Jefferson, Roosevelt, and Lincoln carved into Mount Rushmore came to mind. Ethan smiled.

He still had almost two hours to kill before he was to meet with Ben

Lui. The extra time was much preferred to running late, as he looked for Ben Lui's office number in the directory hanging beside the elevator. "Ben Lui Inc." was near the top of the alphabetic listing. Ethan could feel the buildup of anxiety as he read down the various companies listed on the directory. Could he ever fit into all this? It was easy to be intimidated, but he couldn't afford the luxury. There was no way he could walk around in here for another two hours. He'd be completely overwhelmed. He had to be fresh and excited and not overwrought by the enormity of it going to his head.

You better get rid of this sensitivity shit, he told himself. *You've one chance here. Enough fucking lollygagging. Get yourself together.*

With that he turned from the directory and headed back to the front entrance. On exiting, he was greeted by the late afternoon's smothering heat. He didn't know where to go and turned left outside the ten-foot glass doors.

The sidewalks on both sides of the street were busy with people—lots of people. There were many more than he had noticed on his way in, coming and going in every direction, in a rush to get home or simply to an evening of freedom. Ethan found it exhausting just walking in the flow.

With so many around, he sensed he was going against the flow, only to be pushed when he stopped momentarily. He kept moving, not looking for anything in particular. There were people of every sort and an abundance of beautiful women—a cornucopia of faces, arms, legs, and other more distinguishing body parts. It was exhausting just being there. His head was spinning, reeling from excessive stimuli. It was a paradox—a mass of people all viewed as the same, yet each person was unique and individual. By chance, he glimpsed an overhead sign for books. Like wading through a strong river current, he made his way to the storefront advertising Books at Large. Above the window were the same three words in four-foot letters.

The front of the store was packed with people grabbing the best-selling books by the hottest authors, almost as fast as the shelves were stocked. Ethan recognized some of the authors but none of the titles. He paused, however, when the cover of one novel in particular caught his eye. On the jacket was a painting of a diner, revealing the action inside. The book was called *Browning Station*, and the jacket notes described a character struggling to hold on to reality in his everyday life. For no particular reason, Ethan stuck it under his arm and proceeded to the back of the store.

En route, he noticed a small barista off to the right and ordered a long espresso. It had been a while since he'd had one, but it would serve to sharpen his alertness in his meeting with Mr. Lui.

The film and movie section was where he was headed. Shelf upon shelf seemed to contain every book imaginable on Hollywood and anything affiliated with Tinseltown. The actors, the directors, and the movies filled the many books and captured his full attention. He couldn't get enough of the photos and anecdotes, reaffirming his reasons for coming to California in the first place. There were indeed many paths to take him where he wanted to go.

He browsed through some of the biographies. Most of the celebrities featured had a strong desire to act or entertain people. Some came by way of live theater; some through music; others through television and commercials; and still some had gone directly into the movies. There was no single road to stardom but a common thread did emerge— they all had stuck to their guns. Despite doubt, criticism, and many other discouraging events and hardships, they never gave up. Without knowing when or even if they'd get their break or reach their goals, they simply were unwilling to stop. It was part of who they were.

Ethan picked up a large coffee-table book titled *Homes and Cars of the Stars*. He flipped through a few pages that contained fabulous photographs of celebrities alongside the fruits of their success. The homes were incredible estates, custom-designed and built to the individual desires of the star. Ethan fell in love with several that captured the essence of space and simplicity in modern architecture. The automobiles were no less remarkable. Ethan loved the exotics. Two photographs, in particular, were magnificent: one was a bright-red Ferrari parked outside a multicar fieldstone garage, with the front wheels turned sideways in a position of stealth and majesty; the other was a Lamborghini Diablo, also turned sideways, in striking yellow, like an exotic parrot from deep in the Amazon rainforest. In a sudden impulse, Ethan closed the book and took it and the copy of *Browning Station* to the cashier.

On seeing sixty-eight dollars light up on the cashier's screen, he hesitated—nearly seventy dollars was a lot of money, considering his current financial situation. But he saw the time on the cashier's watch. Twenty minutes was all he had to get back to Ben Lui's office. Without time to think about it, he handed over the cash and left.

The pedestrian traffic outside had declined. He cursed his impulse to buy the expensive books with his limited resources. If he wasn't careful, he'd be back begging Sven for another fuck job, and that wasn't going to happen.

On entering the giant concourse again, now almost deserted, he headed for the chrome elevators. With his focus on meeting Ben Lui and somewhat unaware of his surroundings, he didn't notice the security guard approaching from his right.

"Excuse me, sir," announced the young man, who was built like a Chippendale's dancer and wearing a professional fuck-off-and-die smile. "Can I help you?"

Ethan turned around so quickly that he nearly dropped his book purchase on the polished granite floor. "No thanks," Ethan replied, quickly and tight-lipped, shifting his books from one arm to the other.

"The elevators are locked out after five thirty, sir," the man stated sternly. He was twirling a key fob in his right hand. "Sorry, but I can't allow you to go up without authorization."

"I have an appointment with Ben Lui at six o'clock," Ethan told him.

"Well, I guess Mr. Lui won't mind if I call him to confirm your admittance."

"No, I don't suppose he will."

Ethan followed the security guard around the corner to a small office tucked into one of the monolithic walls of the entrance. *If this guy fucks me around, I'll head to the stairway.* The clock on the wall showed six o'clock.

"No one's answering, sir," stated the security guard, crossing his arms and revealing gym-sculpted muscles as his short sleeves tightened around his biceps.

Ethan was unimpressed. His face became hot. Looking at the guard's heavy, laced-up boots, Ethan was pretty sure he could outrun the guy.

"There's nobody there, chief," the guard announced, replacing the receiver. "Maybe some other time."

I don't think so, Ethan thought, trying to remain calm. "Please try again," Ethan said in his best low and professional voice. *There is no chance in hell this doofus is going to keep me from meeting with Ben Lui.*

"Maybe come back tomorrow," the guard suggested.

"Could I leave a note?"

"Do you see a secretary?"

Ethan was ready to go through the roof. There was no way he was going to talk his way past this asshole. He was at the point of tirade when Mr. Security's pager went off. At the same instant, a person exited the elevator. Ethan took off and was around the corner before the security guard looked up.

"Hold that elevator," Ethan hissed as a small, plump man stepped out. The man, who appeared panic-stricken, did as he was told, holding it open long enough for Ethan to reach it. "Thanks," Ethan said, sliding into the elevator and slamming his shoulder into the wall to stop himself. He punched the floor number repeatedly to get the doors to close. They finally moved just as the guard came into sight. There was nothing Ethan could do but watch; he was caught. But as fate would have it, as the guard passed the corner, his hard-soled boots slipped on the polished marble, and he hit the floor hard. The guard's curses and frantic shouting faded as the elevator door closed. Ethan closed his eyes and leaned back against the gray lacquered panels inside as the elevator rose. He was breathing hard, and his face was lathered in sweat. He'd made it by the skin of his teeth. Taking a several deep breaths to regain his composure, he wiped his hand across his wet forehead. Using the chrome midsections between the gray panels as a mirror, he ran his hand back through his hair and straightened his shirt. He placed the bag containing his recent purchase on the carpeted floor and tucked in his shirt. As he rechecked himself in the chrome, the elevator came to a stop at the designated floor.

The doors opened to a deserted hallway, with an arrow and sign opposite the doors indicating the direction to Ben Lui Inc. The white walls of the hallway were bare and clean, with a recent application of paint. Gray carpet lined the floor.

Ben Lui's office was at the end of the hall. Ethan knocked twice on the heavy oak door to no avail; there was no one there. It never occurred to him that Ben Lui might actually stand him up. His forehead fell against the door. It just couldn't be.

The bell on the elevator rang down the hall. Ethan froze. Had his buddy downstairs followed him? *Fuck.* He'd not thought this out very well. There was no one around, and that jerk wouldn't think twice about taking liberties with his fists. Ethan knew he didn't stand a chance against the muscle-bound ape. There had to be a way out. The knob on Ben Lui's door hardly budged. Quickly, he tried another door across the hall. Locked. *There has to be a stairwell somewhere*, he thought. *Every building has a fire exit stairway.* The elevator door opened. Ethan pressed himself as close into a door well as he could. He held his breath.

The person who exited the elevator was not the security guard but a small, chubby man wearing John Lennon rose-colored glasses and a white fedora. He leisurely strode across the new carpet in beige leather shoes. He was carrying two coffees in a disposable paper tray. Ethan's entire body relaxed as the man approached the door he'd been knocking on.

"Hi," the man greeted Ethan, who stood in front of a nondescript office door opposite Ben's.

Ethan was trying his best to look relaxed. "Hi," Ethan replied. "You wouldn't happen to be Mr. Lui?"

"As a matter of fact, I am," the little man answered, turning to face Ethan while balancing the two coffees in one hand and holding the key to his office door in the other.

"Ethan Jones," Ethan said, stepping forward to extend his hand and then retracting it on seeing Ben's full hands. "Let me help you with that," he added and retrieved the paper tray.

"Thanks," Ben replied, opening the door and gesturing Ethan inside. "We must have just missed each other," Ben added, closing the door. "I realized after we talked that you might have difficulty getting past security, so I went down to meet you. I stepped out for a second to get coffee. When I got back, our security guard was cursing. Said a—" He stopped, his expression saying it all. "It was you, wasn't it!" he exclaimed, laughing out loud. "Ha! Now that's funny. You got the big fucker pretty upset."

Ethan didn't know what else to do but smile.

"I can see I'll have some explaining to do on this one," Ben said, directing Ethan into a white office, "but it'll be worth it. I shouldn't laugh. We've some of the best security around. It's hard to find."

Ethan nodded. He'd keep his comments to himself.

"So what can I do you for?" Ben asked, sitting down in a seat at the end of a small conference room table. The room was bare except for a few paintings on the walls. It looked to be a room that wasn't used very much.

Ethan smiled again. "Well, Mr. Lui ..."

"Ben, please."

"Ben." Ethan began again. "From our conversation earlier, I was given your number by Randy Baseman, who said you were looking for unknown talent."

"Yes, yes, sorry, Ethan, of course." He stopped talking for a moment and looked around the room. "This room needs some windows. I find it hard to think without windows." He paused and stood up. "Like right here. There should be a window right here." He traced the outline of a window with his index finger. "What do you think?"

Ethan, not knowing where Ben Lui was moving the conversation, agreed.

"Ethan, I've already selected the actors for my project," he said directly.

Ethan nodded, indicating he understood, but Ben had said he still wanted to meet him. Something was there. Ethan had to find out what it was and, for once in his life, be patient. He would let things unfold. With a mild kind of amusement, he thought of Sven and acknowledged to himself that he would leave if Ben's project had anything to do with removing his clothes.

221

Unexpectedly, as if a fire bell had sounded, Ben rose to his feet. "Excuse me for a minute," he said and walked out of the room. He came back in as much haste as he'd left, placing a thin purple folder in front of Ethan. Contained in the folder were a number of untitled pages.

"I would like to you read for me," Ben said, handing the open folder to Ethan. "Take a few minutes and prepare yourself. Interpret the character however you like. Call me back when you're ready."

Ethan looked over the material and knew at once what he wanted to do. The folder contained the story of a man, in dialogue with himself, attempting to overcome the loss of his wife.

After one read he was ready, and from the doorway of the conference room called Ben back in.

Over the next several minutes, Ben Lui's demeanor changed from a reluctant, do-a-friend-a-favor attitude to an interested, here's-what-we-do-next mode. Ethan remained in his chair. He'd roughed up his hair a bit and leaned back on the rear two legs. He spoke with candor like there was no tomorrow with subtle hints of fear and sadness, but his look of crazed insanity—his hazel eyes lighting up—was what grabbed Ben Lui's attention.

"God, I wish I had the camera!" Ben Lui exclaimed, beaming like a new father holding his firstborn. "Ethan, I'll get back to you tomorrow. What a look." At that, he rose abruptly, as if to leave.

"Do you have something for me?" Ethan asked, amazed by Ben's enthusiasm but more than a little confused.

Ben Lui stopped and turned just as hastily as he'd initially left the room. "Yes, Ethan, but I need a day or two to figure it out." Then he murmured, as if to himself, "I should know better than to question Randy's instincts."

Ethan thought Ben seemed hesitant, distracted in some way and thinking about something else, even though Ethan had amazed him. Ethan concluded he was about to become the casualty of yet another audition.

"I'll call you tomorrow," Ethan said, trying his best to stay positive.

"Do you have an agent down here?" Ben Lui asked. Ethan was surprised by the question but pleased. It was his first insight into how

Ben worked. Ben's mind wasn't in the room or even with the current conversation but instead about three steps ahead.

"Yes, I do. Why?"

Ben turned his head slightly before answering. "You're going to need one."

Ethan's face lit up. His dry mouth broadened into a smile. It was a tidbit that meant hope.

"Come back tomorrow," Ben announced, as if talking to someone in another room. He was holding a white piece of paper in his hand. "Have you ever done live theater?"

"It's been a few years, but I did a lot of live work in college."

"Good. We'll see you tomorrow. Same time."

"Count on it," Ethan replied, excited about his prospects and changing luck.

"I'll come down with you," Ben offered, smiling, "to make sure security doesn't detain you further. Can't be too careful these days. I have to go anyway."

At the entrance, Ben turned to Ethan and shook his hand, bidding him a good evening. "We'll see you tomorrow, then."

"Yes, and thank you," Ethan replied. He headed toward a taxi parked at the curb outside the glass entrance doors. There was an added lightness to his step as he thought, *Just keep keeping on.*

CHAPTER 38

Ethan's Timeline
September 1991

The next few weeks brought a number of changes to Ethan's world. He returned to Ben Lui's office the following day without any interference from security. Ben was true to his word and quickly directed him to a low-budget theater production. Ethan auditioned for a part in the morning, went home, learned the lines, and performed live the same evening. The theater group was desperate for an actor on short notice. Ben, through his limitless supply of contacts, made the connection. Ethan came through at the last moment and saved the day. He finally had a stage production for Northum to see—if he could ever reach him.

A week after seeing Ben for the second time, Ethan received an unexpected call from Jamie Scott. Jamie was quiet to the point of apparent disinterest but apologized for not getting back to him sooner. Ethan thanked him for the Northum contact. Jamie wished him well. The conversation was short. As soon as he hung up, Ethan dialed Frederick Northum's number at Paramount. He'd already left half a dozen messages over the course of several weeks without response.

After the fourth ring—as Ethan was ready to hang up and not about to leave another message—Frederick picked up. His voice was high with energy. He apologized for not returning Ethan's calls—it was crazy busy—and wondered what Ethan was up to.

"I'm finally in a show!" Ethan said excitedly. "A different one from my messages."

"Yeah?" Northum replied, sounding surprised. He didn't say anything else.

"Yeah!" Ethan rejoined loudly. "It's too long to explain but something came through."

"That's great," Northum chimed back, his voice regaining its earlier energy.

There were too many holes in the conversation for Ethan to believe Northum was sincere. He didn't let that deter his intentions of getting Frederick to his show, though. Northum was another ticket to making movies, and Ethan wasn't about to squander it.

"It's amazing!" Ethan all but shouted over the line. "So when are you available to see it?"

"Ah … I don't know," Northum answered, his voice slowing.

"Come on," Ethan persisted, surprising himself. "You said you needed to see me in a show. You won't be sorry." He then added, "I will make it worth your while."

"Let me see …" Northum said, pausing again for reasons Ethan could only guess at. He needed Northum, and Northum knew it—it was all part of the game. "Well, okay."

It was all Ethan needed. He set it up so that Cushman would pick up Northum at his office and take him to the show.

Then it happened—one thing followed another.

Ben wanted him to do the first of a series of dramatic commercials on drugs and alcohol addiction. Big-name directors were being hired for the projects. Ethan read for a part but was rejected. Incensed, Ben blew a fuse and went to bat for him. "Some casting people can't find their assholes without a map! Un-fucking-believable!" Ben had said. Things changed. Ethan was offered another part in a second commercial, playing a young parent with a cocaine addiction. Ben calmed down, and Cushman smiled a lot. The commercial was directed by a new female director named Katharine Davenport. No big-name actors were selected for any of the roles in these pseudo-movie commercial spots. The producers—private investors with government money—wanted unknown people in the roles for the stop-you-in-your-tracks effect, without the influence of celebrity personalities. For Ethan, it was an unbelievable opportunity. The commercial started shooting two weeks after his live show's last performance. The timing couldn't have been better.

Ethan phoned Randy Baseman the night after meeting Ben Lui to thank him and invite him to dinner. Randy took a rain check on dinner, as he was deep in preparing storyboards for another trip to Japan. The Japanese company had bought his idea, and he was consulting on production. Excited and exhausted, he spoke so fast that Ethan had difficulty understanding all he said. Randy didn't mention his financial success, but Ben Lui had alluded to Randy's becoming one of America's most recent millionaires.

Christa attended Ethan's first live performance with the theater troupe and continued to be amazed at his transformation. "It's like you *are* someone else," she said, leaning against his shoulder on the cab ride back to the apartment. Smiling demurely, she then whispered in his ear, "It's like I can have someone different every night and still get to sleep with my favorite."

Their schedules were completely opposite during his theater gig. He'd leave for his evening's performance before she'd get back to the apartment after work, and he'd be sleeping when she was readying herself for the day.

Christa gave him a warm wake-up on the morning before his performance in front of Northum. As his anxiety grew, he'd struggled between sleep and excitement, not handling either well. He'd heard her switch off the alarm at seven o'clock; his head was swimming from his consumption of Jack Daniel's. Rolling onto his back, he used his arm to shield the morning light penetrating the slits in the window blinds, and sleep returned to his tired eyes. His dreams were unremarkable until he was overcome by a strong desire for sex. Falling through layers of sleep, he thought he was dreaming, only to find Christa moving gently between his legs. With a sweet brown-eyed look, she held all of him in her mouth. Her cheeks puffed, attempting a smile, knowing the pleasure she was providing. Her fingertips crept around his thighs and up his chest, her nails digging, searching, and pricking. Ecstasy moved through him in waves, like tiny electric charges, stimulating his most erogenous senses, sweeping him to near unconscious bliss, and rendering him helpless to her powers. Like warm, wet honey, she covered him completely.

His body climaxed in unison with hers, every pore sensing, every muscle pushing and pulling, trying to absorb and hold on to every moment. Each instant stretched to infinity and then contracted to zero. Christa climbed up his body, searching for more, further extending herself. Her lips melted into his chest, her teeth biting, bringing him back to his senses, only to be swept away with the brush of her breast against his hand or her erect nipple pressed into his lips. His eyes opened for an instant, only to be kissed closed again and again. His fingers touched her wetness and slipped inside without effort, incapable of resisting. Once inside, he moved to another dimension, outside of humanness—they were like animals in the wild. Christa moaned, as if miles away and inside of him simultaneously. For an instant, their souls were one. Once exhausted, Christa lay on her side, satisfied. Her skin was wet against his.

"I love you," they whispered in near unison, too exhausted to smile. He fell back asleep.

Several hours later, Ethan woke to a warm room and a hangover. Christa had left without stirring him. On his pillow, he found a scented pink envelope. With his eyes barely open, he picked it up and tore open the flap. The scent of Chanel perfumed the air, arousing more than his olfactory senses. Christa had written a note to wish him well in his performance that night.

To my movie star:

May the shining Tinseltown gods look down on you tonight, my dear. You are wonderful. I'm already jealous of the screaming women in your future. I don't know if Hollywood is ready for Ethan Jones, but they better get ready—because he's here.

Your love always,
Christa

P.S. Break a leg.

Tears filled his sleepy, bloodshot eyes after reading her words. He wished she was by his side. The handwriting was that of an angel, each letter perfect, with a flourish at the end of each word. How was it that he'd found this perfect woman? If anyone could actually feel like a million dollars, he did. At that moment, nothing seemed too monumental to overcome. He could conquer the world; another conquest would be on the stage that night.

It wasn't yet eleven o'clock. He flipped off the remaining bed sheet and hung his legs over the side of the bed. His lines for the evening already were passing through his head, as they usually did when he woke up. Over and over again, the words surfaced. Sometimes he would backtrack and repeat a line until the next appeared.

"You just can't stand there and expect something to happen" was a line from midway through the second act. His character was explaining how to build a relationship with a woman to another character. "Sometimes you just have to push." His lines were never far away.

He showered, ate a couple of oranges and a pink grapefruit to offset his early morning bout with Jack Daniel's, and still found himself with four hours to kill before having to depart for the Limelight Theater. Waiting had become the most frustrating part of his routine. Every day, he had any number of hours before a performance with nothing to do. Never wanting to get too involved in anything that might sway his performance, he found it increasingly difficult to keep occupied. He'd vowed never to drink before a performance but often found himself tempted to do so. Today was especially difficult, with the added pressure of Northum's attending the performance.

He hadn't been sitting for more than ten minutes, with the *Homes and Cars* book spread across his lap and orange peel on the armrest of the only comfortable chair in the apartment, when Robbie walked in.

One looked as surprised as the other as the door closed and Robbie crossed to the kitchen.

"How is Mr. Jones?" Robbie asked, smiling. He looked tired but good. Life was agreeing with him. "You've been busy lately. You have the afternoon off?"

"You could say that," Ethan replied, closing the book. "Big show tonight so just kind of hanging out. My usual routine." He picked up the orange peel and added, "You're off early. I haven't seen you in a few weeks. Maybe since I started at the Limelight."

"Probably," Robbie agreed, opening the refrigerator door and pulling out a slice of day-old pizza. "I was out of town last week and had a couple of crazy days at the office." He came back to the living room and flopped down on the gray couch opposite his friend. "You must be working pretty steady."

"Didn't David tell you about the Limelight gig?" Ethan asked, moving the book off his lap.

"No," Robbie replied, shaking his head, "but that's not surprising. We broke up a couple of weeks ago."

Ethan was caught off guard by this news. "Sorry to hear that."

"Say, man, want a beer?" Robbie asked, heading back to the kitchen.

"Sure," Ethan replied. It wasn't often they got guy-to-guy time. "A beer would be good, like old times."

"To college bros," Robbie announced on his return, handing a can of Heineken to Ethan. "Drink up, my boy."

It was an odd moment for Ethan as he sucked back the beer. He didn't drink before a performance but here he was, laying into a can with his friend. He knew better.

"How's Christa doing? Haven't seen her in a while either." Robbie took a sip of his beer. "You guys still good?"

"You bet."

"You're a lucky man."

"I am. She's awesome!" Ethan replied, reminded of what had happened earlier.

Ethan set his can on the coffee table and pulled up his book. He wanted to shift the conversation and not get into drinking. "You should see some of the cars in his book, like this blue Duesenberg that Clark Gable is standing beside or this 512 Boxer."

Robbie gulped down the rest of his Heineken and went back to the refrigerator for another. He opened it and sat on the arm of Ethan's chair to get a better look. His hand gripped Ethan's shoulder as he gulped down more of his beer. "Are you gonna have a beer, just like old times, or not?" Robbie asked, noticing Ethan's can on the table.

"Well, I don't drink before a performance. Mine comes after the final curtain falls."

"Ah, come on," Robbie prodded. "What's one little beer gonna do? Might never get to do this again."

Ethan shrugged, reached for the beer, and took another gulp. At the same time, Robbie's hand moved down his back. It was an odd moment that Ethan could remember sensing only once before, back in college, and it made him uncomfortable. Was this how a woman felt when a man came on to her whom she didn't want?

"So how's work going?" Ethan asked, louder than he'd intended, his voice cracking. With his beer can in hand, he stood up and took another sip.

"Incredibly busy," Robbie said, sounding aloof, like his mind was elsewhere.

Ethan wondered if he had misjudged the situation and that Robbie simply was being friendly. All he knew was that he felt awkward.

"I'd love to talk more," Robbie said, "but I need a shower and some shut-eye in the worst way." He headed to the bathroom. Ethan placed his book on the small table beside his chair and stood up as Robbie opened the bathroom door. "Break a leg, Eth," Robbie said, poking his head between the bathroom door and door frame. "Hope it goes well tonight."

"Thanks, man," Ethan returned with a wave of his hand. "Time to lock 'n' load."

Robbie closed the door.

CHAPTER 39

At four o'clock, Ethan's nerves set in. A small pain started in his abdomen, just below his ribcage on the right side. He pressed and massaged the spot, hoping for relief, but the cramp only tightened.

The park—a ten-minute walk from the Limelight Theater—usually was quiet, where he found a vacant bench to sit on. His lines continued to pester him as he went through different parts of the play. Somewhere between the first lines and the last, he'd drift off. Each time, his concentration was interrupted by some diversion—a swearing cab driver in the street, a cooing pigeon by the pond, or a crying youngster in the playground. He sought quiet—it was why he liked this isolated part of the park—but today he heard everything. If he listened closely, he was sure he could hear earthworms crawling through the dark black earth beneath his feet.

His biggest distraction, however, was the thought of Robbie's advances in the apartment and what he'd done to make Robbie think he was interested.

The harder he tried to concentrate, the worse things became and the worse his stomach felt. The day was beautiful and clear in contrast to his stormy feelings. He had been to the park on several occasions before a show to relax and calm his pre-show jitters. But today was different. Again, he brought himself back to his lines.

"You just can't stand there and do nothing!" he exclaimed to an imaginary Richard beside him on the bench. "And why not?" he replied, filling in Richard's lines in a different voice. "Because it's not the right thing to do, you oaf!"

Another spasm of pain filled his abdomen, disrupting his concentration again. After two and a half weeks, he knew his lines cold, but now he was having difficulty putting three lines together. Even his hand hurt where the nail had pierced it weeks ago.

You have to relax, buddy, he said to himself. *It's going to be fine.*

From somewhere else came the voice of his mother: *"Don't screw up your face like that."*

He could not remember being as nervous as he was now. *But Eth, you've never had this much at stake before.*

He closed his eyes, trying to ignore the pain and recite Richard's line. But nothing appeared on his internal teleprompter. He bent over and pressed his fists against his stomach. One good fart would do the trick, but the gas would have to work its way down. It felt like a bent hanger was snagged inside his intestines. His hand probed his abdomen for a protrusion but found nothing. Waiting would have to suffice for now. His stomach often pained him before a performance, but this was unusual.

He shifted and lay flat on his back on the bench, his feet extending over the gray cement arm at one end, while his head rested on the other. The cement felt rough against his skin but offered a good resting place for his head.

His mind could not leave that night's performance. He needed to impress Frederick Northum—stand him on his head with his performance.

Richard's next line popped into his head. Ethan spoke the lines before he'd even thought them through. The words he'd rehearsed again and again over the past few weeks began to flow from his mouth as if on autopilot.

Ethan could feel his body begin to calm. He tried again to sit up on the hard wood beams of the bench, but his stomach still was cramped and tight. He lost his lines and silently prayed they would all stay in his head that night.

He got up, shook his arms, and walked around, trying to move the gas inside his stomach around. His mind was boiling his stomach. He somehow had to switch off the growing pressure.

Be cool, he told himself.

His stomach tightened. He had never been this nervous prior to a performance before. The more he tried to compose himself, the less he could relax. He returned to the bench and sat with his back straight, shoulders back—perfect posture. Slowly inhaling through his nose, he took in as much air as his lungs would hold, closing his eyes as he did so. After holding his breath for several seconds, he exhaled the air from his mouth. He repeated the process five or six times, and each time, the hard tension in his stomach seemed to loosen. Christa had shared this breathing method with him after attending a yoga class. Ethan had paid little attention at the time, but after a few more inhalations and exhalations, he was more at ease.

He let a few more minutes pass before opening his eyes. Still without a watch, he wondered what the time was. No doubt someone would be by soon enough, and he could ask. More relaxed, he leaned forward and farted. It was louder than expected, but when he looked around, no one else was present. The pains in his abdomen dissipated. He closed his eyes again and leaned back, his face to the sun.

His lines returned. He wished for a way to foretell the future, wanting to see how everything would turn out. Frederick Northum would come to the small dressing room after the show with a contract in hand. His face would be alight with the evening's dazzling performance. So excited with his new prospect, he would hardly be able to hold his pen still enough to hand to Ethan to sign the contract. Ethan would buy him a scotch at the bar next door in celebration. They'd discuss Paramount's plans for his first project. It was hard to sit still, just thinking about it.

"It's yours to grab hold of, kid," his character told the drunken brother who lay unconscious on stage near the end of the third act. "And yours to lose too."

Tonight was to be his night.

CHAPTER 40

A minute before showtime, the theater lights dimmed, silencing the audience. There was no sign of Cushman or Northum. The stage manager counted down with his fingers in the shadows backstage, and the show's recorded music began. The stage was set. This was one of the most exhilarating parts of theater. The electricity of the crowd's anticipation saturated the air, feeding the cast backstage. A performance was the re-creation of human events by other humans, a duplication of another time and place. It was an event that took people away from their busy, mundane, everyday lives and placed them somewhere else—like a dream, only more tangible, an escape of sorts. Here, the audience could peek behind closed doors and watch others interact without their knowledge. They could experience another's life and adventures without leaving their own. People loved to watch others interact in any form, good or bad. Most liked to be spectators, at least once in a while, without having to participate—like watching television or watching someone through an undraped window. Though socially unacceptable, curiosity often was stronger than etiquette. The inclination to watch the acts of others was more important than what was right or wrong. At the theater, all was acceptable; that was the purpose—to watch and observe through another's eyes and experience and make judgment without persecution.

The brother of Ethan's character hustled up the back stairs and onto the stage as the show began.

Ethan's entrance came about five minutes into the first act, and his

234

timing was perfect. *No room to mess up tonight*, he reminded himself. His delivery was magnificent, his focus and concentration were uninterrupted. Tonight was his night. He planned to make the most of his opportunity.

By the end of the first act, Ethan had not seen Cushman or Northum in the audience. Disappointment was beginning to distress him. They should have been there by eight. He prayed it wasn't a no-show. The best opportunity he'd had to showcase his talent seemed to be evaporating before his eyes. As the music began for the second act, he glanced into the audience again. His heart started to pound as he watched Cushman assist Northum to a seat near the rear. He had no time, however, to get nervous, as he was cued on stage. He nodded to indicate he was ready, afraid opening his mouth would cause his heart to pop out. All that faded as he mounted the steps to the stage. The show was his as the second act began.

Pausing on the stairs, he stopped and took a deep breath. Someone tapped his shoulder. He turned as the stage manager frantically pointed him to the stage and mouthed, "You're on." Two steps, and he was on the stage. The music stopped as he sauntered into position with his first line easily on his lips. "I just can't imagine how someone with that kind of talent can treat it so ... so ..."

And the words were gone.

CHAPTER 41

Cushman walked in the dressing room as Ethan was blow-drying his wet hair in front of a cracked mirror.

"You know that's bad luck, don't you," Steve said, forcing a smile. His face looked like cold cement, his forced smile cracking the smoothness. "Tough night."

"Fuck, it would have been better if I'd just pissed on the stage and shut up."

Almost nothing went right after stepping onto the stage for the second act. After his first line, he'd drawn a blank, as if he'd unintentionally hit the "delete" key in his brain. He'd recovered the first line by stepping forward, as if his character was searching for the right words to say, rather than the actor searching for his lines. *I just can't imagine how someone with that kind of talent can treat it so …* "Commonplace," he'd ad libbed quickly, "like a scrap of food or a disposable razor." His next lines were no better. His rehearsed lines were just gone—a blank slate in his mind. Like a child learning to ride a bike, he'd get started again, go for a bit, and then bang—he'd be on the ground. From his first spoken words, he'd wanted to get off the stage. He could not recall being so embarrassed or humiliated in all his life.

"How long did he stay?" Ethan asked.

"About forty minutes," Cushman replied, shifting from one foot to the other and looking nervous and anxious. "Said he'd call."

The woman who played Ethan's sister in the play passed behind him and caught Cushman's eye. He immediately perked up. She was wearing a bright red bra that helped display her latest breast work. She'd been after Steve to represent her since Ethan had started with the group.

"Eth," he said, slowly pulling his eyes away from the attractive blonde, "you're still the only one on stage with charisma. You've got it. Northum even said so. He wanted to stay but had another—"

"Prospect," Ethan interrupted. "Face it Steve. I sucked. I choked. I fucked up." He slammed his hand against the wall. "I never miss my lines!" he exclaimed. "You know what scares me? It's that I won't get another chance like that."

"You'll get as many as you want," Steve replied, glancing back at the woman now brushing her long blonde hair. He turned back to Ethan. "Nobody does what you're trying to do." Then he lowered his voice. "There are actors in here who have been working twenty years to get a break. And they'll work another twenty, trying."

"That's what I'm afraid of, Steve," Ethan hissed; his face was flushed. "I don't want to be here for twenty years, grabbing for scraps that fall off the big-screen table." He sighed heavily. "That's why I hired you."

"Come on, Eth," Steve said, turning the doorknob. "Let's grab a drink. I think you need one."

The words were a welcome melody to Ethan's ears.

Steve opened the door and nearly walked into a man dressed in green khaki shorts and a yellow golf shirt. His California-tanned face smiled and revealed a set of very white teeth. "Sorry," Steve said, hastily stepping back.

"No problem," replied the stranger.

Ethan stepped out from behind the mirror. His mind already had switched to savoring that first taste of alcohol. Who better to help ease his woes than his good pal Jack Daniel's?

"Listen, can you—" began the tanned-faced stranger, but then he stopped abruptly and looked straight at Ethan, saying, "This is the man I'm looking for."

CHAPTER 42

"Lou Royson," said the man, extending a tanned, manicured hand. His grip was solid and locked into Ethan's hand with purpose. Ethan was reminded of his father's repeated advice in shaking hands: *Be firm—make sure they know you're there.*

"Really enjoyed your show tonight, Mr. Jones."

Ethan nodded. "Thank you, it's one—" He'd begun to make a deprecating remark but changed his mind. "Glad you liked it."

Never dump on the audience no matter how bad you want to, came Mila's voice.

"Where you from, Mr. Jones?" Lou Royson asked before Ethan could say another word.

"Ottawa, Canada," Ethan answered. "Please call me Ethan."

"Could have guessed that. I was in Ottawa a week ago. How long have you been in California?"

"About two years, I guess."

"What brought you to California?"

Ethan looked at Steve, wondering what to make of this guy who seemed overly interested in him. "Hollywood," Ethan all but blurted out, his eyes returning to the sharp emerald eyes of Lou Royson. "I'm here to be in the movies."

Royson continued to stare directly into Ethan's eyes, like he was searching for some hidden message. It was beginning to make Ethan uncomfortable, but he held his own.

"I've been here to see you for the past four nights," Royson said, his smile broadening with glistening teeth. "I'd like you to come down and do a test with us next week."

Ethan stared at Lou Royson unbelievingly. He did not say a word. It was Steve who jumped in.

"Mr. Royson, Steve Cushman," he introduced himself, turning to shake hands. "Good to meet you. I represent Mr. Jones. I'm his agent."

"Great," said Royson. "That was actually my next question. If he didn't have one, I was going to suggest he get one."

"Excuse me, Mr. Royson," Ethan asked, his head leaning forward, "but what test? What are you talking about?"

"I'm sorry," Royson said, retrieving a small black leather wallet from inside his jacket. He pulled out two cards and handed them to Ethan. "Maybe I could get you to jot your number down on the back of one of these."

Ethan took the card and stared for several seconds at the printing on the front face. It was difficult to believe what he saw:

Louis Royson
Columbia Pictures, Inc.
Casting Director

The address and phone numbers were in the bottom right-hand corner.

"I work for Columbia Pictures and am always on the lookout for new talent," Lou said, handing Ethan a gold-plated Cross pen with the initials LHR on the clip. "We're working on a number of projects. I'd like to see how you look on screen."

Ethan's face expressed a mixture of emotions, reflecting what was bubbling inside him. Was this real? It seemed too easy. He'd had one of his worst nights yet—a truly mortifying experience by any measure. Yet here was a casting director—from Columbia, no less—inviting him to come down for a screen test. *Go figure.*

Ethan wrote down his phone number on the back of one of the business cards and handed it back. "I can be reached here. There's an answering machine."

"I have a lady waiting in my car," Lou said, passing his hand through thick brown hair. "I'll be in touch." He shook hands with Ethan and Steve and left as quickly as he had appeared.

Ethan looked at Cushman and held up the second card Royson had given him. Steve's beaming face said it all. "Well, about that drink, Eth. It's on me."

Steve bought two rounds that night, but Ethan was too agog to even feel the alcohol. Sleep did not come easily.

The Limelight show was supposed to close that Sunday but was extended another week after Saturday night's show sold out. Ethan waited all weekend for Lou's call. By Monday afternoon, he still hadn't heard. *Another short wick*, he concluded, *that burns bright for a moment and then goes out quickly.* That was Hollywood.

After four o'clock, he dialed Lou's number from the pay phone in the back of Rosie's Bar, across the street from the Limelight Theater. His mind was not on the evening's performance. *Fucked again*, he thought, dialing Lou's phone number. Royson was going to hear an earful, if the number even worked. Why hadn't he called Lou the next day and saved a week of hopelessness? Unbelievable. He was pissed for letting himself get sucked in yet again. How many times was he going to fall into these goddamn traps? Would he never learn?

One ring. No answer.

Two rings. An answering machine would soon click in.

He anticipated a third ring that never came. Instead, Lou Royson answered the phone.

"Lou?" Ethan replied, surprised. He thought he might be listening to a good electronic copy of Lou's voice.

"The one and only," Lou quipped. "As far as I know."

"Lou, Ethan Jones."

"Ethan!" Lou nearly shouted over the receiver. "It's about time. I thought I'd lost you."

Ethan stood dumbfounded in front of the blue pay phone, shaking his head. "What do you mean?" Ethan queried, confused by Lou's exclamation.

"I've been trying to reach you for four fucking days!" Lou's voice was loud with frustration, but Ethan was pretty sure he heard a tinge of relief as well. "I'll tell you what. Get your ass down here if you're even thinking about the movies!"

Ethan stood in shock. "I haven't heard a word from you," he replied, incredulous that this could in any way be his fault. "I only called today because I hadn't heard from you."

"Really?" Lou sounded stunned. "You better get your damn answering machine fixed then. I must have left a dozen messages in the last week."

"Fuck," Ethan hissed, wondering what could be wrong with their machine. How many other calls had he missed? Christa and Robbie hadn't passed anything on to him. "So ... when?" Ethan asked Lou.

"I think I said tomorrow at eleven in my last message," Lou said. Ethan could hear commotion at the other end as Lou seemed to be searching for something. "Damn these computers. I can't find shit ... here it is. Yes, tomorrow at eleven."

"Sure, I'll be there."

Lou gave him the address, and Ethan did everything he could to lock it into his memory.

"I'll be there, Lou."

"Great. Knock 'em dead tonight. *Ciao.*"

CHAPTER 43

Ethan's Timeline
September 1991

"I've been waiting a long time for tomorrow to happen," Ethan said to Christa in a low voice. It was past 3 a.m., and he didn't want to wake Robbie. "I can't believe it."

Christa rolled over on her side in the bed and kissed him. Her long fingernails brushed across his chest. A light sheet covered both of them. Her tired brown eyes stared back at him as she pulled the sheet up to her shoulders. His palm brushed against her nipples. The room was warm, but her skin was cool, almost fragile, and so soft to his touch. He traced her full lips with the tip of his index finger.

"I'm so happy for you, Ethan," she whispered, unable to keep her weary eyes open. "I just know it's gonna go well."

Ethan wondered whether he'd be able to sleep at all. Tonight's performance had been nothing short of spectacular. The audience had erupted at the end, giving him a rousing standing ovation. He'd been on, hitting all but one of his lines perfectly. The entire performance simply flowed out of him. As one cast member said after the show, "Eth, man, you were in the zone!" Several people from the audience approached him after the performance for autographs. Usually, it took him a couple of hours to come down after a show, but tonight was different—his mind was in no hurry to let him relax.

"I sure hope so," he whispered next to Christa's ear. The essence of Givenchy perfume was around her neck. The fragrance never failed to excite him. As he pressed his lips against her ear, he noticed she was wearing the gold dolphin earrings he'd given her earlier in the evening.

He'd found them in the jeweler's display window across the street from the Limelight. After his phone conversation with Lou confirming Columbia was interested, the first thing he'd wanted to do was get something special for her, to share his good fortune. The fourteen-carat gold dolphins represented freedom—a wild freedom—and a celebration. More expensive than he could afford, he bought them anyway, with his eye on the bigger things to come.

"I know it will," she sighed, indicating she was nearly asleep. "I love you." Shifting herself, her skin cool against his own, she kissed him. "Good night, Ethan Jones, and thank you for coming into my life." She rolled onto her other side and went to sleep.

Ethan wasn't ready for sleep. There were too many things buzzing around in his head. After his telephone conversation with Lou, he'd wondered about the many messages he'd never heard. He found his memory was gapping; he was so involved with his work that he couldn't quite recall the order of how things had changed. He and Christa had moved into Robbie's place after her ex's attack. It was Robbie's place but it felt like Robbie was the visitor. They were there more than Robbie was. Robbie, like Ethan, had come into tough times and lost his job. Ethan didn't know the details but Robbie was having a tough time getting his shit together. It seemed odd that Robbie would have difficulty finding another job, especially when he'd found Ethan his first job. Now Ethan was getting confused recalling how it all fit together. It was as if by taking on each new character, he became the character to such an extent that it mixed up his own life. He took on that character's life and made the character's fictional background real, as if he himself had lived the character's life.

He found it odd that Robbie hadn't mentioned any messages recently, as other than Ethan, he was the only one picking them up. A broken answering machine might explain why Robbie was having difficulty in his own efforts to land a new job. *Note to self,* Ethan thought. *Check it out tomorrow before leaving for the show.* Propping his head up on the pillow, he stared at Christa's back. The worn cotton sheet she'd pulled up had fallen away from her slender shoulder, leaving most of her back exposed. Gently touching her soft, smooth skin, his fingertips drew phantom abstracts across her back. Good fortune's eyes were shining upon them now. *Magical* was the only word he could think of to describe the feeling.

Christa stirred. His hand dropped to the bed, his head into the softness of his pillow. He reached down beside the bed and retrieved his book. In the dim light of a forty-watt bulb in his nightstand lamp, he could just make out the glossy photographs. The poor light served to expand the pictures in his imagination. The book was a window out of their small apartment, with its cracked ceilings, faded paint, worn parquet, chipped veneer, and bruised walls, to a world of possibility. It took him from cramped lodging to spacious mansions; from asphalt parks and cement high-rises to unrestricted grass and wooded wilderness. He could step into the pictures and touch that other side. He turned to a page featuring Kim Basinger, attired in hot-red latex at the wheel of Ferrari's 512 Berlinetta Boxer. Kim pouted her bright ruby-red lips and wore matching red-framed sunglasses. The car would be his one day, Ethan decided, with Christa dressed in the red latex beside him.

As he turned the pages, he saw himself standing in the bedrooms and studies, the gardens and driveways, beside the Lotuses, Bentleys and more Ferraris, until the shadows crept over him and closed his eyes. As the first light of morning rose above the horizon, the book fell to his chest and sleep finally claimed him.

A few hours later, he awoke with a start, instantly aware that it was *the* day. He had no clue as to what had awakened him, but the digital clock beside Christa's side of the bed let him know it was 9:45.

"Shit!" he cursed, springing from the bed, only to tangle his legs in the bed sheets. He should have been up an hour earlier. He had no time to mess around; he'd need every second to make his eleven o'clock appointment with Royson.

Christa had left for work. He vaguely remembered waking to kiss her good-bye and then fell back to sleep, although he did recall her warning not to do so. Whatever the case, he now had to hope everything fell into place. There was no way he could afford to be late. He pulled open the bedroom door and all but walked into Robbie in his underwear.

Completely naked, Ethan jumped back in shock. He grabbed Christa's housecoat hanging from the hook on the back of their bedroom door. The discomfort—maybe even fear—he'd felt earlier was unmistakable.

"Good mornin'," Robbie greeted him, his glance similar to one Ethan might give an attractive female. "Sorry to wake you. I didn't think you were home." He looked at his watch. "Don't you have an appointment this morning?"

Hearing the words was like having a bucket of ice dropped down his back. How did Robbie know? Ethan hadn't mentioned it to him. He tied the belt on Christa's robe, not wanting to talk. He didn't dare look at Robbie's underwear, fearing what he might see. "Ah ... yes ... yes," he stammered, looking like he'd been caught in the act with another woman. *Ethan, how did he know? Ethan!* The words screamed inside him. But Ethan ignored it. He didn't have time for crazy questions and doubts. *You've known Robbie for a long time*, he told himself. *Straighten up and get with it! What are you thinking?* "You better believe it," he finally said, regaining his composure. The expression on his face changed as he battled with his emotions. "You have another all-nighter?"

"So to speak," answered Robbie, smiling as if nothing out of the ordinary had happened. The dark circles under his red-lined eyes told a different story. Robbie's flippant response irritated Ethan. He knew about partying, and Robbie recently was doing his share. Ethan was reaching the end of his patience.

"Is it really helping you to find work?" popped out of his mouth somewhat unexpectedly. He didn't mean to speak his thoughts out loud. This was not the time to deal with their issues.

"And what do you mean by that?" Robbie asked, his demeanor shifting abruptly to a snarl.

Ethan knew where this was going. "Nothing, man. Sorry. I'm late and gotta run." Walking past Robbie was uncomfortable, but he couldn't stay. Five minutes was all the time he had, and he had to shower.

"Ethan," Robbie said calmly, stopping Ethan as his bare foot touched the cool tile of the bathroom floor. Ethan turned to face his longtime friend. If he'd thought about it, he might have continued on and answered after closing the bathroom door behind him.

Their eyes made contact, and Robbie took a step toward him. Ethan's heart pounded, anticipating what he hoped would never happen.

"Rob—"

"Eth," Robbie interrupted him, "good luck."

For another second their eyes stayed locked, communicating much more than words could ever manage. Ethan saw a depth of sadness in a face that was becoming increasingly difficult to recognize. It chilled him more than any temperature drop in the air.

Robbie broke eye contact first and walked toward the refrigerator. Ethan stared after him for a moment, unable to speak. What had just occurred stopped his blood cold and pulled the air from his lungs. Despite his discomfort, he stepped into the shower.

As the water flowed over him, he tried to think of something other than Robbie and shifted to his appointment with Lou Royson. But Robbie's countenance remained in his mind, adding an edge to his nervous excitement. By 10:15 he was out the door and hailing a taxi. Thirty-five minutes later, he was at the gatehouse of Columbia Pictures, with security checking his appointment with Lou.

"Free and clear, Mr. Jones," the woman guard announced as she looked back and forth between the cabbie and Ethan. "Mr. Royson will meet you in the lobby of building number six." She then leaned back and pointed at the front of the cab. "Turn left at the stop sign up ahead. Then turn at the first right. Building number six."

"Thanks," Ethan shouted from the back seat, thinking of his last confrontation with a security guard at Ben Lui's office. "Have a great day."

"You too, Mr. Jones," she replied, grinning. Ethan noticed the woman taking a long look at him as the taxi drove under the raised gate.

Well, here's to you, bud, he thought as they approached the building.

When he stepped out, he looked up at the four-foot number six that fronted the building. Dropping his head level with the cab driver's window, his face revealed his excitement as he grinned wide and said, "I'd say things are about to change for Ethan Jones."

The three hours that followed were like a wondrous dream and seemed to last just about as long. Lou met him at the glass doors of the main lobby. He introduced Ethan to their auburn-haired receptionist, who gave him a cute smile and a hand-flip wave while answering an incoming call on her headset. Lou escorted him down a long hall that was lined with movie memorabilia, explaining all the while what would take place over the next few hours. Ethan caught little of the explanation, distracted as he was by the historical movie stills hung on the pastel purple walls and the stars pictured in them.

In his office, Lou asked Ethan to fill out a sheet with his personal history, and he talked non-stop while Ethan tried to answer the questions. The sheet still was incomplete when Lou led him down another hall to a voice studio. The rest of Ethan's time was spent in a whirlwind of activity. He read three times, twice on camera, in three different buildings; met numerous people whose names became a blur; and witnessed several studios filming productions.

Returning to Lou's office, he was surprised that three hours had elapsed so quickly. A plate of sandwiches sat atop Lou's desk. Lou grabbed one and relaxed in his brown leather chair, crossing his brown Gravati loafers on top of the mahogany coffee table.

"Help yourself, Ethan," he offered, pointing to the plate. "There's lots."

"Thanks," Ethan said. He didn't feel hungry, but his stomach barked at the delicious aroma. He picked roast beef and tomato on fresh pumpernickel bread.

"You'll be back before the week's out," Lou said matter-of-factly, as if he was scheduling Thursday night bowling.

"Yeah?" Ethan replied, his mouth all but dropping open. He covered his open mouth with his hand.

"Yes," Lou said, moving his feet to the floor and leaning forward.

"We've a part—a small part, but a part nevertheless. It's a perfect fit for you. There are a few others I have to convince, but I can make that happen. It's just details."

Ethan couldn't believe what he was hearing, but it was music to his ears that he'd waited a lifetime to hear. Concerns about anything had vanished. The unbelievable was becoming believable. "Awesome!" Ethan exclaimed, not knowing what else to say. "I'm totally—"

"Listen," Lou interrupted, "things are going to happen. Cushton. That's your agent, right?"

"Yes, he is, but it's Steve Cushman," Ethan answered.

"Right, Cushman. Well, we have to talk to Steve and you ..."

The rest of what Lou said went right past Ethan, but not because he didn't understand it; it just didn't register. The merry-go-round was turning fast. He was getting his chance to step on, despite the dizzying activity. His dream was exploding.

"So please, Ethan, make sure Steve gets in touch with me," Lou was saying as Ethan's head returned to the conversation.

"No problem, Lou," he replied, snapping to attention.

"All right then." Lou stood up behind his desk. "I'll be in touch. I know you've heard that a thousand times, but I will, so watch your answering machine."

The whole answering machine fiasco returned to Ethan's head. Robbie's disturbing image from the morning came back. "I still don't understand what happened," Ethan replied. He didn't want to admit where most of his answers were leading. He still couldn't believe it.

"If you don't hear from me tomorrow, call me, first thing, two days from now."

With their arrangements set, Lou invited Ethan to take the sandwiches with him. He wasn't hungry, but Ethan accepted anyway; someone would eat them. Lou escorted him back to the front foyer, where the receptionist called him a taxi. On his way back to the apartment, he began to take in the last few hours and what likely would happen next. Lou was sketchy in describing the initial role he was earmarked for, not that it was of any grave concern. Ethan would accept being the mascot for the LA Kings at the Forum if they planned to put it on the big screen. As the cab neared his apartment, he was glad he took the sandwiches. His hunger was catching up with his excitement.

At the apartment, no one seemed to be around ... and then he noticed their bedroom door was closed. Christa must have come back and gone to bed, no doubt exhausted after being up half the night with him. Approaching the door, he could hear the clinking of hangers in the closet. He opened the door to find Christa, standing at the closet, unclasping her white lace bra. Her white satin nightshirt lay on the bed.

An audible sigh passed her lips.

"You look like you could use a little assistance, darlin'," he stated, feigning a western Clint Eastwood accent.

"Y'all wanna give a little lady some assistance," she replied in her best Texan form.

"Sure do, ma'am."

Christa's hands dropped to her sides, leaving the partially fastened bra strap in place midway up her back. Ethan gently rubbed her smooth shoulders and then slid his fingers down to unhook the clasp of her bra.

"Ooh, now that feels a sight better," Christa said, smiling as she turned around. "Whaddya think?"

"It's not real ladylike," Ethan answered, his eyes dropping to her bare breasts, "but I do believe it fits me right good, ma'am."

"Oh, come on, Ethan," Christa cried, wrapping her arms around his neck. "Are you going to tell me, or do I have to pry it out of you?"

"Well, what do you have in mind?" Ethan replied. He held a serious expression on his face as she leaned back to look at him.

"Ethan!" she exclaimed in a louder voice. "What happened? What did they say?"

"Can't tell you. Scout's honor," he retorted.

She poked her fingers into his ribs, rattling his composure. "You better tell," she said, pushing him on the bed, "or you're gonna pay dearly, my friend."

"You're not gonna hurt me, are you?" he taunted. She was sitting on his chest as he stared up into the fullness of her chest. Her knees were on his arms, so he couldn't touch her. "Okay, okay, uncle. I give," he cried as her fingertips continued to drill into his ribs. He couldn't stand being tickled hard. "Christa! Stop already." He was laughing and crying simultaneously, afraid of wetting his pants. "Come on—stop it!" Rolling sideways, he rolled her off his chest and onto her back beside him. He leaned over, kissed her, and fell to his back. "Well," he said as she propped herself up on her elbow, "it's a pretty big deal. I'm getting a chance to do something I can hardly believe—no, I can believe it—that I've wanted for so long."

His hand moved up her arm to her smooth, bronzed shoulder. "Lou's going to call tomorrow. There's a role he's already cast me in. It's incredible. I read three times and did great. I definitely made an impression. My big break is here. I got to make the best of it." Ethan paused a moment, his hands rising to rub his eyes and stubbly cheeks. "It's happening, Christa."

Christa stared at him. Her soft brown eyes were wet with tears. "I'm so proud of you, Ethan," she cried, sliding on top of him and kissing him hard on the lips. "I just knew it. You're something special."

Christa unbuttoned his shirt. The warmth of her skin and the softness of her breasts pressed flat against his bare chest distracted him from any rational thought. That afternoon would stay in his memory for a long time.

CHAPTER 44

With all the goings-on of the day, Ethan had delayed preparing for his evening performance. Then his cab got jammed in traffic, forcing him to run the remaining six blocks to the Limelight. He still was dressing as the music started out front. While waiting for his stage-left entrance, he could feel the rivulets of sweat trickling down his chest and back. His face was damp, even though Daphne, the butch, braless makeup artist, had toweled his forehead off while applying his makeup.

"Shit, this is crazy," she lamented, wiping her own forehead and inadvertently distracting Ethan with the sight of her erect nipples tight against her white cotton T-shirt, inches from his face. "It's like stickin' in a tampon while I fuckin' pee."

"Daph!" Julia cried from somewhere behind Ethan. "That's gross."

"His face is like a fuckin' runnin' stream," she retorted, snorting a guffaw. "It might as well be piss."

"Oh, sick, Daph," Julia cried in mock shock. "Who writes your material?"

Daphne proceeded to wipe his face again and finish with eye shadow. "There you go, babe," she laughed as she pulled the plastic cover sheet off his shoulders. "You're the star. Go knock their socks off."

"Thanks," he replied.

His performance that night was another he'd try to forget. From the second act on, things turned upside down. After walking on stage, he inadvertently stepped into some spilled water. The combination of his flat-soled shoes and the polished wood stage caused his feet to slip out from under him. He found himself on his back in the middle of the set. Landing hard, he could hear the hush sweep through the audience as he lay for an instant on the hard floor, shocked still by his unintentional fall. Without hesitation, his lines were out of his mouth at knee level and all but inaudible to even the closest person to him. His breath was gone and a bolt of pain shot up his back. Locked on the stage, he struggled to his feet, knowing he was hurt but refusing to stop. Everything around him fell into dreamlike slow motion. Even the words from his fellow cast member on stage sounded slow and foggy. His lower back screamed with pain that dulled everything else. The other actor delivered the next line, but Ethan never heard it; he only saw the motion of the other actor's lips. His next line, thankfully, was on his tongue and louder, as he maneuvered into position. Sweat poured from his forehead and down his cheeks, dripping from the end of his nose to the front of his shirt. Every syllable he uttered reverberated down his back and burned, as if bone and flesh were exposed to an open flame. The next half of the scene went according to plan. The pain was tolerable, provided he moved with care. He turned and sat down on a wooden kitchen chair. As the back of his thigh touched the seat, he knew he was in trouble. He could do nothing as the full weight of his torso came down, and he felt as if he was sitting on a six-inch knife blade. His world went gray as he bordered on consciousness. His lines were gone. He could barely breathe.

The stage lights faded to black as the curtain fell to end the second act. Two of his fellow actors were instantly at his side, assisting him up and to the side of the stage, as everyone scrambled with what to do next. Ethan told them he was not about to quit; he walked around backstage under his own strength but was afraid to sit down. The third act was minor for his character. He could rest, walk around, shake it off, and stretch. The pain subsided after popping a couple of codeine tablets provided by one of the stagehands. In his next scene, he climbed the steps to the stage and walked into the spotlight, only to find his mind devoid of anything to say. He couldn't have spoken his name.

Before the fourth act, he repeated his first line over and over, while imbibing two long espressos and a couple of wake-me-up pills. The pain subsided, but he struggled to keep his eyes open. All was going well until he mixed up his lines near the end. The entire cast became flustered. Julia lost her patience—and her lines—and walked off the stage. Ethan, still in pain, had to ad lib the end without all the cast members. The show was a nightmare, beyond anything he'd yet experienced. Everyone disbanded afterward, hoping Ethan would be okay. For the most part, it would remain a nightmare that everyone wanted to forget but couldn't.

"Character building," someone whispered to him in passing. "You know—what doesn't kill you … but let's not repeat it."

Done already, Ethan thought, *but thanks for the advice.*

Just after midnight, he carefully sat down at Rosie's. Christa agreed to meet him there after the show. Not seeing her, he'd walked to the pay phone to call Cushman about his news. He'd been unable to reach him earlier in the day. The show was over, and all he wanted to do was forget, which should have been easy, considering he'd forgotten most of his lines that night. The parts he'd missed now came back with ease on his internal teleprompter, adding further insult to his failed evening. *Where the hell were you when I needed you?*

Steve answered the phone on the first ring. "Ethan, my man," he announced, his voice as crisp as if it were midday. Ethan often wondered when the man slept. "I tried to get you earlier, but that sweet woman of yours said you'd already left. I was hoping to catch the end of the show."

"Just as well you didn't," Ethan replied.

"Somethin' happen?"

"It's what didn't happen that was the problem."

"What do you mean?" Steve asked, the tone of his voice turning serious.

"I'd rather not talk about it. I want to talk about Columbia."

"Hey, you're da boss."

"Listen, you have to get in touch with Lou Royson," Ethan said, excitement rapidly returning to his voice. "Lou's already cast me in a part. He needs to talk to you. Contract stuff."

"No way, buddy! You're kiddin'!" Steve shouted over the line. "You went for a screen test, not an audition!"

Ethan thought Steve sounded shocked. Was Steve really with him or what? The nagging sense of whether Steve was his guy whispered around his head. "Steve, whose side are you on?" Ethan exclaimed, shaking his head.

"My fingers are already dialing."

"All right." Ethan paused, peering at his table and scanning the patio. Still no sign of Christa. "We're just sitting down for a drink. Why don't you join us?"

"I'll see. Depends on how long I'm on the phone with Lou. That is, if I can even get him at this time of night."

"I doubt that'll be a problem." Ethan hung up and walked back to his table. Christa was walking up the patio steps.

"How did it go?" she asked, her eyes wide with anticipation. His facial expression gave it away.

"I didn't break a leg," he replied, leaning forward to kiss her very red lips, "but nearly broke my back." Evidence of his pain was quite visible as he lowered himself slowly onto the cushioned plastic chair. "I landed on my tailbone. It fucking hurts." Over the next couple of minutes he gave Christa the highlights—or rather the low points—of the evening that already sounded comical. By the end, he was laughing hard enough to make his back hurt.

Jen, their waitress, whom the cast in general had gotten to know, returned with their drinks and a plate of nachos. Steve didn't show, which this night Ethan took as a sign he'd hooked up with Lou.

Christa suggested they go after finishing their drinks. Despite the excitement, she reminded him that she still had a day job, which meant getting up early.

"Not for long, though," Ethan said.

"And what do you mean?" Christa asked, her eyes twinkling despite the late hour. "What are you suggesting?"

"Suggesting?" he returned.

"Yes, you have something in mind?"

"Maybe." Excited love filled his heart. Tonight was not the night, but he felt it in the air. He wanted her to be with him for the rest of his life. He stared into her eyes. He could get lost forever in her brown eyes. God, she was beautiful. How had such an angel landed beside him? Without thinking more about it, he decided the time was right to move with his heart.

Pressing both hands on the table, he lifted himself to a standing position. Christa followed his move, but he raised his hand to keep her still. "I'll be right back."

Making his way gingerly across the patio, he motioned for Jen to come closer. His lower back was stiffening from sitting still. The worst, no doubt, was yet to come.

"What's up?" she asked.

"I need a cigar."

"A cigar?" Jen replied, a blank expression appearing on her face. "You don't smoke." Then a smile appeared on her face. "But she does. Are Colts okay?"

He thought for a second. "No, I need a real one." He turned to see if Christa was watching. "I need the thicker band."

He followed Jen back to the kitchen, where she was gone for an instant, only to reappear a moment later with a yellow-banded Cohiba.

"This'll do the trick," he said. Rolling the cigar around in his fingers, he carefully slipped off the band and handed the cigar back. He smiled and headed back to their table.

His back stopped bothering him as he thought about the next few moments and what he would say. Christa had a funny look on her face as he approached.

"What are you up to, Ethan Jones?" she asked, searching for something in his face that would give it away.

"Oh, nothin'," he replied, sitting down slowly and paying little attention to his injured back. He looked straight into her wide eyes.

"Ethan?"

"Christa," he said, bending to one knee and taking her hand in his. He was oblivious to anything going on around them. "Christa," he repeated, pausing for only an instant more, "will you marry me? I want you to be my wife."

For a moment, she didn't say a word. She didn't move; she was locked in his eyes. He watched as her expression softened and her eyes, unmoving, went glassy, turning to water. A teardrop rolled down her left cheek and onto her red lips. The tip of her tongue poked out as if to taste it.

Ethan took the yellow cigar band and inserted it over her ring finger. "I want you by my side, Christa—forever."

She began to flutter her hands. Tears ran down both her cheeks. Her shoulders and head shook as she grabbed his hands, squeezing his fingers. "Ethan," she cried, trying her best to compose herself, "I'm already yours." Then, squeezing his fingers even tighter, she added, "Yes, yes, of course. Of course I will."

An hour later, they were back at the apartment. Ethan couldn't find comfort, no matter what position he got into, but it didn't matter. Standing seemed to be the best and most tolerable position, until Christa pushed their double bed against the wall and propped him up on pillows. Lying on his side took the pressure off his tailbone and eased the pain to bearable.

"Should we set a date?" Christa asked, returning to the bedroom.

"Yes, or let's just do it," Ethan replied, wincing as he shifted the wrong way against the wall. Sleep was closer than he expected.

"You okay?" Concern showed on her face.

Ethan tried another position and became more comfortable. "You're an angel," he replied, paying no attention to her question with his eyes half closed. He'd taken some Tylenol on return to the apartment and promised to be checked out if it was worse in the morning. But now, sleep had the upper hand and was taking him down. "See you in the morning," he mumbled, hardly cognizant.

"Forever, Ethan," she whispered, kissing his cheek. "Forever."

Those were the last words he would hear her say.

ACT IV

Talent is cheaper than table salt.
What separates the talented individual from the
successful one is a lot of hard work.
—Stephen King

CHAPTER 45

His dream was odd but very real.

Ethan found himself inside their apartment. Someone was standing motionless behind the entrance door. He didn't know how he'd come to be there, only that he was there with someone else. He heard a key inserted into the apartment door's lock. He felt rather than saw the person's lips form a broad smile, as a plan was coming into play. Clear plastic, like Saran Wrap, was wound around the fists of the person standing nearby, ready for the strike. It was then he became confused as to where he was; it wasn't their apartment yet seemed like it. But he'd been here before. Maybe it was because his eyes hadn't fully adjusted to the darkness. The door opened, just missing the person standing in the dark behind it. He watched as a woman let the heavy door close and reached for the light switch. Hearing the door latch click, he watched as the intruder brought the plastic up over the woman's head and, in a split second, pulled the plastic over her face and back around her slender neck. Ethan was moving before the man completed his motion with the plastic but to no avail.

The attacker pulled back with such force that Mila lost her balance and fell back against him. At the same time, she kicked backward, slamming his head hard against the steel apartment door. Rage flashed through Ethan like a charge of electricity. The attacker's arm went rigid, as did the plastic around her neck, cutting off not only the flow of air but blood. As the monster pulled harder, Ethan was certain he would see Mila's head severed. His scream was nightmare silent as he imagined finding her severed head in their bed.

Her legs kicked wildly as her attacker held tight. Ethan recognized her attacker but refused the image. Her strength was remarkable but not overpowering. Though the attacker held her above the floor, he could do little to stop her flailing legs, instead holding tight to the plastic until her oxygen was depleted.

Ethan watched in agony as her legs began to slow. In her last futile effort, her hands grabbed at the plastic over her face. Instinctively, she searched for leverage over her attacker's locked arms. With her legs continuing to strike her attacker's, she madly grabbed for his head with her hands and tripped him up. As he fell, his arm clipped the light switch, instantly lighting the entranceway as the two fell to the floor together.

On landing, her head turned sideways and allowed her to see her attacker. Ethan saw the shock and horror of recognition in her eyes, giving her attacker an immediate advantage. A quick turn of the wrist further tightened the plastic. In the light, Ethan watched as the familiar figure forced the remaining life from Mila's eyes. As blood flowed from her neck, the tension in her rigid body eased, and her lifeless form fell limp. He watched the toe her ring was on quiver and then become still.

Ethan shuddered, unable to put together all that he was witnessing.

He watched as the man moved like a panther—smooth, precise, and efficient—his movement without wasted energy. Sliding his legs out from under hers, the monster stared at the slender shape before him. Ethan wanted to turn away, but the horrific spectacle made it impossible; he needed to know the violence dealt to his love.

Mila was so beautiful. But the toe ring—the toe ring was Christa's.

He heard the madman say, "Oh, how beautiful you are. Such a shame you had to get in the way—such a shame. Wrong place, wrong time."

The man carried her into their bedroom, laying her on her back, her pretty face tinged in the gray-blue of death. Blood fell everywhere. Ethan saw Mila's dark, lifeless brown eyes stare blankly at the ceiling.

The monster sat down beside her on the bed and as gently closed her dead eyes.

Ethan again heard the monster speak. "If I can't have him, you can't either," he whispered.

It was then that Ethan realized what was about to happen.

He could see Christa in Mila now. *Why had he never noticed before?*

The monster sat beside her corpse, observing as an art lover might study an intriguing work of art. This was his art. Two buttons had popped open on her white cotton blouse—Christa's blouse—revealing more of her breast than Mila would have been comfortable with. But that didn't stop her attacker. He seemed captivated by the lifeless form in front of him and with the freedom to do as he pleased. He proceeded to undo two more buttons and spread her blouse open. Mila's breasts were full but loose, nipples shrunk and withdrawn. Blood ran down her shoulder. Ethan watched as the monster removed the surgical glove on his right hand. Then gently, like a lover, he touched the end of her soft nipple with his bare index finger.

Ethan was frantic. His neck muscles strained as he tried to overcome his silenced screams, trying harder and harder to make himself heard.

The man's left hand went to his crotch, squeezing his erection, excited by the lifeless form at his disposal. Ethan couldn't bear what was sure to happen next, but the attacker instead stood up and hurried to the door. He picked up a bag, stripped off his clothes while still excited and noticeably erect, and changed, placing his soiled clothes into the garbage bag. He was returning to Mila's lifeless form when something scraped the apartment door.

"Fuck!" Ethan heard a familiar voice seethe. The monster froze.

Ethan heard the key inserted into the lock on the apartment door and the sucking sound as the door lifted off the frame. He was shocked to hear his own voice.

"Hey, Mila, are you—?"

Ethan's heart fell, hearing the sound of his voice, watching himself enter her dorm room. His emotion went hard, blank, and closed off, like cauterizing a wound.

Silence.

He watched himself immediately recognize the now-masked murderer at her bedside.

The attacker headed toward Ethan with the plastic wrap around his fists, as if preparing for his next kill. Instead of attacking, he handed the plastic to Ethan and disappeared out the door with the bag under his arm.

"Mila?" Ethan asked, his voice quiet as if trying not to be heard as he approached the bed. He knew what he was going to find but couldn't accept it.

Something then shifted inside him. The room he was in was white. He woke up.

CHAPTER 46

Lifting his head, Ethan was shocked to find himself in their bedroom beside Christa's bloodied corpse. Above her shoulders, there was little left that was recognizable. Her long, slender fingers were bent inhumanly atop what was left of the back of her head, as if she had tried to protect herself.

Havoc had been unleashed throughout the entire apartment. A chill ran up his back and arms that he couldn't control, yet he could do nothing to affect the situation.

He saw the bloody handprints marking the walls he'd seen before.

Although he was alone, Ethan could see the attacker in his mind, still excited and noticeably erect. Ethan knew the man had changed his clothes, put his soiled ones in a garbage bag, and then disappeared out the door with the bag under his arm.

Ethan felt his energy diminishing, as if the very room was sucking the life out of him. His legs were heavy. Violence was done, and the killing was chasing him.

He somehow got to the phone and called the police. He stopped and turned back to the bed. He looked at her lifeless form again. It was Christa. He went back and touched her arm.

You must get there, Ethan, Mila said, as if her voice was coming from Christa, *for all of us.*

He looked at Christa's mangled body again but could take no more. Frightened and confused, he ran to the door and pulled. The door sucked open as if releasing internal pressure.

A moment later, he was in the hall of their apartment building. He couldn't remember getting there. There was a lot of activity and people around.

"Ethan?" Robbie shouted from halfway down the hall. His face strained with concern. "What the hell's going on?"

Ethan looked up, recognizing Robbie. He reached forward and touched his friend's shoulder. Robbie was real. "But I thought ..." Ethan started shaking his head, confused. "Christa's dead, Robbie," he sobbed. Embracing his friend, he sorrowfully added, "How could he hate her that much?"

CHAPTER 47

The events that took place the next day eroded Ethan's recollection of the dream and what he saw in it. It was simply too painful and seemingly meaningless. His memory was unable to track the order of what happened following his walk up Bronson Street. The events were devastating. He could recall returning from his meeting with Royson with his first movie contract in hand. Feeling ecstatic with the turn his pursuit of movie-making had taken, he told the woman in the elevator up to his apartment about his good fortune of being cast in his first real movie. He remembered telling her to remember his name, though he couldn't remember hers.

It was after leaving the elevator that things unraveled in his mind. Did he have the dream and find Christa, or did he find Christa and have the dream? The events and when they occurred didn't match. But to Ethan, it really didn't matter. He'd lost his love again.

The period after Christa's death was the most difficult one of his life. He was a mess on the day of her funeral. All he wanted to do was sleep—sleep away the nightmare he couldn't wake up from. Sleep away who he was. Sleep away and become someone else.

Nothing mattered. He woke up bleary-eyed, his face puffy and swollen from his ten hours of sleep and lots of JD. His first thought was trying to remember what party he'd attended to make him feel so awful. But before the thought had gone far, the answer exploded in his head. Christa was gone—forever! She would never lie by his side again. He fell into a conscious doze of depression, hoping and praying he could conjure her back into existence one more time. Where was his friend Jack? He needed more of Mr. Daniel.

Robbie and Ethan's father managed to pull Ethan together enough to make it through the service. They were surprised when he asked to speak. He distanced himself from his emotions, pulling everything from his acting toolbox and then some, and delivered a short, comforting eulogy to his love. There wasn't a dry eye as he spoke of their short time together and his love for his angel. He was certain she heard his words. He spoke to her in the eulogy as if she were standing beside him. Gone was a beautiful, exquisite woman, statuesque in form and person, who cared more deeply for others than anyone he'd ever met. Questions of her death and why she'd been taken would plague him forever. She knew how much she meant to him.

He'd never met Christa's family until the funeral. They had made their way down from western Canada to bid her farewell. Christa rarely spoke of them, other than to say they still resided in Calgary. He met her older sister and a younger brother. Her brother was a bodybuilder whose handshake nearly crushed Ethan's hand; he said all of two words the entire time. Throughout the proceedings, the brother kept adjusting the jacket that stretched over his enormous, disproportionate shoulders and narrow waist. Ethan couldn't help thinking of the Incredible Hulk miniatures on Randy Baseman's dashboard. Christa's sister, whose straight, waist-length hair reminded him of Crystal Gale, was the lead soprano in a Calgary choir. ("They've toured the world," her mother was quick to note.) Nearly as quiet as her brother, she was quite thin, with plain, hollow facial features. Her eyes were set deep into her face and seemed sullen, a look that was exacerbated by her lack of makeup. Throughout the time Ethan was with them, her mother continually doted on Christa's sister with food or drink, asking often if she was comfortable.

Ethan looked for some resemblance to Christa but found none. It was later during the reception that he learned that Christa was adopted. Christa had never shared that with him. Although faded by age and—as Ethan observed—her husband's imperiousness, the woman's past beauty was evident. She did not wear makeup either. "None of my girls are going to look like sluts," the man told Ethan outside of the funeral home's small chapel. Bunny, as her husband introduced his wife, shook Ethan's hand politely and retreated to her husband's side. Their eyes met but once and only for a second. Her dark eyes, darkened further by the circles under them, looked to the ground whenever Ethan turned her way. She seemed a very frightened woman.

Christa's father, a tall, strapping man, who towered over Ethan, was one of the most vulgar people he'd met. Ethan disliked him immediately. Balding and greasy, Ethan noticed the end of a tattoo that extended beyond the cuff of his sleeve when they shook hands. They met after the service in the men's room. He spoke of Christa like she was a woman he'd read about in some tabloid.

"So, Ethan—it's Ethan, right?" he said, unzipping his fly in front of the urinal. Ethan nodded. "That's a strange one. Never met an Ethan before. How long you been seein' my daughter?"

"About six months," Ethan replied, not really thinking about it.

"You been livin' in sin for half the year, have you?" The man spoke without any remorse or feeling over his daughter's murder.

Ethan found just being in the man's vicinity nauseating. "We've shared an apartment with another friend," Ethan replied, not wanting to be where he was.

"Where you from, Ethan?" the man asked, speaking into the white ceramic tile on the wall.

"Ottawa."

"Eastern Canada, eh. Whadaya know? So what brought you here? Fuckin' babes in bikinis, I'll bet."

Ethan didn't know whether to smile or frown but could have puked into the urinal in front of him. "Actually, no. I work here."

"Where'd you meet Christa?"

"At a party."

There was a pause while the man stepped back and shook himself in front of Ethan and the urinal. Ethan did his best to focus on the white ceramic wall tiles. "I'll bet. Did my little Christa have her boob job done? It's hard to tell, looking at her in the box."

Ethan couldn't believe what he'd just heard. Rage brewed that he couldn't contain. The man zipped up his fly and moved toward the sink as if he'd just asked for the score in last night's Raiders game.

"Listen," Ethan said, collecting himself as best he could, "I'll pretend I didn't hear what you just asked me. Christa deserved much more out of life than she got."

"Oh, come on, Ethan, I'm just shootin' the shit. We both know why Christa left home and came down here." The man who represented Christa's father stepped toward the door without washing his hands.

Ethan was having difficulty peeing because he was so upset. He wanted to get as far away from this guy as possible. "I don't think you know shit about your daughter," he hissed and zipped up without finishing.

"Don't you fuckin' tell me what I know 'bout my daughter," the man retorted, sticking his big tattooed arm up to block Ethan's exit. "I know you were fuckin' her out of wedlock."

Ethan's face flushed. His composure was gone, and he knew it. This sorry excuse for a man—much less a father—was testing every nerve in his body. "If you don't move your arm this second, I'll remove it for you."

"You little fuck! Don't threaten—"

The man never finished his sentence. In a flash, Ethan's arm came down on top of the older man's elbow. Ethan was not a fighter, but he had incredible fight. The man may have been tattooed and tough-looking, but he was fat and slow after too many nights in the local tavern or in front of the tube in the old La-Z-Boy, sipping back one beer after another. Ethan loved Christa more than his own life, and no one was about to tarnish her image. The man grabbed his elbow. Ethan lined a left into his face, not knowing what he connected with but feeling the crunch under his knuckles. He pounded two more quick punches into the man's soft belly and then left, too enraged to utter another word.

He didn't see much of the father after that. At the gravesite, the family kept to themselves; the left side of the man's face was swollen and already bruising. He had found some sunglasses. Ethan stayed close to Robbie for the rest of the day.

A work friend of Christa's—Ethan had only met her once and

didn't know her name—held a small reception at her home after the ceremony. She introduced herself and told Ethan how much Christa would be missed.

A couple of veggie finger sandwiches and a thin slice of key lime pie were all Ethan could manage. His stomach was mush. He kept imagining Christa's killer, certain of who it was. He would recognize her ex's silhouette. It was the familiar sense of the monster in his dream. If only he'd known sooner. He didn't want the police finding him now. They'd had their chance. His love was gone. He'd start the manhunt himself.

CHAPTER 48

Two weeks after Christa's grizzly murder, Ethan was back at his father's home in Toronto, ready to quit Hollywood. He wanted his old life back. His movie was to begin shooting three weeks after the funeral, but without Christa, it just didn't seem important.

At first, he couldn't bear to think about the movie after seeing Christa's casket lowered into the dark brown earth. He couldn't actually remember seeing it; he only had the feeling. Images of earthworms and grubs eating their way through her eye sockets and crumbling ribcage ate away at him. He yearned for his beloved Christa. The days after her murder ran together like a blurred movie loop. He pictured their story in storyboard format, where one scene blended into another, and he stood on the sidelines as a spectator, no longer a participant. It was like grabbing a handful of sand and having it fall through his fingers. Time dripped by. He could find no purpose or reason for pursuing movies—or for that matter, much else—any longer.

On the third night, his father invited him to dinner at a small restaurant on Rideau Street. Ethan wasn't much in the mood to talk, but his appetite was returning. His father drove, proud of his new black Cadillac. The car was beautiful, with its supple black leather seats and smooth ride.

"So you're ready to pack it in?" his father asked. Neither had said a word since leaving his father's downtown condo.

"Pretty obvious, isn't it?" Ethan replied, his heart still heavy. Sooner or later, he would have to deal with it but hoped for later—much later.

"I really don't know what to say, Ethan," his father sighed, wanting to comfort his son in his grief, "but I'm here for you."

Ethan looked at his father and smiled. He didn't know how to respond, but the sound of his father's voice comforted him. It had since his childhood days in hockey, when his father would talk earnestly about how well he'd played. It was the timbre more than the words.

"Dad," Ethan replied, now seeing his father as just a man who was trying. "Thanks."

There was little said until they'd finished dinner. They talked a little about hockey and football and his dad's new car but nothing important. When his father returned from the men's room, he surprised Ethan with a question.

"What was Christa like, son? Tell me a little about her. I know so little about the woman who stole my son's heart."

Ethan thought for a moment before he answered. "Dad," he started, raising his coffee cup and then setting it down again without taking a sip. "She was perfect. She was very beautiful and intelligent, and I loved her. She was the angel I never thought I'd find after Mila." He paused and this time took a sip of his black coffee. "She encouraged me. Told me I would make it when my time arrived. Now she won't see it, and I don't even want it." Tears ran down his cheeks. "Dad, I loved her," he sobbed, wiping his wet eyes. "I can't stand her not being here. I can't do this again." His head dropped forward in his hands as sobs of grief shook his body.

After several minutes had passed, his father said simply, "Grieving, Ethan, is good."

Ethan heard the words and smiled. He knew what his father was trying to say. "I'm glad it's good," Ethan replied, the hint of a smile curving his lips. "I just wish it would go away."

His father returned the smile.

"I met Christa at an industry party," Ethan began, remembering much of his troubled times in his first year in California. "We drank a lot, and I woke up the next morning in her bed. We've been together ever since."

Their waitress came by. His father ordered two more black coffees.

"Her ex was nuts. I'm sorry I never told you. He came after me. He shot at me one night after finding out she was staying with me."

His father seemed to shrink upon hearing of his son's attack.

"Fortunately the bullet only grazed me," Ethan continued, touching the faint scar on his cheek, "but he thought I was dead and took off. The police never found him. Christa and I moved back to Robbie's place. It was supposed to be temporary, but things worked out. Somehow her ex found us again. I don't even know what he looks like."

The waitress returned with their black coffees. Ethan grabbed his and took a sip. His mouth was dry.

"Aren't you concerned for your own safety?" his father asked.

"Not at this point," Ethan said blankly. "It should have been me."

His father shifted in his seat and then asked, "When does your movie start shooting?"

"In about two weeks," Ethan answered, not wanting to think about it. "There's a script meeting later this week."

"Are you going?"

"No," he said quickly and then added, "I don't know. It's so hard to think about. Christa's gone."

The two sat in silence. Ethan's eyes welled up again.

"I'm not sure I ever told you this before," his father said, looking at his son. He was bent forward with his forearms flat on the table. Ethan knew that what his father was about to say was difficult for him. "I had a chance," his father continued but then stopped to sip his coffee. "When I was nineteen, I was invited to the Toronto Maple Leafs training camp."

Ethan's hazel eyes widened. He leaned forward. "You never told me that."

"It was my big disappointment. I've hidden it for thirty-five years. I didn't even try out."

"You were invited to the Leafs' training camp and never went?"

"As unbelievable as that might sound, I didn't. I got scared. There was a lot of pressure. The guys were big. They shot harder. I talked myself out of it. I blamed your grandmother for years, but it was my decision not to go." The hardness of his father's eyes softened. "I've hidden it too long. You need to hear it." He again paused to collect his thoughts. "Don't let it go, son. You've been through hell, I know. But come back. Life happens, one way or another. I'll tell you something else. You know I'm not religious, but we never seem to get more than we can handle."

Ethan watched as a tear ran down his father's cheek. He'd never seen his father cry. He didn't know what to say.

"Take a couple of days. Do some walking. But go back and set the world on its ear. Christa's spirit won't leave you. She wouldn't want you to quit."

Ethan didn't respond. He could not remember ever seeing his father in such a light. His grief was muted, replaced by something like hope. He turned and looked at a woman sitting alone two tables over, surprised he hadn't noticed her earlier. The teased brown hair looked familiar. Almost simultaneously, the woman turned in his direction and caught his eye.

Mila? Here? She smiled as only Mila could, knowing its effect. Her lips parted as if to say something, but then her attention was drawn to something else. She rose to reveal a tight yellow-silk dress and looked at him again, motioning to him with her red-nailed index finger to follow her. It wasn't possible, yet he followed, leaving his father at the table without saying a word. She disappeared out the front entrance. When he got there, she was gone. The maître d' didn't know what Ethan was talking about; no woman dressed in yellow had passed by him.

Ethan returned to the table, with his father looking for an explanation.

"It's nothing," Ethan lied. "Thought I saw someone I knew."

"Wow, she must have been something."

"She was," he heard himself reply, somewhat distant.

For a moment, he was somewhere else but slowly returned. He knew he had to go back. For Mila and now for Christa.

There was no answer for why they'd been taken. He would respect and uphold their memory. He would not give up, just like his father hadn't.

His father's pain was of lost dreams—the pain of choices made long ago, not the pain of success that sat before him. Ethan made his decision; it took but an instant. He wasn't going to be an actor. He needed to find Christa's killer.

CHAPTER 49

Ethan's Timeline
November 1991

Ethan went back to Redondo Beach, intent on following through with his decision to leave Hollywood. His father's words were etched into something deep inside him. He would move on, just not in acting.

He booked himself into the Holiday Inn for the week. He couldn't go back to the apartment. His heart could not bear it. There simply was nothing there for him. The hotel was comfortable and gave him a home base.

Most of what he owned was at the apartment and was required for the police investigation. All he took with him were a few photos of Christa, what remained of his book of *Homes and Cars of the Stars*, and some clothes. The rest he didn't care if he ever saw again—it could all go to charity.

On returning to California, he didn't see or hear from Robbie at all. He left several messages, but Robbie wasn't good at returning them.

He called Lou Royson at Columbia, as well as calling Cushman. He told them both he wasn't returning; he had something else he needed to do. Lou tried to talk him into a pre-rehearsal, just for fun, but Ethan declined. Later on, in his hotel room after a couple of glasses of Jack, he found the script in his bag. He'd been carrying it with him since bringing it home after the meeting with Royson. He ruminated on what his father had said: "Don't let it go, son." Two hours later, he put the script down and called Lou. He was in.

As the rehearsals began, he found his way back into his character's personality—as well as finding a reprieve from his grief. The intensity he gave the character skyrocketed.

The afternoon before the first shoot, he received a call from the LAPD's Officer Barnes, the officer assigned to the shooting incident with Christa's ex.

"I've finally tracked you down," Barnes said after identifying himself.

"Yes, you have," Ethan said, suddenly interested. "Has something happened? Have you found Christa's …" His voice trailed off. His throat was tight and his face hot. He sat down on the duvet covering his queen-size bed. The air had been knocked out of him as he anticipated what he might hear.

"No, Mr. Jones, we haven't," Barnes replied, "but I have an interesting discovery that I'd like to share with you. Can I come by in an hour or so?"

Ethan's tongue felt like a rock in his mouth. The image of Christa's limp, bloodied body lying face down in their bed rushed to take him down. He struggled with coherency.

"Mr. Jones? Hello?" said Barnes. "Are you okay?"

Ethan stiffened, unable to speak. Only his breathing was audible over the open phone line.

"Mr. Jones, is something wrong?" Barnes asked.

"No!" Ethan blurted into the phone. "I mean, yes—come on by."

Ethan hung up and fell back onto the duvet, his hands cupping his face. What had they uncovered? A growing rage returned to his gut, making his face hot and dark. What would he do if they'd found the monster?

In less than an hour, Barnes was at his door. Ethan let him in and directed him to a chair.

"How are things, Ethan?" Barnes asked with genuine concern. "Pretty tough, I imagine."

"I'm working on it," Ethan replied, taking a beer from the room's refrigerator. He offered one to Barnes, who declined. "You sounded like you had some information."

"Not sure at this point," Barnes answered, watching Ethan closely. "How long have you known Robbie Johnson?"

Ethan looked up at Barnes; his hazel eyes narrowed. "Why is that important?" he asked.

"It may not be. It's just a question."

"We were roommates in college. We've known each other for years; he's probably my closest friend. Why are you asking?"

"Ethan, from what we know, Christa was dead before she ever received a blow." Barnes watched Ethan's reaction closely as he spoke. Ethan shifted on the bed uneasily and gulped his beer. Barnes added, "Are you okay to hear this?"

Ethan sat very still. He wasn't sure how to answer Barnes's question, afraid of what he might learn. His heartbeat was racing in his temples. He'd need his Jack soon. He nodded his head slowly. "I think so," he said, unsure of whether he really was.

Barnes leaned forward as if preparing to whisper something to him. He looked at the floor and then straight up at Ethan. "Christa wasn't murdered from the blows she received," Barnes stated plainly, keeping with the facts. "She died from asphyxiation."

Ethan didn't move; his heart pounded in his ears. A fog clouded his thoughts. Blotchy red images began to flash into his head. He saw Christa lying face down in their bed. A red handprint appeared on the wall. Blood was splashed around much of the ransacked apartment. The images came on like still photos flashed up by a slide projector, but he couldn't control the projector. Each photo displayed another bloodstained image in chaotic order, causing him to relive the nightmare. The intensity of the images tore at his emotions, adding rage to his overloaded circuits.

He forced himself to breathe slower and tried to relax. "You mean she was strangled?" he breathed, his mind trying to grasp what Barnes had stated. An image of thick, giant hands squeezing Christa's smooth, slender neck that his lips would never kiss again flashed before his damp eyes.

"Yes," Barnes replied, his voice unwavering. "We've found no trace of this other man you've talked about—her ex-boyfriend. We think he's out of state. No one's seen or heard from him in months."

"That's because he's hiding, waiting for the right moment!" Ethan cried out, angered by Barnes's apparent lack of belief in who the killer was. "Which he found. I'm telling you—he did it."

"Ethan, you've said you've never seen him."

"And why exactly is that important?" Ethan shouted. He couldn't believe what he was hearing. The whole thing was ludicrous. Ethan stood up. He'd had enough. It'd be days before he got over this meeting as it was.

"Ethan, please sit down," Barnes requested, his voice even-tempered and controlled.

Ethan hesitated and stood beside the bed. "I'll sit down when you fucking guarantee me the hunt for Christa's killer doesn't stop until her ex is brought down."

"Ethan, you've got my word," Barnes replied without hesitation. "We're getting closer."

Ethan sat back down. "I thought you just said you couldn't find the killer."

"No," Barnes interrupted, "I said there's no trace of her ex-boyfriend."

"But he's the one," Ethan insisted, squinting his eyes, trying to understand the homicide detective.

"Ethan," Barnes concluded, standing up, "we're doing all we can. We'll find who killed Christa. Count on it."

CHAPTER 50

After Barnes left his room, Ethan stepped out into the dreary rain, lost as to what to do next. Emotions boiled inside him. Rage to kill was building. Confusion and turmoil over the killer overwhelmed him. Alone, he couldn't hold back his tears.

His head was overflowing with what Barnes didn't say in the course of their twenty-minute discussion.

The questions didn't stop, and most he couldn't answer. Was he in danger himself? Barnes indicated nothing of the sort. Was Christa's ex no longer a suspect?

Ethan walked several blocks from the hotel. When he stopped to get his bearings, he didn't recognize anything. Tears blurred his vision. As they cleared, he came upon a gray brick building fronted by two wooden doors with large, black wrought-iron handles. Not knowing why, he stopped and pulled one of handles. Fully expecting the door to be locked, he was surprised when it swung open.

Inside was a small foyer with another set of large white doors that were partially open. Pushing one of the doors further, he was amazed at what stood before him: an expanse so great that it caused him to question his sight. His footfalls announced his entrance as they echoed through the cavernous hall, which he soon recognized as the interior of a wondrous cathedral. The ceilings were vaulted high overhead, with paintings and sculptures lining the walls. The depth of quiet was awe-inspiring. His initial disquiet turned into fascination and shifted his thoughts. He walked across the marble floor toward a wooden pew, staring wide-eyed at the grandeur of architecture that surrounded him.

He sat down in the pew with his eyes fixated on the altar. The significance of the moment was not lost on him. He was not religious in the sense of attending church, but his need was apparent. God, how he missed her. His eyes absorbed the sheer magnificence of what he saw. Exalted by the immensity of the structure, he was aware of a pervasive inner strength. Unsure of what he should do, he caught himself speaking quietly, asking questions on what to do next—who or what was he to believe? He asked that Christa might hear him and tell him what to do. The pew was surprisingly comfortable as he slid against the wood back and listened to the loud silence, hoping for an answer. Whispered prayers of others drifted through the air around him, creating a sense of tranquility. Motionless, he sat with his eyes closed, lost in the serenity.

It's your turn, Ethan. I know it is. I'll be with you, but it's bigger than that.

The words came from someone nearby. He was certain he could feel her light breath on his cheek. He turned to see a woman stand up, a familiar brown head.

He closed his eyes. It couldn't be. Not again. She was real. But her voice was again beside him, that voice he would never forget.

It is your turn. Take it for me, for you, for us.

Silence reigned. She said what she needed to say. He turned again. Mila was waiting, dressed in white silk, at the end of the pew. Abruptly, he rose to follow her. Back through the entrance doors and outside, he kept her in sight. Sun was breaking through the tired rain clouds. Time was not present as he watched her cross the street. His world was returning. He had to get back. There was a lot to go over before the morning. His lines still needed work.

He followed her for several blocks, not knowing where she was headed, and then he recognized first one building and then another. Walking a little further still revealed the top half of the Dorothy Chandler Pavilion. In the pew where he'd sat in awe of his surroundings, he had whispered a cry for help. He realized with the suddenness of a thunderbolt that his plea was being answered.

Oblivious to those around him, he stepped into the street, and a passing motorist locked up his brakes to avoid running him down. The screeching tires served only to push him on faster. There was no hesitation in his step as he crossed the street, walking quickly to catch up with Mila this one time.

A gray cloud passed in front of the sun, threatening more rain as he lost sight of her.

Ethan approached the front of the auditorium as he had on previous occasions. Although only a few people actually were in the area, he saw hundreds. They were packed along the street and on the sidewalk, in the building alcoves, the open windows, and other niches surrounding the entrance. People and fans were everywhere. Camera flashes exploded like a Fourth of July celebration. Television cameras and handheld microphones were everywhere. Most eyes, however, were focused on the luxurious stretch limousines arriving with their famous passengers. Ethan turned and saw the red stretch BMW he'd just exited, the door held open by a young brunette driver who smiled and waved a white gloved hand. Christa stood beside the open door, waiting to take his arm. He imagined a loud cheer erupting from the crowd as he stepped onto the red-carpeted sidewalk, engulfed by the throng of hysterical movie-goers. Scanning the crowd, he searched to see who was inspiring the applause. Everyone seemed to be staring at him. He nodded his head and winked at a teenage girl, who held out a black marker, with her white T-shirt stretched out for him to sign. Christa was at his side as he continued toward the entrance, signing more autographs while giving and receiving handshakes and kisses.

As he approached the auditorium's entrance, he caught a glimpse of his own reflection in the glass doors. He wore a black tuxedo jacket with an expensive Armani black mock turtleneck. His black Gucci shades ignited screams of delight when he removed them. He saw Christa's reflection in the glass—or was it Mila? He was alarmed at how similar they looked to him. Despite the unseasonable heat, he felt good, even cool. Inside, he searched for his father in the mass of ticket-holders.

Then suddenly, the nominations for best actor were being announced. He heard his name. A moment later, the crowd was standing. All eyes were on him. In a blur, he was on the larger-than-life stage receiving the gold statue and waving to the crowd. It was then he saw his father beaming near the front. Tears were rolling down his cheeks. He was there.

It's yours, honey, came the sweet sound of Mila's voice. *You are the one. The world is waiting.*

Without warning, something hit him from behind as he waved.

"Mr. Jones, it's time to wake up for your ..." came a voice from somewhere beside him.

Something turned inside his head, and he found someone was shouting, "Hey, sonny! Where the hell are you?"

Ethan looked around to find a woman speaking to him. She was dressed in white with matching hat and shoes. It wasn't Mila.

The crowd and stage were gone. He found himself on the sidewalk with a few people milling around.

"Sorry," he said, feeling disoriented.

The woman glared at him like he was a stray dog who had pissed on her leg. She walked away, shaking her head.

Ethan smiled as he looked at the building in front of him. The answer to his question was here right before his eyes, as vivid and clear as any reality. He understood what he had to do. It was time. He started walking and then looked across the street. Mila was standing at the curb, dressed in white and waving. He waved back as a taxi pulled up in front of him.

There was a lot of work to do.

He saw her mouth open and heard her words.

It's yours, babe. Always has been.

CHAPTER 51

Ethan's Timeline
May 1992

In short order, Ethan's life turned into pure craziness. Nothing excited him like the production of *Browning Station*. Scheduled to be completed in five weeks, they were only halfway there in six. Despite being well over budget, after the producers screened some of the early footage, financing ceased to be an issue.

None of it worried Ethan; it was a special film. The story enthralled him, as did his character, William Avery. If there was one thing that all great films had in common, it was a great story. For Ethan, what added to the excitement was his character's evolution and how he was able to capture it. The picture was transformed, as was the story, as Avery's character developed, and Ethan pushed the envelope. From the smaller supporting role he'd signed on to play, he became a major character in the story, and his already unbalanced world was turned even further upside down. As with most great projects, no one knew how it would turn out, but the cast and crew bonded and knew they were on to something special.

Ethan's character, William Avery, was a madman in Mr. Average American clothes who assimilated well within societal norms. With two children and a beautiful wife, Avery had never learned to deal with envy or, for that matter, life. A chemical imbalance in his brain intensified his sickness.

The character seemed weak on first analysis, but Ethan and Cushman saw potential in what the role could be—if Ethan could pull it off. But something else drew Ethan to the story. *Browning Station* was the novel he'd picked up, coincidentally or not, at the bookstore before meeting Ben Lui. He couldn't help but think that forces much larger than himself were at work. In reading the novel, he was engrossed by William Avery's character.

Four weeks into the project, Ethan became Avery. Though loved by all, William Avery was a very malicious and demented man, the incarnation of evil in a gentleman's shoes. The Jekyll and Hyde transformation was so convincing that even the cast members were awed by Ethan's performance, some even shying away from him off camera.

The director experimented as the cast transformed the picture from a teenage horror flick into a deep, near-epic psychological thriller. Ethan was creating and bringing to the screen a new and original madman—a pathologic piece of average, middle-class America.

Ethan put himself through a myriad of versions of the human condition. He suffered through a stretch of four days without sleep to try to achieve a pure, uncluttered madness. He didn't eat for days, and then he over-ate for days. He drank heavily for two days under doctor's supervision in an attempt to get closer to the edge of a reality that he hoped to capture in the camera's eye. He fought for the look and the feel of insanity, wanting to ride the lunatic fringe, if only to capture a few key moments on celluloid. He wanted to achieve believable madness by showing a man who moved seamlessly from the creature comforts of suburban life to the dark edges of evil.

He pored over books, tapes, and videos on schizophrenia, personality disorders, and psychotic neurosis—anything he could get his hands on to give him insight into the character of William Avery. A friend of the director's even arranged visits to psychiatric wards in the Los Angeles area. Toward the end of production, Ethan was so engrossed in the project that at times he questioned his own mental state. When filming wrapped up, he was warned to get away and let Avery go.

Following the last day of filming, a small cast party was organized outside of LA, close to the director's personal residence in Pasadena. Ethan didn't go. Exhaustion had set in, and Cushman had booked two first-class tickets to a private resort in the British Virgin Islands. He pleaded with Ethan to get completely away for a while and clear his head. Cushman knew that big things were in the works for his future star client. He didn't want him derailed in another actor's psychosis of drugs and alcohol. Alcohol already was growing roots.

"Take two weeks," Cushman had told him. "Come back if you're itchin' to get going, stay if you're not, but you have to get away." He added with a smile, "Life is about to change, my friend. Mark my words—you'll be glad you did this."

Three nights before the end of production, Ethan called his father. "Hey, Dad," he said, his voice surprisingly serious and emotional, "it's Ethan."

"I know who it is," his father chortled. "You're in Hollywood, but you're still my son. How are you?"

"Good." Tears rolled down his cheeks. His father's voice brought an unexpected emotional release after all Ethan had put himself through during the weeks of filming. Steve was right. The past few months had taken their toll.

"Ethan, what's wrong?" his father asked, clearly concerned.

"What's wrong?" Ethan repeated, regaining his control and laughing. "I'm finally living my dream. There's no better feeling in the world." After an extended pause at his father's end of the phone, Ethan wiped tears from his face and said, "Seriously, I'm fine. We're done shooting. I wondered what you were up to in the next couple of weeks."

"Well, just wrapping up another deal with a developer in Atlanta. I'm—"

"Have you ever been to the British Virgin Islands?" Ethan interrupted, knowing his father was never too busy for anything he really wanted to do. Still, Ethan sensed his father's hesitation. "I have in my hand two tickets to an exclusive resort in the Virgin Islands. You wanna go?"

"You want to take your old man to an exotic resort?" his father asked. Ethan could picture the smile on his father's stoic face. "What's wrong with you, son? Have I taught you nothing?"

Ethan laughed, "Well, I didn't think you'd want to go, but I knew if I didn't ask—"

"Hold the phone there, boy," his father interrupted. "You asked. I accept. Don't even think about retracting the offer."

"Well, I was sure you'd be too busy," Ethan teased. "I was asking out of politeness. I've already got a couple of bodacious babes waiting to go."

"I'll bet you have, so bring them along. I'm packing my bags."

CHAPTER 52

It was difficult to fathom the beauty of the islands. They were beyond anything Ethan had ever experienced. The aquamarine water was so clear that it almost seemed like an enhanced photograph. He'd always figured publishers of vacation magazines and travel brochures airbrushed the photos to sell the dream trips. Living it was a different story.

One afternoon, Ethan and his father hiked out to the edge of a two-hundred-foot cliff overlooking a shoreline of jagged rocks and foamy sea. Even with the breeze, sweat dripped off both of them. As he stared over the side of the precipice, Ethan had to step back, as the effect of vertigo offset what the view was worth.

His father didn't hesitate and stepped forward to take in the full expanse of land, sea, and air. "Incredible, Ethan!" his father cried, shifting slightly to his right to look back at his son. "I've never seen anything so beautiful. I wish I could paint."

From Ethan's vantage point, he couldn't see the rocks below, but he could look out across the sparkling blue water. He knew where his father was coming from. "So why don't you?" Ethan replied, squinting a smile into the bright sunlight.

"Maybe I will."

Ethan laughed and turned to look at how the bluff jutted out from the coastline of the island. Stretches of long green grass separated the darker island jungle from the edge of the shore for the full distance of his sight line. "Dad," he said, turning to look at his father, whose stare was locked far out across the sea, "what's your best memory of me, growing up?" Ethan surprised himself with his question, not really understanding why he'd asked it.

His father stepped down from the outcropping and moved closer to his son, unable to pull his eyes from the ocean view. "Now there's a question I can't recall you ever asking before."

Ethan fell back in the long grass and stretched out. His hands were behind his head. The billowing cumulus clouds overhead were like giant puffs of bleached white cotton. Watching the sky relaxed him.

"Besides the day you were born?" his father asked.

"Yeah."

"Well, there are lots. But if I were to pick one … it was in the winter—a Saturday, I think—and you came in the house as I was coming down the front stairs. You'd been shoveling the driveway. You might have been twelve. I realized you were no longer my little guy; you were getting older. I hadn't asked you to shovel the snow. You'd just got up, knowing the driveway had to be cleared."

Ethan's eyes closed as he listened to his father. "I did that?" he queried with a laugh. "Was I ill?"

His father laughed too. "You know, I was pretty sleepy that morning. I never thought to check. Imagine that, and I've held on to that memory all these years."

There was a long pause where neither of them said a word; they just enjoyed the sound of wind and water.

"Another time, when you were younger, you came home from school, crying because you weren't chosen to be the front end of the dragon for a school play. It broke my heart. I hated seeing you unhappy. The next day we found out you'd instead been chosen to play the prince. It was the lead part in the play."

Ethan laughed again, remembering how he'd had to kiss a girl at the end of the play. He'd avoided it until the final performance in front of his parents.

There was another extended period of quiet between them. Ethan was almost asleep.

"I'm not sure how to say this, son," his father began. Ethan could tell his father was having difficulty finding the words he wanted to say. "But you're gonna be a star. I know it like I knew you were going to be born. I hope it's all you imagined."

Ethan didn't know how to reply; his father had never said anything like that to him before.

A few more minutes passed before Ethan sat up. He listened to the ocean crash against the craggy rocks below. A light breeze blew into his face. He looked over at his father and smiled.

His father embraced him for the first time in twenty years. "Ethan, I love you."

Ethan was unable to speak as his eyes filled with tears. He hugged his father, feeling an unexpected strength come over him. For seconds they held each other and then stepped apart. Ethan wiped his eyes with the back of his hand.

"Whadaya say we go find a couple of beers?" his father was quick to say in the awkward moment that followed. "On me."

"You're on, old man," Ethan replied, smiling, his cheeks shiny with tears.

"Eat my dust, sonny boy," his father added and jogged away.

CHAPTER 53

Ethan stayed in the islands for two weeks. His father left after eight days. It was the best holiday his father had ever had, but he simply became too anxious about his business goings-on back home. Ethan understood the feeling. Cushman had called a dozen times, wanting him to come back. Things were heating up.

Hoping to miss the busiest part of the day, Ethan flew back on a Wednesday evening. One flight attendant said he looked familiar but couldn't put a finger on why or where she might have seen him. It would be the last flight on which he would go unrecognized.

The jet landed at LAX without incident. Steve met him in a stretch, jet-black Lincoln Continental. They had hardly greeted one another before Steve's mouth was exploding. Despite being the fastest talker Ethan knew, even Steve had difficulty talking fast enough to get everything out he wanted to say. His flow of words never slowed for the entire ride back to the hotel.

"There's so much shit goin' on, Ethan," Steve continued as the limo swung onto the interstate. Ethan paid no attention to where they were going, excited by Steve's excitement. "I must have a dozen scripts at the office. Things are on fire, my friend. Everyone seems to know about *Browning Station*. They're already callin' you Madman Jones. The Holiday Inn will not be your residence much longer. You'll be living in Beverly Hills, my boy. An early fall release is in the works—definitely before year-end. It's crazy. Talk on the town is, where have you been hiding? Lou is about ready to kill me. He can't believe you left town.

The phone's ringing off the hook. I've never seen anything like it. Get ready. Your schedule's jammed." Ethan didn't say a word. Steve wasn't finished. "They also want to re-release anything else you've done."

Ethan looked at Steve. "Why?" he said, the smile on his face dropped as Sven came to mind. "Why do they want to do that?"

"'Cause you're gonna be a star, my boy!" Steve nearly screamed. Ethan was excited but something hard and uncomfortable was growing in his stomach. "Why the long face?" Steve asked, disbelief showing on his face. "You're supposed to be jumping and popping champagne corks!"

"Steve," Ethan said, crossing his legs, his face all seriousness, "I haven't done anything else. You know that."

Steve looked back at him and smiled. "Good point."

"But I think you need to know something." Ethan paused and then was out with it. "I've done porn."

Steve winced noticeably, as if ice had been shot into his bloodstream. "What!" he exclaimed.

"I worked—" Ethan started to say.

"You never told me that." Suddenly, a grin broke out on Steve's face. "So you did do some character building. Well, well." Steve seemed to relax, as if he'd thought of something else. He smiled. "Can't be any more of that, buddy boy. Sorry, but once, in this case, is more than enough."

"What if it gets out?" Ethan asked, concerned his success might end before it started.

"It will get out," Steve stated, somewhat nonchalantly. "That we can count on. But something else to think about: bad publicity is better than no publicity. It even provides more back story for the idea of William Avery." Steve thought for a moment and then added, "Royson, however, likely won't see it that way." Then he laughed.

"Yeah, I know," Ethan sighed.

Steve was not about to be driven off his course. "You know how they talk," Steve said confidently. "Don't worry about it. We'll figure something out. More important is what we do next. You've already promised Columbia two pictures, with an option on a third. Half the scripts are from them. I'm already talking with their lawyers about a new contract with new terms. There's lots of money on the table, Eth. The time to deal is now, but let me worry about that. We have to focus our efforts on handling your next move—getting you in the right places. I must have twenty invitations on my desk for parties and special openings. The word is out!"

Ethan didn't quite know what to say. His thoughts still were on the white sand beaches at his resort. He was experiencing what could best be described as relaxed excitement. There wasn't a better feeling in the world. What Steve had just explained, Ethan had dreamed of for as long as he could remember.

I know you'll be a star, Ethan Jones, whispered inside his head. They were Christa's words. God, he missed her. Out there, somewhere, she was with him—he had comfort in that—but he missed her, desperately at times, especially now, as he became poised for success. If only he could hold her, touch her one more time, and share the moment.

"I've some other news," Steve said, interrupting Ethan's thoughts as his voice became suddenly serious and his rapid-fire speech slowed. "Robbie is ... is dead." Steve seemed to be waiting for Ethan to say something. Ethan didn't. He hadn't heard from Robbie in a long time. Robbie seemed to have shut himself off. Ethan knew that he had done the same. He looked at Steve to say more. "They believe he drowned, Eth. That's what the police report said. They'd found a shirt, a pair of expensive slip-ons, and a note inside one of his shoes on a beach outside Ventura. A tourist on a morning stroll found them." Again, Steve waited. Ethan didn't say anything; he just stared out the window. "They haven't recovered his body. He left a note, but the police haven't released what was in it. They're still searching. Foul play is not suspected. I don't know what to say, Ethan. I'm sorry."

"It's okay, Steve," Ethan finally replied. "I haven't heard from Robbie in months. The police said he disappeared after questioning. With all the other shit going on, I just didn't know what to believe. I have to keep going, or it'll knock the shit out of me."

"Right on, bud."

"I've had a lot of time to think over the last little while. Barnes questioned me after Robbie disappeared. He asked me how close we were. At the time, I thought it was bizarre. I'd lived with the guy for years. But you know something? It fucking shocked me when I found out he was gay. I'd been his fucking roommate, for Christ's sake, and didn't know. Call me blind, call me naïve, call me whatever the fuck you want, but it seems really odd to me." Ethan had no idea why, but the words just kept coming. "I think back now—in school, I never saw him with a girl, although a bunch of us hung out together."

Silence followed. Steve broke the quiet. "Well, Eth," he said, eager to get on with their next line of action, "right now I'd be fucking thankful for no memory at all. I met Robbie at a party a few months back, and it's … well …" He was about to say more but thought better of it. "We've got a lot to do. Take these scripts back with you." Steve handed Ethan a black athletic bag. "Go over them in the next few days and see what you think. I've taken the liberty of setting you up in a suite at the Four Seasons for the next two weeks—a little gift from your friendly agent. We'll need to get back together tomorrow and go over a few things."

CHAPTER 54

"Hello? Hello? You—yes, you," Rubinstein pointed at Ethan. "Move out of the way. You're blocking the shot!"

Ethan didn't know where to move, but he moved anyway, angry at being singled out in front of the cast by the director. He wanted to be noticed but not that way.

"Who allowed him on the set?" Rubinstein demanded.

"He's playing Johnson," someone shouted out.

Ethan turned and waved to the director.

Rubinstein made eye contact with Ethan and acknowledged his wave with a slight nod. Rubinstein made sure Ethan knew he was singling him out on the set. Ethan faked a Tom Cruise smile back at the director. But Ethan was fuming. One day, he told himself, he'd eat this guy for lunch. There was no need for Rubinstein to speak to him as if he were a child.

The bushy-haired Rubinstein was respected for the remarkable pictures he created. Most actors felt it was an honor to work in his films, but it usually meant sucking up to him and putting up with his moody and emotional brutality. Rubinstein didn't much care what he said or to whom he said it, but he did everything for a reason. Right now, Ethan didn't much care for the man's reputation. He was tired of the bullshit and the director's ongoing demands.

Cushman had warned him—Rubinstein was tough and domineering. "He won't even remember who you are," Cushman had said, "but he will find a way to get the performance he's after." For

Ethan, thinking of what could happen during rehearsal was usually more worrisome than the actual experience. With Rubinstein, he found the exact opposite. He could never be prepared enough. The man just thought differently, and that likely was the reason for the extraordinary performances he captured on film.

"He'll belittle you," Cushman cautioned, "in front of everyone. But just take it and shut up. The worst thing you can do is do battle with him. He'll cut you down like a pig in for slaughter."

Ethan had nodded, half listening to Steve's counsel. He could handle it.

Now as he looked around the set, a number of people were looking at him. His discomfort grew by the second. His face was hot. *For Christ sake, all I did was stand by a camera,* he said to himself. But remembering Steve's counsel, he didn't say a word. His game face revealed nothing of his anger. He stood and waited, wondering what was next. This was his fourth movie, discounting his desperation porn flick. None but the first, however, had been particularly noteworthy. With each he'd gained experience; each was a stepping stone to the next. This was his first real role since *Browning Station*. He shared the trailer out back with two other actors. They would shoot at ten locations. Ethan would go to nine of them.

"Where's Johnson?" cried Rubinstein. He was sitting in his green canvas chair, wearing two sets of headphones—one set partially on his head and the other wrapped around his neck.

Ethan looked up and moved quickly to the set. He wasn't supposed to be in this scene.

"Ethan," Rubinstein said, standing up. He grabbed Ethan by the arm and pushed him in front of the camera.

So he does know my name after all, Ethan thought. Rubinstein rarely called actors by their first names on the set. This surprised Ethan and made up for his earlier embarrassment.

"Stand here and pretend for a minute that Jessy is your sister," Rubinstein directed.

Ethan didn't say a word; he only did as he was instructed.

"Roll it!" Rubinstein shouted. Ethan watched as a man wearing a nylon mask ripped Jessy's dress. "Cut!" screamed Rubinstein, hurrying to Ethan's side. "How'd you feel?" Before Ethan could answer, Rubinstein added, "That's how Johnson has to feel throughout this picture. Mad as hell and crazy nuts. Now get off the set."

CHAPTER 55

Ethan woke slowly as the cobwebs of a hockey practice dissipated. His eyes opened to a dark room he didn't remember. He could only discern different shades in the dark grayness. He couldn't remember where he was, as skates and hockey sticks retreated from his conscious mind, like water dumped from a bucket. Soon he'd have no recollection of the dream and his time spent returning to the hockey arena where he'd spent many hours in his youth. His one-time dream of becoming a hockey star evaporated as he became fully awake.

His hand automatically reached for the light on the nightstand.

He was again on location but this time back in Canada, very near a locale where he'd vacationed as a kid. They'd been filming every day for two weeks and had planned a two-day break to enjoy some of the local geography. Ethan's character had been fighting an FBI agent after being discovered watching his son play hockey. It was something of a different role from the crazy characters he'd been playing.

Their location was grand. Ethan had many fond memories of summers camping in the area. The hockey game took place in a natural outdoor rink between two glacial deposits that had formed a natural triangular amphitheater. Covered in snow, two vertical seventy-foot rock faces made up each side of the field and overlooked Rice Lake at one end. It was a spectacular setting.

Ethan was playing a villain wronged by society. In the end he would die, but not without first saving his son's life.

As a kid, he'd usually visited in summertime. All likely would be fine if it had been summer now, but they were in the middle of December, with Christmas two weeks away. It was cold—colder than Ethan could ever remember it being when he was growing up. Many of the cast members had laughed, watching him shiver in the makeshift dinner tents between scenes. They knew he was from Canada. How could a Canadian boy be cold? He never heard the end of it—"He's not a real Canadian."

Ethan's character initially watched the game from high up on the rock face, near the lake end of the field, to avoid being seen. The scene was set for him to climb down lower, risking being caught, to get a closer look at his son. They'd taken three shots of Ethan on the rocks, attached to a safety harness and choreographed exactly as to where he was to move. Each shot had his character moving closer to the game. On the third shot, Ethan twisted his ankle and required medical attention, causing a break in the schedule. He winced now as he moved his foot under the warm blankets. They'd continued filming, using his stunt double to move down the sheer face.

Steve, seeming to know Ethan's spirits were down, made arrangements for him to stay at Bear Lodge, a resort his family had only dreamed of staying at when he was a kid. Its luxury was comforting, and he enjoyed lobster and cognac and many of the amenities he'd favored at the more luxurious hotels he'd stayed in.

Ethan raised his arm and looked at the time. His new watch—a silver Phillipe Patek—was a present from Cushman for Ethan's work on *Browning Station*, which had received rave reviews since its release.

It was five o'clock in the morning. Ethan had slept for four hours. He wouldn't get any more; his mind was too alive.

He rolled out of bed and flicked on the gas fireplace. The mini-bar beside his bed was fully stocked. He grabbed a Heineken and then thought better of it and took the bottle of Glenfiddich18 that he'd started the night before. Things had changed from the days of sleeping in a cramped tent, boiling drinking water, and cooking on a wood fire.

The phone rang, vaulting him from his memories of late-night campfires. He dropped the bottle of single malt on the floor but retrieved it before spilling its contents. He was pretty sure who was calling and wondered whether Steve had given up sleep altogether.

"Hello?" he answered, his voice cracking and rough.

"Ethan!" shouted Steve excitedly from California. "You better sit down."

Ethan already had dropped to the bed but was on his feet again with Steve's raised voice. "Fuck, what's wrong?"

"Man, oh man," Steve went on, his voice in something of a controlled excitement. Ethan knew the information was important when Steve made such an obvious attempt to slow down. "Tell me—if you could have anything in the world, what would it be?"

Ethan was dumbfounded. He could only think of one thing— Christa. "Well, I think you know—"

"Ah, don't think so much. An Academy Award!" Steve screamed into the phone.

"What the fuck are you talking about?" Ethan shot back.

"Eth, the nominations are slipping out," he said. "You're on the list, buddy! You're gonna be nominated for Best Actor, man! Can you believe it?"

"Steve, that's not funny," Ethan replied, "especially right now."

Browning Station had been released in mid-November to critical acclaim and a lot of press, although not all good. But one thing had remained constant: Ethan Jones's work was remarkable. Ethan had tried not to believe his own press, but he had become surrounded by it. The rumor mill around town, so said Steve, was that a newcomer would be given the nod for the nomination. Ethan had been constantly on the road since finishing *Browning Station*, so he had not been part of the gossip and hubbub. Cushman thought it best to let the momentum build and stay busy.

Steve had repeated over and over again: "Just watch—it'll pay off like you won't believe." Both of them were careful with Ethan's appearances. Cushman kept the interviews to a minimum—and refused press releases. He wanted Ethan to remain an enigma; "keep them wanting more," he preached. He also knew that if Ethan kept busy, he wouldn't have time to think about other personal things that could send him in a tailspin.

"I told you, buddy, you're on a roll. The best thing you did was stay busy on location and outta town." Steve was talking faster than ever. The words were flying out of his mouth. "Everybody's asking questions. 'Where is he? Who is he? Where did he come from? Ethan Jones—who's that? Have you seen *Browning Station?*' It's incredible, Eth. You couldn't be in a better position or getting more publicity. The award is yours. It couldn't be better timed either. You're on your way, like a bullet. Just keep doing what you're doing." Steve paused to take a breath. Ethan pictured Steve with gills in his neck.

"You're serious?" Ethan stated, looking back at his watch. "Steve, it's five o'clock in the morning. Who's picking nominations for any awards now?"

"Actually, Eth, it popped out late this evening at one of the socialite parties in somebody's mansion on the beach. Several of the nominations slipped out. Your name was one of them. The nominations are actually not officially announced until later next month, but you're on the list. Don't doubt it for a second. How are things going in Canada?" Steve paused momentarily for his answer.

"Good," Ethan replied, still struggling to believe what he'd heard. Steve didn't leave much in the way of space to talk before he was back into it.

"Listen, Eth, let's keep the ball rolling. You're next shoot is in Chicago, three weeks from now. It's a new director. I can't remember her name—something like Dovenport or Portacall. She did *Tensions.* An up-and-comer." Steve paused to take a breath and then went on. "Listen, it's 2 a.m. here. I need to get a few hours of shut-eye before the day begins. I just wanted you to hear it from me first. Congrats. Keep well, Madman. We'll talk soon."

"Sleep fast, man," Ethan advised and hung up the phone. He sat motionless on the edge of the king-size bed. Numerous thoughts ran through his head, returning him to his first evening in town. Nothing much was happening in the sleepy small village in December. Christmas decorations and colored lights were on display to celebrate the season but had done little to lift his melancholy mood. Christmas was a difficult time for him. Any reminder could send him spiraling downward into a pit of loneliness. He missed Christa something terrible during any celebration. He'd driven up from Pearson International in a rented Toyota 4-Runner to get him through the anticipated snowfall. Stopping to grab a coffee, he'd walked up Main Street to stretch his legs after the three-hour drive. A few people were out walking and shopping, but the place was pretty quiet. Walking past an outfitter's store, he caught a glimpse of his reflection in the front display window that was filled with stuffed animals and mannequins wearing red toques and fuzzy white beards. A pained frown was on his face. As if on cue, he smiled and straightened up, unaware of his depressed demeanor. At the same time, the reflection of a yellow sign caught his eye across the street. Turning, he stood stock-still and read, "Catch Canada's own Ethan Jones in *Browning Station*" on the town cinema's marquee.

Standing in front of his en suite's bathroom mirror, staring into sleepy bloodshot eyes, his emotions overwhelmed him even more than when he'd looked at the sign above the cinema's entrance. He'd stared at the black letters that spelled his name. Here he was in a town where he knew no one, yet they would recognize him. Many, after seeing the movie, would think they even knew him. They might even venture up to him in the street and say hello, as if they were longtime friends. It was disconcerting to think that people he didn't know and would never meet would recognize him. He was approaching the point he'd dreamed of for as long as he could remember—fame was hovering—but it scared him. Tears trickled down his cheeks as he shuffled back to his empty bed.

The room still was dark. His head was full, trying to put everything together, and it wasn't yet six o'clock in the morning.

CHAPTER 56

Katharine Davenport stepped forward and looked at Ethan. Her eyes were magnificent blue crystals that wouldn't take long to get lost in. With the sense of recall that comes from hearing a song from the past, he knew he'd seen her before. But he couldn't put his finger on where. Her face was expressionless as she extended her hand.

"Hello, Mr. Ethan Jones," she said, a mysterious smile curving her bare lips. "Nice to see you again."

Mr. Ethan Jones. He'd heard that voice before. It was said in the same way, the same inflection. Where did he know her from?

Cushman had called him late the previous evening with an invitation to dinner with, among others, director Katharine Davenport. As he'd mentioned while Ethan was on location in Canada, she was relatively unknown, but her recent film, *Tensions*, had received a lot of attention at last year's US Film Festival. Ethan knew nothing about her, and hadn't seen the picture. Steve wanted them to meet prior to any table meetings with the producers and other cast members. Ethan wasn't excited about meeting for dinner; he'd have preferred an evening alone for once. But the producers forced Steve into action when he learned that final selection for the role was still undecided. Ethan needed to get in front of Davenport and convince her that he was her man. Like it or not, Ethan was going.

Sitting beside this mystery woman, he tried to figure out where he'd met her before. The alarms were sounding. Her greeting of "Hello, Mr. Ethan Jones" echoed a discomfiture that was driving him crazy. Still, nothing seemed to connect the dots. Confounded by his inability to remember their meeting, he prayed for it not to be one of his less savory party moments. Her presence beside him only increased his unease.

He managed a few quick glances sideways and hoped for something tangible to register in his brain.

She sat very still and erect beside him, seeming to study each person at the table. Her straight blonde hair was cropped just above the line of her shoulders and shimmered in the restaurant's lights. The evening was warm; despite living in California for the past few years, Ethan still had difficulty adjusting to the warmth in January.

Ms. Davenport was not wearing a wedding band but had plain gold rings on each index finger. She wore a white cotton shirt under a loose tan silk blouse and Versace dyed-brown jeans with a white rope belt—comfortable clothes that were impeccably clean and crisp. Her nails were short and matched her jeans for color. A thin gold necklace looped in the front of her cotton shirt. Her skin was tanned and lit up her face. She wore little makeup. It was evident she could combine business and pleasure.

Cushman had the movie's two producers deep in discussion when Ms. Davenport turned and remarked quietly, "So Mr. Jones, I don't suppose you remember our last meeting." She smiled as she spoke. "Maybe in an elevator before you were famous?"

Ethan's face flushed slightly, wondering what had occurred on an elevator that he couldn't remember. In the same instant, it came back to him. His head moved closer to hers. A whole kaleidoscope of emotions confronted him. His mouth opened to speak as the horror of what followed that first meeting resurrected itself before his eyes.

"Yes," he said, slowly exhaling as the tidal wave of feelings drew nearer. "That was you!" His words could have been a question or a statement. His tone made it unclear. He spoke again before she could answer to evade what threatened to crush him. "You were the one in the elevator?"

"Yes," she said with a tight smile on her thin lips. "That was me—a little younger, a little greener, and—"

"Just as attractive." Ethan finished her sentence without hesitating.

The words were out of his mouth before he could check them, as often was the case when he'd had a few drinks. It didn't seem to bother her.

"Well, thank you, Mr. Jones," she responded, her bare lips separating to reveal her whitened teeth. "And no less reserved, I see."

It was Ethan's turn to smile. Behind his smile, however, were the brooding memories of the tragedy that followed their meeting. His mind rapidly assembled his wall of defense against the memories of that fateful afternoon. The monsters clawed at the door, anxious to get out and take him down—down to the place one didn't return from easily.

"After leaving the elevator," he heard Katharine say as he struggled to fight off the anxious tentacles reaching out from the depths to reclaim him. They were close but short as he held the upper hand. His smile was an effort, and he missed most of what she said while holding back his demons.

"Are you okay?" she asked. Her face expressed concern for her star actor. "You look pale."

"Yes," he said, doing his best to stay present. "Yes, Katharine, I'm fine. Just tired. I apologize."

Before they could continue, Cushman noticed their discourse. "You two know one another?" he asked in surprise—and surprise was something Cushman rarely expressed. It was his business to be in the know, especially when it involved Ethan Jones.

"Yes, we've met before," Katharine replied, smiling and looking at Ethan as if for permission to tell the story. Ethan nodded.

"Please tell," Steve encouraged her, sitting forward with his elbows on the table.

"It's kind of a funny story," Katharine began and then explained how they'd met in an elevator after Ethan had received his first role in *Browning Station*. As Katharine recounted their experience in the elevator, Ethan continued to ward off his gnawing menace. A red handprint, like a child's kindergarten finger-painting, flashed before his eyes, diverting his attention from Katharine's storytelling.

"I remember this strange man being over the top with excitement. I'd just been fired. I remember him saying something to the effect of, 'Just remember you met Ethan Jones before he was famous.' It was like he knew exactly where he was headed. It inspired me. Two weeks later, I was working at Paramount, editing scripts. In a way, it changed where I was headed."

By this time, Ethan had downed two double-ryes and was ready for a third. His flashbacks to the elevator and the hallway were enveloping him. He tried his best not to recall the room number or that the door to the apartment was open. He saw the small blood spot on the carpet in front of the apartment door. A drop of blood was on the door just above the doorknob.

"That's unbelievable, Ethan!" exclaimed Jerry, the producer sitting beside Steve. Jerry's words were enough to shock Ethan back to the conversation at the table. "It's funny how you know when you know."

Ethan pinched a smile and nodded his head. Words came out of his mouth that allowed him to drop anchor back in the present. "It's a strange thing," he said, feeling somewhat like a marionette as he pushed the words out of his mouth. "I came to California to act—to become a motion picture actor. I knew what I wanted to do. I just had to figure out how. Nobody was giving it away—I found that out really quick. But others had succeeded before me. There had to be a way."

"Well, you're here now," said Robert, the other producer for *Blood Signs* who was sitting between Jerry and Katharine. He winked at Ethan. "Looks like you figured it out." Robert laughed, which prompted the rest of the table to join in. Unbeknownst to Ethan, Robert had handpicked him for the lead. "Ethan, I can't tell you how pleased we are to have you on board for this picture. I enjoyed your work in *Browning Station*. You really hit your stride on that one. I love your subtleties— they make all the difference in an actor. Insanity is often subtle in its existence in society. Some—apparently very few—actually can peel off the skin and reveal the pulpy mess inside."

Ethan listened to Robert's words but was uncomfortable discussing his work in an open forum. He preferred to let his work speak for itself. If people were inspired by his performance, he was pleased. If they enjoyed the film, he considered it a success.

Ethan then saw her broken hands held behind her head in what looked like an attempt at protecting herself. Her long, beautiful brunette hair was a gory mess of coagulating blood. He prayed. ...

Katharine touched Ethan gently on the forearm, but it was enough to bring him back into the conversation at the table. "I want to capture the subtleties in this character," Katharine added, with her fingers spread across his forearm. "The story is magnificent, but what will make the picture is the strength of Jordan Crossing's character. He is likeable, but likeable and evil are not mutually exclusive."

Ethan smiled, nodding his head. He spoke very little during the rest of the meal. It was all he was capable of in order to hold the darkness at bay while the others discussed the film. He focused on Katharine—looking at her helped prevent his nightmares from overwhelming him. Her ideas were different, but they were intriguing and distracted him. The more he heard, the more excited he got about the picture and working with her. It was almost as if the role had been written around him—a natural extension to his work in *Browning Station*.

He felt a connection to Katharine he'd not anticipated. Whether this was because their initial meeting had preceded the tragic events or something else, he didn't know, but he enjoyed her company. Between courses of fresh Pacific salmon, scallops, and capers, Katharine's knee brushed against Ethan's thigh. An electricity seemed to pass between them that he couldn't ignore. She smiled whenever their eyes met.

"Take it wherever you think he can go," Katharine stated, as Ethan scooped up his last piece of espresso cheesecake. "It's going to be fun. I can hardly wait to get started."

As she finished speaking, she looked at Ethan, and he felt something move him—a realization, although it would take months to admit it to himself, that he could love again. The woman who spoke to him and would direct him over an energy-depleting two months of filming could be his friend. The more she talked, the more he wanted to get to know who she was. There was a depth to her that caught him off guard.

Ethan ordered a second Spanish coffee to finish off his meal. In his effort to relax, he'd consumed several drinks over dinner, more than he usually would have—their server replaced each half-empty glass with a full one. He rarely drank enough to feel the liquor anymore, but tonight he'd had a lot. No doubt he would feel it in the morning. He tried to focus on keeping balanced and alert, but the alcohol had flattened him. Fortunately, Cushman, always on the alert, noticed his client's wavering and explained they had another appointment yet to keep.

Cushman had become more than an agent to Ethan. Good at what he did, he also was a good friend. They were in the process of writing a new contract that would be beneficial to them both. There was no doubt in Ethan's mind that Steve was instrumental in getting him where he was and in directing where he was going.

Paying close attention to his words, Ethan excused himself from the table and headed to the restroom. Upon his return, Katharine met him in the lobby.

"It's good to see you again," she said. She wasn't drunk—she had sipped Perrier with lime for most of the evening. "I was really looking forward to this dinner. I remember that elevator ride like it was yesterday."

Ethan smiled. "Me too," he replied as he bumped into a restaurant patron who was leaving. The man turned and gave Ethan a disgusted look. "Sorry about that," Ethan apologized.

The man seemed ready to give Ethan a piece of his mind, and then his face took on a more affable expression. He hesitated for a moment and then said, "You're Ethan Jones."

The woman beside him stared at Ethan as if he was a prized work of art and she was admiring each stroke of the artist's brush.

"*Browning Station* was amazing!" the man exclaimed. "If you don't win the Oscar, the Academy's full of shit. Honey, do you have a pen?"

A piece of paper and a pen was thrust into Ethan's hands, and he scribbled out his name and best wishes on the paper.

"I can't believe it!" cried the woman. "You don't look so scary. You were so real in that movie."

Ethan smiled. It was exciting yet discomfiting that people recognized him on the street. It was strange living the life he'd dreamed of for so long. "Glad you liked it," he replied, not knowing what else to say and a little embarrassed over his alcohol consumption—he was sure the couple could tell he'd been drinking. "Nice to meet you," he added as they alternated their stares between him and the piece of paper he'd signed.

"You too, Ethan Jones," the two of them said, almost in unison. "Thanks again."

The rest of the group joined them in the lobby.

"We get started in a week," Jerry stated, adjusting his blazer. "Get rested. We'll see you then." With that, he moved toward Ethan, his hand extended. "It's great to finally meet you, Mr. Jones. I truly look forward to seeing what you do with this picture. We have big expectations."

Ethan smiled, trying to stay on an even keel. "I appreciate the confidence. I don't intend to let anyone down."

They shook hands. Robert was behind Jerry, and he shook Ethan's hand as well. "Good to have you aboard," Robert said.

"I can't stick around any longer, Eth," Steve interjected, shaking Katharine's hand. "It was great meeting you, Miss Davenport. Don't keep our star up too late." He patted Ethan on the shoulder. "I'll call you in the morning."

Cushman followed Jerry and Robert out the door.

Ethan and Katharine stayed for another hour, going over different parts of the script that she carried with her. Ethan had never worked this way before. He had heard about her unorthodox practices but hadn't anticipated experiencing them so soon.

She pointed out three specific lines as the turning point in the story and indicated how his character's dementia was to come across on the screen. She further explained why she wanted him for the role.

"There's something about your eyes, Ethan," she said, staring at him. "As soon as I saw you in *Browning Station*, I remembered your eyes from our chance meeting that day. I want to take Crossing on a different ride but keep the edge—the edge, that narrow band, that line just before you lose your balance and go over."

Ethan was surprised and inspired by what Katharine explained. She captured exactly what he had tried to attain with William Avery in *Browning Station*. It was the line between there and not there. He'd heard the edge described in car racing when negotiating the apex of a curve. The best lap times were found on the edge, but God help those who went beyond it. Touching this existence and then leaving it; the seconds that pass as one falls from the forty-fifth story, knowing the end is an instant away yet still alive. It was his goal to take that moment that bridges life and death—that insanity—and pull it into his character. It was nerve endings; it was severed limbs; it was connecting the real and unreal but not separating them. Ethan had captured that sense on the screen. Katharine wanted to transform it into Crossing's character.

"He can't just touch it either," Katharine said, her soft face alive with expression. The film was in her heart. Her belief spoke volumes and provided her the confidence of where she wanted to go. "He has to be it. This subtle, zero, infinite 'it', yet he can't get there. You're one of the very few actors I've seen display it. It's in you. It comes through your eyes."

Ethan was spellbound and drunk—or maybe just drunk. His mind was jumping with thoughts and ideas, and it helped him form the character of Jordan Crossing. For some reason, he kept picturing Robbie's face, except it was more than that; it was Robbie's person or what Robbie's person wasn't. And where were those thoughts coming from? Ethan put it down to the liquor doing his thinking and speaking again.

"I think so," he replied, checking his voice to hold it steady. "I know where you're going. Crossing … is a compassionate man but struggles with the emotions of love, anger—even hatred. He struggles with life. Whereas Avery struggled with the imbalance of envy and jealousy, the imbalance here is more subtle, in that Crossing fits into the status quo of society but can't adjust or align to it past a certain point. Then bingo—he crosses it and bad things happen."

A faint trace of color rose in Katharine's cheeks. "Precisely!" she exclaimed. "That … that's what I'm after. That's what I want." With that, she pushed out her chair. "Ethan, I'm very excited about this project," she said, standing up. "We can pull it off."

They walked together to the front entrance of the restaurant. Ethan held open the heavy front door, allowing Katharine to pass in front of him.

"Would you like to grab a drink somewhere?" he asked as they stepped out into the warm evening. He really didn't want her to leave.

"I don't think so," Katharine replied, squinting as she spoke. "I've quite enjoyed the evening, but I've a number of things to prepare for the morning."

"Some other time then," he answered, trying his best not to reveal his disappointment.

"Can I drive you anywhere?" she offered as they descended the restaurant's marble steps.

He hesitated but then accepted, much preferring her company to an unknown cabbie. They spoke only about the film on the fifteen-minute ride to his hotel.

"Ethan, thank you," she said, extending her hand as he opened the passenger door of her Volkswagen Passat. "I couldn't be more pleased that you're doing the film."

The softness of her hand in his was paralyzing. He found himself momentarily locked in her presence. He let go of her hand, not prepared for what was happening. He didn't want to leave but knew he must.

"See you in a couple of days," she called through the open car window and rippled her fingers in a wave, as if playing piano keys in the air.

He waved and climbed the steps to the entrance of the Four Seasons.

CHAPTER 57

The day of the awards was everything Ethan had dreamed it would be. From his wake-up call in the penthouse suite of the Hollywood Roosevelt Hotel to their arrival in a stretch red BMW at the foot of the red carpet in front of the Dorothy Chandler Pavilion, it was a dream. The entire day was a mixture of memories, recollections, and celebrations of where he'd come from to where he now found himself.

It was difficult to mark the specific point where things had shifted into hyperdrive, and he'd become a certified actor. His days and nights merged and became another week or even a month before he stopped and took notice. Since January, it seemed that his feet hardly touched the ground, and it was difficult to tell where he was, minute to minute. Being nominated for any award was an honor but recognition from the Academy was the ultimate. He was beside himself—things like this didn't happen to Canadian boys from the Great White North. He constantly assessed his wakefulness and questioned the reality he was living. Every day was like Christmas morning, with a load of new experiences to unwrap.

In the mornings, he'd go shopping on Rodeo Drive with Katharine. In the afternoons, he'd study lines in a trailer for an early evening shoot on location. Almost everywhere he went, people recognized him, often referring to him as "the Madman."

When he arose on the day of the awards, he headed into the mammoth en suite where a full-sized Jacuzzi tub awaited his arrival. The en suite was the size of an average living room and was equipped with a fireplace and entertainment center, along with an abundance of exotic sundries on the vanity. He lacked for nothing—except Katharine. It seemed ironic that he could have everything, yet without someone to share it, it somehow lost its luster.

After pouring a cup of coffee from the chrome carafe that room service provided, he walked naked to the Jacuzzi, stepped in, and switched on the jets. The water was warm as he stretched out in the bubbling flow that massaged the ache of alcohol from the night before. It was the smell of brewing java, however, that nudged his growing wakefulness to full bloom. *What a way to start the day.*

On finishing his first coffee, he climbed out of the Jacuzzi and into the shower stall. Six brass showerheads extended from the Italian marble ceiling and walls, splashing water over his head and body. It was like standing in the center of a waterfall. Ethan was lost in his own imaginary world, somewhere between his lines in *Blood Signs* and the red carpet in front of the Dorothy Chandler Pavilion, when he heard the ring of the room's phone.

He didn't answer, held blissfully hostage by the steaming water. It might be Katharine, simply telling him to get started without her. He stayed in the shower another fifteen minutes.

Upon exiting, he dried, dressed, and ate breakfast in a small sunlit atrium opposite the bedroom. From his position on the top floor of the hotel, he could see much of downtown LA. It didn't seem so long ago that he'd arrived with little more than some engineering experience and a dream to be a movie star. He smiled into the sunshine as he brought the second cup of black coffee to his lips.

The phone rang again. He ignored it as he stared out into the blue cloudless sky.

Columbia had hired a chauffeur and the stretch BMW to deliver Ethan and Katharine to the Dorothy Chandler Pavilion. As Ethan got out of the car, he saw Frederick Northum approach him to shake his hand, congratulating him profusely on his nomination. Ethan took another step forward, and Ben Lui was at his side. Ben, his hand on Ethan's back, gushed over Ethan's success—"I can't say enough about your talent"—and hoped to see him on stage.

Blinding camera flashes were nonstop, often creating a strobe effect in front of them. Everywhere Ethan looked was bright lights and showbiz. It was an incredible feeling.

Further on, as they moved closer to the entrance, a man wearing black sunglasses and a black leather blazer ducked under the ornamental gold ropes surrounding the red carpet, seemingly blocking their passage. Ethan checked for security personnel, as images of knives and guns burst into his head, and he grasped for recognition of the unknown figure he'd seen only silhouetted in his dark apartment. But before he could do more than stand stock-still, Randy Baseman lifted his shades and flashed a smile. Without a word, the two men embraced.

"I thought you were living in Japan," Ethan cried above the din of the crowd.

"I am!" Randy shouted back, "but I wasn't about to miss this for the world. I just got off the plane."

As quickly as he appeared, Randy disappeared, swallowed into the surrounding crowd like a sandcastle swept away by an ocean wave.

Ethan's stage was set.

CHAPTER 58

Real Time—April 11, 1984
Ethan's Timeline—April 1993

The applause was loud—deafening, in fact. Ethan did and didn't hear it. The sound would fade out as everyone around him stood and clapped as they looked his way. Then the roar of staggering applause would hit him.

Katharine shook his arm. He turned. Her usually clear blue eyes were sparkling with tears. "Ethan!" she cried. "I knew it." Then she was on her feet, clapping.

"And the winner is ..." repeated itself again and again in Ethan's head. For years, he'd heard those words while watching the Oscars. Only in his wildest dreams could he imagine the words announcing his name.

Katharine was pulling at his arm.

Why are you doing that? he thought. Yet seemingly from another side of his head, he was asking, *Who won? Who won? Katharine, who won?*

Like trying to tune in a radio station signal, his present suddenly became clear.

"Ethan, you won!" Katharine screamed. She was on her feet, hauling him up, talking crazy. "I can't believe it! I can believe it! Ethan, it's incredible!"

It was like being part of an explosion. The noise was overwhelming. Ethan was bewildered.

She kissed him.

In the next thirty seconds, many things flashed in front of his eyes.

He saw Mila and Robbie at university. Then Christa and Robbie and something strange—maybe it was Mila. Then he saw Robbie alone.

Katharine was beside him, and for an instant, she looked like someone else, someone familiar.

An instant later, he was shaking and touching as many extended hands as he could. There were smiling faces of celebrities he recognized and admired. Many, he had only dreamed of ever meeting. It was the most incredible hundred yards he'd ever walked. All the hardship he'd endured seemed suddenly worth it—better than his most incredible dreams.

Time seemed to stand still at that moment for Ethan Jones. It seemed for that instant, he could both hold time forever and make it the truth that had always been.

While all this was going on in his head, he continued to move toward the stage.

As he climbed the carpeted steps to the podium, he turned and looked out at the audience. He had been there, envisioned it already a thousand times. It was as if he was where he was supposed to be and, in an odd way, had returned home from a long journey. He wanted to savor every second, like a Davidoff cigar and hundred-year-old cognac.

Dolly Parton and Sylvester Stallone awaited Ethan's arrival on the stage. Stallone was holding the Oscar in his left hand. Dolly was beside Stallone holding the envelope, with Ethan's name, in front of her low-cut black dress. Ethan had never met them, but he loved Stallone's work in *Rocky* and Dolly's beautiful voice. As Ethan approached, Stallone extended the Oscar statue toward him. Stallone's face was alight with his famous pout and coifed hair. Dolly's larger-than-life-ness dazzled him. Stallone handed the Oscar to Ethan and shook his hand. Dolly's bright face looked up into Ethan's as he leaned forward to kiss her cheek. Ethan then stepped back and with the prized gold statue in hand thrust it into the air above his head as he turned toward the audience and screamed "Unbelievable! This is unbelievable!" to a massive ovation. The roar of the audience drowned out his words. Ethan beamed from ear to ear, not knowing what to do except wait. He turned back to Stallone, who patted him on the back and leaned toward him.

"Congratulations, Mr. Jones," he said into Ethan's ear. "I love your work."

"Thank you!" Ethan shouted, humbled by the compliment. "Thank you very much. I'm very pleased."

Stallone then pointed to the podium and stepped back to give Ethan the stage.

He was doing fine and in control, despite the overwhelming and intimidating circumstances, until he saw his father in the audience. His emotions flipped, and he turned away to get a grip on the things he wanted to say.

As he moved to the podium, the sense of honor and privilege of his place among these stars suddenly struck him. It didn't seem possible. Something buckled in his stomach. Again, he glimpsed his father in the distance, still on his feet, his hands coming together in slow motion, like part of a movie that emphasized the moment. His hands came together over and over again, with his eyes glued to his son. For a moment, they locked eyes. Ethan watched as his father's lips parted as if to say something but instead smiled larger. For an instant, Ethan pictured his father as a young man, standing on the Toronto Maple Leaf blue line as a defenseman, upright and proud. As quickly as the weight came upon Ethan, it vanished, just as his lines sometimes would disappear during a shoot. And then he was back. It was such a grand, ostentatious affair. He loved it.

Ethan's focus returned to the curved column that extended into the microphone he stood behind. He pulled a folded page of notes from the breast pocket of his tuxedo jacket. He made a slight and nervous adjustment to the position of the mike as the hall went silent, and people sat down in their seats. The floor was his. He was terrified and exhilarated simultaneously.

"Good evening, ladies and gentlemen," he started, hearing his voice amplified into the large auditorium. And then he spoke in character, reciting his most recognizable line from *Browning Station*: "You better believe I'm here." The words were out of his mouth before he had time to check them. The audience erupted. The line had made him famous and was imitated regularly. The words set him at ease.

316

The audience quieted, and he started in again. "This is the most fantastic moment of my life," he said, looking out at the famous faces. "It's been an incredible journey since coming to California—to Hollywood—to pursue a dream." He extended his arms as if to hug the entire hall. The audience responded with another round of applause. As the hall quieted, he saw Katharine staring up at him. Their seats were five rows from the front. He watched as she stopped clapping—one of the last to do so. She sat very straight in her seat, as she had during their first dinner together, and began to rock back and forth with excitement. Her smile would weaken the knees of any man. As he continued, he spoke to her, about belief and a dream and what could happen—and what was happening—and what an incredible feeling it was.

He glanced at his notes. The words he was looking for were not quite right. All eyes were on him. He could feel the weight of the television cameras and was aware of the need to say the right thing.

"I'm standing in front of you tonight," he continued, using only the first line of his written notes, "as someone who wanted to go somewhere with his life other than where he was headed." He paused a moment to find his father. "I'm a long way from Ottawa tonight, where I left a good job to pursue a passion."

Again, he paused to catch his breath and collect his thoughts. Though calm, his emotions were close at hand. "Seems to have worked out okay though," he said and chuckled. The audience erupted with another ovation. "I didn't do it alone," he added and then hesitated for a moment before continuing. "Tonight is an important evening for a very special person who is no longer with me. Her name was Mil—" He broke off suddenly, confused by his own words, his mind seeming to collide with an invisible wall. He began again. "Her name was Christa White, whose constant encouragement and belief allowed me to get through ..."

Ethan's voice cracked. Trembling, he took a breath as his eyes welled up. He would make himself get through this. "Through the hardships of getting here. Mil—" Again, something shifted in his head, like a switchgear that changes the direction of a train. He looked to the ceiling. "Christa, this is for you. Thank you."

Tears rolled down his cheeks. He stepped back from the podium. The audience responded with a quiet round of applause, allowing him to continue. Shaking his head like a boxer who'd just received an unexpected left hook, he fought for control. He pointed at his father. "And last but certainly not least, my father, whose words of wisdom helped me realize what's important." The audience responded with another ovation but quieted quickly as Ethan's eyes fell on his father. It was his father's secret that inspired him to come back to Hollywood. "You're the best, Dad."

His father waved from his seat. Ethan raised his Oscar. Another round of applause filled the hall, as many turned to search for Ethan's father.

"There are many more I need to thank, but that might take the better part of this evening. Instead"—he paused and folded up the list of names he had written out the night before. This was not the time—"I would like to end with a short poem I discovered a long time ago. 'Sometimes in one's life …'"

The sound of an electronic crackle filled the hall, interrupting him. Ethan stopped, as if he'd received an electric shock, and looked behind him.

"Excuse me, Mr. Jones!" interrupted a loud voice that reverberated throughout the pavilion. Ethan froze in horror, recognizing the voice instantly. A loud murmur passed through the audience. *"Haven't you forgotten someone?"*

Ethan was shocked. He couldn't move. His hazel eyes scanned the hall, searching for the source of the voice. He glared at the stage escort, standing erect and motionless at the side of the stage. The escort shrugged her shoulders as if to say, *What's up?* which reflected Ethan's own thoughts. Ethan didn't know what to do; he hoped it was some sort of sick joke. He leaned forward with one hand on the microphone.

"Excuse me?" he asked tentatively, unsure of his part in this crazy attempt at some kind of humor. The voice haunted him—it just couldn't be. He must have misheard it. Robbie was dead. Ethan's face grew pale. How could anyone be so unfeeling as to think such a thing could be funny? Like a nightmare, it seemed so real yet too crazy to believe. But it wasn't a nightmare. Whoever perpetrated this stunt was sick and needed serious help.

The audience's unsettled chatter grew louder.

It was then Ethan noticed LAPD officers coming through the entrances. They were moving slowly, surrounding the audience.

Something was wrong.

"Ethan!" screamed a woman from the balcony. "The poem!"

The show must go on, buddy, echoed Mila's voice in the back of his head.

Ethan leaned forward to the microphone, visibly shaken but forcing himself to continue. His hands were trembling, making it difficult to hold the paper still enough to read, but he started again. "Sometimes in one's life, he comes to a—"

"*Mister Joneeessss!*" sang the all-too-familiar voice through the hall. It wasn't a joke. Ethan was certain who was speaking but didn't know how it could be possible. The voice continued in a gruesome parody of song, "*Aren't you forgetting someone very special to you?*"

All television station feeds had cut to commercial. No one knew quite what was going on. Something was jamming circuits in the building, and the only audible signals were the hall's PA and the stage microphone.

Music started to play in the background, the loud, driving beat of a familiar tune by Tranquility Release.

"Yes, I'm sure I am," Ethan answered, surprised by his response. The words came from somewhere inside him.

The pounding music continued to play. The LAPD directed people in the back rows out the rear exit doors. Lines of people were filing out. It wouldn't be long before mass hysteria swarmed the audience, with people panicking and rushing the doors. The police were subtly trying to keep control in place.

"*Well, who is it then?*" said the voice.

Ethan paused, trying to stay rational while his brain was transmitting a five-alarm emergency to the rest of his body. Panic was hammering on his chest, wanting out. He knew who was talking to him but didn't know how it was possible.

Then, for a split second, everything became clear, and he knew what to do.

"Why, of course," he said, his own voice all but alien to him. "How could I have forgotten my dear friend *Robbie Johnson?*" Ethan screamed Robbie's name out.

He sensed Robbie's eyes on him from somewhere. He imagined a loaded gun pointed at his head. As Ethan screamed out Robbie's name, something shifted inside his head. It was like watching TV when electrical interference distorts the screen and picks up images of another station's signal. He saw Christa's murder scene before his eyes, only it wasn't Christa in the bed. It was Mila. It wasn't the first time he'd been there. Robbie was standing at the bedside, covered in blood. The image caused Ethan to lose his balance and fall forward, breaking the microphone stand on his way to the floor of the stage.

The M43 projectile whizzed past the top of his head, blasting a hole the size of a small pumpkin into the stage, twelve feet behind where he had been standing.

The microphone stand had snapped backward before breaking and catching Ethan across the face with force enough to fracture his nose. He landed on his elbows on the hard surface of the stage. He was close enough to the stairs that the momentum of his fall carried him over the edge. He rolled down the carpeted steps to the bottom. His right arm caught awkwardly under his body, cracking his wrist and breaking both his index and middle fingers. Noticing none of this, he lifted himself up and ran for cover at the side of the stage.

Tranquility Release continued to blare through the PA in a gruesome soundtrack of adrenaline-pumping music. Mass panic overtook the audience in a scene of absolute insanity.

"*That's right, folks,*" echoed Robbie's insane voice throughout the hall. "*Mr. Best Actor can't remember who got him here! Oh well, what the fuck. You know now!*" Robbie screamed the last words as loudly as he could.

Ethan's brain was on fire. Robbie was dead. Robbie killed Christa. But Mila—why was she in the gruesome scene in the bedroom? And what was this? Robbie rising from the dead? Was this a fucking joke?

No joke, bud. It doesn't get any more real, Mila's quiet voice reminded him.

Replaying what he heard in his head, Ethan thought the person using Robbie's voice sounded out of breath, as if he was running or doing something physical. Was he even in the building?

Unexpectedly, Katharine appeared at his side.

"Ethan! Ethan!" Katharine shouted, panic all over her face. "Are you okay?"

"I think I'm supposed to be dead!" he shouted at her.

"My God!" Katharine cried. "Your face!" She grabbed him in her arms and pulled his head to her chest. The pressure of her hug brought a spike of pain to his head. Her strength was incredible.

"Katharine!" he screamed. "Let go." It took everything he had to pull himself free. "I think my nose is broken," he exclaimed, seeing his blood smeared across the front of her once-beautiful gown.

They rose together as Officer Barnes appeared before them. "You okay?" Barnes yelled. The entire hall looked like a frenzied party as Tranquility Release's single "Unbalanced" continued to reverberate throughout the auditorium. People were running and screaming all around them.

"Yeah!" Ethan shouted back, his eyes passing a questioning glance at Barnes.

"He's not in the building, Ethan. We're tracking somebody who ran from the back exit a few minutes ago."

"Who's not in the building?"

"The shooter!" Barnes shot back. Barnes helped Katharine to her feet. "We're clearing the building."

Ethan winced as Katharine grabbed his broken hand. She gasped when she saw the odd way his fingers were bent.

"The rifle was triggered remotely and hidden in an unused maintenance closet that shared a wall with the inside of the auditorium," Barnes told him.

Ethan winced again as Katharine bumped into him after their abrupt stop.

"He wants me," Ethan said. The whole thing now was clear in his head. Robbie was alive and wanted Ethan. He could see Mila as pristine and clear as life could present her. Like an angel from the heavens, she smiled and nodded her head.

The heavy bass rhythm of the music was alive and loud in his ears.

"He wants me," Ethan repeated.

At almost the same instant that Ethan spoke, Robbie was back on the PA system. *"If I can't have him,"* he screamed, *"you can't either!"*

The music changed to Dolly Parton singing "Here You Come Again."

"Oh, my God!" Katharine screamed as she squeezed Ethan's arm, "This can't be real!"

As they ran together toward the rear exit of the building, Ethan's past flashed through his thoughts. His and Robbie's days as college roommates seemed impossible to believe now. All the parties and jokes, even the studying and exams—Ethan struggled to put it all together. Robbie's hidden secret was matched only by Ethan's own naive blindness. There was nothing left to connect. Ethan wanted to go farther in his memory but couldn't. At least not now. He pushed the thoughts away.

The radio in Barnes's hand crackled into transmission. "We've found it!" shouted an officer from somewhere in the building.

Barnes raised the radio to his mouth. "Larson, where are you?"

"Maintenance, directly below the stage," came the answer. "Holy fuck—there's enough shit down here to blow the block out."

"Get the bomb squad down there now!" Barnes looked at Ethan.

Ethan ignored him and kept moving toward the rear entrance. He had to find Robbie.

They were just through the back entrance of the Dorothy Chandler Pavilion when an LAPD car squealed to a stop, inches from their legs.

"Get in!" Barnes shouted. There were fewer people out here but the air was alive with screaming sirens and panicked shouting.

Ethan didn't say a word as he opened the rear door and let Katharine climb in. He closed the door after her and thumped the roof to signal the driver. Then he was gone, running before the cruiser even moved. He knew once he was in the cruiser, his personal chase for Robbie would be over. He couldn't let that happen, but he could keep Katharine safe.

The sound of several shots rang out in the wet darkness. The shooting stopped. A cold quiet followed, a silence that seemed louder than the actual gunfire. Ethan crouched beside an idling cruiser. Drizzling rain kept everything slick and shiny. He could hear the hard leather soles of the police officers' boots slapping the damp pavement or splashing in puddles as they moved into position. Robbie would not come out of this alive. Shoot to kill was the order of the night.

Ethan couldn't bear to watch yet couldn't turn away.

A dozen LAPD cruisers surrounded the amusement ride inside Paradise Park, a mile from the Dorothy Chandler Pavilion. The lights were back up. Bright fluorescent-green letters identified the Mind Bender ride that lit up the area. To Ethan, the whole scene was like a movie set. He almost expected to see movie cameras placed in strategic locations around the action. It was all disconnected from any sense of reality. Only the pulsating pain in his hand kept him in the now. Shifting his weight sideways, his back against the wet fender of the cruiser, he turned to face the ride, searching in the wet dimness for some sign of Robbie.

He thought of Katharine, safe in a cruiser somewhere in the distance. Without thought or reasoning, he began to run. Numb to his broken bones, blind to any thought of danger, Ethan's mission was to find Robbie.

He looked back at the haphazard line of police cruisers, an intimidating line of firepower with rifles and handguns at the ready. Legs that hardly seemed his own carried him through the nightmare, beyond anything that could be real.

A scream of terrified horror stopped him in his tracks as he approached the Mind Bender, the neon sign on the ride crackling with an electric frizzle. Ethan ran toward the scream, his mind ahead of his feet. He pictured the monster that had replaced his friend. Angry shouts came from behind him as he compromised the LAPD's position. His legs didn't stop.

The midway came alive around him in a mind-numbing display of bright lights and loud music, even though it was deserted of people. He was alone, running through the nightmare.

As he approached the Bender's entrance platform, he saw a man standing at the top, holding someone under his arm. The woman's long blonde hair hung down like a shaggy mop. A gun was pressed against the woman's temple. To Ethan's eyes, it seemed distorted, almost as if it was a gasoline nozzle filling the woman's head. The woman was in shock; her face was locked in a scream.

Ethan was shocked to realize that Robbie had somehow taken Katharine hostage. "You motherfucker!" Ethan screamed, running toward the platform.

Robbie turned and snarled, "What the fuck is wrong with you?"

Ethan stood mannequin-still, thirty feet below the man he thought he knew.

"You're fuckin' brain dead, Eth. Always smart enough to be dangerous."

Shocked beyond words, Ethan could only stare at the man he had called his friend. He couldn't help but feel a twinge of sadness. Robbie was standing on an eight-foot-wide metal platform, holding Katharine tightly against him. Ethan didn't think Katharine was dead, but she wasn't fighting. She wasn't moving, for that matter; she was as limp as a Raggedy Ann doll.

"Don't you fuckin' move!" Robbie screamed as Ethan adjusted his footing, his heart pounding to its own heavy beat. Katharine moved her head—she wasn't dead, thank God.

Ethan remained still, realizing he was staring into the face of evil. The moment was surreal. Everything seemed like that. At any second, Ethan expected the director to yell, "Cut!" He struggled to believe it wasn't a film shoot.

Robbie glared back at him. Despite the distance between them, Ethan was sure he could see tears in Robbie's eyes. His head was shaved. He looked like Bobby De Niro in *Taxi Driver*. The Robbie that Ethan knew was no longer in the eyes that stared back at him. Try as he might, Ethan couldn't convince himself it was the same person. His Robbie was gone, devoured by this apparition that stood on the entrance platform to the Mind Bender.

"Look what you've done, you motherfucker!" Robbie shouted down, leaning forward over the steel railing. His eyes bulged. "You fuckin' paid no attention to me when I wanted you, and now—fuck, I can't get away from you?"

The Robbie thing cackled. It was a sound that would haunt Ethan whenever he closed his eyes. It was the kind of eerie laugh that wasn't human. It came from the bowels of hell, at the very formation of evil.

Ethan watched the gun held against the side of Katharine's blonde head. The scene was unimaginable. He prayed for Robbie to release her.

"Robbie!" Ethan shouted, amazed he could speak. Even from thirty feet away, Ethan could see the dark crimson blood dripping from Robbie's pant leg onto the platform.

Robbie had been hit. He was moving because he had to. He could barely stand up but knew if he stopped, he was dead. "Don't fuckin' talk to me!" Robbie yelled, his voice rough. He spat out a mouthful of blood. Ethan realized Robbie could easily blow him away from where he stood. A trickle of blood ran down Robbie's already wet chin. It seemed incredible to Ethan that Robbie still was upright. He coughed again, clearing his throat. "I wanted you. You fuck. From the first day we met. But you couldn't give me the fucking time of day."

The Robbie thing's foot slipped in his blood pooling on the platform. Katharine's head lifted suddenly, causing the gun barrel to jab hard against her. Several terrifying screams followed until her head dropped again. Robbie almost lost his grip on her.

"Why couldn't you just love me?" Robbie shouted, his face contorted in painful emotion. "It's just so fucking …" His voice trailed off as he choked out a cough. He spit out a gob of blood that fell to the ground five feet in front of Ethan.

Ethan heard the footfalls of the LAPD hastening their approach in the shadows behind him. He opened his hand behind his back to signal them to slow down.

Robbie's foot slipped again as he dropped to one knee, but his hold on Katharine remained firm. She was his life support system at this point; he wasn't about to let her go. If she'd been conscious, he would have leaned on her. As it was, she was like hauling around a heavy sack of potatoes. If he let her go, however, he would be instantly ripped apart by a barrage of police bullets. Whether he knew it or not, his situation was hopeless.

Still, they had to save Katharine.

"But I do love you, Robbie!" Ethan shouted, his voice and the idea coming from somewhere out of his control. "Ever since the first day we met."

His words seemed to reach the monster's attention. Robbie looked out into the darkness as if searching for who had spoken.

Robbie's grip tightened on Katharine as his other knee dropped to the platform. He shifted her in front of him like a shield. Gravity pulled him down as he weakened. His blood dripped from the platform to the ground below.

Robbie then looked up into the darkness. He moved his lips, but the strength to speak failed him. Blood bubbled over his bottom lip. He continued to hold Katharine's head in the crook of his arm with the gun against her temple.

"Please don't let him fire that gun," Ethan whispered.

You're in the role of your life here, bud, so act! Mila said from inside him.

"Robbie, how can I prove my love for you?" Ethan called out, searching for the character Robbie was looking for. "You've misunderstood. I've always loved you."

A long pause followed as Robbie seemed to muster together all his strength. His face smiled his confusion.

"I want to hug you," Ethan said in as caring a voice as he could manage. He pictured a camera off to his right, adjusting to his facial expression. He could see himself on the set. "I'm afraid of you now. I don't want to get hurt."

Ethan heard the sounds of the midway in the distance, clashing metal music mixed with screams of excitement and barkers' voices. The scene was real enough—the flashing colored lights of twirling rides and games of chance. His mind conjured up all sorts of amusements to match what he heard. The stage was set.

He tried to make eye contact with Robbie's drifting sight. It would be the last chance he had to save the life Robbie held in his arms. He read another line. "You've had so many others, Robbie," Ethan called out to him. "I was jealous."

Robbie cocked his head like a dog and then looked in Ethan's direction. His chin was covered in blood; his mouth opened without words.

"Please don't let the gun go off," Ethan whispered. Then he cried out to Robbie with clear emotion in this voice, "Please let me hold you!" His words had never meant more.

With the heaviness of a falling tree, Robbie fell backward. His grip on Katharine held, but the gun slid to his side, away from her head. Ethan moved forward with the swiftness of a cat. He had to get to Katharine. He nearly had reached the platform when Robbie moved … and aimed his gun at Ethan. What followed was the fleshy *thunk* of two bullets taking Robbie down to stay—one shot through his eye and one high on the left side of his chest. The silence that followed the clatter of Robbie's gun hitting the platform signaled it was over.

Ethan needed nothing more to be on his feet, climbing to Katharine's side. He prayed she was still alive.

The air was filled with the sound of an army of heavy footfalls reverberating across the steel platform as the police took over. Cops were everywhere. Paramedics were at Katharine's side, attending to her. Her beautiful gown was drenched in Robbie's blood, but she seemed uninjured, outside of bruising on her head from the gun barrel.

Crouched beside his one-time friend, Ethan looked over at Robbie's open dead eye but had to look away. It was then his legs gave out as he lost the strength to stand. He fell sideways onto the platform beside Katharine. Catching his balance, he reached up and grabbed the platform's steel railing. For a moment, the railing looked different, as if the chrome was there to assist him. He pulled himself up, coming face-to-face with Katharine. But it wasn't Katharine in a bloodied gown. She was dressed in white, like a nurse helping the paramedic.

Ethan leaned closer.

Katharine was whispering something to him. Blood was on her face and splashed on her neck.

"I knew it. … I knew you'd come back. You saw it all …"

Ethan was close enough to feel her breath on his face; feel her lips on his.

"Is he gone?" he whispered, his strength all but spent.

"Yes, Ethan," Beth replied. "It's over."

He closed his eyes with the knowledge that his nightmare was ending.

A short while later, Ethan found himself standing beside the open rear door of a Los Angeles ambulance. Lights were flashing everywhere, like some kind of macabre Fourth of July celebration. Camera flashes, bright video camera lights, popping red, white, and blue emergency vehicle lights, and the strobes-of-life atop the ambulance were more display than Ethan needed. He couldn't recall getting to where he now found himself standing; it was a point in time, like waking from a bad dream. A young crowd had gathered in the area as the calm that follows violence took over. Two efficient paramedics wheeled Katharine on a stretcher toward him. Her eyes were open. Blood—Robbie's blood—was smeared across her shoulder. Though still in shock, she smiled at Ethan. Ethan stepped aside to the let the attendants move her inside.

"That's William Avery," cried one of the many teenagers loitering around the scene. Ethan held on to the door handle of the ambulance for balance, pretending not to hear the comment. The attention of the crowd shifted quickly from Katharine's being lifted into the ambulance to him. Without notice, a hand suddenly grabbed his arm and pulled him backward, almost off his feet.

Before he could manage a word, Barnes was escorting him toward another ambulance.

"This time, I'm making sure you get to the hospital," Barnes said, holding back an obvious smile. "Enough with the action-hero stuff for one night ... but nice work."

The screaming sirens caused Ethan to stumble.

Barnes chuckled. "Whoa, hold on there, cowboy. This posse has reached its end for today."

The ambulance with Katharine inside started forward as people moved out of the way. Once clear, her ambulance sped away in the midst of screaming sirens and flashing lights.

Cops were in abundance. Ethan couldn't help being reminded of the *Blood Signs* movie set. Barnes assisted him into the back of another waiting ambulance. People were trying desperately to get a look at the star being whisked away. Barnes slammed the door shut once they were in. As the ambulance moved away, Ethan waved out the window at the people who recognized him.

The police who remained on the scene began to disperse the crowd. People hovered near and around the yellow police tape surrounding the periphery of the crime scene and the spot where Robbie's body lay covered by a yellow blanket.

"Well, Mr. Jones," Barnes said from the front of the ambulance. A sense of relief seemed to lift his voice. "The Academy can credit you all they want. We just witnessed your best performance of the year, maybe of a lifetime."

Ethan made his best attempt at a smile. It was all too incredible for him to even think about. "I want to go where they're taking Katharine," Ethan said. "How is she?"

"She's okay," Barnes replied. "Just some bruising around her head and neck. One knee was scraped up a bit."

After that, Ethan missed the rest of the trip to the hospital. He came in and out of himself, his mind unable to remain in the present.

The shock suffered from the events of the evening did little to change his state. There was a sense of relief, of a saga ending, and gratitude to be alive. The trip to the hospital seemed to take seconds.

At the hospital, Ethan found himself alone in the whiteness of an emergency room with white curtains drawn around a white-sheeted bed. He was retracing what had happened, trying to piece together what led to his being there. His broken fingers and wrist throbbed. His broken nose was swollen, and it ached. Both served as reminders of the ordeal he'd suffered earlier in the evening. It seemed like someone else's life.

Closing his eyes, something shifted. He could sense things taking shape around him, yet had no energy to open his eyes or do anything about it. Sleep again took him away.

CHAPTER 59

For Ethan, the world seemed to shift around him. He found himself in another room, a room that looked familiar yet reminded him of another time—maybe not as distant as memory might presume. His eyes were closed as his thoughts drifted to a time before California. It was a feeling that didn't seem that far off. He even felt younger.

Barnes's voice interrupted his thoughts from a distance, like he was in the room but the room was large, and Barnes was not at his bedside but across the room.

Ethan sensed that others were around him, yet the energy to open his eyes evaded him.

"Ethan," said a familiar, soft-spoken voice. "Can you hear me?"

Ethan opened his eyes. The light was bright, coming from a window and mixed with the overhead fluorescent light. What he saw was from a memory. Katharine was sitting on the bed beside him. A man stood at his bedside on the left, dressed in a white lab coat.

"Ethan," said the man with Officer Barnes's voice.

Ethan thought for a moment, trying to figure out why Barnes was dressed like a doctor. "Yes," Ethan replied, trying to hold tight to what he was seeing to avoid getting lost in what his mind was thinking—he knew that despite the voice, the man was not Officer Barnes. In that instant, he realized the woman sitting beside him on the bed seemed a lot like Beth and very similar to Katharine. The woman wasn't dressed as Beth would be, in a professional skirt and matching jacket; instead, she wore the white lab coat of a doctor. It couldn't be Katharine, she was in … another room.

Ethan felt a sense of release, like returning home after a difficult journey.

"Ethan," the Beth woman spoke. "How are you today?"

Ethan looked back at her, curious about the question. "I think I'm fine," he replied, wondering why she was asking the question. "How are you?"

"Do you know where you are?" asked the Barnes look-alike in the white coat.

"Well, yes, of course, I do," Ethan responded, as if it was a simple matter of fact. "Why do you ask? Is this a test?"

There was a pause as Barnes turned and raised an aluminum clipboard from the bed. He flipped through several sheets of paper.

"Ethan, can you tell us where you are?" the Beth woman asked, looking him straight in the eye.

Ethan smiled, not knowing quite what to say. He found it difficult to understand why they wanted him to explain the obvious. "I'm in the hospital being checked out," he replied.

"Be patient for a moment, Ethan," the Beth woman said. Her eyes were as blue as Katharine's. "You've been through something of a traumatic experience."

Her opening was just what Ethan needed. "I was pretty lucky tonight," he started, looking from Barnes to the Beth woman and struggling to hold on to something—though he wasn't quite sure of what. "I think I'm lucky to be alive. That first bullet was meant for me."

Ethan noticed a visual exchange between the two people in the room. Vague questions came to mind that he couldn't answer. How could Katharine be in his room, asking him questions, as if she was a doctor? Why was he noticing now how much she looked like Beth? Why had it never occurred to him before?

"Can you describe something of what happened?" asked Barnes, holding a pen in his hand and writing something on the clipboard.

"What? You don't remember?" Ethan shot back, staring at Barnes in disbelief. "You were there for most of it."

The expression from the man with Barnes's face in the white lab coat gave it all away, despite his attempt to cover it up. "Well, I meant from your point of view."

Ethan shrugged his shoulders. "I was accepting my award for …" As soon as the words came out of his mouth, he realized something didn't seem quite right.

"Go on," urged Barnes. "It's okay."

"I was in the Dorothy Chandler Pavilion in Los Angeles …" Ethan continued. "I'm in LA. This happened just …"

Silence filled the room. The Beth woman stood beside him. He recognized her but not as someone he'd not seen in a long time; it was in a much more familiar sense. His recollection of the events of the evening became more of a story he was telling than something he'd lived through.

"Go on, Ethan," the Beth woman encouraged him. "You were saying, 'This happened just …' What did you mean?"

He thought for a moment before answering. There was something going on here. His mind was relaying what happened that night. He was standing on stage at the Academy Awards, accepting the award for Best Actor, when he was interrupted over the auditorium's PA by his longtime friend, who he thought was dead. A short time later, a missile shot meant to kill him exploded on the stage. But the more he thought about the events, the more they seemed unreal. He now couldn't actually remember them as personal experience. It caused him to pause as he explained it. The Beth woman stood beside him. Barnes remained at the end of the bed. Both seemed more real than what he was remembering and the story he was telling.

"Where am I, actually?" Ethan asked before trying to remember any more. He knew as he asked the question that he wasn't where he thought he was.

"You're in the Royal Ottawa Hospital, Ethan," the Beth woman replied. "You've been a patient with us for almost six months. I am Dr. Beth Katharine, and this is Dr. Steve Barnes."

"But I'm in LA," Ethan said, despite the sudden difficulty he was having holding on to where he thought he was or the event he was describing.

The realization that overcame him shut off whatever else he could recall. Like the automatic doors that close on a ship to prevent it from taking on water, the realization inhibited his ability to remember anything else.

Ethan watched as the two doctors exchanged glances, unspoken dialogue passing between them. Before either spoke, another woman with a face Ethan didn't know entered the room. She was dressed in a nurse's uniform of light green. Her entrance broke their silent stalemate.

"Ah, Janice, perfect timing," Dr. Katharine announced, turning from the entering nurse back to Ethan. "Janice is your new nurse. She'll be replacing Christa."

Ethan looked at Dr. Katharine, somewhat shocked by hearing Christa's name. "Christa?" Ethan whispered.

"Yes, Christa went on leave a few weeks ago. We've had a few challenges finding the right person to replace her."

"Good afternoon," Janice said, smiling. "And how is 'the actor' today?"

EPILOGUE

Real Time
April 1984

Ethan was to learn that he'd been hospitalized shortly after the violent murder of his beloved Mila Monahan. Clinically, they had difficulty diagnosing what had happened. A debilitating form of shock had taken over his mind, incapacitating his ability to face any form of reality. They didn't know if or when he'd come out of it.

Ethan later met orderlies Jesse Gonzales and Jamie Scott.

Other patients to whom he was introduced included Louis Benjamin, Randolph Baseman, Roy Sonlu, Jackie Carlson, and Sven Ironside.

Robbie Johnson was charged with the murder of Mila Monahan. His trial date was set, but he never went to trial. He was killed in a vehicle accident in transit between a holding cell in the Ottawa-Carleton Detention Center and Milhaven Penitentiary in Kingston. The vehicle transporting him lost control and rolled down an embankment during an early morning winter storm in March 1984.

Ethan woke at just after two in the afternoon from a short nap. Katharine was standing at the closed blinds of his trailer. He could see only her silhouette against the light penetrating the blinds. He could look at her silhouette forever.

"It's about time you woke up," Katharine said with a smile. "You're supposed to be on the set in half an hour. Makeup's already knocked on the door once."

Ethan sat up. The couch was small but big enough for the two of them to snooze on. He loved being with Katharine. She was beautiful to look at.

"You better enjoy the view today," she warned. "I'm headed to Oregon tomorrow for two weeks."

"Don't remind me," he replied, standing up and pulling on his boxers. "We'll be here at least that long." He then broke into his lines for the next scene he was about to shoot. "Don't look at me like that," he snarled, furrowing his brow and then pressing his lips together.

"Like what?" the doctor replied, trying to keep a lid on her patient's reaction.

"Like you don't understand," Ethan's character replied. "Like you don't know what I'm talking about."

"Maybe we should take a break."

"Take a break," Ethan replied, his face tightening as his lips pressed against his teeth. "I don't need a break. I need a doctor."

He winked at Dr. Katharine.